Revi
Book On

♦

Writers often pen tales of fiction but only those who lived their work can write like this. RoadBlock, as he has been known for decades, lived the club life and ran in those circles that either made the man, or killed him. Reading about the main character's rise to power in the fictional Regents Motorcycle Club only gives me pause to think of what this author has seen in his life.

---Steve Murrin, The Original Biker Lawyer, Full Throttle Magazine, Atlanta

♦

This fiction novel will take you through the probationary period of the seventies, the trials and tribulations of proving you're righteous, and again remind us that a Brotherhood is and always will be a Brotherhood.

Everybody needs something. A biker finds that something in the form of a good motorcycle; and a good brother; and a good dog. This is a damn good read.

---Victor "Preacherman" Shurtz

♦

Mr. Harrell gives us the story of a good ol' boy from Florida, circa 1970, haunted by a past, as he discovers a love of motorcycles and the brotherhood of serious bikers. If you have even a passing interest in motorcycles or the '70s, the last gasp of American freedom, you won't be able to put this book down.

---Glenn Sheldon

♦

Other Novels by
W.T. “RoadBlock” Harrell
In the Regents Motorcycle Club Series

THE PROBATE

(BOOK ONE)

NEW ORLEANS REVENGE

A NOVEL BY

W.T. "RoadBlock" Harrell

ROADBLOCK COMMUNICATIONS LLC

NEW ORLEANS REVENGE

First Edition 2013 Published by RoadBlock Communications LLC
Second Printing 2014

Author Photograph: Krisan Harrell
Cover Artwork: PigPen RSMC

ISBN: 9780988435629
Printed in the United States of America

DEDICATION:

For the kids and grandkids of my old GBNF friends

Acknowledgements:

This book would not have been possible without: My wife, my family, my Brothers and the many friends, individuals and clubs from the biker community who were there for me through a dark period in my life and are still there today.

A special thanks from us to the people who lent a helping hand when they didn't have to: Gerry and Marilyn Wilfong, Rick "Boomer" Murrhee, Charlotte Bassett, Buzzy and Sandy, Van and Sam Evans, Dale and Jan, George and Sandy Umphress, Jerry Clarke, Beverly and Tom Roberts, Tom Barbee, Jim and Helen Nolan, Deborah McEnteggart, Doc, Clarence Smith, Guy Smith, Jessie, Cookie, Karen, ChainDrive, Biker lawyer Steve Murrin, Tim Daley, Blake Fincher, Roger White, Denny Payne, Jamie Landers, Howie & Heather of White Eagle Lounge, Missy Lybrand of Adamec HD, Chris Vorhees of Saints and Sinners Pub, the Lytles of Gainesville HD, Roy Dove of Mind Ride Cycles, John Malik of Gator HD, Meri Beth Dudich of Tampa HD, Marta Rose of Panama City Beach HD, Willie of Willie's Tropical Tattoos, Jack and Ann Schenck of Knuckle Draggers Bike Shop, Carl Williams of Tattoos by Carl, Ludie Bond SSMC, Tommy Sue of Tuff Girl Designs, Carol Crowson of Caney Creek ABATE, Rita of Skully's Saloon, Michelle of Ellie Ray's Lounge & Resort, Benny Brantley of Blue Duck Events, and Don Seeley.

W.T. "*RoadBlock*" Harrell

NEW ORLEANS
REVENGE

To Pete,

come ride with me
back into the 1970s.

RoadBlock

PROLOGUE

New Orleans, 1971

There had to be a way out of the office without looking like a first-rate pussy. Meth and sweat soured the insides of his nostrils. The odor settled on his dry tongue like a cat had backed up and pissed in his mouth. There was no sign of relief, either. Sleaze had finished his beer ten minutes ago and said all he was going to say, but Leon still sat there at the desk like some hulking Italian buzzard

Big guys were like that. They just parked their fat stupid asses and didn't leave until they were damn good and ready. Or until somebody took a baseball bat to them. Sleaze was very good with a bat, but he quickly put the thought aside before it showed in his eyes.

Across the desk, the two deep lines engraved down both sides of Leon's hooked nose made it look like he was smiling. Maybe he was happy. He had packed enough meth up that beak to keep him flying for days. Or maybe the smile was directed at the True Detective magazines thumb-tacked to the walls. On the covers, the captive women sprawled bound and bug-eyed in their scarlet nighties and torn nurse's uniforms, while some guy with a shiny knife lurked in the background.

"I want another beer. How about you?" Sleaze wiped his nose with his arm and glared at the closed door.

Under normal circumstances, his men never left him alone.

"Where's this, boss? What should we do about that, boss?" The interruptions that drove him crazy would be damned welcome right about now. Christ, any excuse at all. He wanted to get back to the bar, see how things were going out there for the Bayou Runners.

His men were partying with the Trogs, a hardcore one-percenter club who could turn on them in an instant. The longer he stayed in the office, the bigger the problems could become. But he was stuck in here with the president of the New York Trogs chapter and could not run out of there like some chicken-shit punk, at least not without a good reason.

The silence stretched. Leon watched him with those deep-set eyes, waiting. It was an old cop trick, but Leon was not a cop. He wore a cut-off denim vest with *Troglodytes MC* stitched across the back. Sleaze knew what the patch meant. In his world, it was the ultimate badge of honor.

Across the room, the door edged open. Sleaze glanced up hopefully, then reared back. A metallic guitar riff chopped through the humid tension in the room like a steel cleaver. *Shit*! The businesses down the street would raise hell if the bar noise overpowered the music halls and strip joints. People came to New Orleans for jazz and blues, not Led Zeppelin.

A small girl peered around the door, her eyes wide in a sallow face.

"Sleaze? Hermy wants to know if you wanta call for more beer. He's almost out."

Filing cabinets rattled under the barrage from the Seeburg juke box and the paper women fluttered on the wall. Sleaze marched to the door and yanked the girl inside.

"I wanta know why that mother-fuckin' juke box is so loud," He snapped.

"It…it just—I d-don't know," She chattered, her knees wobbling.

"Christ. Fucking idiot." Sleaze turned to Leon. "Ya want some face?"

Leon shrugged. "Why not?"

"Take care of him." Sleaze slung the girl in the general direction of the desk and scurried out of the office.

He spotted the Cajun manager huddled at the end of the bar, bracing against Rare Earth's onslaught "I Just Want To Celebrate."

Sleaze shoved through the sweaty bartenders to reach the man.

"Hey! What's the matter with you? Turn that juke box down."

Cringing, the manager shook his head and leaned over to yell in his ear.

"They said they break my arms if I touch it. They turn it up, not me, no. They done broke the Six key, too. They gonna tear up dis place, Sleaze, you don't find a way to get them outta here."

Across the crowded room, from the pool tables to the sidewalk, his men glanced furtively his way. The Troglodytes had roared into New Orleans without notice that afternoon, swarming into the lounge like they owned it. Caught off guard, the Bayou Runners had no time to organize back-up, weapons or a welcoming party. Sleaze warned his men not to mention heading to their club house for a more private party. The Trogs had a reputation for repaying hospitality by destroying property, stealing motorcycles and carrying off the dancing girls who kept his boys in beer and smoke.

"How long this bunch staying this time?" Guidry, his Vice President, joined him behind the bar. Surrounded by Trogs, he switched to a Cajun dialect. "Our boys are nervous."

"They should be. That wop cock-sucker acts like he ain't going nowhere until I tell him about my pipeline. Fat fuckin' chance."

"Watch your face, Sleaze, they lookin' to see how upset you are."

Shit, easy for him to say. Guidry played poker at the private clubs twice a week, almost a decade now. The boys had a running joke about no one ever seeing Guidry blink, even his girlfriends. Sleaze, however, lived with a molten forge in his head and would burn up if he tried to contain all that liquid energy. Keeping a calm impassive expression was beyond him, and would scare the shit out of his men. They knew better. But those damn Trogs--

"Some of them are talking about a place to crash for the night."

"Then we need to get 'em out of here while we can," Sleaze blazed. "Hell, I still ain't sure what what Leon wants."

"He wants to take over the business, get us dumb-ass swamp rats to do all the work while they get all the money."

"No shit." Sleaze knew that much. The marshes south of New Orleans offered a lot of financial opportunities for those who could navigate using cypress trees for landmarks. And an alliance with the Trogs would be big, if he could make himself act like the dumb coon-ass these sons-of-bitches always assumed he was.

Being smart enough to act dumb was hard, though. He wanted some respect for what he had organized in a place known for vice since the first traders screwed over the Indians. British, French, Spanish, and fuckin' Andrew Jackson had all fought over Louisiana territory, but his people were still there, hanging on to a tiny bit of swamp through pure grit. That was worth some respect.

Sleaze grimaced, sucking on a bad front tooth. The Trogs respected what he had, but not him. They still needed him to make it all happen, though.

He surveyed the room, his eardrums cracking from the thumping bass. As soon as these assholes left, he was changing out the 45s back to Nathan Abshire and Floyd Cramer. He loved "Paranoid" but it made him want to smash glass with his bare fists and eat it. He'd been choked once, and his crushed larynx already sounded like he had downed a few busted bottles of Jax. Edgy and tired, his Bayou Runners watched him over their beers for a cue. The Trogs eyed him, too, gloating in their deadly confidence.

"There's too many of them to feed to the gators. We'll have to think of something else to do with their New York asses," He told Guidry, who grinned slightly.

Around the room, the Bayou Runners saw the grin and relaxed. Sleaze was still in control. The Trogs had a national reputation as one of the baddest motorcycle clubs in America, but here in south Louisiana, the Bayou Runners knew the swamps, the alleys and where tons of pot were unloaded on a regular basis. It was still their game.

"Leon say anything about their last visit?" Guidry asked hesitantly.

A shadow passed between Sleaze and the front doors, like the lights had dimmed slightly. He ignored it, and shook his head. Last time Leon and the Trogs visited back in June, three of Sleaze's men disappeared. Without a trace. Not even a bone sliver left to pick his teeth with. He and Guidry had hashed it over for weeks, and couldn't agree on what happened.

Muller had been okay, just a few rape beefs, rough on the women but who wasn't? He left one night with two hundred bucks to buy some reds for a party and never came back. Some figured he split, but Muller made much more than that on other deals Sleaze cut him in on. Taking off with two hundred bucks was bullshit.

Then the night after Muller vanished, Lem and Jitters walked down an alley, rode off on their bikes, and did not return. Sleaze didn't miss those two. He'd seen their kind before, tag-team drifters who cruised America's underworld for prey. They were good for nasty work, but never quite understood that their Bayou Runners' patch meant brotherhood, not status for themselves. They did what they wanted and shrugged him off when he questioned them. When they disappeared, he hadn't tried too hard to find them.

The one thing that Muller, Jitters and Lem all had in common was an incredible act of idiocy. At gunpoint, they had forced the owner of a local tattoo shop to give them one-percenter diamonds on their chests. The other Bayou Runners noticed the welts under their cut-offs and were stunned by the disrespect. Like those stateside fucks who wore Purple Hearts or Navy Crosses even though they had never seen a war, that arrogant trio hadn't earned the right to wear a one-percenter tat. The diamond represented an old code understood by all the motorcycle clubs. Furious, his men waited for Sleaze to handle it.

But the Trogs were in town that week, without warning or invitation as usual. He couldn't get distracted for a second, so he warned the stupid bastards they were on their own if the Trogs saw the illegal tats. Before he could figure out what the hell to do about it, the trio disappeared.

It must have been the Trogs, rough justice for the insult to all, but Leon had not made a single comment about it, which was unlike him.

"Nobody's said shit," Sleaze admitted to Guidry.

Guidry stared out the door at the ongoing party on Bourbon Street.

"It had to be the Trogs," Sleaze insisted, knowing Guidry thought otherwise.

"Hope so."

Sleaze scratched at an undercurrent tickling the back of his neck.

"Damn already, Guidry, ain't it complicated enough?" Sleaze glared, and considered his choices to solve the current nightmare. "Go call Old Man Plesseur, tell him I need his back pasture for some campers from New York, and to keep his house lights off. I'll give Leon a chance, see what kind of deal he wants to cut. The Trogs might come in handy, keep the Regents from coming back."

Guidry glanced at him, but said nothing. Back to a poker face, him and his fancy mustache.

Sleaze took two cold beers and a deep breath, and headed for the office. This was some nerve-wracking shit, always playing roulette with the big one-percenter clubs. Leon had switched on the metal floor fan. He and the girl sat huddled at the desk, their knees touching, looking at the pictures in a Front Page Detective.

"This one's kinda cool." The girl smiled tightly to hide a gap in her front teeth.

"You like that?" Leon smiled back. "You think we could find a tree some place, tie you to the tree? You'd like that?"

She giggled and squirmed in her chair. Sleaze set the beer bottles down with a thump.

"Get outta here," He told the girl.

Leon stared up at him, one eyebrow raised. "I ain't done with her. We're gonna find us a tree and some duct tape."

"You're looking for a tree around here, you're gonna be awhile," Sleaze retorted, his voice harsher than he intended. He struggled to tone it down. "I found ya a place for everybody to crash tonight, get some shut-eye."

He didn't want to sound too anxious but if he kept on, he would lose his temper and screw things up. If he hadn't just done so.

Leon closed the magazine and handed it to the girl.

"Go wait behind the bar for me, toots. Anybody fucks with ya, tell 'em you're waiting on me. Shut the door on the way out."

Sleaze worked hard to keep his face straight. Meth had whittled him down to five feet nine inches of bare gristle. He had grown up where kids got a boat before a bicycle, and not always with an outboard. He could—and did—row all night if he had to. He was also good with a knife, but for the knife to do any good, he had to get close enough to use it. Leon was at least six feet four, and about a yard wide. Getting within reach of those massive paws wasn't a good idea.

Sleaze waited while Leon slumped across the desk and let the fan spread his road funk around the small room.

"So. Where are we with this?"

"You still ain't said what you want," Sleaze pointed out.

"Neither have you." Leon pulled a pack of Lucky Strikes from his pocket and lit one. "Seen the Regents lately?"

Fuck almighty, here we go with that shit again.

"No."

"After that ambush last year, none of 'em came back to settle it? You tryin' to tell me Big Alec never came back?"

"I wouldn't be standing here if Big Alec had come back to New Orleans, would I?" Sleaze thought bitterly, but boasted: "He's probably still nursing that broke leg I gave him. He ain't coming back. He didn't get that deal cleared with his national boss. The deal was between me and him. He thought he was gonna score and instead we made 'em look like pussies."

Leon picked up the beer and took a swig.

"Pussies that kept their patches 'cause their probate stood up to you, way I heard it," He declared. "Here's how I see this, Sleaze.

Not everybody gets a second chance. In fact, not everybody wants you to have a second chance. We stopped on the way down here, talked to some of your friends in St. Louis. If you can't help us out, they'd be happy to reach an understanding."

He took another loud swig of beer, giving Sleaze a few seconds to realize he had been betrayed by a federation club.

"Thing is, you had the balls to try, even if it went bad. I still think you can manage the one thing that would swing this deal your way. I think you can bring me the Regents patch from my dear old friend's back."

Sleaze gritted his teeth. "It'll be a lot harder to get to him now."

"You'll think of something. You're a smart man, Sleaze." Leon's eyes narrowed. "It suits you to play both ends of a game and you're real good at it, but you're out of options. I've got a big demand for your product in my area. You already got the business in place, the respect of the cops and the locals. Me and my guys, we could take over your operation tomorrow if we wanted, but a bloodbath just delays progress."

And men on both sides would die, and Leon would get rid of Sleaze first. Fury swept over him. Not after all the shit he'd had to do to get to this point.

"We can make this work in a big way for both of us," Leon said. "You don't like leaving your swamp, fine, I'll handle the national shit. But you gotta prove to me you ain't gonna let me down."

Ah, there it was. *Proof.* Him and this damned vendetta against Big Alec. Sleaze wasn't supposed to know about it, but Big Alec once hung out with the Trogs for a summer. Then he went to south Florida and started a Regents chapter down there instead of a Trogs chapter like he was told. Worse yet, he'd made a success out of it. And the Trogs didn't forgive.

Leon stubbed out his cigarette. "When I go to the other guys back home and talk about an alliance with you, I got to have something that proves your loyalty to us."

Sleaze remained silent. Why didn't Leon just go to Miami and get Big Alec's patch himself if he was such a bad ass? It had taken four of Sleaze's best men to wrestle Alec to the floor even with his leg broke and his head busted open. If it hadn't been for that damned Regents probate pulling a .38 and screwing it all up, Sleaze would have had that damned patch.

Sweaty and gritty, the ultimate prize, he'd been sawing into the blue denim cut-off with his favorite knife when the kid stood up with a pistol in his hand. His men thought the kid was going to kill him, and the kid thought Sleaze was about to cut Alec's throat. A dozen bullets sizzled through the air, and the world changed a little in New Orleans and Sleaze couldn't undo it.

Leon seemed to be reading his mind. Black eyes glinting, he waved the dead cigarette in the air.

"Ya bring me that patch, Sleaze, and we'll do business. And ya know what? I'll sweeten the pot because you did try. You almost had it. You risked your neck for it. So I know you're no bull-shitter. I respect that." He paused, leaned forward slightly, and dropped his voice. "You bring me his patch, and I'll trade ya even."

Uncertain if he heard him right, Sleaze didn't move.

"You bring me Alec's patch and I'll give *you* a patch," Leon almost whispered. "I guarantee a hundred-percent vote on it. No probating, no hassles. You'll be the first Trog in Louisiana. You wanta wear a Trog patch, Sleaze? You wanta be a one-percenter in the baddest fucking motorcycle club in America?"

Sleaze picked up his Jax beer, his hand quivering. The bottle thudded against his rotten front teeth but he didn't feel it. He managed a swallow down the tiny opening in his constricted throat. A Trogs patch. Jesus. People crossed the street to avoid a Trog. They had been around over thirty years, in the newspapers, even a movie, working their way over from the west coast. Jesus. But how the hell could he get to Big Alec? The man would kill Sleaze on sight if he saw him again, and the son-of-a-bitch never went anywhere without his loyal Miami Regents chapter.

"A smart man does not wait for opportunity, Sleaze. A smart man creates opportunity."

Someone knocked on the door, and Leon chuckled.

"There you go. That could be opportunity knocking."

It took awhile for Leon to stand up. He had to gather his bulk, put tremendous pressure on his knees, heave, straighten his back, his body rising up toward the acoustic tile ceiling, out toward the walls. Sleaze, however, couldn't move. Leon lumbered over to the door and opened it himself. The bar manager gaped at him and stepped back.

"They…they got a place for you to camp, Mr. Leon. Some of your men wanta leave, say they're tired."

"They can go," Leon said. "I got a motel room. I'll be back tomorrow. We got a deal?"

Sleaze had been bracing himself on the beer bottle. He left it on the desk and walked toward Leon, offering his sweaty hand.

"Deal."

♦

The bar emptied itself rapidly of the unwelcome visitors, boots clumping on the wooden floor and voices drifting outside. Suddenly it was quiet. The juke box volume dimmed, Ringo Starr agreeing that nothing came easy. Sleaze sat motionless behind the big desk, listening. He could finally hear empty bottles clinking as they were tossed in the trash, the whirring fan, a cue stick scattering billiard balls into distant pockets.

Two faint raps sounded at the open door. The bar manager peered cautiously inside, followed by Guidry.

"Saved you a beer, Sleaze. Them sons of bitches took every last one."

"Thanks," Sleaze said quietly.

Open-mouthed, the manager exchanged a shocked glance with Guidry.

"You okay, boss?"

"Yeah." Sleaze looked at a nurse with flaming red hair, her short skirt scrunched up to reveal a black garter belt. "You think women like getting tied up like that?"

"Huh?" The manager followed his gaze. "Oh. I don't know."

"Then why do you have all those goddamn magazines tacked to the wall?"

"I jus' like looking at them. They pretty when they scared. They bother you, I take 'em down. You never said nothin' before."

"I never been staring at 'em over Leon's shoulder for five fucking hours before."

Anxious for a diversion, the manager pointed to a side desk drawer.

"I never had time to tell you, no. Didn't wanta say nothin' in front of Leon, neither. Mailman brought a package here today for you. I put it in dat bottom drawer."

"Package?" Sleaze frowned.

He couldn't make his brain work except to visualize a Troglodyte patch on his back, tourists veering off the sidewalk in terror as he approached, all those snotty bastards at the Courthouse turning to gape, everybody in the Quarter wanting to make him happy. But Guidry and the manager were looking at him funny. He had to snap out of it. Sleaze popped the latch on the bottom desk drawer and rolled it open. A small parcel neatly wrapped in brown paper nestled among the peppermint candy and whiskey bottle.

"Like *The Sound of Music*," The manager smiled. "You know, a few of your favorite t'ings tied up in strings."

"Fuck *The Sound of Music*. The mailman handed this to you or one of the guys?"

"He ast for me, waited outside. He wasn't coming in here, no."

"Take it out of the drawer and put it on the desk."

"What?"

"You heard me." Sleaze said and rolled back in the chair.

The manager awkwardly bent over Sleaze's boots and plucked up the small parcel.

"Dere ain't nutten wrong wid it." The man's accent deepened as he became more nervous. "See? Him's got stamps on him. Done been t'rough de U.S. Mail. And look. Dat's educated handwritin'. It ain't Cat'lic school but it is educated. "

"There's no return address," Sleaze observed. "Pick it up and throw it on the floor. Over there."

Guidry pressed himself hard against the wall.

"It might be fragile," The manager protested. "It don't hardly weigh nothin'."

"Throw it!"

Scrunching up his face, the manager picked it up by the strings and flung it across the room. The box struck a screaming blonde in the forehead and bounced lightly to the floor without bringing down a single thumb-tacked nurse.

Sleaze held his breath but the parcel sat quietly on the floor.

"Okay, bring it here."

The manager scooped it up and set it down in front of Sleaze with trembling fingers.

"Don't tell me to cut it open 'cause I cain't, my nerves is gone."

"Shut up." Sleaze pulled out his pocket knife and sliced through the strings, then checked the address once again. "Mr. Sleaze Minarde."

Somebody was being funny. Hardly anyone knew his last name. Had to be from way back, some joker that knew his family. Or somebody who served in the Navy with him. He got mad. The brown paper was three layers thick and glued in place. He tore through it until he could see a Hav-A-Tampa cigar box taped shut.

He pushed at it with a pencil. Something inside shifted. Guidry crossed his arms, squinting, waiting for a blast.

"Dear Lord," The manager breathed.

Exasperated, Sleaze slit the taped edges with his knife and pried off the lid.

The manager frowned at the slightly curled objects inside. "What is dem, fortune cookies?"

Sleaze dumped them out of the box. There were three of them, light-colored, leathery. He pushed at them with the tip of his pencil until one turned over.

"Fuck," Guidry said in a strangled voice and stepped back from the desk, crossing his arms tighter across his chest. "Mother-fucker."

Tonsils glued to the back of his throat, Sleaze stared as the one-percenter diamond came into focus. Black ink. On pale tanned leather. No, not leather. Skin. Dried skin. Three of them. Muller. Lem. Jitters.

The manager squinted in bewilderment.

"What dem is?"

Sleaze wheezed as his meth-scalded lungs tried to inflate. "They are the answer to a question I been asking wrong."

He studied how carefully the edges had been cut, how the skin had been prepped. The precise work mirrored the educated handwriting on the package.

"How does it feel to be right, Guidry? Wasn't the Trogs after all."

"It ain't feeling so hot right now," Guidry admitted.

Sleaze touched the faded black ink with his pen. "Shit. Wonder how long the son-of-a-bitch has been out."

"He ain't just out," Guidry said. "He's been *here*."

Sleaze considered that, unable to break his fascinated, horrified stare with the three souvenirs on the desk.

"Well, guess we oughta be glad he didn't stop by to say hello. It don't look like he was in a good mood."

CHAPTER ONE

Atlanta, August 1971

Neon signs glowed along the Strip, deep reds and greens trapped in the dust rising from the street. Hippies and cops moved slowly down the sidewalks, pretending it was business as usual in this part of Atlanta, even though they knew better. They eyed the dark upstairs windows in the old brick buildings, the passing cars, and each other. A week ago, a young policeman had been murdered.

Slain cops had reached epidemic proportions in other cities, courtesy of the Weather Underground or Black Liberation Army, but that was elsewhere. Here in Atlanta, students protested, police arrested marchers, and the occasional youthful outburst turned into a riot, but luring cops into an ambush didn't happen here. Until now.

Determined to have a good time, tourists strolled from dance lounges to liquor stores, ignoring the tension. They were in Atlanta to party and gawk at the hippies, not worry about what the hell else could go wrong in America. Thanks to Walter Cronkite, they had seen enough of Charles Manson, massacres at Kent State and My Lai, and weekly skyjackings to everywhere but Mars. The death of one young cop wasn't even a small blip on national radar. Whatever happened a week ago was already history.

That's what they wanted to believe.

"If you don't honor the dead, they'll never leave you alone."

Joe Wilson watched the procession from the front seat of a '62 Impala: the enraged cops in commando mode, the paranoid hippies, and those grinning tourists, determined to see only the bottom of their shot glass as the lights began winking out down Peachtree.

"Pretending it's okay won't do you a damned bit of good," Joe warned silently.

It had been ten years since the Fates got his attention on an Air Force flight-line. He did whatever it took to keep that memory at the back of his skull--some people thought he went to extremes-- but the dead wouldn't stay dead.

Joe glanced at his watch. Two in the morning. Only one more stop before heading back to the clubhouse. He wanted to ditch this mood. A lot of men would gladly have traded places with him at the moment. The big Impala was packed hip to hip with young dancers, the air a tangy mix of pot and White Rain hairspray. The girls were tired but sassy, chattering about their night and the tricks: the good-looking ones, the big tippers and the weirdos.

Beside him, two young women in mini-skirts sat crammed together, their legs jackknifed in heels. Not that he was looking. Despite the booming 8-track player, he heard an exasperated sigh from the small tawny-haired woman snugged hip to hip against him. Or maybe he felt it. He knew what that hip looked like when it wasn't hidden by a lime green mini-skirt.

"Pay attention." She gazed out the windshield.

"I was," He assured her.

"She meant, eyes on the road," The brunette beside her clarified.

"You know, why is it you want us to act like men, then you get mad when we do? Can one of y'all explain that to me?"

"No, we can't. It's a chick secret," Kitty said.

Inside the purse on her lap, the grip of a Colt 1911-A poked out, within easy reach if Joe needed it. With his left hand on the wheel, he pulled up behind Hank and Jerry's Lounge. He knew the bouncers, dishwashers and short-order cooks. They watched out for the girls, and usually waited around to make sure a taxi or ride showed up before going home themselves. It kept the predators in the shadows, gave them time to get nervous and go find easier prey among the runaways.

Nobody in their right mind would snatch up a Regent's old lady. It was the "wrong mind" factor that Joe looked for when he scanned the parking lot for potential trouble.

The back door of the lounge opened, and two girls skittered to the air-conditioned car. "Make room. My feet are killing me."

"We're full. Sit in Joe's lap while he drives."

"Y'all want to get home tonight or not?" Joe grinned.

A tiny blue-eyed redhead in the back seat leaned forward to run her fingernails across his neck, slowly.

"You've been so serious tonight, we thought something was wrong. Tell you what, I'll get a motel room and we can all make you feel better," She purred, and the other girls laughed, glad to see Joe finally grin. "My treat. I got a big tip from the Professor. That man loves the way I do 'Lola.' "

"Maybe he's impressed you can spell," Joe said, trying to ignore the hot peppermint breath in his ear.

"Aw. Isn't he the sweetest probate we've ever had?" She smirked. "And damn sure the best-looking one."

"Keep on, Dorrie, you'll get me kicked out before I get kicked in. Settle down or I'll turn off the tape. I know that's why you're behaving inappropriately."

"Yeah, she's usually so dignified," Kitty sniffed.

The big car purred down Peachtree Street, the worn 8-track tape thumping out "Ramblin' Gamblin' Man." During a run to Detroit, Dorrie had fallen in love with the rugged lead singer of a local band, the Bob Seger System. Just in case the guy never made it big, she stole the tape.

"He ain't good lookin' but ya know he ain't shy," She gyrated in the back seat.

The air inside the Impala warmed up, musk overpowering marijuana. The raw male voice grunting from the speakers wasn't helping. Joe wanted to get them back to the clubhouse before it got crazy. If they were late, the Regents might pull him from taxi duty, and this was definitely one of his easier assignments.

"What's going on at home?" A tall blonde asked. "They sleeping or partying?"

There was a mood-crusher.

"Dudley was getting a meeting together when I left."

The girls grew quiet. Joe reached for his cigarettes and rolled the window down an inch. Their unspoken sympathy was embarrassing. The Regents trusted him to make sure their women got home okay every night from the titty bars, but he had to stand outside the clubhouse like a scolded kid when they held a meeting. As they often reminded him, he was a probate, almost at the bottom of the club hierarchy with the dancing girls.

His patience, never a strong point, was wearing thin. He hadn't been in Atlanta long, but he had already proven himself worthy to ride with the Regents as a patched member, not some punk bringing up the rear. He was getting antsy again, and that wasn't good.

"What are they doing over there at The Bird, celebrating another issue?" Kitty squinted.

White glare poured from the front windows of the radical newspaper office. Inside, several figures danced wildly, paper flying everywhere. Dorrie leaned forward to gape at the waltzing hippies.

"Oh no, *oh no*, is that Bobby? Joe, look!"

Joe stopped the car in the middle of the street. In the Air Force, they had nicknamed him Scopes because of his incredible vision. Through the dusty windshield, he followed the wild dance until the revelers separated. A teenager with a blonde Afro and Nehru shirt ran from the open door. Behind him, fearless and staggering drunk, came a stocky man shouting curses.

"Shit." Joe jumped out of the car.

Terrified, the kid ran crazily, his pale hair bouncing behind him like a dandelion, his tennis shoes digging for traction. Bobby wore heavy boots, but fury gave him an edge. He gained on the kid, grabbing a handful of hair just as Joe caught up and tackled them.

"Mother-fucker!" Bobby roared as he hit the pavement. "Lemme go."

"Stop him!" A gaggle of hippies in prairie dresses stormed down the sidewalk. "Somebody call the pigs! He's killing Mickey."

"You little shit." Bobby found the kid's neck somewhere in the hair and used it as a handle to pound his head into the concrete.

"Billy was a friend of mine, you hear me?"

"Bobby, stop." Joe pulled one arm loose and twisted it up behind his back, forcing him face-first into the sidewalk. He didn't want to hurt him unless he had to.

"No," Bobby panted, even though the kid had pancaked beneath the weight of the two grown men. "Didn't you see…what he wrote…in his fucking commie newspaper? The little bastard..."

"It's freedom of the press. We write the truth," A young editor shrieked and marched over to kick Bobby in the ribs with her gestapo boot. "Your pig friend was a terrorist persecuting the Liberation Army. Killing him was justice!"

Joe grabbed her ankle and twisted it, dumping her on her ass.

"Shut up," He advised.

With feral cries, the hippie girls surrounded them and launched a frenzy of kicks. Before Joe could move, the doors on the Impala flew open and the dancers hurtled out. An eager crowd of spectators materialized, hanging on the edges of the brawl, hooting as the hippies' hair-pulling techniques failed miserably under round-house punches delivered by the dancers.

Joe felt Bobby's rage slacken, and heard him groan. Not from physical pain—he wouldn't feel his aching shoulder until the booze wore off—but from a deeper place.

"Let go, Bobby. Save it for another time."

"Fuck him," Bobby said, but uncurled his fingers and closed his eyes.

Joe carefully eased off him, making sure he didn't erupt again. Bobby rolled to the curb on his back, wheezing. The blonde kid sprawled unconscious, an unhealthy blue color, with one ankle turned inward like a sawdust doll. Sobbing, the battered female radicals took him by the arms and dragged their vanquished comrade to an unlit doorway for safety.

"You want some more, bitch?" Dorrie taunted, stamping her size-five foot at them. "Huh? Do ya?"

Surrounded by slender legs on acrylic heels, Joe sat down beside Bobby. He had no room to lecture anyone on impulse control, and tried consolation instead.

"They're just a bunch of stupid naïve kids trying to be important. If they live to grow up, the smart ones will be embarrassed by what they didn't know. And you taught 'em something. If they print it, you've got a right to let 'em know you disagree."

"Billy was a good guy," Bobby said. "Instead of putting me in the drunk tank, he'd take me to the clubhouse, ya know? He wasn't an asshole. He was twenty-seven fuckin' years old, man. He didn't deserve for some gutless mother-fucker to shoot him in the back of the head."

"Joe," Kitty said. "We've got company."

Blue lights swirled in the haze, and a siren cranked up, echoing between the buildings. Down the sidewalk, two beat cops were hurrying up from the far end of the Strip.

"Get the girls back in the car. Bobby, where's your bike?"

"Oh man. Shit. I don't know where I parked it. Shit, man." Now came the maudlin wailing part of the drunken binge. Joe didn't have time for therapeutic counseling. He forced Bobby to his feet and walked him to the car, shoving him into the back seat between the women.

"Sit there and shut up. If you get me arrested, I won't forget it," Joe promised.

"I want my bike." Bobby kicked the seat in front of him.

The girls shifted in the cramped car, hair wilting and cheap polyester outfits chafing. Dancing naked for strangers was hard work. "Would you settle for me, Bobby?" Dorrie eased into his lap. Two girls flanked him, effectively sealing him in the car just as two beat cops walked up.

The Impala was hemmed in by the crowd so Joe leaned against the hood to wait while the cops interviewed the hippies. Kitty sat beside him, legs crossed and smoking a cigarette.

"You always park in the middle of the street?" The cop wore sergeant's stripes, and was tall enough to look Joe in the eye.

"My friend's had a bad night," Joe said. "I'd like to take him home."

"That's Bobby Boozer. He's a Regent." The cop worked a toothpick in the corner of his mouth. "You a Regent?"

"No, I'm a redneck from Hazlehurst. Just visiting."

"Oh. An innocent bystander," The cop said, then gazed at the boneless kid sprawled on the sidewalk, encircled protectively by young women with bloody noses and scraped knees. "They said your friend just walked into their office and started trashing the place."

"From what I understand, Bobby took exception to an article they wrote."

"Everything they write pisses people off. They wouldn't be happy if it didn't."

"I don't read the shit myself but the article was apparently about the young officer you recently lost, and it wasn't respectful," Joe said, his dark eyes watching the cop's face.

The man shifted his toothpick and glanced at his partner.

"They wrote an article about Billy?"

"Billy the Pig."

"Is that so?"

This time, Joe looked away. He didn't want to witness the change working over their faces. It was too personal. "If you don't mind, I'd like to take my friend home," Joe said quietly.

The sergeant shifted the toothpick again, his gaze on the red-eyed sobbing bunch against the building. Now that they were safe, they were working themselves into an indignant frenzy over the violation of their civil rights.

"Have a nice night," The cop told Joe softly, and walked off.

CHAPTER TWO

In the former dining room of a 1920s bungalow, Savoy Brown pulsed from eight speakers mounted around the ceiling. The music hovered low in the hot corners. The occupants of the house wanted to hear any potential threats from the street.

A dozen men sat at a plywood table, their boots angled around the metal frame beneath it. Ash trays hopscotched among the beer cans down the eight-foot length. On the makeshift bar behind them, a lava lamp oozed red blobs, throwing a scarlet glow across the walls.

"That lamp looks like embryos, you ever notice that?" A small monkeyish man with long slick hair peered at the bar. His single eyebrow slid into a knot.

"Greasy, I don't wanta know how you know what embryos look like."

"I seen 'em in a carnival once. They were in jars." Greasy pointed across the room. "Look, there's a leg dangling, see?"

"You are one sick bastard. I ain't looking." His muscular back to the bar, Ugly refused to rise to the bait. "It's just wax, okay? I busted one to see."

"You broke the last one?" Greasy gaped. "Did y'all hear that? Ugly broke my damn lava lamp. That's ten bucks you owe me, you stupid grunt."

"Here's your ten dollars." Ugly bounced a bottle cap off Greasy's forehead. Disappointed when it didn't stick, he slung another one, harder.

"Ow! That's gonna cost you more."

"Okay already. This meeting will now come to order," Smitty, their Vice President, interrupted as the situation deteriorated.

"We can't start yet. Bobby ain't here."

"I'm not waiting on Bobby's drunk ass."

Dudley, the boss of the Atlanta Chapter of the Regents MC, leaned forward in his creaky cane chair, shifting his weight to his upper arms. He lived in pain from hips shattered in a helicopter crash. It hurt to sit down, it hurt to stand up, and it hurt to ride his '68 FLH, even with the swing-arm. He refused to resort to the morphine needle ruining the lives of his former infantry brothers, but felt like shit most of the time. By 2 a.m., his patience was gone.

"Enforcer, you want to get everyone's attention?" He suggested.

Conversation stopped when Ugly reached inside his jacket. When he pulled out a pack of Camels, the men relaxed.

"Okay, gentlemen, I've got good news and bad news. Good news first. We're hosting the next National."

They didn't react with great enthusiasm. Three hundred club members descending on their small clubhouse meant the place would get trashed, if not burned to the ground. Things tended to happen during Regents MC Nationals.

"We just went to a National," Greasy pointed out, bewildered.

"Yeah, and now it's our turn. More good news, it won't be here. The National's gonna be in Talladega at the A.M.A. races."

They finally grinned. The Talladega Super Speedway was two hours away in Alabama, putting some distance between their clubhouse and trouble. The motorcycle races would be a bonus. So what was the bad news?

"Some intel reached me today that we'll have company. In fact, we're gonna put together a little welcoming party."

The smiles faded.

"Trogs?" Ugly ventured.

"Nope. Almost as good."

Grins broke out around the table.

"Bayou Runners?"

"Bingo."

"Hot damn! I'll go clean up my Cajun decoder ring. I want to know when Sleaze says please stop, Mr. Regent, it hurts!"

Every man at the table laughed, except one. Blue eyes like ice, Jess Whitley rocked back in his chair until it teetered on the two rear legs, bumping the wall.

"They don't come out of their swamp without a very good reason," He said.

"Yeah, it don't make sense," Long tall Country chimed in. "You really think they're going there for the races? Is somebody from Louisiana running?"

"I seriously doubt they're making the trip to cheer for the A.M.A. guys," Jess said, moving his beer bottle around an ash tray like a chess piece. "But even if they do, Sleaze is mine."

His Regents brothers became quiet.

"Big Alec might have something to say about that," Dudley remarked.

Jess shrugged. "Talladega's a long way from Miami. He may not show up."

"For a chance to pay back the Bayou Runners for last year? He was packing when he called me. He's the one who got the tip."

Jess acknowledged Dudley's token protest, proper procedure for a boss, then looked around the table at his Atlanta Chapter brothers.

"If he wanted revenge, he should have taken care of it before now," Jess said. "It was his chapter they disrespected. Me and Smitty went along because we knew the territory."

"He wasn't in no shape for revenge for a few months. Alec sorta had a broken leg, remember?" Smitty chortled. "Sleaze and those Cajun boys worked that knee cap of his, too. He couldn't ride for shit."

Jess picked up a toothpick, and said softly: "Sleaze is mine."

No one argued. They knew why Jess wanted Sleaze. So what if the Miami boss, Big Alec, also had a score to settle with the crazy bastard? The Atlanta Chapter didn't have a problem out-maneuvering their Miami brothers to insure Jess got first crack at the treacherous Cajun. After all, old friends made the worst enemies, and Jess and Sleaze went way back. Rumor had it, all the way back to Vietnam.

Beneath Jess's boots, a small black and white bulldog pup suddenly lifted her head. A minute later, they heard an engine thrumming up the street. Headlights slowed in front of the bungalow and washed across the walls.

"There's our probate."

"With our old ladies." Greasy lifted his eyebrow. "Running late, ain't he?"

"Probably took 'em for ice cream," Ugly huffed. "I don't know who's spoiling who."

"Would you want to be trapped in a small space with them for an hour?" Jess said.

"You gotta keep their mouths busy so they can't talk," Ugly cracked, listening to the tires crunch up the rough concrete driveway beside the house. He stubbed out his cigarette and glanced at Jess. "Is he going to Talladega?"

At the end of the table, a small pug-faced man frowned and sat up straight.

"He hasn't been a probate long enough to go to a National. You trying to give him a patch already? It took me six months to get one. And look what happened last time we had a National and you left him alone here."

Several men raised their eyebrows. Others looked away at the breach of protocol. They left the rebuttal to the one with the most at stake.

"What happened, Bugsy?" Jess looked long and hard at him.

Bugsy squirmed. Despite his best effort, his moist, protruding eyes shot over to the trophy wall behind the bar, where a dozen patches hung. Bayou Runners, Maulers, and a solitary Troglodyte. One Mauler patch still had a strong feral odor. He opened his mouth, then thought better of it.

"Whatever happened, he ain't been here long enough to go to a National," Bugsy insisted. "He don't exactly have a good track record and you guys let him go pick up your women. You really think that's a good idea?"

"You really think our women are any of your business?" Ugly retorted.

A glare from Ugly usually inspired most people to leave the room quickly. At six-foot-four barefoot, he carried a massive muscular frame straight out of a super-hero comic book. His deep-set eyes and blocky face looked like fists would merely bounce off him, if someone was suicidal enough to try. But Bugsy had lived his short, miserable life airing his many grievances, and wasn't about to stop now.

"Maybe you ain't worried about him getting some pussy, but I know you give a shit about their tips. That guy's had spending money ever since he got here. Where the fuck's he getting it? Those cunts go in heat if he walks across the back yard without his shirt."

He finally had their attention. They already knew the girls liked Joe, and only a few minded if their old ladies wanted to party with the probate. It kept the girls from straying outside the club, which prevented problems for everyone. But they had never considered where the probate got the funds to indulge his other sweet tooth: a gallon of butter pecan ice cream twice a week, not to mention gas money for his motorcycle.

Greasy slammed his beer can down, splattering himself with Pabst.

"Boss! Is there a rule says the old ladies can't get wet panties around the probate? Has no one informed me of this new rule? What the fuck kinda club is this?"

"Sounds to me like somebody's a bitter bastard because none of the girls want to fuck his itty bitty pug-dog dick," Country drawled.

"If you're done with the pussy debates, can we get back to the National?" Dudley said. "We seriously outnumber those assholes, but we'd be stupid not to figure on Sleaze pulling something. It's guaranteed there's gonna be trouble."

"It's guaranteed there's gonna be trouble if Jess takes his new probate," Smitty declared. "What do you think, Jess? You're his sponsor."

"I got shot last time I went somewhere with him," Jess admitted.

"I don't remember things going too smooth, either," Ugly spoke up. "But the son-of-a-bitch always had my back no matter what."

"Didn't we agree it'd be a good idea to take him to a National first chance we got? Before he gets into any more shit?"

"I don't know about no agreement." Country carved a frog in the plywood with his pocket knife. "I think it was a suggestion in the heat of the particular moment."

"So? He can't get a patch until he attends at least one National. This'll let the rest of the Nation see how he operates."

"I know that ain't a good idea," Country grinned.

"Talladega's starting to sound like fun." Greasy smacked his lips.

Dudley's aching hip sockets reached their limit. "I didn't call the meeting to discuss the probate. He's going. It's a national, we'll need him. That's it. Right now, we've gotta figure out what to take with us. Greasy, get in touch with that friend of yours at the base--"

The back door thumped open, hard. The pup raced around the corner to the kitchen with high excited yips. A second later, she hurtled back to hide under Jess's chair. A wild gurgling yell followed a crash in the kitchen.

"What the hell?" Ugly was on his feet in a second, a .45 in his hand.

Around the table, pistols came out of boots and shirts. Dudley reached for a pump shotgun in the corner.

"Don't shoot!" A man yelled from the kitchen.

Bobby Boozer came staggering into the room. Arms and face crusty with fresh scabs from skidding down the sidewalk, his bleary gaze latched on the lava lamp.

"I hate that thing. It looks like pickled pork tongues. Where's my pistol?" He growled. "It's on my fuckin' bike, wherever that is. Hey Probate, what'd you do with my bike?"

"I let Dorrie ride it home," Joe said, standing in the doorway, his forearms and elbows bleeding.

"What happened?" Smitty gaped. "My old lady rode his bike?"

Joe shook his head. "Bobby decided to express his freedom of speech down there at the Bird. I got him home but I don't know where he parked the bike."

"Any arrests?"

"Nah. The door was open so it wasn't breaking and entering. Wasn't really assault, either, more like Texas two-step with Bobby taking the lead. But I'm guessing they're going to miss their print deadline."

"God Almighty," Dudley said and stowed the shotgun back in the corner.

"Where's my pistol?" Bobby wailed.

"Shut up." Ugly gave him a shove.

He landed on the floor and sat there for moment, fresh blood oozing from the scraped scabs, then crawled over to the couch.

"Everything's gone."

"Yeah, including your dignity." Country handed him a beer.

"You'd have been proud of your old ladies," Joe grinned.

"How come?"

"Me and Bobby were under attack from the radical left and the girls jacked 'em up. Wasn't much of a fight, but we appreciated the effort."

"Oh yeah? Where are they?"

"Outside, waiting to see if you want them to come in or go home."

"Tell 'em to go on home. We're busy," Smitty said, but grinned at Joe through the cigarette smoke. "Dorrie got in a few good punches?"

"Shit. She laid one out. Lois Lane was laying there on the sidewalk with her granny glasses knocked off her head and a nosebleed."

Smitty cackled. "That's my girl. I taught her that."

Dudley's face twisted into a yawn, and he looked up at Joe with bleary eyes. "We're not done with our meeting. Step outside, probate."

The mood in the room went from jovial to sour. Joe shut down. This was something he would never get used to. As a teenager in boot-camp, he took it because they made him believe he had to. But it had been years since a man talked to him like that and got away with it. He picked up the squirming puppy, who clung to him like a fat baby and licked his face anxiously. Some of the tension left him. He didn't want her picking up on his mood.

"Come on, Smokes, let's go pee."

He stepped back outside and set the puppy in the grass. The women waited wearily by the car, shifting from one aching foot to the other.

"You are free to go," Joe announced. "You can pick up your boxing trophies tomorrow."

For several dancers, home was right across the driveway at the bungalow next door. Plastic heels clattered across the rough concrete to the back door.

"Good night, Joe, see you tomorrow."

Mina lingered. She had a good-natured homely face, the sort seen in the mountain coves north of Atlanta, with dimpled cheeks and a sharp chin.

"Kitty, you wanta walk with me or you gonna hang around and wait for Jess?"

Greasy and Mina rented a house a few doors down, the backyard opposite to a two-story Victorian owned by Kitty and Jess. Day or night, they took a shortcut through the back yards of the houses, strolling under the trees with familiar confidence. But the cop murder reminded them the world was not so safe, even for the street savvy.

Kitty scooted to the driver's side and swung her legs out. A fat joint glowed between her fingertips, down to a half inch of paper.

"I'll wait on Jess. I'm too jazzed up to go home yet." She said, green eyes like crystal.

"We kicked some ass, didn't we?" Mina grinned.

"Joe could have sold tickets."

"Not without someone's tit falling out. Maybe next time, huh."

Joe leaned against the Impala and watched Mina open the gate and vanish into the darkness. Fragrant smoke swirled as Kitty exhaled, but he shook his head when she offered him a toke. The puppy ran around the wilted azaleas and gardenias, sniffing along the chain link fence. She stopped in front of Kitty, sneezed, and took off on another circuit behind the garage. The old neighborhood panted softly, resting before another day beneath a harsh sun.

Kitty bent forward and lifted a handful of long tawny hair off her neck. "Were they still at the table?"

"Yep."

"It's hot tonight. Are you spending the night at my place?"

Yes, it was at least eighty degrees, but that kind of heat didn't bother him. What bothered him was sleeping in the small room next to the master bedroom she and Jess shared. Even with the door closed and the stereo on, he didn't sleep worth a damn. Sometimes the noises seemed to be for his benefit, one male gorilla letting the new gorilla know that the alpha male was back in the jungle after a long captivity, a primate challenge as to whose skill and gymnastics could please the female the best. Joe doubted if Marlon Perkins would do a Wild Kingdom show on it, but he got the message.

"I'll crash in my apartment," He said. His so-called apartment consisted of a sleeping bag and fan on a workbench in the old two-bay garage.

"They might be awhile," She gazed up at him with lazy eyes half-closed. "Come on over, I'll turn on the air-conditioner and we can wait for Jess."

He shook his head.

"Three's a crowd, Kit. Your old man's home now. It's kind of awkward. I'm an old-fashioned redneck. I don't know the rules for all this open-minded sharing shit."

"Jess didn't expect me to sit still while he was locked up. He doesn't mind what I do as long as he knows about it."

"Have you asked him lately?" Joe said, refusing to look down at her pouty little mouth, the perfect small teeth that could nip—*stop thinking about it*!

He was not going to give in. He had been in a weird mood all night, a hot tension wire humming along his nerves. Revved up from the fight, rowdy sex was the natural conclusion to an evening of violence, blood and victory over an enemy. Another era, another time, he would have flung her over his shoulder and stalked off cave-man style to a field of tall rustling grass to give her what she wanted, and she damn sure wouldn't be jumping back up to ask for more any time soon.

But Jess was home now, and Joe had to rein in the blind lust. It also irked him that Kitty thought bribing him with sex would keep him around through the bullshit and humiliation of probating for the Regents. He wanted respect from Jess, to mend what he had done, and he wanted a friendship with both of them. Which wasn't easy when she knew how to turn him into a rabid dog with a hard-on.

"What are you thinking about?" She took the last hit from the paper fragment.

"You laying naked in a moonlit field with a bunch of grass pounded up your ass."

"Ow. Did I enjoy your little fantasy at all?" She stood up, arching her back, and pouted. "Why do you want to make things so complicated? I'm just talking about physical release, not a marathon. You know, a quickie in the shower."

What the hell was in that weed? Jess could walk out the back door at any second. Kitty took a few teasing steps toward him, the hem of her mini-skirt brushing his thigh. Oh hell, there he went. He had to stop this.

"It isn't complicated at all, Kitty. If someone handed you a gun and said you had to shoot me or Jess, you wouldn't hesitate to blow my brains out."

She stared at him, her mouth falling open, the calm marijuana glow evaporating. She backed up, clenching her fists, then leaned forward to hiss: "You asshole! How can you say that? How can you even think something sick like that?"

"Because it's true?" Finally. He had pissed her off.

"You shit!" She slugged him in the stomach."I would never—how can you say that to me, after everything I've done? You're a shit."

He hadn't counted on tears. She wasn't a weeper. She must be tired.

"Kitty," He relented, reaching for her hand.

"No." She stepped back, gathering her rage and dignity. "You can just go fuck yourself, or whatever whore around here wants to get laid. I've got better things to do than get grass up my ass."

She yanked up her purse and slung it over her shoulder.

"And by the way. If some son-of-a-bitch came up to me and told me I had to shoot you or Jess, I'd shoot the son-of-a-bitch! Damn. I hate you. I hate all of you."

The puppy peered anxiously around the corner of the garage, her black velvet ears down.

"Except you," Kitty said. "Come on, Smoky, you don't have to put up with his shit either."

The two of them marched through the gate toward her house, Kitty unsteady in the heels, the puppy staying close.

Joe reached in his pocket for a pack of cigarettes. "Good night, girls."

"What's that all about?"

Joe turned to look at the man standing at the back door.

"She says she hates anything with a dick."

"Must be that time of the month. You're such a suave motherfucker, it couldn't be you," Greasy declared. "Come on, meeting's over. Let's have a beer."

CHAPTER THREE

He couldn't remember what led up to it, only that he had tumbled off a cliff and was now hurtling through rushing air. Eyes shut tightly against the impact, Joe gripped the cushions and jammed his boots against the upholstered arm, hoping the couch would somehow break his fall. Instead, he jerked awake in mid-air, heart hammering and sick to his stomach.

Panting, he rolled onto his back and stretched his hand down, touching dusty wood, not hard-packed clay. He was not at the bottom of a canyon. Blowing out a long breath, he opened his eyes. Shit. A witness. Barely two yards away, a man sat in a chair, straddling the seat backwards, his arms propped across the back. Morning sun poured in the window behind him, lighting up his blond hair and classic profile.

"Something wrong?" Joe asked, determined to gain the advantage, if he didn't throw up first.

The Regents and their old ladies rarely went to bed before 3 a.m. Barring disaster, no one stirred before noon.

"You tell me." Jess held a big mug of coffee in one hand, the rich smell of Louisiana chicory giving Joe caffeine high. "You're the one going into cardiac arrest in your sleep. Did you watch a scary movie after we left? Lavinia the Lascivious Lizard Girl always gives me nightmares. I think it's the green tail."

Joe ignored the jab and leaned back into the cushions. "Me and Smoky are guarding the clubhouse."

"Yeah, you're quite a team. She almost licked me to death at the back door and you were snoring your ass off up until you started kicking the shit out of the couch."

"Got you in here, didn't we? She's probably in the kitchen sharpening her teeth on some kibbles, waiting for my signal."

A grin twitched at the corner of Jess's mouth. Joe relaxed. That was a good sign, maybe. Jess didn't smile or laugh much.

"Nah, I think she's in the kitchen making coffee."

"Now that's a damn good dog."

"Are you seeing that hippie chick in the park?"

Surprised by the change of subject, Joe contemplated a hairline crack snaking across the plaster ceiling before saying cautiously: "Seeing is about it. We don't have a place to go or the time. Why?"

"You haven't smelled like sandalwood incense in awhile." Jess stirred the coffee before taking a sip. "And it's easier to get pussy from the girls around here."

His tone was reasonable but Joe knew this was going somewhere. Were they finally going to have it out over Kitty?

"If it's what they want and it's cool with their old man."

"But you've banged a few."

"That would be telling on the lady involved. You got something you want to talk to me about?"

Jess rubbed an itchy new scar on his face. "Where have you been getting your ice cream money? If it's one of the girls, she'll get her ass beat. Somebody brought it up last night at the meeting."

Joe waited a second, then another four. It felt like he'd been punched.

"Do you think I'd take their tip money?" He glared. "I had cash when I moved up here, but I had enough damn brains not to advertise it."

He wanted to ask who had made the accusation, but if he knew for sure, he'd wind up in trouble. He had no patch and no status. Just a cut-off denim vest, with an Atlanta GA bottom rocker, that told the world he was a rookie. It didn't tell them he was a rookie with big plans. Joe bit down his temper. The Atlanta Regents respected him for the things he'd done since his arrival. But if he stomped the hell out of a Regent, even that little son-of-a-bitch Bugsy, the rest of them would make sure he left Atlanta in little pieces. He had learned that the hard way.

"I had to ask," Jess said. "I'm your sponsor. I'll take care of it."

He lit a cigarette, his eyes fixed on the trophy wall. "We've got bigger problems than who's screwing who."

"What's wrong?"

"The meeting last night. Some decisions had to be made. We're having another National," Jess paused, then looked directly at him. "And you're going."

Joe sat up slowly, boots thumping on the floor to ground him. He still felt like he was falling.

"Are you screwing with me?"

"No," Jess shook his head. "But going to a National is no guarantee, Joe. It's just one more step toward getting a patch. Even with everything you've done for the club, you most likely won't get a hundred percent vote the first time. Some guys probated for six months."

Some guys maybe. But not him.

"Where's this National gonna be?"

"Alabama. The A.M.A. races. We're hosting it, too."

"They just got back from a National."

"Shit happens. This one isn't about partying. We heard the Bayou Runners are going to the races."

Joe hesitated.

"They're the ones who killed your probate. The one before me."

"Yeah. That would be them."

Joe's dark eyes traveled to the trophy wall and a ragged muddy patch with "*Maulers*" stitched across the back. He had personally added the patch just a few weeks ago, stunning the Atlanta Regents. The battle had been the turning point for him -- the point of no return.

"Is this gonna be a replay of the night we got Smoky?"

They couldn't talk about it, and didn't need to. It had been personal, ugly and screwed up. Not a clean fight, but effective and necessary, righting a wrong. They caught a few bullets and lived to walk away, with little Smoky as a souvenir.

"The Maulers were ignorant white trash. The Bayou Runners have bigger numbers, more expertise, more to lose, and their boss Sleaze doesn't respect limits," Jess said. "And they don't leave Louisiana if they can help it, so there's a reason he's doing this."

"What's his deal? Why would he want to screw with a big club like the Regents?"

"Good question. I've been asking myself the same thing. He has it made. He's got a good business going, with local protection and not too many problems. So why would the dumb bastard start shit?"

"You've known him a long time. What do you think?"

"He's heavy into meth from what I hear, which is wrecking his judgment. But he isn't stupid. So if he's risking his neck, he's trying to impress somebody who can do things for him," Jess said. "And if he's crazy enough to keep opening the door to the tiger cage, he needs to be stopped."

"You know who the tiger is?"

"I've got a pretty good idea," Jess stared out the window. "But the tiger needs the monkeys. So he can't eat them…"

"Did you like riddles as a kid?"

"I was never a kid," Jess held out the empty mug. "Coffee should be ready."

Once a probate, always a probate? Not damned likely. Joe got up, reached for his cut-off, and headed for the kitchen.

"Tell Smoky I take mine with two sugars," Jess called.

Joe made himself a peanut butter and jelly sandwich to go with the coffee, and listened to the sound of a lawnmower firing up outside somewhere in the neighborhood. He squinted through the wavy glass panes. Probably the bootlegger next door. Should have scythed the grass down to a mowable length first. That little 2-stroke couldn't handle the thick Bahia. He lingered by the window, listening to the end-of-summer sounds. But his mind was on Talladega.

"If you're not coming back, could you send the dog with my coffee?" Jess finally said.

Joe meandered back into the dining room and handed him the mug, along with an observation guaranteed to irritate.

"Just giving you some time to work on your tiger riddle. And I was trying to remember where I recently saw a tiger. I was over at Greasy's when Mina got Kitty to do her cards with that Asian deck. Lots of monkeys and snakes, too." Joe commented, certain Jess would never admit he had consulted Kitty and her tarot cards about the situation. It was club business, off limits to the old ladies. And to do so also meant something about it troubled Jess. He wasn't remotely superstitious. Everything had a scientific reason, a logical explanation not found in a deck of old hand-painted cards.

"You should have asked her how many years you'll have to probate before you get a patch," Jess said, putting him back in his place. "Speaking of which, what did you say to Kitty last night? She's all pissed off this morning, says you're a stupid bastard."

"Huh. Maybe she really is psychic," Joe smiled faintly. "Doesn't matter what she thinks about me anyway. She's your problem, not mine."

Like he could make it so just by saying it. Jess sloshed his coffee, confusion shifting his cold handsome features. *Ha ha*, Joe gloated. The stupid probate just knocked the star quarterback on his ass.

"But what did you say to her? She was hopping mad."

"Sweet little Kitty losing her temper? Unbelievable. And it's not really a hop, it's more like a stomp," Joe said. "All I said was, if she was forced to shoot you or me, she'd plug me in a second."

"Where the hell did you come up with that?"

"It's true. I'm just the Knight of Swords, remember? You're the king or duke of sticks, or whatever her cards said. I'm not shit to her. Hell, I don't even know her real name."

"Neither do I," Jess retorted. "And for that matter, neither does she."

Joe almost dropped his sandwich.

"Don't ask. It's a long story and we don't have time," Jess stood, stretching. "Go pack a cooler with some beer and put it in the car. And bring your Colt. We're leaving in about thirty minutes."

"Where are we going?" Joe inquired cautiously.

"Talladega. I want to check out the place ahead of time. I don't like surprises."

"Don't know why not, because you're sure full of 'em."

♦

Lawnmowers growled across the steep yards up and down the street, trimming the grass for what the homeowners hoped was the last time that year. The air felt and smelled good, Indian summer at its best. Joe lugged the cooler down the steps while Jess slung a long lumpy duffle bag into the trunk. The back door on the bunkhouse suddenly banged open and Ugly stomped outside.

"Where ya going?"

"Talladega," Jess said. "Recon."

Without warning, Ugly strode over, yanked open the back door of the Impala and thumped down heavily in the seat.

"What are you doing?"

"I'm going with ya," Ugly declared. "I'm outta shit and Shirley's little pusher says some new people in town stole his shit. So I need to go for a ride."

"Instead of a fix? What purpose could you possibly serve if I permit you to come along?"

Ugly grinned. "You might need a linebacker, Doc, to save your pretty teeth and handsome nose for another fight. I'm in the mood to kick some ass. Why should the probate have all the fun? Hey, do you think they'll put Bobby in their paper?"

"I didn't see anybody taking pictures," Joe advised and set the cooler down. "I'll be right back. We're going to need more beer."

♦

Heading west out of Atlanta, the morning sun trailed them across a blue sky. It was a day made for riding motorcycles, but the car was a necessity this trip. Ugly rolled the windows down and wedged his big frame across the seat.

"Lemme know when you get there," He said, and closed his eyes.

Joe propped his arm on the door, savoring the sun's heat on his skin. The unfinished interstate soon dwindled down into an old highway. Houses and trailers dotted the countryside close together, families settling within walking distance of each other. Joe saw two little pot-bellied kids in bathing suits dancing around a sprinkler in front of a trailer. A few miles down the road, a young pregnant woman was hanging up overalls on a clothesline behind a farm house. In the pasture beyond her, a man drove an old German tractor, white cow birds following the bush hog to seize insects startled out of the grass.

"Tallapoosa," He said as a city limit sign announced a small town. "Were those Indians?"

"How would I know?"

"You're so much smarter than everybody, thought you went to college. Talladega, Tallapoosa, Tallahassee…it must mean something. Aren't you interested in history, where things come from?"

"If you question where things came from, then you also have to worry about where you are, and where you're going," Jess stated. "It's too Zen for me."

To Joe's way of thinking, Zen or not, it was hard to find answers without asking questions. As the oldest of a houseful of kids, he dropped out of school in the eighth grade to head to the pulpwood camps for work. It was expected of him, and the tedium of school had been difficult for a boy with twitching feet, but he regretted not learning to read or write well enough to pore through the old Zane Grey and Louis L'Amour paperbacks an uncle gave him. So he just went slow, doubling back over a tricky word until he figured it out.

"What was the longest you ever stayed awake?" He said to Jess, deciding a scientific tack might work better.

"Thirty-eight hours. It wasn't much of a record there. We didn't have a choice."

"I stayed awake for six months once," Ugly spoke up, examining the tracks on his arm.

"I guess two days isn't shit then. I'm getting used to it. Hey, what kind of purple flowers are those?"

"Weeds," Jess said shortly.

"You're a real drag on a road trap, Doc," Ugly said.

"Yeah," Joe echoed, glad to have some back-up. "Didn't you ever play games in the car when you were a kid on vacation?"

"I told you earlier, I was never a child."

Ugly snorted. "You know, I can sorta see that about you. You've always been snotty and superior, you were just shorter."

Joe gave up on philosophical discussion, his attention diverted by a pretty brunette in a candy pink dress walking down the sidewalk in front of a Western Auto store. She carried two bags brimming with groceries, a pink purse dangling from one wrist.

"She looks like peppermint."

"We're not giving her a ride," Jess said.

"I was just gonna whistle at her."

"I'd like to lick her," Ugly growled.

"Don't get us arrested, we've got shit to do."

Downtown Tallapoosa consisted of brick stores, a water tower, churches and railroad tracks running parallel with U.S. 78.

"Possum Snout," Jess said when they slowed for a blinking caution light.

"What?" Bewildered, Joe searched the signs on the buildings.

"It used to be called Possum Snout. This road," Jess pointed to the cross street, "Used to be a stagecoach road, and before that, the Creek Indians traveled it. It was called the Sandtown Trail."

"I'm having a nightmare," Ugly said from the back seat. "I'm back in school and the teacher's about to beat my ass because I don't know what year Fort Sill was built."

"1869," Jess said.

"Holy shit. Ya know, if I get out right now, I can walk back to Atlanta before dark."

"You wish. We're almost to the Alabama state line."

"I'll run, then."

"Everybody knows linebackers can't run, you're only good for the short term. Besides, where's your sense of adventure?"

"It ain't in Possum Snout," Ugly declared.

"We seem to have cleared Tallapoosa," Joe said. "What's next, navigator?"

"Muscadine, Alabama," Jess said without missing a beat.

The hills around them rustled with longleaf pine, the sky glazed a perfect blue. The rural landscape resembled middle Georgia where his people came from: miles of barbed wire fences, white farmhouses, red-feathered roosters strutting along ditches ready for a fight, and chestnut horses content to stand in the sun. The land made Joe feel like his old self, confident and optimistic, before the Regents rolled into his hometown and changed everything.

"Keep your eyes open," Jess said.

"For what?" Joe asked.

"Louisiana license plates and people that talk like they've got a mouthful of gumbo."

"If we get close enough to hear them talk, we're screwed," Ugly said.

They had passed a scant mile into Alabama when Jess pulled over into a Baptist church parking lot and parked under a cluster of maples.

"Your turn to drive," He said.

He and Joe got out, arching their backs and rolling their shoulders. Jess studied the old wooden building, the moss-laden oaks, and the cemetery on the far side of the hill. Joe wondered if he ever turned it off, or if he always expected trouble. When he was satisfied the place held no threat, Jess unlocked the trunk and swung the green duffle bag out.

Time for business already? Joe hoped there would be no sign of the enemy, or conflict to ruin the day, and sure as hell no action in broad daylight. He didn't know where any of the side roads went. Highway 78 looked like the only fast way back to Georgia, and he didn't like having just one way out.

"Don't hot rod and get us pulled over," Jess warned, and set the heavy duffle bag in the back floorboard.

"No kidding," Joe slid into the driver's seat. "What kind of numbers are we looking at? How many chapters do the Bayou Runners have?"

"Just one. But it's big. They had about three dozen members last I heard. And they all show up for a fight."

"And if the three of us run into them?" Joe eased the car up to speed.

Jess took his time, lighting a cigarette.

"That depends," He finally said. "But no matter what…"

"We know, we know," Ugly interrupted from the back seat. "Sleaze is yours."

"I don't even know what the guy looks like," Joe said.

"A starved fuckin' rat," Ugly replied.

"He's the smallest one in the club. Wired all the time, can't sit still. But he doesn't miss much. He holds that club together, and the men I knew weren't easy to manage. The Runners are local, grew up working on shrimp boats or gator poaching. I knew some of them from the service."

Joe heard the regret in his voice. From what he had been told, the ambush in New Orleans last year had destroyed friendships and worse, a sacred trust conceived in battle. If it came down to a war, both clubs would have to fire on men who had once fought beside them in combat. He couldn't imagine any vet he knew drawing down on a survivor, a brother, stateside.

Lost in thought, Joe was startled when a fluttering tangle of torn bloody rags suddenly swooped across the windshield. Flight suits, the sleeves beating at the glass, clinging to it.

He jerked back and sucked in a breath that he couldn't release, strangling despite the warm currents blasting in the window. Zippers clattered against the glass, the coveralls rippling as if alive. Joe gripped the steering wheel. *Get the hell away from me.*

"What is it?" Jess sat up, staring ahead at the road. "Probate, what do you see?"

In the back seat, Ugly snatched up the duffle bag and had it unbuckled in two seconds.

"Where the fuck is it? What do ya see? Doc, do you see anything?"

Wind tugged at the rags, the flight suits popping, hanging on until they jerked away, sailing by his window as quickly as they appeared. The blacktop stretched out before him, safe and grounded, but overhead, the blue sky was feathered with vapor trails. How long ago had those planes flown overhead, minutes or years?

"Where are they?" Jess barked. "What is it?"

"Nothing," Joe said hoarsely. "It's nothing."

"Must have been something," Jess retorted, still braced against the dashboard.

"No." Joe clutched the wheel.

Why couldn't he crush that shit out of his head? *Not now, you bastards!* He could have wrecked the damn car, killed all of them. Ugly and Jess both stared at him. They knew he had perfect eyesight, almost uncanny. They didn't know he also saw things from years ago.

"It…it wasn't what I thought."

"It never is. Pull over."

Hands shaking, his teeth chattering, he had no choice. He couldn't drive and he knew it. Joe turned in at the next farmhouse driveway, nearly hitting the mailbox. He wouldn't blame them if they dumped him out and left him. God Almighty, it felt like the temperature had sank twenty degrees, he could not stop shaking.

"Wait a sec," Jess told him and turned to Ugly. "Hand me that flask in the duffle."

Ugly rummaged through the weapons until he found a battered copper flask. Jess unscrewed it, and had to help Joe bring it up to his mouth.

"This is the good shit. Go slow or you'll puke it back up."

Too sick to be embarrassed, Joe banged his teeth on the rim, then managed to get a sip down his tight throat. Peach-flavored moonshine. Jess waited, watching, then offered him another hit. Joe took the flask into his own hands, wrapping his fingers tightly around the cool metal. He focused on the feel of it, the rich penny color, trying to lock his trembling wrists and elbows into place so he could lift it.

"Damned chicken-shit yellow belly," He cursed silently.

The silver Impala emblem on the steering wheel glinted, the antelope frozen in mid-leap. He couldn't do that. He had to go forward. And he had to find a way to stop going back before it killed him. Deceptively mellow, the peach moonshine brought a halt to the tremors but did nothing for a headache now trying to crack his skull open. His blood pressure had probably set a record. He couldn't bring himself to look at Jess, or acknowledge the concern on Ugly's crooked features in the rear view mirror.

"The headache will go away after a while." Jess tugged the flask from his hand and gave it back to Ugly. "About the time mine does."

He stepped from the car, once again did a sweep of the countryside, and then walked around to the driver's side.

"Slide over and enjoy the buzz. Talladega's waiting. You ever been there?"

"No," Joe said, and made the mistake of shaking his head.

The highway rocked, and Ugly laughed when Joe reached for the dash to steady himself.

"The valley is supposed to be haunted," Jess said, sliding behind the wheel, not giving a damn about the silver Impala's predicament. It was all in what a person saw. "All kinds of weird shit happens there. If you see anything other than a Bayou Runner, keep it to yourself. Don't bring more ghosts there. And don't tell Kitty. She's got enough of her own without others showing up."

CHAPTER FOUR

When the speedway came in sight, towering above everything for miles, a tingling swept across Josiah Kelley Wilson. He couldn't blame it on the moonshine. His redneck heritage made him sit up straighter and gawk at the ultimate tribute to racing.

"Damn," Joe stared in awe, his heavy heart finally lifting

The Alabama International Motor Speedway was the biggest track he'd ever seen, and Joe had seen a few. He wished his best friend Buddy could see it. "Look at that place!"

They had raced on the small tracks in north Florida and south Georgia for years until he totaled his car. This soaring new track, however, literally put the others in the shade. Surrounded by a skirt of thick grass, then a forest of dense hickory and pines, the outside framework resembled a fortress. Drivers and crews in the late model sportsman class circuit had told him about it. Even the big-name drivers found the high curves intimidating.

Dust swirled across the road in front of him, stirring a memory of the steady roar of a big block engine, passing, dodging, closing in. But this? What was it like to race all day here? Five stories high and over four thousand feet long, the immensity of the structure in the rural Alabama landscape was staggering. Joe desperately wanted to get inside.

Jess drove slowly down the main road, circling beyond the track until he reached a large grassy expanse. Tents and camper trucks had already set up on the eastern acreage, leaving a vacant section close to the road.

"Ugly, hand me the binoculars."

They remained in the car while Jess checked out the other visitors.

"See anybody you know?" Ugly yawned.

"No. But it's still early in the week."

"Which way would they come from?"

"The fastest way from New Orleans would be up to Meridian, then catch 80 to 5 to 25."

Ugly frowned.

"They'll come from the southwest," Jess explained.

"Why didn't you just say so? I didn't need the bus schedule," Ugly retorted and thrust open the back door. "What are we waiting for? How about a Pabst?"

"Sounds good to me," Joe said, glad to have his feet on the ground again.

Jess tossed him the trunk keys, then made a slow circle around the car.

"This end of the track will be a good place for us to set up. We can see almost everybody else on the field, the new arrivals, plus have the woods flanking us for some shade."

"And ticks and poison ivy," Ugly grumbled.

"Ex-Marines can't handle a tick?" Jess taunted.

"There's no such thing as an ex-Marine, Doc," Ugly retorted.

Joe noticed a silver Airstream already set up on the far side of the track, with lawn chairs and little kids kicking a ball.

"It's going to be here? The fight?" Just how crazy were the Bayou Runners?

"If they start it here, we'll finish it," Ugly said. "Don't worry, probate. That's why we're gonna get here first. When they see us, they'll turn tail and head back to their bayou. It's a show of power. They wouldn't be dumb enough to turn it into a war in a place like this."

He scratched his neck, then frowned. "Right, Doc? Three dozen of them and two hundred of us? That's suicide."

"It's hard to second-guess Sleaze. Even if you know him. Of course he knows us, too." Jess found a stalk of onion grass and broke it in half, jamming part of it in his teeth. "It's easier to forgive an enemy than to forgive a friend. William Blake."

"Nah. I can forgive a friend most anything," Joe said. "But I never forgive an enemy."

"What if they're the same?"

"You two scholars can discuss philosophy all by yourselves," Ugly said, exasperated. "I've gotta find a tree."

The big man stalked off into the thick forest.

"They're real tall, and have branches and leaves on them. Good luck," Jess called and Joe grinned.

Cradling a bottle of beer, Jess sat on the trunk and craned his neck to survey the pennants on top of the track.

"Bobby Allison just won twenty grand here. Can you imagine anyone winning that much money in a race?"

It surprised Joe that Jess followed racing, but maybe it had something to do with that middle-Georgia accent he tried to tone down.

"I'd say he earned every nickel of it. It'd take some guts to race on a track like that against all those boys who grew up running shine."

"What's the point of it?"

He already knew. It was a test for Joe.

"Running a hundred miles an hour drafting off the wall an inch from somebody else's car. Showing what you're made of, even if you don't win enough for a six-pack later."

"Was it that bad for you?"

"I won my share, but it meant someone else didn't. I've seen a driver's kids sleeping on the race car hood because nobody could afford a motel. But you don't give up. Buddy Baker set a world record here last year, breaking two hundred miles per hour. Wish I could have seen it. I'd like to do that."

"Still wouldn't be fast enough," Jess said.

To outrun your demons.

"Well, screw you. Does that mean I'm not supposed to try? Giving up ain't what I'm made of," Joe retorted, then grinned. "When I wrecked my Chevy, I went and got a motorcycle, didn't I?"

"And look where it got you," Jess said.

Another race track, Joe mused, watching Ugly return from the woods, studying his arms for ticks.

"How does this work, a probate going to a National?" Joe inquired, as casually as possible.

"You do what you're told, same as anywhere else. Count on working your ass off," Jess promised. "And don't disrespect anybody. It makes your sponsor look bad, and your sponsor doesn't have a sense of humor."

"Yeah, I heard he was never a kid. I meant, say…after the National. How soon would I know something?"

Ugly chortled and reached for a beer.

"Assuming you actually do not fuck up, Dudley will call a meeting," Jess said. "Then we all vote on the probate getting his patch."

"That doesn't sound too positive."

"No point in getting your hopes up. What are the chances of you not getting into some shit?"

Joe ignored him, musing: "And it takes a hundred percent vote."

"And you're not likely to get it the first time."

Joe didn't answer. He knew Bugsy would vote against him. But there were ways of handling such problems. Like cramming the little shit into a garbage can, and chaining and padlocking the lid on tight. He smiled slightly at the imagined screams.

"Don't go getting any brilliant ideas. You've already used up your quota for the year."

"I was just getting started," Joe advised.

♦

He lit his last cigarette at midnight, the white lines of the highway guiding him back to Atlanta while Jess and Ugly dozed. The same small towns they had passed through earlier were silent, the traffic lights turning red for ghost cars at empty intersections. After dodging several raccoons, a frantic possum and a pair of slender does who bolted at the last minute, he was grateful to finally reach the interstate.

It had been a long day in the sun, drifting southwest from the racetrack in a futile search for Bayou Runners. They had stopped at country stores where hounds dozed in the pot-holed parking lot by the gas pumps and saucer-eyed children shadowed them, fascinated and terrified by their long hair and bloodshot eyes.

Ugly and Jess usually waited outside while Joe bought jerky and orange marshmallow circus peanuts, and dumped bags of real peanuts into his RC Cola as he roamed the aisles. With his rumpled dark hair, tilted black eyes and tanned skin, he easily passed for a Cajun-Indian mix. He flirted with the female store clerks and said he was looking for his wild motorcycle-riding cousins from Thibodaux, coming up for the races. Without fail, the women smiled and assured him they had been there all day and had not seen anyone but local people and tourists with normal haircuts.

On the way out, Joe dropped a few shiny quarters in the dirt just outside the door where the children would find them.

After a looping trail of over a hundred miles, with no reports of long-haired strangers except themselves, they headed back to the race track and sat in the shade, devouring a bucket of fried chicken and finishing off two six packs, taking turns dozing. By ten p.m., more campers had rolled in and set up, but there was still no sign of the Bayou Runners. Wearily, they made one last attempt under cover of darkness, this time driving slowly through motel parking lots and campgrounds, scanning license plates for Louisiana.

"You think Alec's source knew what he was talking about?" Ugly grumbled. "What if it was Fat Jack? He's only right half the time."

"Fat Jack isn't answering his phone.I called *my* source this morning. I was told Sleaze and his club are definitely not in New Orleans," Jess assured him. There's a few hang-arounds at the bars, just for show, but the rest are gone."

"Wonder if they're on their bikes." Ugly shifted in the back seat.

"If they're crazy. Too easy to spot and no way to carry big weapons."

"Can the probate say something?" Joe inquired.

"Help yourself."

"If there's only a few of them and a lot of us, they're not planning on confronting us at the race track. Too many tourists and no fast way out. I've been to a few big races, and it'll be bumper-to-bumper two miles from here in a few days. So where are they going to pick us off? If it was me, I'd do it from a side road somewhere close to the state line. And they don't need bazookas. All they need is a couple of men raised squirrel hunting who hit what they shoot at. They pick off a few Regents from the highway, cause a big pile-up and haul ass on their bikes in a dozen different directions."

Joe waited, and when they didn't respond, he shrugged. "That's the way I'd do it. If this is all about a show of power, that is."

After a long day drinking beer in the sun, Ugly couldn't process it. He looked questioningly at Jess. Yellow porch lights from the motel turned their faces sallow, and he drummed his fingers on the window sill.

"Damn," Jess said softly. "Take us home, probate. I've got to sleep on this."

CHAPTER FIVE

Activity around the clubhouse rose to fever-pitch chaos. They were leaving tomorrow for Talladega. The women scavenged the kitchen for food to take, while some of the men drove to an unofficial firing range in a rural county to practice.

"Anybody calls, come get me." Smitty cornered his number one old lady, Dorrie, on the back porch. "I couldn't reach the ones who ain't home yet from the last National."

"Should I pack my pea shooter?"

"Of course. Don't forget the hotdogs, either. I'm not buying sirloin for two hundred of my closest friends."

Outside, several forward-thinking Regents squatted in the driveway beside their bikes, making adjustments to increase the odds of getting there and back alive. Smitty surveyed the bodies until he spotted a blue bandanna and a dark head of hair on the far side of a mint '47 knucklehead in the garage.

"You're in an awful good mood today, probate."

"Are you about to ruin it for me?" Joe grinned.

"Nah, I got a project for you," Smitty handed him a set of keys. "I should have done this earlier but oh well. We've got to make sure the van is mechanically sound. Go over it with your fine-toothed comb and see if you can tear it up."

"You want it torn up?"

"No, but if a hose is gonna bust, I want it to happen before we go to Talladega. Take it up there on the interstate and run the shit out of it."

"He's helping me with my bike," Jess interrupted sourly.

"Oh. Excuse me. Since when have you needed help with your bike? If you'd ride something newer than this piece of shit, you wouldn't be working on it all the time. You've become really useless since you got a probate again, like you don't want oil up under your fingernails."

Jess was used to cracks about his Hollywood good looks, but joking about the black and white knucklehead was asking for trouble.

"This is the van you want me to check out, right?" Joe headed for the only van in the driveway.

He had money in his pocket, the keys to a vehicle and orders to take it for a spin. Or tear it up. Whatever happened first.

♦

"Cracked engine block," He told Smitty later.

"Shit."

"It's not that bad. We keep pouring oil in it, Talladega won't be a problem and I can change the engine out later. Maybe something a little faster? Leave the outside looking like hell but have a surprise under the hood."

"Now there's a plan. There's hope for you yet, probate, you Air Force fly boys occasionally think ahead. You might find it a useful skill to develop one day."

"So where do we get an engine?"

"You have to ask?" Smitty looked pained. "Think. Where does this club get their shit?"

Joe smiled.

"Greasy's Trading Post?"

"That-away." Smitty pointed down the path.

Greasy and Mina were in their back yard in a child's plastic wading pool, reasonably submerged. Mina wore an over-sized tee shirt and Greasy had stripped down to his briefs. Joe tried not to look at what was floating.

"Cochise!" Greasy lifted his beer. "Just in time. Help yourself to a beer, they're in the fridge. Bring us a couple more while you're at it."

"I've been sent. We need some stuff."

"Do the acquisitions require stealth and cunning?"

"Why else would I be here? That's your department. I'm just the worker bee."

"Don't the queens kill the workers when they're served their purpose?" Greasy retorted, glancing through the big shade trees at Kitty's house, then realized what he'd said. "Bees, that is."

"Smooth, honey," Mina sniffed as Joe went inside the house for more beer.

"Shit, everybody knows he was screwing Kitty while Jess was in jail. So what?" Greasy shrugged.

"Joe's just kinda old-fashioned. I think it bothers him."

"Have you bumped your head? Every time I turn around, somebody's old lady is sneaking in or out of that garage. He gets more pussy than any of the damn Regents."

"Except you," Mina smiled sweetly, her hand patting his soggy briefs.

"Your loyalty is understandable."

"Should I come back later?" Joe inquired as he came down the back steps and handed them two cans of Pabst Blue Ribbon.

"Desist, wench," Greasy told his wife. "What are we fixing up this time, Probate?"

"The van. We'll need an engine, for starters. I'm thinking a 350 instead of the 327. And some shocks."

Greasy leaned back, his monkey face reddened by the sun, and closed his eyes. "I see where this is going. And will I be rewarded by my chapter for my labors?"

Joe gazed down at him, a faint smile on his face.

"I'll make a list of what we need."

"Umm…have we got to do this before we go?"

"If we keep pouring oil in it, we can drive it to Talladega as-is, but it sure wouldn't hurt to make it a little more comfortable in the back. The bare metal is rough, and noisy. Noise isn't always good."

Greasy thought for a minute, took a chug of beer, burped.

"I know where there's a couch," He said. "We could slide it in through the back doors. Quick fix."

Joe glanced at Mina. Was he serious? Mina rolled her eyes.

"A couch?"

"And I know where there's some carpet," He mused.

"I've gotta go," Joe shook his head.

"Suit yourself. We're having hamburgers later."

"Oh yeah?" Joe hesitated. "What time?"

"Whenever you get back from A & P with the meat," Greasy grinned.

"Why do you stay with him?" Joe asked Mina.

"Right here," She patted Greasy's floating shorts.

They all paused to listen to a pair of Harleys coming up the street. It was second nature, identifying the bikes and riders as they came and went. Greasy frowned, listening to the approaching motorcycles, the combination of engine and pipes, even the rider's style of gearing down.

"I don't know the loud one. Sounds like forty-inch straight pipes."

The sound echoed off the clapboard siding as the bikes turned up the driveway two houses down.

"I'll go see," Joe said and headed down the path toward the clubhouse.

Before he cleared the property line, he heard female screams. On the run, Joe pulled the .380 from his boot, dodging in and out of the trees until he could see the driveway behind the clubhouse. Two Harleys had pulled up outside the garage, pinging and chugging. The girls hopped and shrieked, but he quickly realized their cries trembled with desire, not dismay, as they waited impatiently for a tall lanky rider to shut off his motorcycle. He wore a Regents patch with a Chicago rocker, and pried his helmet loose with a gasp of relief.

"Damn it's hot!" He drawled in a thick East Texas accent.

When the tall apparition turned sideways, Joe saw a beaked profile that only a mother buzzard could love. A grin spread across his face. Stowing the pistol, he headed for the gate. Jess and Smitty let the man dismount and secure his bike before back-slapping and greeting their Chicago Chapter brother. When the Regents finished their insults, the gleaming-eyed women rushed him, leaving anxious fingerprints on his sweaty brown arms.

"Well I'll be damned." Towering above them, the newcomer spotted Joe standing in the shadows of the big magnolias. "Get your ass over here, probate." Shaking off his unofficial fan club, he strode up to Joe, took him by the arms and turned him left, then right. "Gawddamn, son, you look rough. But a helluva lot better than last time I seen ya."

He stuck out his hand, crunched Joe's and slugged him on the arm.

"Good to see you again, Denny," Joe grinned.

"Hey!" A war whoop sounded at the gate.

They turned to see Greasy running across the concrete in his soaked jockey shorts.

"Do not touch me, man, I mean it!" Denny warned.

Joe was the first one to see a flicker of movement to Denny's right, then a large man in a flak jacket and camouflage pants rushed in front of Denny and planted himself there. Greasy tried to stop, but had too much momentum and careened hard into the stranger. With a loud "oomph!" he ricocheted backwards and skidded across the concrete, the rough pavement savaging his shorts and skin.

"Oww," Greasy gripped his back and rolled over, then screamed when his water-wilted package made contact with the blistering pavement.

"What the hell?" Dudley stepped out the back door.

The man in the camo glared up at the newest possible threat, his stance ready. Denny hastily put a hand on his shoulder.

"It's okay," He said. "It's cool, man, stand down."

"Denny, what is that, a probate?" Smitty asked.

"What? This?" He gestured to the silent man standing in front of him. "Nobody knows. He never introduced himself. He just kinda adopted me."

"Is anybody else from Chicago on the way?"

Denny grinned.

"You got us. You don't need anybody else."

At Denny's request, they adjourned to the air-conditioned clubhouse, where he shed his sweat-soaked long-sleeved shirt and shrugged bare-chested back into his cut-off. His friend carried in a large duffle bag and set it down on the floor beside the couch.

"Joe, this is Silent Sam. You got a lot in common except he ain't stupid and he doesn't talk. How about giving him a tour of the place? Like the front porch?"

That was fairly diplomatic for Denny. Joe snagged two beers from the refrigerator and led the stranger through the house to the front porch. He was gratified to see Denny eying the latest Maulers patch on the trophy wall, and hoped Jess would give credit where credit was due.

"They might be awhile," Joe pulled up a scavenged rocking chair and tested it before sitting down.

The stranger did not remove the heavy flak jacket and sat on the edge of the wicker couch. Sweat poured from his bushy dark hair, a single streak of white at his temple. He aimed his sunglasses at the street and took a long swallow of the beer. Apparently Sam wasn't much on conversation or comfort, which was fine with Joe. This was his last chance to kick back and savor a beer without constant demands and harassment. The National was a necessary step in his quest for a patch, but it damn sure wouldn't be fun. The empty cut-off would make him a target, with no place to hide. But that was okay. He planned to have the Regents patch on his back before the end of summer.

The break didn't last long. Denny stuck his head out the front door and motioned Joe inside.

"Give us a minute," He said to the silent man on the couch, and handed him another beer.

A Regent rarely showed consideration for a visitor around a clubhouse but Denny didn't care about rules. His actions weren't subservient, either. It was more like somebody making sure a dog had some cold water on a hot day. Joe followed him inside. Smitty and Dudley got up and walked out the back door, leaving Jess alone at the table. Uh-oh.

"Sounds like you've been busy up here." Denny flopped down on the couch lengthwise, his snakeskin boots hanging over the arm.

"Shit tends to happen," Joe said.

"Shit tends to happen at nationals, too," Denny watched a crack in the ceiling in case it moved. "Your sponsor would like to talk to you about something."

Jess raised an eyebrow at him. "I knew once you hit that couch, you wouldn't be worth a damn."

"I been on that bike since Chicago, man, wasn't like we had a lot of notice for this. Besides, you wound up with the redneck. He didn't want to probate in Chicago, said he didn't like the cold. So handle this." Denny set his beer bottle on the floor and closed his eyes.

Jess crumpled a potato chip bag and tossed it at the couch, then looked up at Joe. "Okay, bullshit aside, there was something no one mentioned to you about this National. In case you forgot protocol, attending a national is mandatory for all Regents."

"Unless someone is in the hospital or jail. And I'm not," Joe said, puzzled.

"Neither is Big Alec."

They were expecting a reaction, and he almost obliged them. His ribs seized, remembering pain deep in the bones, but Joe reined in the quick retort that would betray just how much he hated that bastard.

"Big Alec and the Miami Chapter are coming up for Talladega. Stay away from him," Jess warned. "We'll keep you busy so you won't have any reason to get near him. And don't give him a chance to get you by yourself. Do not fuck up getting your patch because of him, understand?"

A drum beat started in his head. That son-of-a-bitch Big Alec was half the reason he was here now, determined to get a Regents patch. As an equal, it was the only way he could meet him on neutral territory and finish what Big Alec had started.

"You do remember why you're here," Jess said. Was he reading his mind, or just the fury on his face?

As if he didn't think about the whys and wherefores of his reckless decision a dozen times a day.

"I appreciate you asking me to probate, Jess. It may not seem like it, but I'm trying my damnedest to hold it together."

A good neutral answer, even though these two men were best qualified to question it.

When he accepted Jess's invitation to probate in Atlanta a few months ago, he was ready for a change, anxious to be among men who understood about brotherhood and outrunning war ghosts. But everything went to shit the following day. And instead of a rival club, it was Big Alec, boss of the Miami Regents, who provoked him to detour to a place he'd never been, and intended to never see again.

The only chance of settling the score was to meet the enemy on equal footing. To Joe, that meant one thing--getting a Regents patch, hunting the bastard down and choosing his time wisely.

"Did you hear me?" Jess said impatiently. "I'm not screwing around. He would have killed you if it weren't for Denny and Smitty."

"I'm well aware of that," Joe said.

Denny remained silent on the couch, his arm across his forehead. But he was listening.

"I want your word you're not going to do anything to Alec, or even try," Jess insisted.

"I'm not going to stand still for another beating. Nobody's ever done that to me in my life, ever."

"The solution is pretty simple. You won't get your ass stomped again if you'll stay away from him. Do you want revenge more than you want a patch? What the hell is wrong with you? We've got enough to worry about with the Bayou Runners. I want your word, Joe."

Damn. Why did he keep insisting? Of all people, Jess should understand some things couldn't be forgiven. Joe pressed on.

"Why is this different than what you're doing?" He said.

"What do you mean?"

"They killed your probate last year, and you still want revenge. I want to make things square for Alec busting Pooch in the head and stomping my guts out my backbone."

Jess stared at him a long time, his pupils shrinking to dots. He held up his hand, ticking off his fingers.

"The main difference is, Big Alec is a Regent, not a Bayou Runner. The second difference is getting smacked with a beer bottle isn't the worst thing that ever happened to Pooch. The kid was in fuckin' Nam, for Christ's sake. At least he's still alive. Third, you were warned by several people not to go to that party. And fourth, mother-fucker, you are a *probate*."

"You left out dumber than a lug nut," Denny said, exasperated.

"I'll give you five minutes to think about it," Jess said. "If you don't want your patch any worse than that, you're not going to Talladega."

Joe stared, panic overwhelming his temper. "Are you serious?"

"What do you think? You can stay here and guard the palace and we'll take Bugsy instead. He's a dick but at least he knows not to fuck with Alec."

Stalling, Joe reached for a pack of cigarettes and shook one out. Another National might be months away. He'd never last that long. He was fed up with eating shit all the time as a step-n-fetch-it for a dozen men. Life had been a lot less complicated back home. If somebody started some shit, he finished it. If someone in his neighborhood came to him about a problem, he took care of it. But here--Damn damn *damn*!

Joe waited a few seconds, like he had to consider it, then said: "Okay, Jess." Without adding: *This time.*

But the discussion wasn't quite over. Denny sighed, a sound like a horse clearing its throat.

"You know what, probate? I'm laying here listening to you, wondering if you're the kind of guy who'd put up with all this probate shit just to get back at somebody. Not because you want to ride the bike you built with your own hands from a damned basket case in a barrel. Not 'cause you want to belong to a club that's been around since the Depression and has one hell of a history of brotherhood and hell raising."

He opened his eyes, and favored Joe with an uncomfortably sincere glare.

"So why don't you go give it some thought before you waste gas money on a trip you don't need to take? You might want to tuck your tail and go home instead. You're down to three minutes by Jess's watch. And personally, in case it matters to you? I'd be ashamed to call you brother if you get that damn patch and Alec is the only reason you wanted it. Now go get me another beer before your time's up."

CHAPTER SIX

Just outside Meridian, Mississippi, heading for the Alabama state line, the traffic on the old two-lane highway slowed down. Guidry saw blue lights in the distance and wondered if there had been an accident. He glanced down at the gas needle. About half a tank left. The Bayou Runners rounded a curve, sputtering along in second gear behind creeping semis and station wagons. Up ahead, several cars were parked zigzag by the side of the road. The cars sported blue flashers and State of Alabama decals.

As the pack approached, a dozen state troopers carrying shotguns suddenly stood alert. The Bayou Runners watched Sleaze for a signal. *Keep going, don't slow down. It ain't us, they're looking for a fugitive or escaped prisoner.*

One trooper with lieutenant's bars pointed the nose of his Mossberg 12 gauge into the pack and swung the barrel slowly to the left. *Pull over.* Guidry's jaw locked and a high singing started in his ears. From previous experience, he knew that if Sleaze handled this, the Bayou Runners would wind up face down on the steaming asphalt getting stomped. Or splattered by the Mossberg into bite-sized pieces for the buzzards.

Guidry shut off his shovelhead chopper and pulled his helmet loose. This was not the time for a cold poker face. They had already decided he was a threat. Walking toward them, he held out his hands so they could see he was unarmed, and sized up the three officers closest to him. The lieutenant stood slightly to the side so he could drop and roll out of the way if he had to, and let his men open up.

"Something wrong?" Guidry forced a smile.

"Turn around," the Lieutenant said.

His back constricting under the leather cut-off, Guidry slowly turned. He realized they wanted to see his patch, but it didn't make him feel any better. Sleaze and the other Bayou Runners watched in disbelief from their motorcycles, hands on the grips.

"You the boss of this here gang?" The lieutenant questioned.

Guidry caught Sleaze's eye. *Handle it.*

"Nah, he's back home."

"Where y'all headed?"

"A.M.A. races at Talladega."

"More of this gang on the way?"

"We're it. We come up from Louisiana to see the new track."

The state troopers didn't budge. Guidry counted a dozen of them, all with pump shotguns.

"You're not going to the speedway this weekend," The lieutenant said. "I don't need your bullshit in Alabama. Get those motorcycles out of my state."

Guidry had a hard time containing his surprise. Some of the Bayou Runners shifted nervously in their seats. The cops knew? What the hell had happened? He tried again.

"Is there some kind of problem, officer?"

"Only if you waste another minute of my time."

Without breaking eye contact with Guidry, the Lieutenant spoke to his men.

"Looks like we're gonna have to do a license check," he said.

One by one, the troopers adjusted their stance.

Oh shit. Not here in Alabama, where they didn't have second-cousin bail bondsmen or uncles in the robbery division.

"We meant no disrespect. We're just out for a nice ride on a nice day. We'll go on. A pleasure." Guidry turned and walked stiffly to his bike, a dozen barrels aimed at his spine. He watched his fellow Bayou Runners for a clue, desperately hoping one of them would yell "hit the deck" if necessary.

"Don't do anything stupid, you sons-a-bitches," He silently pleaded. "Don't nobody reach in your pocket for a cigarette."

The troopers forced the slow traffic to a complete halt in both directions. With Guidry leading the pack, the Bayou Runners circled around and headed back into Mississippi, shaken and furious. They didn't slow down until he signaled them into a truck stop outside Meridian.

"Mother-fuckers!" Sleaze jerked his sportster to a halt under a big concrete arch. "Fucking pigs!"

Guidry let him rage. Now that he could breathe again, he had to sort this out. That roadblock didn't make any sense at all.

"Gas up and cool off 'til we figure something out," He told the men. "Come on, Sleaze, we got to talk."

He headed for the restaurant inside the truck stop, the cold air chilling the sweat on his face. He'd see those damn shotguns in his sleep for the next month.

"I ain't believing it." Sleaze stormed ahead of him. "Do you believe it?"

"I believed those damn Mossbergs and Ithacas in my face." Guidry found an empty booth in a back corner and slid down on the tattered vinyl seat.

Outside the plate glass window, the Bayou Runners talked angrily among themselves at the fuel pumps. Sleaze picked up a menu, then tossed it aside and started tapping his black fingernails on the table.

"What the fuck?" He fumed. "How did the state cops know we'd go this way? For that matter, how the hell did they even know we were going to Talladega?"

Guidry reached for his Marlboros, grateful his hands weren't shaking. "Now you're asking the right questions."

A waitress with faded blonde hair and brilliant blue eye shadow walked up, her pencil posed on a pad.

"Get you fellas something to drink?"

"You got beer?" Sleaze said.

"Sure," She said. "We ain't a dry county."

Sleaze's beady eyes and long wispy hair did not impress her. Broken countless times since childhood, his nose dangled over a thin mustache and yellow gums littered with cracked brown teeth that reeked. Guidry, however, was a different matter. He kept his coal-black hair combed straight back, and she wouldn't mind that mustache tickling her neck one bit. She decided to overlook the motorcycle gang patches; the sleeveless vest allowed her to measure his shoulders and working man's biceps. By truck stop standards, he was well above average. He smiled at her, and the tired shadows under her eyes lightened.

"We'd appreciate some cold ones, cher. We come a long way."

"I had an uncle from Lafourche. You sound like him."

"Oh sure, I know Lafourche. Been t'rough there a lot."

"Y'all visiting us to see the grave of the gypsy queen?"

"No, I ain't much on cemeteries. We were going to the races in Alabama."

She paused, tapping her pencil, and suddenly smiled.

"The motorcycle races? Sounds like fun. Wish I was going."

"What you got to eat around here?" Sleaze interrupted.

"The hamburgers ain't bad. The Big Rig Special is double burgers all the way with French fries for $2.25. Cheese is an extra ten cents."

"Bring four of 'em," Sleaze said irritably. "And bring us the beer now."

When she walked off, he lit up a cigarette, took a deep steadying inhale, then resumed tapping his nicotine-stained fingers on the table.

"I must be fucked up because I can't connect the damned dots," He frowned. "How did the pigs know we were coming this way? Who the hell tipped them off?"

"The same person who told us about the race?"

Sleaze shook his head. "If Leon's playing a game, I don't get it. If he wanted us out of New Orleans for a week, why tip off the cops to send us right back? And there ain't nothin' he can do in New

Orleans without us. He don't know anybody there or he'd 'a' already burned us out. He needs us, and he wants that patch bad."

"Yeah, he wouldn't screw that up," Guidry admitted. "Well, if it wasn't Leon running a game, who else cares about us getting to the race?"

"Somebody in the Regents, wanting to make sure they won't have no problems this weekend?"

"Shit. Fat Jack couldn't wait to haul ass back to his shop and call 'em when I let on we were going to the races. If they don't want a fight, they just wouldn't show." Guidry scratched his jaw. "Count on it, they're waiting on us, not running to the cops."

"And nobody but us and the boys knows all I want is Big Alec. Hey, you wanta bet on who collects the bounty? I bet fifty bucks Virgil gets it." Sleaze was quite pleased with himself for coming up with the idea of offering a cool grand to any of his men who handed him Big Alec's patch. It took the pressure, and personal danger, off him. "Virgil wants the cash, and he's fired up about getting into the Trogs. Bet he's the one who plugs Alec. Fifty bucks?"

"Done told you a t'ousand times, I don't gamble."

"Yeah, yeah, you play poker 'cause you like to play cards," Sleaze taunted. "It's got nothing to do with the money you win. Or lose, if the bosses out there on Jefferson Highway tell you to lose. You get paid no matter what."

"You trying to piss me off?" Guidry leaned across the table, his black eyes blazing. "Told you before, this ain't the way to do business with the Regents. You done forgot your little cigar box wit' your very own one-percenter patches? That was just Jess's way of telling you not to step over the line like them three dumbasses. Somebody messes up Alec, the whole nation's gonna come down on us."

He gazed out the window at the Bayou Runners. Virgil thought he was ten feet tall and bulletproof, but the rest of them had some brains, when they remembered to use them.

"And your friend Leon don't care how many of us wind up dead as long as he's got one Bayou Runner left to show him where everything is down home. It's win-win for him, and he ain't had to bring nothing to the table. You really think he's gonna give you a Trog patch?"

Sleaze glared at him. They had already had this argument before they left New Orleans. Guidry hated taking chances. He was forever second-guessing someone's motives and working his contacts to see a situation from all angles. His way of thinking made him successful at cards, and very much in demand among the gambling clubs for their private poker parties, but irritating as hell among friends.

"Are you saying Leon would bullshit me? He don't think I'm good enough for the Trogs?"

Guidry shook his head. "Leon thinks you're good enough to take care of a problem for him. The Regents ain't ignorant, Sleaze. Hell, they got to be wondering why we're doing this."

"They don't wonder shit. They think we ain't nothing to worry about. Even their damned probate got the draw on us. I'da had Alec's patch if it weren't for that punk," Sleaze rasped bitterly, and narrowed his eyes. "I don't know any other way to draw out Alec but this. I sure as hell ain't going to Miami. If we get his patch and Leon makes us a Trog chapter, nobody will ever shit on us again. Didn't you get tired of people shitting on us growing up?"

Guidry did not reply. It would have been harsh to remind Sleaze of their differences. Guidry came from a poor but well-respected family. His fragile mother died young, and he was grateful she never had to bear knowing her oldest son died from burns in a helicopter crash in Vietnam. His father, a decent hardworking man, drowned when a shrimp boat got caught in an unexpected squall, and he had tried to save two young nephews.

Etienne Guidry found himself without a family much sooner than was almost tolerable, but at least had known their love and wisdom. His father taught him first and foremost that a man had to earn respect, and to pay no heed to ignorant people who wanted to belittle him because of his Acadian heritage.

Sleaze, however, had not been as lucky. Drunks, thieves and addicts, the adults in his family craved self-destruction by any means possible. No one cared if he died in his crib. Demons in their blood latched on to the weak yellow Minarde infants at birth and waited. An aunt remembered to feed the listless infant, and Guidry often saved the undersized Sleaze from savage beatings by schoolyard bullies. Guidry's father fed Sleaze at their own table, gently correcting his foul language, and gathered hand-me-down clothes from the neighbors so the boy wouldn't have to wear rags to school. Guidry still had no idea if Sleaze ever resented the charity.

Sleaze had avoided his family's curse for years, doggedly determined to make something of himself, but Guidry watched the meth change him, and wondered how long his friend could do battle with himself.

"Where's the beer? I'm getting a headache. I thought we were gonna get shot back there."

"We? I didn't see your ass doing shit," Guidry scowled.

"You did all right. They'd 'a' killed all of us if they had the chance, been big heroes in the newspapers," Sleaze sneered.

"Wonder if they did the same thing to the Regents," Guidry mused.

Sleaze drew in a startled breath. "Then we'd know!"

"What would we know?"

"We'd know if the info got leaked to the cops, if they're behind this. Shit, we musta told two dozen people we were coming up here so it'd get back to the Regents," Sleaze said. "We've got to find out if the cops let the Regents through from Georgia. Where the hell did Kenny go with the car?"

"They waved the cars on through. Kenny had to keep going."

So now Kenny and the car were somewhere in Alabama, along with the weapons and disguises they planned to use.

"He'll come back," Sleaze said. "Go tell the boys to park out front so he can see the bikes."

"And?"

"We're gonna go to Talladega in the car. Leave some of 'em here to guard the bikes. We'll cut north like we shoulda done anyway. We can't get 'em on the way there, we'll get them on their way home. Might even be easier. But I wanta see if the cops stopped them, too."

"We get caught and the cops recognize us, we're dead."

Sleaze considered that for a moment, then glanced up at the cash register.

"See what time that blonde gets off work, and if she's got a car."

"You taking her damn car?" Guidry frowned.

"*We're* taking her car, and her too. Flirt with her a little until we get into Alabama good, just in case."

"Then what?"

"We don't need her."

"You're pushing your luck with me." Guidry's lip curled under the mustache.

"You getting soft over a skaggy old cunt you ain't even fucked?" Sleaze sneered and squinted out the big window. "They're leaving the gas pumps. Go tell 'em to park out front where Skelly can see the bikes."

Guidry stood slowly.

"This is our chance to turn around and go home." He lowered his voice. "We never shoulda done that last year. We was friends with them."

"You wasn't there anyway," Sleaze accused. "You had one of your big poker games. You think I believed that? Shit. But I didn't say nothing 'cause I knew you didn't wanta fight your old buddies. Nobody was supposed to get killed anyway. But I'll tell you something. Our old buddies have looked down their noses at us ever since they patched over to the Regents, like they're better than us. We let them join our club, and go riding and partying with us when they first come home, and then they take off when the Regents come recruiting down the east coast. Jess and Smitty and them had to be hot shot one-percenters, pushing and pushing."

"Like you're trying to be?"

"Leon said we could stay in Louisiana. He don't wanta yank us all over the United States like the damned Regents. He knows we're fine right where we are."

"We had a truce with the Regents until last year. Jess ain't forgot what you did to his probate." Guidry leaned over the table, pressing his palms flat so they wouldn't curl into fists. "Armand once told me Jess could take a hundred pieces of blown up guts and bone and skin and put 'em back together and send a boy home alive. I guess he knows how to take somebody apart, too."

With that, he walked off.

"Didn't help Armand any, did it? Him and Jess both wound up fried, and Armand came home in a box, black and stinking. And for what?" Sleaze ground his cracked teeth until one twanged all the way down to the root. "Some fuck-hole country." He would have hurled the sugar shaker at Guidry's back for making him remember it, but the tired blonde looked the type to call the cops if she had to clean up Dixie Crystals and broken glass. One near miss with the cops today was enough. He wasn't going to screw up a chance to get to Talladega.

The blonde bitch finally brought the beer. Since Guidry wasn't there, she didn't say a word and walked away.

"That's all right, you dumb whore, right about sunset you'll wish you had been nicer to me."

He fished some downers out of his pocket and swallowed them before his heart blew up. *Cool it, don't get sidetracked.*

He didn't want to think about the tattooed skin in the cigar box. He damn sure didn't want to think about how bad it must have hurt. *Fortune cookies*, the bar manager had said. Sleaze belched up something sour. Not his fuckin' fortune, not if he could help it. Damn Guidry for harping about it all the time. And Christ, Vietnam, like he could forget months waiting to die. And it didn't stop when they came home, for none of them. Some still waited for the bullet but not him, hell no.

Sleaze swallowed, rubbing his aching forehead. He leaned back in the booth and became still as the downers did their magic. Around him, the clatter of dishes and voices receded. A weight settled on his bones like cold heavy dirt.

He shook it off. He wasn't dead yet. Nobody was burying his ass until he was good and ready. Not Vince Minarde. He had been one of the lucky ones, making it home to start over.

CHAPTER SEVEN

The rumble shook the summer air, super-heating the humidity until a violent thunderstorm billowed out of their wake. Joe rode at the back of the pack with the stranger from Chicago, blasted by a full chorus from dozens of pipes. It had to be something in the male wiring that hungered for speed and noise. Hot wind battered his face, and the sun heated muscle and bone, turned his skin coppery-brown.

Just as they swerved onto a scrap of I-20 heading west, two chapters from North Carolina fell in with them from the east, and Joliet and Milwaukee bore down from the north. Stunned tourists pulled to the side, certain they witnessed an ancient Teutonic Goth horde roaring out of the past, hair flying, chrome horses jamming down the interstate. All they lacked were battle axes waving over their heads.

Five miles later, Indianapolis and Dayton thundered up behind them, vying for position, fast and relentless while the sun rose overhead.

The van stayed back thirty feet, which wasn't far enough for Joe with Dudley's old lady Flossie at the wheel. Windows down, her blonde hair in a braid, she had the 8-track blaring "Highway Star," the frenzied chords encouraging her up to warp speed. The black and white bulldog pup sat in the passenger seat, occasionally rising up to peer over the dash and check on Joe.

With Kitty snug behind him, Jess dropped back to ride beside Denny. Then he fell back next to Joe and swerved to see if he'd fall out of formation. Joe didn't budge. His '65 panhead roared steadily six inches off the white line, his right boot three feet from Jess's left. Kitty smirked and Jess hit the gas, rejoining the patched members in formation.

Joe wished he had an old lady on the back, firm thighs bracing him, living for each mad second clicking off. "One day, man," He promised himself. "Maybe a redhead. And she'll be hot and ready to go riding anywhere. Blue eyes. Long legs."

When I-20 narrowed down into State Road 78, the feverish din startled cows in a nearby pasture. Joe grinned when he saw a pretty white-faced heifer kick up her heels and bolt. Dorrie sat up straight behind Smitty to flash a passing pulpwood truck, setting off a chain reaction among the girls.

Their final stop for gas was on the outskirts of Oxford, Alabama, at a red Texaco station. Across the road was wilderness. Behind them rose the foothills of the Blue Ridge Mountains. The gas station only had two pumps. Hank Williams yodeled from a radio in the office and Smoky began howling a duo from the passenger window of the van. A white-haired man shuffled from the bays and approached Jess, feeling a kinship because of their matching overalls.

"Will y'all be requiring any mechanical services today?"

"No, just gas. And maybe some cigarettes and soda pop."

"The Co-Colas are right there." He pointed to a large red ice case inside the office door. "And I got boiled peanuts for sale. I'd be obliged if you'd wait for me to hand out the cigarettes. I'm by myself today."

"I'll take care of the cigarettes for you," Jess said.

The man looked at him a long moment, then nodded.

"All right, son, I'll take care of the fuel."

The Regents rolled up two at a time, fueled up and paid the old man waiting by the pumps, then walked the bikes out of the way to wait. They chugged down ice-cold bottles of Coke and stocked up on cigarettes. No one tried to coerce Jess out of a free pack. A few Regents shopped the new arrivals to see what dope they could score, until the bosses put a stop to it.

"We're not going in there stoned. Not until we see what's going on with the Bayou Runners. You've gotta wait on that buzz, ya hear me? I ain't pulling your ass out of a cluster-fuck."

Dudley ordered the Atlanta girls to ride in the van from that point on. The men could respond to a battle or ambush with fewer distractions if their women weren't getting shot off the back of the bikes and causing a pile-up.

"Where'd you find the pup?" Denny ambled over as Joe poured a hubcap full of water for Smoky. "I seen her at the clubhouse."

"Long story."

"She ain't very old. She's still at that wiggler age. I miss having a dog."

"It appears to me you have a watch dog," Joe glanced over at the man standing near the garage bays.

Silent Sam stood straight, his head lifted to scan beyond the trees across the highway. He had taken his sunglasses off and whatever he saw in the pulsing sky engulfed him. The men and women milling around the parking lot simply weren't there.

"Is he going to probate?" Joe said.

"Nah," Denny said. "He's not consistent. Sorta like you. Can't take a chance."

"Where'd you find him?"

"He found us. Showed up at a party and started hangin' around. He stayed out of the way so they didn't run him off. He can ride like a son-of-a-bitch."

Smitty walked up, and followed their gazes to the man oblivious to the traffic around him.

"Reminds me of someone I saw once. Got hit, knocked his guts out his back, and he just kept standing there, like whatever he saw up in the clouds suddenly didn't make sense. Didn't scream, didn't yell for a medic or his mama. Weirdest damn thing. Took forever to fall. I can still see him, plain as day."

He shook his head in an effort to empty it, then swung around to look down the highway. "Wait a sec. I'm hearing somebody else. Miami? Or Louisville?"

"Nah, that sounds like Marv's bike. My Chicago brothers have finally caught up," Denny smiled faintly.

With the arrival of the Cook County Chapter, the bosses stepped into the shady garage bays and called a hasty meeting. Then Dudley called Joe. He studied their faces for a clue, and found nothing but grime and sunburn.

"You're running scout," Dudley informed him. "The Atlanta old ladies are going in the van. Stay close to them, and maybe you can get in there without getting noticed. If there's any sign of the Bayou Runners, we want to know where they are and how many. Get your ass back here as soon as you can without attracting attention."

Dudley then summoned his old lady.

"Flossie, if those punks are there, park out of the way and wait. Do not leave unless there's big trouble."

Joe shook the last of a peanut pack into his Coke and handed his cut-off to Jess. The girls climbed into the van and reluctantly settled in among the coolers, grills and bedrolls. They sat cross-legged and motionless in the heat, but Smoky trembled near the doors, her rapid panting betraying her anxiety.

"What's going on?" Kitty said, winding her hair up off her neck.

"I'm your escort and official spy for the club."

"What an honor."

He rubbed Smoky's chest, waiting for the puppy to relax. "Take care of her for me if something happens."

"You've watched too many Disney movies. Besides, you're the one who insisted on bringing her instead of leaving her at the clubhouse."

"She doesn't like Bugsy and I bet she has a good reason why. She just can't tell us."

"I'll see if I can get her to rap with me," Kitty said. "Stay close."

♦

Traffic thickened into one slow steamy lane, the road sucking at tires like hot taffy. Joe stayed a car-length behind the van, watching for Louisiana tags and sizing up anyone else on a motorcycle. Vehicles inched along bumper-to-bumper by the time the track came into view, then the van abruptly rolled to a stop. Dorrie gave him an "okay" sign with her fingers from the rear window. Nothing wrong, just a security guard directing them into the makeshift campground beyond the race track. Joe had already told the girls where to go.

The van crept across the grass, Joe on the far side for cover. Flossie parked in the shade beneath the trees and the girls flung the side doors open, gasping. Pulling her denim shorts from the crack of her ass, Flossie slid from the front seat and gazed out across the clearing. It was early still, and they had this part of the campground to themselves.

Dorrie and Mina unloaded a few webbed lawn chairs, staking out an area in the newly mown grass. Joe shut the bike off and reached down to pick up Smoky as she hurtled dangerously close to the exhaust.

"See anything, Eagle Eyes?" Kitty was the last one to get out of the van, awkwardly crawling across the mattress with a cold beer in one hand.

Joe stepped away from the thick oaks blocking his view and surveyed the race fans milling around distant Scotty Highlanders, Shastas and VW buses. He sure as hell didn't want to lead two hundred Regents into an ambush. His radar immediately honed in on an unusual group too close for comfort.

"I'm seeing men with long hair, past those two trucks to the right of us," He squinted. "Careful, a few are looking this way. They're wearing cut-offs, too, but I can't see the patches. Beyond the green Chevy and black Ford. This side of the U-Haul."

"U-Haul?" Kitty stood up on tiptoe. "Oh shit! Double-damn shit. Get back over here!" She hissed at her bewildered friends.

They didn't ask questions. Abandoning lawn chairs and coolers, the women hastily assembled on the sheltered side of the van, wide-eyed and panting.

"It's Big Alec," She told Joe. "Get the hell out of here before they see you. We'll stay by the van until our guys get here. Hurry, let 'em know the Miami Chapter is already here."

But Joe didn't budge. Kitty's green eyes crystallized.

"Joe…please. Please don't, not now."

He stepped away from the small restraining hand on his arm and moved deeper into the woods where he could see beyond the trucks. A circle of chairs sat in the full sun. He saw the thick black hair and beard of the Miami Regents enforcer, Wolf, who he had once considered a friend. One massive tattooed arm hung over the side of a lawn chair, and he was leaning forward, talking to someone even larger than himself.

The other man sat with his side profile to Joe, his long wiry ponytail and thick beard fiery red. Despite the distance, Joe knew the man's ruddy skin was peppered with freckles from years of south Florida sun. He also knew the man wore size thirteen combat boots, because Big Alec had kicked his ribs into kindling scarcely two months ago.

"Joe, please," Kitty implored. "Our guys are waiting for you back in that little town. Go let them know the Bayou Runners aren't here. That's what matters."

Yeah, the Regents were waiting, but right now, right here, he was two hundred feet from a son-of-a-bitch who had turned his life upside down and made him feel like his skin didn't fit and his skull was packed with metal. No one had ever sucker-punched him, beaten him into unconsciousness, down into a place he didn't know how to get out of. He hadn't felt that way since Korea, when he walked into a hangar to start another day with his friends and instead stepped into a hell beyond a young man's comprehension.

In Korea, the enemy had vanished as quickly as they had come, out of his reach. But here they gathered in one place. He'd never know who had swung first and knocked his head into a wall, who kicked his ribs into kindling, who dragged him relentlessly back to his feet even after his eyes had swollen shut and his brain had no connection with his fists. But he knew who started it. The .380 weighed heavy in his boot, the Colt snug under his denim shirt.

Not now. You could never go far enough away. They'd go after your friends back home. You have a plan. Get the patch first. Equal footing, remember?

"I want to see fear in his eyes," Joe thought. "I want him to know he isn't immortal."

Denny had only been partly right. He didn't want a patch solely because it would give him easy access to Alec. But Alec *was* a big damn part of his motivation to stick with it. Just seeing the bastard reminded him how much. The girls stood by the van in silence, watching him cautiously like he had suddenly become a stranger to them.

"I'll be back as soon as I can," He said. "You girls stay put." He put a finger against Smoky's wet nose. "Including you."

"Oh shit. Too late," Flossie groaned. "Look!'

Wolf was heading their way, eyes shadowed, jaw grim.

Kitty pushed Joe toward the panhead. "Get on your bike, *run*."

"I don't run," Joe told her.

CHAPTER EIGHT

Joe stepped around the van, arms loose, wary, no humor on his face. Wolf came to an abrupt halt, his dark eyes assessing Joe's stance. He relaxed when Kitty and the girls appeared behind Joe.

"Hey Wolf. How did y'all beat us here?" Kitty moved forward slightly so that she was between the two men.

"We drove all night. Where's everybody else?"

"They're on the way. They wanted the probate to check out the place and see if the Bayou Runners were here."

"Probate, huh? Guess you're with Atlanta?"

"Yeah." It was all Joe could say. He knew his eyes showed the fury he felt but couldn't shut it down.

Wolf waited two beats, then tossed his head at the women.

"Get lost."

They retreated to the other side of the van and sat down to wait Flossie gripped the keys and Kitty held onto Smoky, ready to toss her inside if they had to haul ass.

"Alec knows you're here," Wolf said. "And he doesn't give a shit. But your best bet is to stick with the Atlanta guys."

"If he doesn't give a shit, why does it matter?"

"This is coming from me, not him," Wolf said, struggling. "What happened at that Fourth of July party was a bad scene. When I first met ya, I knew you were a stand-up guy. I knew you'd make a good Regent. Me and Jess wouldn't 'a' spent all that time talking to a lame. I'm glad you got a chance to probate with Atlanta."

"Thanks to Denny," Joe said tightly.

"Man, you were told not to go to that party. And I told you to fuckin' leave, several times, remember? Wasn't nothin' I could do when it got heavy. If Denny hadn't stuck his big nose in it, you wouldn't be standing here right now giving me lip," Wolf glared. "Sounds you still ain't learned nothin' so maybe you're not so smart after all."

A dusty breeze from the west ruffled Joe's hair, cooling his temper. He couldn't blame Wolf for what happened. Jess and Wolf had been the first two Regents he had met, and treated him like an equal. His own pride stopped him from listening to their good advice.

"I'm a little smarter than I was that day," Joe conceded, and Wolf relaxed.

"Fuckin' hope so. When's the rest of 'em coming?"

"When I go tell them there's nobody here from Louisiana."

"Well, I guess you'd better beat feet, then, huh. They're gonna miss the party."

♦

Joe still expected them to give chase. Wolf had no control over his boss, and Big Alec acted on impulse. The Miami Regents heard the panhead fire up. A few glanced his way as he circled in the grass and headed up the road. But no one came after him. When he reached the highway, he rode against the heavy traffic, away from the race track. Asphalt heated the soles of his boots and the sun blazed down on his black helmet. Watching his side mirrors, Joe kept a steady pace.

The hard truth finally sank in. What they did to him meant nothing to them. As far as they were concerned, it was history, a Fourth of July skirmish. By the time the red Texaco sign appeared in the distance, he had talked himself down. *Wait. You can make him remember what he did, and regret it. But you've got to wait.*

Regents crowded the parking lot, watching anxiously as he geared down off the highway. The bosses studied his face for a clue. Would there be a war today? Joe pulled up beside Dudley and told him: "No Bayou Runners. Everything's okay. The Miami Chapter's already there."

"All right!" Greasy whooped and ran for his bike.

If a war wasn't available, a party would do just fine. Amid yells and blasting engines, the men mounted up and impatiently waited for the bosses to sort out the pecking order. Joe rolled his panhead to the shade beneath the overhang. As a probate, he would ride at the very back.

His eyes drifted to an open bay and a '65 Ford Fairlane on the rack. Around the bay were crates of oil cans, neat stacks of tires, greasy red rags up on the work bench-- familiar parts of his old life. He saw Jess shake hands with the old man, who nodded his thanks. He had completely sold out of soda pop, cigarettes and boiled peanuts, and had a hefty roll of cash in his overall pocket. Jess cocked his head at Joe, then walked up to him and handed him the denim Probate cut-off.

"You ride at the back of the pack with Denny's freak. When we get there, set up a place for Atlanta to camp and get some firewood."

Near the pumps, Denny spoke to Dudley, dipping his head slightly to be heard. They knew what the Miami Regents had done to Joe. Denny walked over to where Joe sat on the panhead.

"Do not forget for one second you gave your word to Jess. My hang-around has been through enough. I don't want him getting killed because of you doing something stupid. You hear me, probate?"

Joe glanced over at the hang-around, who stood ready, his big shoulders bowed from a heavy weight only he could feel. He had taken off his sunglasses, and the man's clear blue eyes were so full of pain that Joe wanted to look away. The man gazed at Denny. *"What do we do now, Sarge?"* Joe heard it, though the man's lips didn't move. In a place like Camp Lang Vei or Khe Sanh, when it was really important, his Sarge never got a chance to answer.

"I hear you, Denny." Joe pulled his helmet on and looked straight into the hang-around's tortured eyes. "The club calls me Rider but my name is Joe Wilson. I was in Korea for awhile, Cold War. Air Force, Ninety-Second Combat Defense Squadron."

The man blinked. Some of the tension ebbed from his face. His throat wobbled, as if some rusty words were creaking upward, an introduction, remembering who he used to be. Joe shook his head.

"It's all right, pard, maybe later. Let's ride."

♦

Thirty minutes later, the first wave of motorcycles reached the race track. The military pairing split into chaos as Harleys bounced across the grass in every direction, some bearing down straight for the Miami Chapter.

"He-e-e-e-ey mother-fuckers!"

The Miami Regents jumped up and ran straight at the bikes, roaring and waving their arms. Joe veered off behind the van into the woods, and didn't stop until he reached a stand of dogwoods. He parked the panhead where it could not be seen, but he could hear it if a thief cranked it up. Since the very first time, riding it took him out of the bad place, him and the pan outrunning the clutching hands only he could see. So he took care of it now. He had a gut feeling that the Bayou Runners had not suddenly decided to go home.

The girls once again piled out of the old Chevy van, their faces pink in the heat.

"There goes the neighborhood." Flossie fanned herself with a True Confessions magazine."Have a beer, Joe, they won't last long."

Joe sat down in the driver seat and watched as old friends reunited, backslapping each other and trading insults. He wanted to join in—he had met the Milwaukee crew at the Atlanta clubhouse a few weeks ago—but their probates stood by nervously, also awaiting orders. Unconcerned with rank, Smoky ambled up to him and nudged his boot with a wet nose.

"Who put the pink bandanna on my dog?"

"She *is* a girl, you know," Dorrie reminded him.

"Yeah, but I don't want the other dogs making fun of her."

"They won't for long. She'll show 'em who's boss."

Spreading across the field, the different chapters staked out their preferred patch of grass, circling it with bikes and bedrolls. The old ladies and probates got to work setting up the campsites. Hoarded speed, pot and pills were swapped and bought. Mildewed tents unfolded and the Dayton girls stretched several king-size sheets among the lower branches of a small oak for shade. Civilian campers gaped in astonishment at the invasion, then gathered their kids and beer and edged away to the east side of the track.

As the host, Atlanta was responsible for booze and food, but because of the last-minute notice, the other chapters weren't taking any chances. Denny rolled out a big jar of peanut butter and a bottle of Jack Daniels from his sleeping bag, and another Chicago Regent pulled two smashed boxes of glazed donuts out of his saddlebags. The shell-shocked hang-around set down his large duffel bag, but didn't open it.

Kitty peered across the grass. "Damn, Big Alec bought those two stupid whores, the peroxide twins."

A U-Haul box truck glared orange from two hundred feet away, the back door open. Big Alec's men had already settled in, their bedrolls and lawn chairs and coolers in a circle.

"Ain't no room in there for their bikes. They must have actually rode 'em up here instead of hauling 'em," Mina observed.

"Bet Alec came up in a limo. Or flew in," Flossie said, but not too loud. "You know those whores aren't gonna get their hair messed up in the wind."

Joe smiled faintly as the claws came out. He wasn't the only one with a grudge.

Smitty left the frenzied greetings and stalked over to the van, wiping the sweat from his face with his boonie hat.

"Probate, you and the old ladies get those hot dogs going. Set up the grills over there. I want 'em to have to walk by us to get to the food, but not through us. I'll collect some money this evening, and you can escort the ladies to the nearest grocery store tomorrow. We got enough to last us tonight if they don't get greedy."

Denny ambled over, clutching his peanut butter jar.

"Can I leave this over here without y'all making it evaporate?" He set it down behind the driver's seat in the van.

"You usually share," Kitty said with a faint smile. "If you'd get an old lady, you wouldn't have to farm out your peanut butter."

"Yeah, wouldn't you rather have an old lady than that weirdo following you around?" Dorrie asked under her breath, scrutinizing the stranger who shadowed him.

"The weirdo isn't nearly as complicated as a woman. Any of y'all wanting some Texas peanut butter later, draw straws to see who goes first," Denny told them, then looked at Smitty, "See you in my office a minute?"

They walked off together in the general direction of the Miami crew, leaving the girls to smirk and giggle.

"Shit, why draw straws? There's enough of him to go around for all of us," Dorrie snickered, but only after Smitty was out of earshot. "That's the only man I've ever known that could wear a five-pound belt buckle without it sliding down."

Shaking his head, Joe hefted a cooler from the van.

"You're embarrassing me," He said, though he'd heard the rumors about Denny since he first met him. Women zapped up to him like his Regents belt buckle had a magnet in it, or just below it.

"Oh you'll always be our favorite probate," Dorrie assured him, but her gaze slid sideways, watching Denny stride across the thick grass, Levi's slung around his hips and an unbuttoned denim shirt shifting in the breeze. "That's just dessert."

CHAPTER NINE

"Care to join us?" Denny stopped by the old knucklehead.

Jess paused while unloading his bedroll and eyed the sweating group standing beside his bike. "Depends on what your committee has in mind. Looks like trouble to me."

"Hell yeah." Denny grinned. "Gonna talk to your favorite person, see if him and his boys got rid of the Bayou Runners for us so we can go ahead and party."

Jess glanced at Smitty. "Was this trip all a big waste of time?"

"A party is never a waste of time, just a waste of money," Smitty said. "Come on."

They weren't the only bosses sauntering through the thick grass toward the Miami encampment. Some wanted answers, others followed their noses. In the shade of the U-Haul, heat waves smeared the air above two green metal grills. The scent of charcoal sizzling with dripping meat juice was almost unbearable for the new arrivals. Three of Big Alec's old ladies wielded forks and spatulas, their hair pulled off their necks, and denim shorts cut so high the Milwaukee bosses could confirm the women did not have a tan-line.

The Dade County men didn't budge. They sat in a circle and chugged sloppily on their beers, watching their boss to see how he would handle things. Big Alec looked bored, sprawled out in a lawn chair, his long wiry hair kinking in the late-summer humidity. He didn't bother standing up

"How's it going, gentlemen?"

"You tell us," Dudley said."You got here early."

"We wanted to check it out, make sure it was safe for the rest of you," Big Alec said and his men laughed.

"That was damned nice of you," Denny drawled. "So did I just ride down from Chicago for nothin'?"

"I'd rather ride to a party than an ambush," Big Alec retorted. When a slight smile twisted Jess's face, he realized what he'd said. The Miami Regents stopped laughing and the others shifted uncomfortably.

Quick to redirect the blame for last year's New Orleans disaster, Big Alec narrowed his eyes at Jess. "Heard you got yourself a new probate. Think you can keep this one alive long enough to get his patch?"

Jess stared at him a long moment.

"I'd say he's one tough son-of-a-bitch to still be alive and probating. As long as he doesn't get caught up in one of your brilliant ideas, he might make it."

Dudley glanced at Smitty, but both decided not to intervene.

"Well, the problem, Jess, is Atlanta has a different standard for tough. When Milwaukee came to visit us, they said your probate was a regular little Suzy Homemaker, tidying up the place," Big Alec taunted.

"They told you that?"

"Sure did."

"Well, if they stop by Atlanta on the way home, they'll see a new patch on the trophy wall. Any of your Betty Crocker probates bring you a patch in their first month?"

Before the pissing contest got to the point of a brawl, Dudley interrupted."The man's been an asset to the club, Alec. He's done everything he was told to, and then some. I don't want any shit."

"There won't be any shit unless he gets jazzy with me again. Why are you giving me grief over a probate?"

"He's an Atlanta probate now," Dudley emphasized, his patience wearing thin. "Anybody has a problem with him, come see me or Smitty first."

"And if you can't find them, make sure you find me," Denny suggested with a menacing grin.

"I thought we were worried about the Bayou Runners, not some fuckin' probate," a Miami Regent grumbled.

"We aren't worried about shit, Jonesy," Big Alec said. "But Atlanta does seem more concerned with their probate than Sleaze. Something sweet that guy does for you, in addition to cleaning the clubhouse? Pretty boy like Jess, I always wondered."

"If you want your dick sucked, Alec, I'm not loaning out my probate," Jess said. "Get one of your Dade County boys to drain your weasel."

"Fuck you!" Jonesy started up out of his chair.

"Settle down," Alec told his man with a faint grin. "And it isn't a weasel. I have a fucking bull alligator."

His old ladies, who weren't supposed to be listening, shrieked with laughter.

"Your alligator ain't shit compared to ours," The Chicago boss crowed, and thumped Denny on the back. "Show 'em!"

Denny shook his head. "I'm not whipping out my dick around this bunch. One of 'em would latch on to it."

"You wish," Wolf chortled.

A pot-bellied man with a thin brown ponytail ambled around the corner. Mustard and mayonnaise ran down his chest like bird shit as he tore into a thick cheeseburger. "Hey Alec, you want me to go find a payphone and call New Orleans?" He stopped dead when he saw the visitors.

Smiles fell off their faces, replaced with incredulous stares.

"Are you shitting me?" Jess glared.

The man worked a jaw full of cheeseburger and bread to his cheek, and said hesitantly: "Hey Jess. How ya doing?"

"ChristAlmighty, what's the world coming to?"Smitty exclaimed. "Turn around, let me see that probate patch."

"It ain't a probate patch, Smitty. I got the one that counts." The man bumbled through a half-turn, peering over his shoulder anxiously, then stumped back around. "See?"

Big Alec grinned smugly, enjoying the dumbfounded shock.

His men, however, couldn't hide their embarrassment.

"Let me get this straight." Smitty smacked his lips. "The Miami Regents have a new member. He did not have to probate, and he still lives in New Orleans? Have I got that right?"

"The part that's any of your business," Big Alec said.

Denny stuck out his hand, but the dark fire in his eye warned that he would not forgive.

"Fat Jack. You'll fit right in with the Miami crew. They need men like you."

"It's a good arrangement for everybody, Denny," Fat Jack said eagerly. "There's a lot of shit going down in New Orleans we need to keep track of. I can do that."

"No, we need to leave shit in New Orleans alone," Jess retorted. "We didn't have a problem there until Alec decided to cozy up with Sleaze and got himself a broken leg, got my probate killed, and made us all look like idiots!"

Big Alec stretched his fingers and gripped the arms of his chair, his smile morphing into a sneer. The old ladies abandoned the grill and headed for the other side of the U-Haul.

Jesus. Denny waded in, sweeping out a big hand. "And where are the Bayou Runners? Is this your gig, Jack? Were you the one with all the information?"

Fat Jack took another bite of his cheeseburger, his eyelids fluttering nervously as he sucked mustard from his fingers.

"Ain't my gig. I don't know what's goin' on. I can't even wear my patch in New Orleans, Sleaze would kill me."

"Fuck." Denny shook his head and turned away in disgust. "I gotta take a shit."

Jess, however, wasn't ready to leave.

"It's kinda funny, Alec, I keep wondering why Sleaze would come this far to screw with us. My probate pointed out that maybe we weren't asking the right questions. I had to think about that. What does Sleaze want so damned bad?" Jess smiled. "My guess?

The one thing he didn't get last time—your patch. If I were you, I wouldn't sit around waiting for a bullet."

"That little bastard wouldn't dare come after my patch!" Big Alec retorted.

"He already did," Jess assured him. "And if it wasn't for my probate—the dead one—Sleaze would have it."

♦

When the afternoon sun tracked overhead and seemed to stop, Dorrie pulled three large umbrellas from the van. She invited several wilting Milwaukee women to share the shade. They sat cross-legged in the grass, catching up on gossip while hot dogs cooked on the grills behind them.

Unfazed by the relentless Alabama humidity, the Atlanta Regents set up twenty feet from the grills. Jess stretched out in the grass and leaned against his bedroll, his '47 knucklehead parked behind him. Denny and a few old friends from Chicago settled in with their beer. Joe saw them passing around pills and pot, and kept his distance, roaming the woods for kindling and small limbs for a campfire later, if anyone could stand more heat.

Across the campground, radios and tape decks played a mishmash of country and rock. Eric Clapton's raging pain over Layla fought for volume over Cher and her gypsies, tramps and thieves. Country fans rocked blissfully to Freddy Hart and Bobby Bare, Merle Haggard and Tom T. Hall. Joe discovered he knew the words to the country songs far better than the rock tunes. Maybe rednecks just couldn't change.

"What the hell is that?" Two men with Dayton rockers stopped by the Atlanta circle.

Denny's silent friend squatted beside him, a plate loaded with hot dogs, chili and relish balanced on his thigh.

"Is that hang-around eating before I do? That's bullshit. Gimme the plate." Dayton swiped for it.

"Leave him alone," Denny said through a mouthful of hamburger.

“He don’t have a patch. How come he’s eating before me?”

“He was hungry. He went and got something to eat instead of standing around yanking his dick.”

“Hang-arounds don’t eat until members do.” The man swiped for it again. Silent Sam crouched over his food. “Give it here, asshole.”

“Ya see the grill over there?” An old Chicago Regent pointed in exasperation. “You can’t walk twenty feet?”

“I don’t have to walk. I got a plate right here,” He snatched at it, missed, and knocked it into the grass. Then he screamed and went down on his knees, clutching his shin.

“Told you to leave him alone,” Denny set the wrench down.

“You asshole! We’re Regents.” The other Dayton man helped his wailing friend to his feet. “You sticking up for this bum?”

“The bum is my guest. I, however, am a Regent, and I told your friend to leave the man alone,” Denny said. “Any more fuckin’ questions about the rules?”

Silent Sam scraped up the hotdogs from the grass, put them back on his plate, and resumed eating. The pair from Ohio hobbled off, muttering. Kitty walked up, waiting until the two were gone, then held out a squeeze bottle.

“Anybody want a Coppertone tan?”

“I’d say we’re already well-done, darlin’. But you can slather me with lotion if you want,” Denny said, cocking an eye at Jess. “You wanta watch?”

“She already knows you have a big wrench and tend to use it spontaneously. She’s on her own.”

♦

An hour later, Wolf stalked by, heading for the grill.

“We want to talk to you about your new Miami member,” Jess called. “Stop by on your way back.”

“I can’t, thanks to your big mouth.”

“Can’t what? Hang out for a minute?”

“Exactly. Alec doesn’t want me to leave his side,” Wolf sulked.

"I'm supposed to take a bullet for him if Sleaze runs out of the fuckin' woods with a M-16"

"Didn't mean to screw up your party," Jess said, reeking of insincerity.

"Of course you didn't. Congratulations. You wanted to shake him up, you did." Wolf reached for a beer floating in a galvanized tub of melting ice. "He'll barricade himself in the motel room tonight."

"You're in a motel?" Smitty cracked. "Oh, what am I thinking? Of course Alec rented the Presidential Suite at the Holiday Inn for the weekend."

Wolf popped the cap off a beer and looked at Jess.

"Anything to that shit you were running?"

"All theory. But it makes sense. Why would Sleaze screw with us? He doesn't have enough men to take us on."

"Sleaze was getting squirrelly last time we were in New Orleans, remember? Too much crank," Wolf pointed out. "Coulda burnt out more brain cells since then."

"He was smart enough to wait 'til you went to take a leak before he set his dogs on Alec," Jess said.

"There was something in my beer. I couldn't stop pissing, even when the fight started," Wolf protested.

"Alec's the one with no brain, giving Fat Jack a Regents patch," Denny interrupted. "That puke don't look out for anybody but himself."

"Aw, leave Wolf alone," Smitty protested. "You'll never get him to admit his boss is an idiot. He's loyal, ya gotta give him that."

He stopped, and frowned at the sky. A small plane broke the tree line, the humming engine suddenly loud. It stirred the pennants along the top tiers of the track, and banked to circle back over the Regents. Terrified, Smoky bolted and scurried under the van.

"Fuckin'cops. They're starting already. That son-of-a-bitch is low." Denny squinted, his Adam's apple working as he craned his neck. "Those are cops, right?"

Jess waved at Joe, who was working on a Detroit member's sportster. "Probate, can you see who's in the plane?"

"Bastards," Wolf spat. "Here they come again. Why don't they just ride in here and take pictures? Chicken-shit assholes."

"I ain't kidding about making sure those are cops." Denny got to his feet and shouted harshly at Joe. "Can you see 'em?"

The plane dipped lower during the second pass. Anxious faces across the campground tilted skyward, watching with dread as it soared by, then climbed over the trees to bank again.

"I can see them, but I can't tell what they're holding," Joe said.

Panic rippled across the encampment. No one wanted to be the first to run, to become a joke, unless running meant staying alive. Joe focused on the tiny windows as the Cessna reappeared over the pine trees.

"There's kids down here," Denny fumed, panic in his voice. "Sleaze better not be that stupid. I'll pull his head off. Damn it, what do you see?"

"I'm not sure." Joe started.

He heard Jess shout "Holy fuck, stop him!" and caught a movement near Denny. Silent Sam had lunged into his duffle bag and brought out a Soviet AK-47. Before anyone could move, he lifted it and blasted away at the plane, tearing the air apart. The Cessna veered sharply, wobbled and began streaming black smoke.

"They've got cameras!" Joe yelled. "It's cameras, not guns."

Jess and Denny tackled Sam, fifteen seconds too late, while the campground erupted in panic. The vast majority of race fans had no idea where the gunfire came from, and didn't care. Parents yanked up their kids and tossed them inside trucks and campers, following hastily behind them. The ex-military hit the dirt, hands over their heads, too familiar with the sound and damage of an AK. Wolf took off running for the Miami encampment before they began firing back.

Two confused security guards sprinted for the track entrance, while the old ladies darted into the woods behind the van. Smitty planted a boot on the AK's barrel, forcing it into the dirt. "Get his finger off the trigger!"

"Stand down!" His knee in the man's back, Denny shouted: "Stop! Sam, cool it."

Jess grabbed an arm and bent it backward until Sam was face down in the grass while Ugly slammed across the man's legs. Joe watched in horror as the plane shuddered out of sight, listening for a crash but it was impossible to hear over the screams and shouts. He tried to wave the girls into silence but they were beyond hearing him. Denny pried the AK loose from Sam and tossed it to Joe.

"Get rid of it," He panted. "Holy Jesus. If that plane crashes, we are fucked."

"Round up the bosses," Dudley told Smitty. "We've gotta figure something out, fast."

But Smitty stared at the road, his mouth hanging open.

"Do you hear that?"

There was no mistaking the rumble of a dozen Harleys, heading their way.

"Shit!" Bobby Boozer gasped, sprawled across Sam's feet. "Where's our look-out? I put a look-out up there by the road!"

Anyone with a spare hand reached for pistols. In the middle of a nightmare he couldn't control, Joe raised the AK-47, ready to cut down if he had to, waiting for the pack to clear the corner. He wasn't about to let anyone slaughter his friends.

"Wait." Dudley waved at his men and shouted: "Hold it!"

They stood ready as the Harleys came slowly into sight. Holding his breath, Joe studied the faces and patches, and sagged with relief. *Louisville.* He relaxed. The first two bikes chugged up beside the sweating, panting tangle on top of Silent Sam. They pulled their helmets loose and surveyed the armed Regents crouched behind bedrolls and tents, and old ladies peering from the big trees.

"Our damned bikes kept breaking down all the way here. Did we miss something?"

CHAPTER TEN

That night, a full moon rose over the foothills, washing the Alabama countryside in silvery-blue. Bombed on chocolate mescaline, a cluster of Atlanta and Milwaukee girls sat cross-legged in the grass, their backs against the van. They gazed across the field at the spectral sight, bloodshot eyes mesmerized. Dozens of tiny campfires flickered, hot orange sparks rising like escaping souls. Some of the girls saw faces in the sparks, and had to grab the grass to keep themselves from floating away, too.

Laughter rippled raw and loud as the moon lifted. Guitar riffs from the Allman Brothers, Marshall Tucker and the Nitty Gritty Dirt Band echoed off the looming track from dozens of radios. Somehow it worked, the words and rhythms running along the same southern chords.

"Chomp!" At the next camp, the Chicago girls goose-necked to 'Polk Salad Annie.' "Chomp chomp!"

They eyed Joe as he passed by, their invitations obvious, but he was safer with the females he knew, even if they resembled a row of wild owls with their enormous pupils and pivoting heads.

Kitty sat at the end of the row, the unofficial guide. She didn't indulge in hallucinogens; she didn't need them to see things. She extended a brownie on the palm of her hand. "It's the last one. Straight pot, no peyote. It'll help you relax."

"I'm so relaxed now I'm almost dead," Joe opened the driver's door and sat heavily on the edge.

The dome light had been disconnected, and the door's shadow made it difficult for a Regent to spot him. He desperately needed a break. The van trembled, disorienting him, then he heard the sounds of violent grappling and moaning in the back. Whoever it was didn't care, probably stoned out of their gourd. He looked across the field to see who was missing.

Ugly swayed slightly to a thumping Led Zeppelin tune, a half-smile on his face, his eyes almost closed. With the sputtering Cessna long gone, he and the Regents soothed their jangled nerves by partying hard. Next to him, Bobby Boozer and Greasy gestured and laughed until they convulsed and gripped their stomachs. They appeared to be reliving the plane fly-over and tackling Silent Sam.

Denny had confiscated the duffle bag, assuring Sam "Just for now, man, you've upset some people." He gave it to Joe, who carried it into the woods, set it down beside his panhead, and secured a dark tarp over both revered possessions.

Long after the Regents and tourists stopped watching the sky and roads, Joe remained edgy. So did Silent Sam, banished to sit beneath a rough-barked old pine with a six-pack. Sweltering, the man remained alert, his big head moving like a mastiff waiting for lions to descend. He looked at Joe once, a deep searching gaze, like "you, too?" They both sensed a presence waiting and watching, and it kept his shoulder blades tight.

After a hot hectic afternoon on alert, repeatedly checking his Colt in the privacy of the van several times just to reassure himself, Joe finally reached a stage of exhaustion he couldn't fight. He slumped forward, forearms propped on his knees to prevent him pitching to the ground on his face.

"You want some speed?" Kitty said, concerned.

"Been doing 'em all day. I'm gonna blow my heart out if I don't lay off."

He hadn't indulged in them in a long time. The military passed out amphetamines by the bucket load to keep soldiers wired for battle. A lot of men brought the bad habit home, but Joe shied away from drugs. Falling asleep was hard enough without speed pumping through his veins. Until he moved to Atlanta and could not adapt his blue-collar body to the Regents' late-night schedule. He still didn't like to do dope; he knew what happened when the inevitable crash came. He let people down, people who depended on him for their safety, and sometimes their lives.

Joe sank his hands in his hair. In Korea, coming down off a four-day high buried him into dry-mouthed oblivion, deaf to the sounds in a hangar only a few yards from the bunk room. He slept through the whole thing. When he woke up, longing for coffee, he opened the door and took two steps into a nightmare that still refused to let him turn around and shut the door on it.

The silver moon gave him something soothing to rest his stinging gaze on. If it wasn't so late, he'd go for a ride. The farm houses and highways would be lit like daylight.

"There's a dozen other probates on duty," Kitty said. "Why don't you grab your sleeping bag and crash?"

"I keep thinking something isn't right," Joe admitted, running his hands through his hair. "I can't figure out what happened to the plane. Why didn't it come back? I didn't hear it crash."

"That isn't what's bothering you." Kitty leaned in close so only he could hear her, her eyes locking him in to a Cheshire cat gaze crystallized from cannabis sativa. "This place is haunted."

Joe smiled. Trust her to admit it. Before the plane, before they had settled in, back to about the time he parked his motorcycle deep in the woods, he had felt someone steadily watching him. He tried to dismiss the notion, certain it was because he was a probate and constantly on call. It only made sense the Regents would watch him nonstop. But once the sun gave way to that dappled moon, turning the shadows deep blue, the sensation became stronger, like the constant humming of crickets.

Joe said: "I know it's haunted but I'm not supposed to talk about it with you."

"Says who?" She peered up at him.

"Jess. He says you've got enough ghosts."

She scowled slightly at the campfire, where Jess shared a bottle of Jack Daniels with Denny.

"Shit, he's one to talk. I can't believe he doesn't trip over all those damn things following him around."

Yeah, a combat medic would have a regular entourage trailing him. Joe wondered how Jess handled it. But he couldn't ask outright. It would have been weak, admitting he had a problem. So he did the next best thing.

"What do you see here?" He asked quietly.

She shrugged and bit into a brownie. "I don't see things with my eyes. It's more like in the back of my head. When my neck starts tingling, I know they're here. Flossie's from just a little ways north of this place. She says this valley is old. People have lived here for thousands of years. And there was a World War II Air Force base here. So it might be the boys who can't find their way home from wherever they wound up. Maybe…maybe they want to talk to you."

A cold rush of air swept over Joe, numbing him, and he gripped the beer bottle.

"I've already got others who won't leave me alone," He said hoarsely. "I can't handle any more. If you can see them, tell 'em I'm sorry but for God's sake, leave me alone."

"Oh shit," Kitty turned to touch his hand, her fingers small but warm. "I'm sorry, Joe. I shouldn't talk when I'm high."

"It's okay. I started it." He waited a minute, then asked her: "I'd like to know. What is it you see?"

"Shapes, colors," She struggled to explain. "Sometimes when someone gets close to me or when I'm doing the cards, I get impressions. Do you…actually see them?"

He knew what she meant. "Yeah," he said. "Yeah, I see 'em."

At 3 a.m., if his nerves were bad and he couldn't sleep, Joe would give in and let them come forward, young, grinning and sharing jokes on the flight line. And sometimes, he saw them the other way. The real way, the way it ended.

Like a bad movie, with no sound in the hangar except for metal creaking under the weight of the dangling airmen, bound and sprayed with bullets. He didn't know if other veterans were weak like this, unable to stop thinking about it or let it go. She was the first person he'd ever been able to talk to about it. No, not "it." *Them.*

"They'll fade after a while," She promised.

"It's been ten years, and I can still smell the blood and the shit." He wanted her to understand. "I don't try to remember, Kit. I never know when they're coming. That's the bad thing."

"When doesn't it happen?"

He had to think.

"When I'm at the beach or a river. Or on the bike." He smiled faintly.

"The wind keeps them away," She mused. "Cool. Wonder why?"

"I wonder what a shrink would make of it."

"You ever been to one?"

"Are you kidding? They'd stick me in the state hospital," He said. "But it isn't my guys tonight. It's not the same. Whoever's here tonight is older."

"I think this place was a passageway, once. For people who understood the earth better than we do. Maybe they know something about you." She held her arms out, resting them on her knees, her palms up. "You're special, Joe. You've got a lot of energy, if you can just figure out what to do with it."

"I was hoping you could tell me," He said.

"We have to find our own answers. There's no magic fix," Kitty smiled. "Go lay down. You're tired. Tomorrow's going to be rough. We've got to find a grocery store and fight thousands of tourists for whatever's left on the shelves."

That didn't sound like fun. Last count, there were over two hundred Regents and old ladies here. Joe closed his eyes for a second. If he could just get through the weekend without ghosts or Bayou Runners or Big Alec starting some shit, he had a very good chance of getting rid of his rookie status. He wanted to attend the next National as an equal.

A distant radio picked up the ominous "When the Levee Breaks," Led Zeppelin's hard percussion version. Joe listened. If the slow pounding didn't summon ancient Indians, nothing would. He saw Denny stand up, weaving slightly, firelight shadowing his dark face into a rugged Mephisto. Jess frowned at him and shook his head. Denny waved him off and unsteadily made his way across the sprawled bodies to the van. He walked down the line of slack-jawed women until his shadow fell across Kitty.

"Hey, darlin', got your cards?"

"Sure I do. But I can't see out here."

"Sure you can. I can read by that moon. Let me pull a card, I wanta know something."

Reluctantly, she dragged a leather purse around to her lap.

"I'm kind of burned out right now, Denny. I don't think I can do it very well."

"Nah." He looked over his shoulder at the moon, his hawkish profile dark. "You couldn't turn the shit off tonight if you wanted to."

Joe didn't move. Denny was the last person he expected to be a mean drunk. And that was the bad thing about mean drunks. By the time you found out, it was too late. He glanced at Jess. Joe didn't dare touch Denny unless a full patched Regent said so. He was relieved to see Jess's crystal chip eyes aimed directly at them.

Kitty stalled, her fingers uncertain on the slick surface of the tarot cards. This wasn't her favorite deck, a hand-tinted antique set she couldn't afford to lose. She brought this newer one along because the girls always pestered her for readings. Besieged, she'd done light readings all day and was exhausted. But there was no telling a Regent "not right now."

"You have a question in your mind?"

"Yeah. Is he gonna be dead by the time I get there?"

"Don't tell me," Kitty shook her head, shuffling the cards.

"But that's what I want to know. Am I going to a funeral in Texas when I leave here, or is the son-of-a-bitch gonna hang on?"

Kitty held the deck in her lap, relaxing, her gaze on the dark shadow towering over her. She fanned the cards, then lifted the deck. “This isn’t how I do it. But go ahead, pick one.”

Denny set his jaw and his long fingers swooped down to pluck a card. He held it out to her defiantly, daring her to tell him what he didn’t want to hear. She gave it a glance, but only for a second. She didn’t need it.

“You should go home for your mom’s sake.”

“I already know that. If it wasn’t for her…what did that card say?”

She toyed with the card, taking her time before poking it back in the deck.

“Stalling won’t change what’s already happened, Denny. Yes, he’s dying, but you know that, too. Go home for your mom. It’s very important to her,” She hesitated. “She wants to see you.”

Denny stood there a moment, thumbs hooked in his belt loops.

“It figures,” He said cryptically, and headed back to the circle around the campfire.

Joe waited until Denny settled down on a ragged sleeping bag before creaking to his feet. He couldn’t fight it any longer. He had to find a place to bunk down, preferably where he wouldn’t get stomped or run over.

“I give,” He announced to Kitty. “You gonna be all right?”

She gazed thoughtfully at the sky, her leather purse across her lap, her hands crossed over it.

“I always see kids around him. Little kids.”

“Who? Denny?”

“Yeah.”

“Why don’t you tell him?”

“They’re Asian,” She said simply. “And if I can see them, they’re dead.”

A shimmer passed over her eyes.

“And he already knows who they are.”

Which explained why he panicked when the plane flew over earlier. And why Silent Sam kept vigil in the roots of the old pine. Could he see them, too, or just the wild pain that kept a bottle of Jack Daniels in Denny's hand?

"Good night, Kit."

"Sweet dreams, Joe," She said.

♦

He had his answer. He wasn't the only one with demons and nightmares and places he didn't want to visit. He thought too much, his girlfriend back home always told him. Joe dragged his sleeping bag from under the van and rolled it out. Certain he'd dream about ancient Indians and Spaniards and will-o-the-wisps, he settled into the lumpy cotton.

He slipped the Colt from the back of his jeans and wedged it between the fabric. Smoky waited patiently until he stopped moving, then curled herself into a ball next to him, her pink bandanna rustling against his arm. He wasn't sure who was protecting who.

"Good night, girl," He whispered, and was rewarded with a puppy kiss just before he fell asleep.

CHAPTER ELEVEN

A diesel engine rolled out of a bizarre dream about school buses, waking Jess instantly. School on Saturday? He was hearing things. Kitty's rump rested against his thigh, her hair tickling his arm. Nasal snores sawed through the morning air in every direction. Despite the lead weights on his lids, he forced his eyes open a cautious quarter-inch. Gray light hazed the campground into shadows, a Civil War battlefield rising with the dew. Lumpy bodies lie scattered on the ground, the tents silent and still. Except for telltale snores, everybody looked dead.

Denny sprawled next to him, open mouth gurgling, a jar of peanut butter upside down on his sleeping bag. Over by the van, Joe slumped unconscious, Smoky curled up against his chest. Jess couldn't see the grills behind him without moving his head, but a row of women trailed across a few blankets near Joe. No one was up making breakfast.

So what had he heard? Jess edged his head slightly toward the track.

"Kit," He said. "Don't move."

"Mmm?" She didn't stir.

"Can you see the track?"

She stopped breathing, then he felt her heart pick up steam.

"Yeah."

"What do you see?"

"Men. With rifles. A lot of them. All around the top."

At least he wasn't hallucinating.

"What do we do?" Kitty whispered.

"Hold still." Jess wished the probate was nearer with that telescopic eyesight of his. And where the hell was his pistol? Stuck between layers of the sleeping bag. Could he get his hand on it?

"Must be cops. They're wearing hats and gun belts," Kitty said. "Aw shit, do you see what's heading this way?"

Flashing blue lights materialized out of the silvery dawn, creeping toward them down Speedway Boulevard. Jess didn't have to play possum anymore. Before he could warn anyone, a bullhorn blasted the birds out of the trees.

"Attention Regents Motorcycle gang. You are *surrounded.* Stand up and put your weapons on the ground."

Bodies across the field jerked to life, yawning and dazed.

"This is not a joke," The bullhorn advised from the top of the track. "Stand up now and place your weapons on the ground."

"Fuck you." Jolted out of a sluggish sleep, Bobby Boozer reached inside his jacket.

Greasy weakly caught his arm, trying not to puke in the grass. "Cool it. There's a million of 'em. Look."

"There's two hundred of us," Bobby retorted. "That's even."

"They'll be shooting down while we're shooting up." Smitty rubbed his aching eyes. "That ain't even."

The Dayton and Detroit Chapters didn't care about odds or trajectory. They staggered to their feet, furious that their short hibernation had been interrupted, and waited impatiently for orders from their bosses.

The squad cars came to a halt in the track's long shadows, lights spinning silently. Deputies stepped out in pairs, shielded by the doors, rifles ready. A Talladega County deputy raised a bullhorn set on full volume.

"Throw down your weapons *now*! You are surrounded."

"Come and get 'em, motherfucker!" Ugly snarled, stirring up threats around him.

They had passed out only a few hours ago, stoned into a deep level of unconsciousness. Now a harsh voice ordered them back to reality, a humid morning on hard-packed grass. Near-crippled from the damp ground, Dudley forced his hips into place and lurched up on his feet with the help of a baseball bat. Wavering for balance, he saw Jess push Kitty toward the van, with the other women hastily following at a running crouch. When Silent Sam got to his feet, his blue stare fixed on the revolving lights, Dudley wracked his aching brain for a plan, fast.

The Chicago boss staggered over, with Louisville trudging behind him. Their hung-over men cursed and sneered at the uniformed silhouettes standing far overhead along the track.

"Half of us are gonna die here if we don't do something," Chicago said under his breath.

"No shit," Dudley gritted his teeth. Right now, it'd be a mercy killing. He was getting too old to sleep on the ground. But he knew they wanted him to go talk to the cops. Hardly a compliment, Dudley appeared the least threatening, hobbling like an old man, his long horse face and jaw jammed with big teeth that made it look like he was always smiling. Unlike the black Charles Manson eyes popping open around the hissing campfires, he was a twin to the cartoon Mountie Dudley Do-Right, with a lantern jaw and weary brown eyes.

"Make sure I don't get friendly fire in my back. I'll go see what they want."

With Smitty trailing, Dudley limped across the wet grass until he was within shouting distance of the first county car.

"What's the problem?"

"You are all under arrest," The bullhorn blasted, cracking his eardrums in half.

"Put that fucking thing down or I'll tell 'em to open up," Dudley glared, certain his skull had splintered from the noise. "Stupid bastards."

The officers had a hasty conference.

"You're all under arrest. Everybody throw down their weapons."

"Under arrest for what?"

"Assault, robbery and attempted rape."

"Attempted?" Dudley glanced at the furious hung-over men behind him.

During their parties, bored housewives would often slink over to sample a big sweaty motorcycle bum while their husbands drank themselves stupid. Even if the husband sobered up enough to realize his bride was in less than pristine condition when she returned, they rarely dared complain.

The cops waited. Dudley narrowed his eyes at the ring of uniforms overhead. At least the rifles pointed skyward. It hadn't gone bad yet. Possibly because of all the civilian witnesses peeking from tents and vehicles.

"Those charges are bullshit. We haven't had any problems here."

"We got reports that you robbed some people. And that you assaulted a colored man who rode in here on a Kawasaki with a girl."

"It was a white girl, to be specific," Dudley pointed out. "We already had enough of those. We told him to go back wherever he came from, since it was obvious he wasn't from around here."

The cops couldn't argue that a black man toting a white girl around on a motorcycle was pure suicide in Alabama. Smitty edged up behind Dudley.

"Those charges are bogus and they know it. They can't prove who did what. They want us out of here."

"Before the race, too. Ain't that some shit?"

A small, neat man with military posture stepped forward.

"We're all going to have a very long day no matter what. So tell your men to toss their weapons in the grass and form a line. The women, too. We've got buses ready, and a couple hundred Alabama National Guardsman and deputies as escorts. If you've got any sense at all, get your people on those buses without any trouble. You can go to the county jail or the morgue, I don't care. But you are not staying here."

Dudley didn't see a good way out of it. He turned, and was met by two hundred furious faces, waiting for an order to wade into an epic battle. His dark eyes slid over to the national president, who kept a low profile for a number of reasons, outstanding warrants being the most important. The man nodded slightly, exasperated. They didn't have a choice.

"Line up," Dudley told his men. "We're going for a bus ride."

CHAPTER TWELVE

Across the campground, spectators silently watched from their cars and tents and wherever they had scurried for shelter when the bullhorns woke them. Sleepy kids were quickly hushed. No one wanted to get noticed or associated with the outlaw bikers, but they all wanted to hear what was said. Far down the road, three school buses idled, barely visible, the last of the Regents outside the doors getting checked for weapons.

With the bikers out of the area, a half dozen National Guardsmen kicked through the empty sleeping bags, dumping what they found on a green blanket. Cash and small items went in their pockets.

“Looters with badges,” Guidry said quietly to the probate beside him. “I never seen Guardsmen do something like this.”

Both had rolled under a truck when the bullhorns blasted the morning into pieces. The absolute dead-last place they wanted to be was locked up in jail with a bunch of furious Regents. No one would know the new probate, but Guidry was familiar to a few. The blue work shirt borrowed from a mechanic at the Mississippi truck stop would not help at all.

He had almost had a heart attack yesterday when he spotted Fat Jack from New Orleans hanging around with the Miami Regents. Not only had Jack taken his race tip to the Regents, he had decided to come along for the fun. Not wise for a man who owned a tattoo shop in the Quarter. The big surprise was Fat Jack sporting a Regents rocker. Sleaze would flip out. Fat Jack had played both sides for years. Apparently he had finally taken a stand, which wasn’t like the gutless bastard, especially on the wrong side. Life would not be easy for the only Regent in New Orleans once word got around.

At least Big Alec and his crew had left last night, probably to a hotel with cold beer and Magic Fingers beds.

"We gotta get to a payphone, tell Sleaze not to come." The probate pushed a few strands of Bahia grass away from his nose. They had been under the truck for two hours.

"Hold still. This ain't over. Wait 'til them buses are gone."

Idiot, he thought. Sleaze had no intention of showing up here.

"This is crazy. What's this all about?"

"Shut up and find out," Guidry told him.

He didn't like the new probate, another high-strung doper with zigzag eyes, but needed back-up for this recon mission. After stealing an extra car, Sleaze had decided to head north and circle around to wait, the men scattered to attract less attention. He ordered the punk kid to go in his place, jamming a ball cap on his head and stuffing his dirty-blonde ponytail down the back of his shirt. Telling him to keep his mouth shut and learn was another thing.

"Damn, now what?" He exclaimed.

A half dozen tow trucks and flat-bed trailers came rolling up and pulled off the road into the grass. The guardsmen made a half-hearted attempt to direct them, then resumed shaking out saddle bags for loot. The drivers and their cronies gazed across the field in amazement. Summoned from three different counties at the last minute, their experience with motorcycles was limited.

"Hurry it up, we don't have all day to clear this place," A state trooper told them.

"There must be two hundred of them things!" They exclaimed, not exactly horrified.

They were getting paid by the piece, not by the hour. The more they towed off, the bigger the paycheck. Eying each other, they hastily split up.

"Let's get to it then."

Toting massive chains, two men walked up to the nearest circle of motorcycles, and began snaking the links around the middle of the frames.

"Aw shit, look at that." The probate grabbed a handful of grass. "Are they really gonna do that? Wish Sleaze could see this, he'd die laughing."

Guidry didn't think it was funny. Neither did the campers. Rusty chains tightened around the bikes, crushing them together, metal banging. And then it got worse. A tow truck reversed down into the grass. A man jumped up on the back and guided the end of the winch to the doubled chain. With a sickening lurch, the hydraulics on the winch kicked in, and the cluster of bikes slammed into each other in a crush of fenders, frames, handlebars, chrome and paint.

"You believin' that?" Even the probate winced when a classic old black and white knucklehead slammed onto the skids.

"No," Guidry said, his stomach tightening against the hard ground.

He knew who that knucklehead belonged to.

All around them, the A.M.A. race fans watched in horror as the motorcycles were dragged up the skids. A flatbed truck maneuvered into place, idling as the bikes were loaded on to it.

"That ain't right," A man said nearby.

"Hush!" A woman's voice chided. "You wanta go with them?"

"I'm just saying it ain't right. Them men didn't cause no problems. And them bikes, Lois, that's a shitty thing to do."

Guidry cringed at the shrill metal shrieks. In the distance, the last school bus chugged away. Were any of the Regents watching through the tinted windows? If even one saw this, they would bust out the glass and run back like old-style berserkers. He had to get the hell out of here.

"Guidry?" The probate's voice didn't sound so peppy.

"What?"

"Where's that waitress?"

Guidry tried to look over his shoulder. All he could see were feet. She'd been wearing white slacks and her waitress shoes. Sleaze hadn't given her time to change.

"Oh Lord," He put his head down.

He wanted to believe she'd gone to the portable toilets, or maybe she was just a few yards away somewhere in the crowd. He really wanted to believe, but thanks to the big-mouthed probate, she had gone from quiet to uncomfortable last night. Odds were she had slipped off to her car when the cops showed up and was now on her way back to the truck stop.

"Guidry, that bitch has booked and took her car, I'll betcha. We better go find her. I can't keep laying on my stomach, I've got to piss like a race horse."

Without waiting for a decision, the probate squirmed out the far side of the truck. By the time Guidry elbowed his way across the flattened damp grass into a crowd of people, the probate had disappeared.

"You about done with my truck?" Sandy-haired and red-faced, an older man sized up Guidry's mechanic's shirt. The man meant it as a joke, but it took Guidry a few seconds to realize what he was talking about.

"Good as new, my friend," He said with a smile. "And no charge."

Another bang, another crash, and an engine whined. They all turned, smiles gone, to stare across the decimated camp. As fast as the tow truck drivers could band them together, motorcycles were snagged, cinched and dragged screeching up onto the flatbeds. Saddle-bags fell open, the contents spilling to the grass for anyone to collect.

Embers still glowed in the abandoned campfires. The guardsmen gathered up the tents, clothes and sleeping bags, and dumped them into the fire. Black smoke began to rise.

"They shouldn't leave them fires going with nobody to watch 'em," A woman said. "They're making a bigger mess than them bikers."

Guidry barely heard her. His dark eyes squinted past the uniformed looters, and he took in a sharp breath. He double-checked the name on his shirt. Larry. Larry the mechanic.

"Yes ma'am, they sure are," He said, and began walking steadily across the grass toward the wreckage.

A deputy plucked at a guitar, testing the strings. Another clutched two transistor radios to his chest while he shook dirt from an overturned cooler full of beer. They didn't even look up until it was obvious he was heading straight for them. They straightened, eyeballing him and the work shirt. He didn't slow down, and didn't smile.

"Runnin' late. Couldn't find nowhere to park my truck," He told them and pointed. "I got to pick that one up."

They turned, looked at the old van parked on the edge of the trees, and exchanged glances. Had anyone checked it yet? A van was bound to have drugs, cigarettes and booze.

"Hold on there a minute, it ain't been cleared yet," said the would-be guitarist.

Guidry shifted into a hard gaze as he passed them.

"Nobody's clearing it but the man who wants it. And I don't have to tell you boys who that is."

Bewildered, they hesitated long enough for him to reach the driver's door. Then he heard a shout, and his shoulders tightened.

"Hey! Hey…Mr. Plant…wait!" It was the damned probate, running breathlessly across the grass.

Guidry turned, black eyes furious. If that stupid son-of-a-bitch screwed this up and got them carted off to jail, he would kill him, if the Regents let him live long enough.

"Where the hell you been?" He blasted back. "We already late. You know we don't keep him waiting."

The probate slowed, confused."I'm…I'm sorry, Mr. Plant."

"Get in the damned van before I bust some sense into you, boy."

"Yes sir."

Guidry turned to the deputies, his hand on the door. "If I was y'all, I'd get that shit you're carrying into Impound real quick. That crowd over there came to see the motorcycles race, and they ain't very happy about those bikes."

"It ain't the same," the deputy jeered. "Them motorcycle gangers kidnap and rape little girls. They're trash, not racers."

"If you don't think they're racers, then you've never seen 'em ride. And those people?" He nodded at the campers. "Motorcycles is motorcycles to them. And there's a lot more of them than you."

"I ain't afraid of nobody. I got a rifle."

Guidry couldn't help grinning.

"I bet they got two for your one."

Behind him, the probate dangled over the console, reaching under the dash. Guidry heard the engine fire up, and the van shuddered. So the boy was good for something. He climbed up into the driver's seat and closed the door. Almost out of there, almost gone.

The probate hurried to the back and squatted by the side doors to yank them shut.

"Where the hell did you get Mr. Plant?" Guidry snapped at him.

"Couldn't remember the name on your shirt. Somebody was playing Led Zeppelin and it was the first thing come to my mind." He suddenly laughed low. "Oh hey there. Been watching you. They missed you, didn't they? Where you been hiding? Come on up here."

"What the hell." Guidry gaped. "Who is that? We got to go."

The probate reached outside the van. In one sweep, he hurtled back inside, fistfuls of black and white fur in his hands.

"Let's go then," He grinned, and slammed the big side door shut. "I got me a fighting dog."

"Throw her out now." Gritting his teeth, Guidry shoved the van into Drive and began to edge slowly between the simmering campfires and torn rope tents. "That ain't no fighting dog, that's a puppy. She ain't mean. You seen how friendly she was running around the camp yesterday. She's scared to death. Throw her out."

"My uncle knows how to make her mean. He got the best fighters in west Louisiana."

"Boy, I'm telling you to ditch that dog now."

"I'll split the money with you. I know dogs. Look at her muscles, she's got good blood. And that big head. She'll make us some money."

"I had dogs before you were shitting green in your diapers and I'm telling you she'll never make a fighter," Guidry declared, determined to keep the rage from his face. The tow truck drivers all knew each other, and were peering through the windshield, checking him out. He could manage this. He'd managed much worse. Guidry lifted his hand, gave them a thumbs up.

Ain't this fun, wrecking bikes and stealing and setting fire to stuff with a bunch of cops joining in just to keep it legal? Hell yeah, sons of bitches.

When the van bumped up safely onto the highway, Guidry dropped all pretense and set his jaw hard. Traffic was thick around the racetrack, but thinned out quickly once he got into the countryside. He rolled down the window, steadying his breathing, and fought to keep his speed down. Getting busted in this county would be lethal. He had to get back to Sleaze, figure out what to tell him, what not to tell him. Without their bikes, the Regents were stranded and almost defenseless. And Alec was at a motel with his men. Armed to the teeth, but alone.

Sleaze was always talking about opportunity. If this wasn't an opportunity, Guidry didn't know what was. Behind him, the probate sat on a mattress, cuffing the puppy.

"Come on, dog. You can be mean, can't you? I can make your little ass mean, turn you into a killer."

"I told you for the last time, probate, leave the puppy alone. She ain't no fighter."

"Aw hell, I'm just having some fun. 'Sides, if she don't get mean, she'll wind up a bait dog for the big ones. She better get tough real quick."

The puppy whimpered and scuttled to a back corner of the van, curling up in misery behind a few pillows.

"Shit, she *is* useless, ain't she? My uncle's dogs won't have no fun with her if she just lays on her belly—whoa!"The van swerved right, bumping along the weeds beside the highway. It finally hit gravel and stopped. "What the hell, man? We stoppin' for gas?"

"No, the tank is full. They smart enough to keep it full for their own emergencies." Guidry stepped back between the seats, shucking his good-old-boy accent along with the last bit of his self-control. He was one hundred percent enraged coon-ass. "What I'm doin', I'm taking me a five-minute break."

The probate stared at him. "Are you crazy? We've got to get out of here. We've got to tell Sleaze what happened."

"No, what we gotta do, probate, is learn you a few t'ings about a probate back-talking a patched member. We gonna play big dog versus bait dog, and you fixin' to be the bait dog. A bait dog keep openin' his mouth, the big dog gonna shut it. Long as you keep talkin', I'm gonna keep hittin'."

"But I was just…" A hard left slammed his head into the door. "Unnh!"

"There you go. Keep talkin', boy, I got plenty of mad I been saving up."

CHAPTER THIRTEEN

"Where the hell are we? We been on this bus an hour now."

"I wasn't watching the signs until we left Talladega."

"Where'd they take the girls?"

Highway Patrol cars trailed behind the three school buses, just in case a crazed biker jumped out the emergency door.

"You're awful quiet, Greg," Denny said to Joe.

Joe managed a smile, his eyes on the countryside. He wanted those green trees to erase what he saw out the back window as they were leaving. He didn't want to tell the others. If they got mad enough to riot and wreck the bus, they'd all get hurt or killed.

"I'm trying to remember who I am," Joe said.

Fairly new to arrests where he didn't know the cops, he had almost given his real name during the processing. Denny had bumped him aside, reached down for something on the ground, and handed him a wallet.

"You dropped your stuff, Greg."

Joe managed to keep his mouth shut until he opened the wallet and checked the name inside.

"Greg McRae." If it kept him from getting a record, he'd answer to it.

Having the dubious honor of first in line during the weapons check, the Atlanta Regents wound up in the back of the bus. At least they were far from the two deputies up front, who stood braced against thin metal poles for the entire ride, their rifles growing heavier by the mile.

When a Childersburg city limits sign appeared in a stand of pines, the deputies exchanged relieved glances and adjusted their grips on the rifles. The buses swerved down a side road, and a compound strung with razor wire came into view.

National Guard and state vehicles passed the buses, parked, and once again formed a shoulder-to-shoulder human barricade, hemming in the prisoners near a set of high chain-link gates, rifles ready.

"One of you rape the mayor's daughter or something?" The Chicago boss glared.

"Man, this blows," Bobby Boozer exclaimed."They took my ax."

"You still got everything else, don't you?" Country consoled.

"Yeah, but my ax. Man, it was sacred. My dad used to kill hogs with it."

"And anything else who came in the yard."

"That was a long time ago. I told 'em back then, if my mom had boyfriends, I never saw 'em."

"That's 'cause you didn't hang around the hog pens."

"Stow the childhood reminiscing," Smitty told them. "A suit has arrived."

A man in a brown suit and black horn-rimmed glasses stepped out a side door, surrounded by men with shotguns.

"Bring them in this back gate."

The buses discharged the passengers one bus at a time. Nobody thought about bolting. Four guards stationed themselves at the narrow gate, while several more herded the Regents down chain link chutes and gates until they wound up in a large recreation yard. Razor wire glistened in the sun, curling around the fence top like a wicked Christmas decoration. Each corner had a tower.

"What's with them towers? This is a jail for midgets? They're barely fifteen feet up. Denny could reach up there and take their guns."

"Denny ain't doing no such thing," Smitty warned.

The grumbling got louder as the rec yard became jammed with restless hung-over men. No shade, no breakfast and no place to piss except through the fence.

"Now what?" Joe asked. This was new to him.

"Good question. This is a first," Denny said. "I think. Hey, Marv, is this the first time the entire nation's been arrested?"

Marv, one of the oldest Chicago members, had to give it some thought.

"I'll be damned. I believe we're making history here."

"I'd rather make it somewhere else."

"Yeah, like wherever fuckin' Alec is."

"How'd they miss him?"

"We don't know they did. Mighta took him somewhere else."

"What if the Bayou Runners show up at the track?" Bobby Boozer asked, stricken. "All our shit is still there."

Panic rippled through the crowd. Joe bit his lip. After he saw the tow trucks in action, he knew the Bayou Runners wouldn't find shit to steal or wreck. And please God don't let anyone find his bike. He regretted not rolling it farther back in the woods or camouflaging the tarp with brush.

"If the Bayou Runners show up, they'll go to the motel after Alec," Jess advised optimistically. "But at least we don't have to worry about them showing up here."

"You're always looking at the bright side, ain'tcha, J.W.?" Smitty smirked.

"Alec and Sleaze and their bullshit got us all here," Jess sneered. "Let them fight it out."

"Kinda like a red ox trying to catch a little nutria," Smitty cackled, and Jess relaxed.

The rickety towers resembled children's tree houses. Each held three guards with shotguns, which was two too many. A row of unhappy sweating Guardsmen hovered on the flat asphalt roof of the old building overlooking the rec yard. Once the black asphalt heated up, they would be dancing in their boots. Beyond the fences, the local deputies sat on the car trunks, their hard uniform shoes dangling, with a few Styrofoam containers discreetly hidden behind a tire.

"They got a breeze." Bobby Boozer wiped his forehead. "How long we got to sit out here in the sun? Don't we get a phone call?"

Unaccustomed to the thick southern humidity, the Milwaukee Chapter pulled off their shirts and draped them over their heads sheik-style. The sun steadily cleared the tree line, burning off the clouds. The smart ones edged to the fence.

"Hey, what about some food?" Bobby Boozer yelled up at a guard tower. "You didn't give us a chance to eat."

"I heard a uniform telling the warden they had 'successfully evacuated' all the work camp prisoners."

"So we got the place to ourselves? Just us and John Law? Hey Denny, call a meeting. I'm hungry. Wonder where the kitchen is."

"Well, it ain't out here," Denny said in exasperation. They were surrounded by woods and grass and fields on every side but one. The building's flat face had one blank steel door.

"Anybody got a crow bar?"

"Right here. Davey's got a shim, too."

"Great. Give Davey some cover, tell him to get that door open."

By the time the men on the roof realized what was going on directly below their feet, it was too late. The big steel door creaked outward, and a dozen men hurried inside. The first room held rusty exercise equipment, basketballs, and stacks of thin towels. The stockade prisoners had been evacuated without much notice.

"Scavenger hunt! Probates, bust through those doors, see what you can find. We want sheets, weapons, and food."

"The guards are coming from the other end, I see 'em through the glass. They look like they wanta kill somebody."

"Screw 'em. I'm not giving up this room." Dudley signaled Ugly, who stalked up to the next door and busted out the small glass window with a bar bell. "Grab what you can. Country, Gypsy, go back to the yard, shove the steel door against the outside wall and wedge it so they can't close it on us."

"This is the laundry room," A Milwaukee probate called over his shoulder.

He and Joe grabbed sheets, towels and pillowcases, and tossed them to waiting arms in the exercise room. Rolling racks hurtled outdoors, and became instant sheet-covered teepees. More sheets were tied flat to the fence, blocking an outsider's view while needles were produced and drugs heated in old spoons. The guards stationed outside the fence waited reluctantly for instructions from their supervisors, content to ignore the action. None of them wanted to take the first step into the rec yard.

During the confusion, the Regents bosses made their way to the supply room.

"Now what?"

"They can't prove who did what at the race track. The best they can do is disorderly conduct," Marv explained.

"The old standard," Dudley said.

"The biggest problem we got is outstanding warrants. They didn't do fingerprints or mug shots. All they got is our names, and half of them are wrong."

"So?"

"Once they run a check, most of us will be in trouble. We've gotta get out of here."

The men stared back in confusion. "How, Marv? We ain't invisible. We don't have our bikes and we've got all those National Guard crazies waiting to gun us down."

"They can't shoot us over disorderly conduct."

"Get real. They shot those kids at Kent State for protesting."

"We're not kids," Marv said. "We are grown men and we are Regents. I'm thinking we wait until after dark, and get some of the men out of here. The cops ain't gonna have shit for night shift personnel around here. They shot their wad putting us in custody, and they need manpower for the race tomorrow."

"So we lull them into a false sense of security?" Smitty sprinkled some pot in a paper and carefully rolled it up. "We just relax, let 'em think they've won, then about two a.m. slink out of here and steal some cop cars? Marv, we don't know where the bikes are and we don't know where the women are. I don't know where I am."

"You have a better idea?"

"We wait. We relax and get some rest, then we make them want to get us out of here, really bad," Smitty grinned.

"But for now we wait?"

"We wait."

♦

The idea of two hundred hung-over Regents biding their time under any circumstances was crazy. But they were exhausted, and word of "a plan" circled the irritated group. Makeshift shelters kept the sun off, and they drowned beer withdrawals by gulping water from the laundry room faucets. The tower guards relaxed, sat down and propped their feet on the rails. On the roof, the cops sweltered until a red-faced deputy stomped downstairs and demanded some relief. The work camp supervisors decided they needed men on the ground in case the Regents continued to "acquire" parts of the building.

"Acquire?" The deputy sneered. "They're gonna do more than acquire if you don't get 'em some soda pop to drink. My sister works at the state nut house and she says some of them people get crazy thirsty 'cause of their meds and drink water until they're water-drunk. Says it's worse than beer."

"We're handling the situation, Deputy."

"Boy, I hope so," He snapped and stalked off to stand in front of an air conditioner.

♦

Inside the rec supply room and laundry room, the Regents rolled towels into pillows and stretched out on the tile floor. A cool draft ran low from a solitary vent and kept the temperature tolerable. They waited, weary from lack of sleep, but unable to shut down. They wanted beer, not water, which only made them piss every five minutes.

About four p.m., a Chevy Caprice drove down the side road and stopped a safe distance from the fence. The outside guards, whose numbers had thinned considerably, rushed over to the car, shaking their heads and pointing back down the road. The two men in the Caprice ignored them, got out and started walking toward the compound.

"Hey. Jeff Cleary with the Florence Times Daily. Anybody want to make a comment for my paper?"

"Fuck off, man. There's my comment."

"I already got that one from the warden," The reporter admitted, and earned a few laughs.

Denny moved toward the fence.

"What else does the warden have to say?"

"You all are charged with aggravated assault, rape, robbery and disorderly conduct."

"It's getting better, not worse," Denny mused. "You talk to any other motorcycle clubs?"

The reporter raised an eyebrow. "For instance?"

"Just wondering if any other clubs showed up at the track."

"No, you're the unexpected story of the day. But," he thumbed back through his notebook, "A source did tell me the cops expected trouble between your gang and a rival gang called the Bayou Runners."

Jess glanced at Dudley. Who the hell were the sources?

"Did they tell you anything about the Bayou Runners?"

"They were stopped by state troopers at the Alabama state line on Thursday." The reporter squinted, the white sheets blinding him. "Can I ask a few questions now? It's like you're interviewing me."

"You're the first person with any answers. We don't know what the hell's going on. How about our women? Do you know where they are?"

Behind the reporter, the photographer grinned.

"Yep, we just left there. They're in the county jail. It sounded like a Beatles concert with all the screaming, although I never heard that kind of language at a concert. We'd have been here sooner but your women set the place on fire. I've got some great pictures."

"No shit," Denny grinned. "Hey, y'all hear that? The girls are burning down the jail."

"All right!"

Since his visit had cheered them up, the reporter persisted.

"Do you have any comments at all?"

"Nothing you can print. Oh yeah, maybe you could say we're all innocent."

"That's original."

"Hey man, can you get us some beer?" Bobby Boozer cupped a ten-dollar bill in his palm so the photographer could see it. "We hadn't had nothing to eat all day. A beer would be great."

"We'll ask but don't get your hopes up," The reporter said. "Well, thanks for an interesting day. I came here to do a story on the races but this is a hell of a lot better. I appreciate it. Hope you don't hold this against the town. From what I can tell, the orders came down from the State of Alabama, and the locals didn't have a choice. Oh, by the way, the people up at the track said to say they were sorry about your bikes."

"What?" Dead quiet settled over the group at the fence.

"Told you not to tell 'em." The photographer quickly stalked to the car, his head down.

The reporter stowed his pencil in the spiral notepad.

"There wasn't anything those folks could do. Apparently the tow truck operators had a bounty per bike. Too much competition and not enough time. Some of your bikes got banged up, to put it mildly."

Joe closed his eyes. Denny jerked his head toward him.

"That's what you saw when we were leaving. Tell us what you saw."

"Gotta go. I'll ask about the beer." The reporter waved and hurried away through the grass.

"What are you talking about?" Jess said. "What happened to the bikes?"

Joe leaned against the fence and took a deep breath.

"They were putting chains around a bunch of bikes and dragged them up the skids. The bikes were swinging in the air, banging shit."

That was as far as he would go. It was bad enough. Humor and hope drained from the weary faces of the men around him. They were once again sunburned and jittery, going through D.T.s and withdrawals, breathing the sour funk of whiskey on empty stomachs. This wasn't what they had planned for a National party at the Talladega Super Speedway.

Denny looked at his brothers, then shouted at the reporter through the fence.

"Hey! You want a story? Stick around."

CHAPTER FOURTEEN

A rumble started low, rippling behind him to the far reaches of the fence.

"Did they get my knuckle?" Jess stared at Joe, stricken. "What did you see? Don't lie, Joe, it's too important."

"I couldn't tell from that distance," Joe lied anyway. "I saw them moving some bikes together, then work the chain around 'em."

"They tore up our bikes?" For once, Smitty's trademark humor deserted him.

Marv had been chewing on a piece of cardboard he'd found in the laundry room. He spit it out. "Guess we're done waiting. Let's make 'em sorry they ever met us."

But Jess was way ahead of him.

"Mother-fucker!" He growled, his face turning purple.

Stunned, Joe watched him shove his way through the Regents, knocking them aside, and disappearing into the rec room.

"Go!" Denny thumped Joe in the back. "Just don't touch him."

They hurtled after him, followed by a thronging mass of Regents.

"God fucking Dammit!" Jess yanked a fire extinguisher off the wall. "Cocksuckers fuck up my fucking knuckle!"

He bashed his way through door after door, leaving broken hinges and glass. In his wake, the Regents roared into the kitchen, the bunk room, an arts and crafts room, the showers. They tossed the bunks for any contraband they could find, shaking loose pot baggies and packs of cigarettes. Bobby Boozer slung open the steel refrigerator and gulped down a gallon of fruit juice, then seized a handful of grapes.

"Muscadines," He breathed. "Hey guys, there's drinks in here."

"Fuck food, I found glue!" A Dayton Regent yelled from the craft room and gleefully ripped into a case of white bottles.

At the end of a long hall, Jess bashed at a steel door with a relentless rhythm.

"Moth*er* fuck*ing* cock-*suckers*!"

"Jess, it's gonna explode. Put it down!" Smitty shouted from a safe distance.

"Should we tackle him?" Joe asked Denny.

"He'd beat your brains out with that thing before you could nail him," Denny said, and shouted: "Jess, under the door! Blast 'em."

"What?" Surprised, Jess backed up, then aimed the nozzle at the one-inch strip between the door and tiles. "Eat this, fuckers!"

Joe couldn't believe the damn thing was still functional, but it shot a frothy hissing cloud into the barricaded room. He could hear furniture crashing, a woman screaming, and another door thumping hard.

"Now would be a good time…well maybe not," Denny recanted as Jess stormed up and down the hall, caving in the plaster walls with the steel extinguisher. "I'm hungry. Let's see what they got in the kitchen."

"Are you sure? He looks like he's going to detonate."

"It's how those quiet people are. You wanta go try to stop him? If they look like they're gonna shoot him, we'll do something."

They fought their way downstream, Joe sliding and bumping into people, but nobody gave a damn or even noticed that a probate had knocked them off their feet. The showers ran full blast, the over-heated Milwaukee and Detroit men shouting and jumping beneath the cold water. They blocked the drains with ceramic plates from the kitchen until the room flooded and spilled into the halls.

Boots splashed, men slipped, and anybody too stoned to get back up was trampled. Joe hugged the wall, gladly allowing Denny the privilege of battering ram. They finally reached the swinging steel doors of the kitchen, crammed with slobbering growling maniacs. One way in and one way out, and little room to move.

"Marv!" Denny yelled and held his hand up for a pass.

From the depths of the refrigerator, Marv lobbed a head of lettuce.

“You’re a funny son-of-a-bitch.”

“I’ll eat it if you don’t want it,” Joe spoke up, and Denny handed it to him.

A crate of tomatoes overturned, rolling across the floor. Joe scooped up four without getting stepped on and dug into the biggest one with his teeth. Pulp ran down his arm and dripped down the front of his shirt, the tartness burning his tongue. The spoils of war had never tasted better. He tore loose the outer layers of the lettuce and ripped a section loose.

“Regents salad,” He told Denny between chews.

“I want meat.”

Marv signaled frantically, and Denny plowed through the crowd. The two of them huddled in a corner, their backs to the chaos, devouring what looked like someone’s barbeque rib dinner wrapped in aluminum foil.

“Outta the way, outta the way,” Ugly yelled unnecessarily from the far side of the kitchen as men scrambled from his path.

His tee-shirt bulged around the waist with weird lumps and his big face was lit with a strange light. Gripping the lettuce protectively to his chest, Joe followed Ugly outside.

“What?” Several tower guards peered down at a host of men in dark suits outside the fence who were shouting up at them. “I can’t hear a damn thing!”

“Can ya hear this?” Ugly grinned.

He put a small round object up to his mouth, appeared to pull a pin, took a few sidesteps and lobbed it into the guard tower. He followed it with two more, jumping up and down and shouting. The younger guard went over the side, the older one slid down the ladder, and the third one froze, shotgun in his arms, then did a trembling, useless hop over the things rolling around his feet.

Joe watched, his mouth open, but the guard towers didn’t explode.

"Spud grenades," Ugly chortled, and reached into his tee-shirt for another potato.

The destruction escalated as the sun set, the Regents working in shifts. Those sated by glue and fruit juice retreated to the bunk room, finally comfortable and relaxed enough to pass out. In the arts and crafts room, two Marvel comic book fans from the Charlotte Chapter convinced Ugly to take off his shirt and let them paint him green, hair and all.

"You'll look just like the Incredible Hulk, man."

Their talent didn't quite match their enthusiasm, and it took much longer than they planned with the small acrylic brushes available. When they ran out of green, they switched to blue and grabbed some sponges to cover more space faster.

The County turned off the water to stop the flooding showers, but quickly realized the toilets wouldn't flush, and had to send a terrified maintenance worker on overtime back to the facility to restore the water service. More sheets were tied around the fence and top secret meetings held, offering creative escape plans. Irritated by the secrecy, the cops brought in huge klieg lights. A few cinder blocks tossed by a growling turquoise monster shattered the lights and everyone's peace of mind.

A makeshift riot squad was called in, but they took one look at the compound and refused to enter. Tear gas canisters were quickly smothered by towels, and the red-eyed snot-faced warriors who braved the pepper were infuriated enough to rip the siding off the exterior and start a bonfire.

A new Regent from Detroit dropped his jeans and waved his lengthy dick like a propeller at the cops, taunting: "Bet your wives would like some of this!"

Rural men accustomed to hunting, fishing and attending church on both Sundays and Wednesdays, the horrified deputies stared at the porn-like proportions, then looked away, embarrassed.

"I think you just got bumped down to runner-up," Smitty told Denny.

"Horse-shit," Denny scowled. "Looks like a damn plumber's snake. What's he gonna do with that? Girls want something they can ride, not get tickled with."

"Is that so?" Smitty mused. "Bet they've got a yardstick in the crafts room. Wanna see? I'll put twenty bucks on Detroit."

"Fuck you. I'm not just a dick. I've got feelings."

"Sure you do. Right down the side of your leg."

♦

At midnight, an administrator with bloodshot eyes reluctantly approached the fence with a bull horn.

"Send your leaders out. I want to talk to them."

A few bleary Regents in the rec yard roused from their tents, uncertain if it was a trap. Even so, finding a leader wasn't going to be easy. The bosses had hung on as long as they could in case things got out of hand before passing out in the bunk room.

"Where's anybody?"

"How about a VP?"

"Shh, man, it ain't none of their business who's who."

"Who we got that can talk?"

Bobby Boozer got up from his comfortable place near the bonfire and staggered inside. In a corner of the rec supply room, Joe sat on a dry mattress, a few cautious yards from the hall mounded with crushed food, chunks of plaster, vomit, wet towels and unidentifiable debris. It was well on its way to smelling like an open dumpster in summer. His back against the wall, Joe sat on the mattress, smoking a cigarette to counter the stench. Next to him, Jess slumped in exhaustion, a carton of chocolate milk and a pack of cheddar crackers propped against his thigh.

"Some suit at the fence wants to talk to a boss. Seen one?"

"No," Jess said, hoarse from shouting. "And they don't need to, either. Go talk to 'em, probate."

Thus, for five minutes, Joe became a Regents boss. The men under the sheet tents smirked and jabbed each other in the ribs when he walked up to the fence, but Joe was okay with it.

"You wanted to see me?"

"And you are?"

"Greg McRae."

"I want you and your men to know that your lawyers in Chicago called and are flying in first thing in the morning. They advise you to cease and desist so that the charges against you won't add up to trials you can't afford."

Lawyers in Chicago? Someone had managed a phone call.

"Okay. I'll speak with my men. I'd appreciate you keeping me posted so we can end this as soon as possible," Joe said.

"Have a good night," The man said grimly and walked away.

"That's heavy," Bobby breathed. "He bought it. You sounded like an authority."

"You just gotta believe, Bobby," Joe said, and walked back to the supply room.

Jess hadn't moved. Joe told him what the man had said and waited.

"You gonna work the deal, too?" Jess pried a cracker loose from the pack, staring at the far wall with a dull gaze.

In blue-green paint, someone had written "Regents Forever, Forever Regents," and signed it with a big turquoise handprint.

"I've never been arrested with two hundred people who destroyed the jail before."

"It's no big deal. The lawyers know what to do." Jess brushed cracker crumbs across his Levi's. "Wish I could go to sleep."

"Me, too," Joe thought, but he'd been on the downside of several crazed adrenaline binges himself. Since Jess had not already collapsed, he'd remain in that zombie state until his brain suddenly winked out and he fell on his face. Until then, he was Joe's problem. Joe said: "I've got to move this mattress outside. I can't take that stink much longer. If you'll grab that end, we can keep it out of the garbage.

"Sure." Jess drank the last of the chocolate milk, tossed the carton in the hall, and got unsteadily to his feet.

Standard prison camp issue, the mattress was hard on the ends and barely two inches thick in the middle. It wobbled like an accordion when they headed for the door.

"Oh. Wait a minute." Jess held his end up out of the gunk in the hall, and reached back for the empty fire extinguisher. "We may need this."

Joe didn't argue, but said a silent prayer that the Chicago lawyers had some experience with Regents and this sort of thing. He didn't want to spend the rest of the year in Childersburg, Alabama. He was certain they had worn out their welcome.

CHAPTER FIFTEEN

The Talladega County Courthouse was the oldest working courthouse in the state of Alabama. Built in 1836, the red brick exterior was trimmed in white, with four white columns encircled with stunning plasterwork. It sat on a grassy square anchoring the small commercial district of neat timeworn shops. For once, however, Joe failed to appreciate the history. He kept his thumbs hooked in his belt loops, overwhelmed with anxiety. He knew this was not the end of it.

Inside the courthouse, a table had been set up in the gloomy hall. A silver-haired female clerk riffled through a stack of documents, her paper clips, stapler and spare pens laid out beside her. She was irritated about missing church, but knew she'd have quite a story to tell at the services this evening.

The Regents walked up to her in pairs, subdued.

"Write your name down here. You're agreeing you'll never come back to Alabama again." The Director of Safety for the State of Alabama stood to the left of the clerk.

A small battalion of federal, state and county officials stood stiffly behind the table, not making eye contact with any of the Regents as they signed off as hastily as possible. For a fifty dollar fine each, they were allowed to walk out the front door to a waiting school bus which would take them to their motorcycles.

An entourage of attorneys flanked one side of the table, their backs to the big doors, not quite preening. On Monday, when the teletype fired up and spit out dozens of outstanding warrants, the gentlemen in uniform currently glaring at them were going to be very embarrassed.

Surprises were on the way for everyone, Joe thought. But his first priority was to get out of here.

"Thank you, Mr. McRae," the clerk dismissed him.

Jess had gone ahead of him, and waited on the brick sidewalk. Parked lengthwise along the curbs, two buses were already full, diesel engines chugging. Sharpshooters stood on the roofs of the old buildings across the street, but the locals had arrived by the truckload and pulled up chairs right in the line of fire, gawking and waving.

An art deco theater across the street had a big "R" on the front.

"You think that's for Regents?" Smitty came out of the doors behind them.

"In a small town, it's always Ritz," Jess assured him. "Why, you want to catch a movie?"

"I want to catch a bus." Joe knew what a rifle could do to the top of a man's head.

Smitty followed his gaze.

"Don't worry about them. Those boys probably grew up knocking squirrels out of trees for stew. If they plug you, you'll never feel it."

Joe had shared a similar history, making every bullet count if he wanted dinner, but somehow the comparison didn't make him feel better.

"The sooner we get on the bus, the sooner we can go."

Rather than risk getting left behind, the last Regents out the door wedged themselves down the bus aisles and sat on the floor. They were tired, satisfied with the destruction and now their redemption. Joe wound up in the first seat, leaning into the aisle to give Denny more room for his legs. Behind them, Jess sat with Silent Sam, their knees jammed into the back of the seat.

"These damn things from the elementary school?" Jess frowned.

"Kindergarten," Denny said.

"It's hotter than hell already and stinks like a locker room. He needs to get this bitch moving."

"It ain't like you smell like a rose yourself, J.W.. At least we ain't downwind. Chill out, man."

"He's mad because they wouldn't let him keep the fire extinguisher for a souvenir," Smitty cracked.

"I'm saving my temper for Alec," Denny announced. "Son-of-a-bitch is laid up in an air-conditioned hotel room somewhere with booze and his broads."

"Thought you had to get home to Texas quick."

"All I gotta do is find his U-haul, which is hard to miss," Denny said. "Then him and me will have a little talk."

"Shut up and enjoy the bus ride," Smitty advised.

"I never got to ride a bus when I was a kid. I had to walk to school," Denny said. "It was at least twenty miles, too."

"Don't tell me you had snow in Port Arthur," Jess retorted.

"There was a hurricane or two. Lucky I was tall or I'da drowned."

"Probably looked like Ichabod Crane trotting along," Ugly cracked from across the aisle, setting off laughter around him.

"Screw you. Joker's got blue hair and he's gonna make fun of a little kid who had to walk barefoot to school on hot pavement."

They had traveled about two miles when they came upon a smaller bus idling beside the road. It swung into the pack, but not before the men saw their old ladies lined up at the windows, their tops yanked up to their necks.

"Haw haw, look!" The men crowded to the right side of the bus, stomping their feet and whistling while the women waved back.

Joe listened, knowing the jeers and joking kept them from worrying about their bikes. They could handle some scratches and dings, as long as the damn things would start and get them the hell out of here. That what they were hoping, anyway, and Joe wasn't about to advise them otherwise.

It was a little strange, though. He had expected a shotgun escort, at least to protect the drivers. The guy in front of him wore civilian clothes, and despite the gusts blasting through the windows, a big patch of sweat soaked the back of his cotton shirt. His skin was white as paper, and his breath came in short pants through a gaping mouth.

"You the regular driver for good old number 55?"

"You noticed?" The man glanced at him in the rear view mirror, then hastily looked away.

"I used to have a race car with that number."

"What happened to it?"

"Got totaled on a pretty Sunday afternoon, just like this."

"Oh," The guy swallowed.

"You do this every day?"

"Weekdays. With kids, yeah. Haven't ever hauled motorcycle people before."

"I bet the kids are scarier."

The man finally smiled.

"Some days, yes sir, they can test you."

"How far is the impound lot?"

"Not much further."

Joe settled back, watching the road ahead. If it weren't for the driver's white knuckled grip on the wheel, the ride reminded him of one years ago to Brackenridge Park. His first weekend pass from Lackland Air Force Base, the seventeen year old men headed to San Antonio. Jostling along, the guys cutting up with each other, all swearing to defend the Constitution without a clue to what it meant.

The men riding with him today understood the cost. If nothing else, he had learned this weekend, this phenomenal first National, that almost every single man in the bus lived on the edge of an abyss, the ground cracking away beneath their feet at the most unexpected times. So, like him, they rode their Harleys as fast as they could from the edge, before they were pulled down into a place they'd never come back from.

He hoped to hell some of them still had motorcycles waiting ahead.

♦

The impound lot sat back from the highway behind a complex of red brick county buildings, surrounded by chain-link fence. Cast into shadow by the noon sun, the front of the buildings looked abandoned. No one came out to greet them. Several wrecked cars and trucks faced them, parked in neat rows inside the gates. Dented bumpers and shattered headlights caught glints of the sun, reflecting it with blinding mockery. Joe hoped Kitty couldn't see it. Whoever had died in those vehicles was still mad.

"Mister, would you let your friends know the county wants y'all to line up outside the gate? They won't unlock it until everybody's orderly." The driver clung to the dividing post, his skin now a metallic gray. "I ain't feeling so good."

"He'd better not go into cardiac arrest. I don't feel like hanging around Butt-Fuck Alabama," Jess groused.

"There you go again, *bac si.* Do you ever stop being a caring, compassionate medic?" Smitty sank a rough paw on Jess's shoulder and pulled himself up out of the cramped seat. "Hey! Shut up and listen. They want us to line up in an orderly fashion before they'll unlock the gate. Think you can do that?"

"Sir yes sir!" Bobby Boozer shot to his feet. "I can do that, sir. I want my bike and I want to exit this county post-haste, sir."

Joe saw the driver slump in his seat.

"Mister, are you okay?"

"Just please get them out so I can leave."

"Handsome ones first, probate," Denny thumped Joe on the arm and tried to stand up in the small space without banging his skull. "That's us. Let's go."

As soon as the last man hit the step, the doors abruptly closed and the school buses thundered away in a black cloud of diesel fumes. The enforcers and bosses hustled to get their chapters organized. Even with the arrival of the women, it wasn't difficult. They all wanted their motorcycles and to get back on the road. If they had to maintain order for five minutes to achieve their goal, so be it.

"Where are the bikes? I don't see them."

"They must be behind those trucks. Denny, can you see 'em?"

"Looks like handlebars and some sissy bars off to the right, past that Dodge."

They fell silent, curious and expectant, when a solitary young man walked out of a dark building about thirty yards away. To their amazement, he stopped short, took a deep breath, then flung a small object with a pitch worthy of Dock Ellis. It landed at Smitty's feet. Before he could bend over to pick it up, the young man spun around and fled back inside the building.

"Somethin' ain't right," Denny muttered.

"Something ain't been right since we got here so let's get the fuck outta here." Smitty scooped up the key and unlocked the huge Master lock.

Joe and Denny shoved the big gates out of the way, and followed the crowd inside. Any resemblance to order dissolved. They wanted to get the hell out of there. The men quickly threaded through the abandoned vehicles, while some of the women scrambled up on top of the cabs and hoods to get a better view.

"Smitty was right up front, he oughta be…" Dorrie's voice faded.

"Oh my god," Flossie said in a monotone. "Oh god."

The tow trucks had simply backed into the lot behind the cars, dumped the motorcycles on the gravel, retrieved their chains, then hauled ass. The roar started low, a tremor gaining momentum until it exploded. Shouts and cursing sent the women running among the junkers for safety.

The men went crazy, roaring at the top of their lungs, pulling the tangle of tires and frames apart, frantically searching for their bikes.

"Gimme a hand, probate," Smitty ordered, furious.

The Atlanta Regents found most of their bikes in two tangled clusters near the back of the lot. Panting and fuming in the sun, they helped each other pull the bikes apart and back up on the tires, rolling them to the side so they could keep digging.

"Aw shit, man," Bobby Boozer shook his head. "Those mother-fuckers need to die."

Jess's '47 knucklehead was at the bottom of the pile. It had taken the brunt of the thick tow chain sawing into it, and the weight of the others. Silently, the Atlanta Regents stood it upright and propped it against the metal fence. Without a word, they turned their backs, leaving Jess alone with it, and headed for the next heavy jigsaw puzzle of ruined parts.

Joe paused beside the knucklehead, hooking his fingers on the fence for support. He couldn't believe it. The knuckle had been a work of art. He had polished it daily while Jess was in jail, keeping it in mint condition for the man who recruited him into the Regents. Kitty stood a few feet behind Jess, not daring to speak. She clutched her purse against her stomach as if she'd been punched, her stunned gaze going from Jess to the ruined bike.

All around them, men cursed and raged until they were hoarse. Dudley cornered the other bosses, and did a quick count.

"I got six men and their old ladies with bikes they can't ride. How are you set?"

"I ain't even found all of mine yet. You don't think they dumped 'em somewhere, do ya?" The Milwaukee boss clenched his fists, his face bright red. "I had custom saddlebags made by a guy who's dead now. All that shit is gone."

"I'm coming back here and burning this fuckin' town to the ground, you got that?" Detroit was so mad he couldn't stand still.

Marv from Chicago came striding up.

"What the hell are we gonna do?"

Dudley shook his head. "My van isn't here. They might have missed it if they thought it belonged to one of the civilians at the campground. I could send somebody to get it, but we're gonna need more than one van."

The rumbling suddenly died down across the lot.

"Holy shit," Bobby Boozer shouted. "Look!"

Out of the heat waves, a steady stream of white and brown sedans poured down the highway, blue and red lights whirling on the racks. State, county and city, they pulled onto the grass across the blacktop from the impound lot and parked, bumper to bumper. Car doors slammed as the men got out and stood behind their vehicles. Rifles settled down on the roofs beside the blue lights, sites aimed at the chain link fence and the Regents behind it. Bringing up the rear came jeeps and trucks in camouflage, more uniforms and more weapons.

"What the hell" Bobby Boozer bounced on his toes. "Those sons of bitches."

"Let's kill the bastards," Ugly growled, and the echo rippled through the crowd.

"With what?" Smitty retorted loudly. "Busted springers?"

"What the hell is going on? They told us we could go. They wanted us to leave."

Dudley gazed across the street, a sense of morbid fatalism settling over him.

"They are waiting for us to do something stupid," He said.

"Personally, I feel like doing something stupid right about now," Denny declared. "But we got nothin' with us that can reach across the highway."

If the Regents could have killed with pure raw hate, the lawmen and weekend soldiers would be lying dead behind their vehicles. High overhead, the sun reflected eye-slicing beams off the twisted chrome and shattered windshields. Two hundred men and women with a hundred ruined motorcycles squinted through the glare, eyes watering, their brains on fire. Some had been surrounded before. Some went back to the heat and elephant grass and amphetamine high.

"Got any ideas, stupid or otherwise?" Smitty said under his breath to Dudley. "Quick?"

"Maybe this day is what I been waiting on, ever since I came home," Dudley said quietly.

"Shit, man, don't lose it now. We got too many people here," Smitty snapped. "Get drunk later but right now, figure somethin' out!"

"Maggots," A voice rumbled.

"What?" They both turned.

Ugly's square jaw glistened with blue sweat. His eyes narrowed into beebee-sized black dots. Men who had not dared to move under the troopers' rifles now edged out of Ugly's way.

"They are maggots," He proclaimed and headed for the fence.

"Stop," His old lady Shirley squeaked, her eyes wide, then instinct kicked in, and she ran after him, her voice stronger. "Stop!"

Joe put an arm out and caught her, binding her thin arms to her sides.

"Stop him, they'll kill him," She shrieked. "Joe, make him come back!"

Ugly kept going until he stood at the chain link, zeroing in on the dumbfounded spectators across the highway. Then he took a deep breath, straightened his massive shoulders and opened his mouth. To the astonishment of all, he began to sing, loudly.

"From the halls of Montezuma to the shores of Tripoli, we will fight our country's battles in the air, on land and sea. First to fight for right and freedom, and to keep our honor clean. We are proud to claim the title of United States *Marine*!"

Two Regents from Milwaukee looked at each other, shocked. Then they walked up beside Ugly, flanked him, and joined in for the second round.

Smitty shook his head helplessly at Joe. "This is why they always send in the jar-heads first. You can't do nothing with 'em anyways."

"This is bullshit," Bobby Boozer declared. He took up a spot near the gate, cleared his throat, then yelled: "I wanna be an Airborne Ranger, I wanna lead a life of danger! Before I die, I'm gonna fuck your sisters, and all you cops can suck my blisters!"

"What the hell, man? Blisters?"

"From his sisters, stupid. Get it?

A heavyset Regent with a Detroit patch stepped up to the fence and shouted: "Fuck you, you pussy REMFs!"

Smitty took off his boonie hat, smoothed his hair, then slapped the hat back on. "I want to be presentable when I die."

"We're dying?" Joe frowned. Not if he could help it. "Look, Smitty, I'll bet most of those cars still have a little gas in them. If I blew up a couple for a diversion, you can get everybody out the back end of the lot."

"Jesus Christ, probate," Dudley was stunned out of his funk.

"If I'm dying, I'm taking them with me." Jess gave the knucklehead one final glance and headed for the fence.

"Stand down. You're doing exactly what they want," Dudley declared.

"What the hell did they think we were gonna do when they trashed the bikes?" Jess scowled.

"You got badges but you ain't shit, I'm a Marine and proud of it," Ugly shouted in precision cadence. "I've fucked your wives good and slick while you were out sucking dick."

A bullhorn raged across the black-top. "Cease immediately!"

"Dudley!" Flossie called frantically from the truck bed and pointed down the highway. "Honey, look!"

The men on both sides of the road craned their necks, waiting for whatever it was to materialize. The flicker of fluorescent orange grew until it looked like a bonfire. A bonfire on wheels. With an enormous U-Haul logo across it.

"Way to go, Ugly. You called out the Calvary."

CHAPTER SIXTEEN

Grins broke out as the U-Hauls crested the hill, then cheering shook the humid air and sent birds flapping out of the trees. One by one, the three big trucks slowed and bumped down off the highway, pulling alongside the fence. In less than five minutes, they had blocked the view of the impound lot and its inhabitants from the highway. The drivers remained in the cabs, windows down and sunglasses on, eying the team across the road. The fourth U-Haul stopped in front of the deserted buildings, changing gears with a clank, and backed up to the gates. The rear door rolled up, and a half dozen Miami Regents jumped out.

The bosses hurried to the gate just as Big Alec stepped down from the cab. He looked like he had just gotten out of the shower, with a fresh white wife-beater under his cut-off and his hair in a long damp braid.

"Where the hell you been?" Smitty said, and stuck out his hand. "Damn, it's good to see your ugly ass."

"You ever tried to find four of these on a holiday weekend?" Big Alec retorted. "Get the bikes loaded. These mother-fuckers rent by the hour."

"Since when have you ever paid for anything?" Smitty snorted, but signaled the Atlanta Regents to claim the first truck before the other chapters could. "Probate, tell 'em to load our bikes, quick. We'll save your Chevrolet Molatovs for another day."

"Where are we going?" The Milwaukee boss weltered.

Big Alec aimed a wicked smile at Dudley.

"Atlanta's closest. We'll head there, and you can figure out how to get home."

Dudley closed his eyes. *Shit.* If that wasn't his idea of hell, dozens of pissed off Regents descending on his clubhouse with no way to leave.

Denny and Silent Sam came wheeling up on their bikes.

"If you've got some beer in these trucks, Alec, I'll take back most of the shitty stuff I ever said about you."

"I'd settle for a little gratitude for getting those lawyers down here so fast."

"Shit. All you had to do was make some phone calls from the comfort of the Holiday Inn to get those shysters here."

"You were glad to see the shysters, weren't you?"

"Sure as hell was. How'd you know about the bikes?"

"Some tourists were talking about it at the motel. Wolf rode by here last night to check things out." His face lost its humor. "I'd say we owe 'em, but right now, we get the hell out of here, and we go together."

"Seen any sign of the Bayou Runners?"

"No. I heard they got stopped in Mississippi. But that doesn't mean shit."

Tall enough to meet him eye to eye, Denny gave him a long look. "One of these days, we're gonna have a talk about where you hear shit."

Big Alec smiled slightly. "A good leader has a lot of sources. Aren't you glad I do?"

"When the sources are right and don't waste my time. I got a funeral to go to back home."

Alec frowned at him, surprised. "What are you waiting for? If your bike will make it, get out of here. We can manage this."

Denny's narrow face tightened into a grim smile.

"It's just my old man. I heard he was dying. With any luck, he'll be dead by the time I get there."

"Suit yourself," Big Alec said. It was none of his business.

Banged and bent, missing kickstands and foot pegs, some of the Harleys were still operable. Those, they rode out the gates and parked in the shade of the buildings, out of the way. After a minute savoring the shade, they reluctantly headed back into the lot to help the others. It was no small sacrifice.

Rescue was at hand, but the Regents were running out of energy. They were desperate to get the bikes loaded, and didn't have the strength or energy to manage it. The old ladies joined in, pushing the six hundred pound machines up the ramps. Flat tires made it a nightmare.

"If I'd known they were this bad, I'd have brought more winches and come-alongs," Wolf apologized.

"I need a drink," Bobby Boozer panted. "And some speed. I ain't been to sleep since Thursday night."

Beside him, gripping the handlebars of a new purple chopper slick with leaking oil, Ugly refused to give in to the shaking sweats. They needed his muscle. A fix could wait. But not too much longer.

A young brunette girl leaned from the cab of the largest U-Haul.

"Alec, those cops are yelling through the bullhorns to move the trucks."

Big Alec shrugged. "We will, as soon as they're loaded."

"Step it up!" Smitty called.

"Shit, Alec, can't your guys help us?" Denny glared, his boots sliding on the gravel.

Big Alec shook his head. "They're in the trucks for a reason."

"Well, if they're providing cover, here's their chance. Here come the bad guys."

"I'm not up to a firefight," His face flame-red, Smitty slapped the side of the U-Haul. "This one's loaded. Get another one up here while we still got room to turn around."

Five sedans bumped across the grassy median and pulled into the parking lot. The Regents weren't the only ones short-tempered in the heat. Shoulders reared back for a fight, a sergeant barely bigger than his badge stomped across the hot pavement to put a finger in Big Alec's face, from ten feet away.

"Move those trucks immediately."

Big Alec had no difficulty looking over his head at the other uniforms. "Who's in charge here?"

"I said move those trucks!"

"And I said, who's in charge?"

Joe paused at the back corner of a truck, trying to catch his breath. He would hate the man with his dying breath, but had to admit Big Alec had balls, standing there without a visible weapon while at least two dozen firearms zeroed in on his chest. Sweat ran down the front of his white tee-shirt, but he didn't look concerned. His infuriating smirk fastened on the cops.

"You don't know who's in charge of your boys?" He badgered. "I'm in charge of my men."

"He'll be here in a second," The sergeant said between clenched teeth.

"I'll wait," Big Alec assured him.

He passed the time by scratching dead skin from his massive sunburned shoulder and drinking a beer, Sunday or not. Ten minutes passed before a brown sedan pulled up beside the U-Haul.

"Hey Dudley, you got a brother? Looks like another Do Right with that hat."

"Man, he's gotta be roasting in that uniform."

"He's mad. Bet they pulled him from the race."

Joe wasn't so sure. With a screw-up this big, the man in charge wouldn't be far away. The new arrival spoke briefly with the sergeant, then walked over just beyond Big Alec's reach.

"I'm Colonel Cooper. What's the problem?"

"Your sergeant wants us to move the trucks. But our bikes aren't loaded yet."

"Somebody decided these men can hang around until we finish running a warrants check on Monday. This is as good a place as any."

"The warrants are your problem. The deal was, the Regents are kicked loose and leave your state. It's a little tough to go since some redneck assholes fucked up our transportation, but we're working on it."

The man flinched as if struck, but held his ground.

"Your people did some damage to the stockade last night."

"If they'd known what you did to their bikes, your stockade and the town wouldn't be standing," Big Alec informed him, and glanced over his shoulder. "They're still not too happy."

Across the compound, the Regents stared, listening.

"We'll be on our way shortly and your boys can still make the last part of the races." *Unless somebody wants to start some shit.*

Yes, he used his size to intimidate, but muscle didn't stop bullets. It was the bored look he gave them, like they were insects interrupting his picnic, which made them hesitate. He wasn't afraid of their guns or badges, or them. So they waited. The Colonel had the fire power to take care of this, and his men were ready, but it would make national headlines. The reporters were camping at the courthouse; they had come to cover the races and instead wound up with a story that would get picked up by every newspaper in the south. The embarrassing details had to stop with the stockade's destruction.

"Hurry it up," The Colonel snapped.

With the damaged motorcycles lashed together and back doors left open for some fresh air, the Regents and their old ladies finally collapsed in dirty exhausted heaps on the floor. The big trucks shifted, lurched heavily onto the highway, then circled and headed toward the racetrack, the remnants of the pack riding behind them. They were sure nothing would be left at the campground, but had to check.

"I'd drink my own piss right now if I had any." Bobby Boozer held his forehead, squeezing his eyes shut. "Damn, this headache is killing me."

Beside him, Ugly and Shirley sat next to each other, yawning and heavy-limbed as the truck bounced along.

"You think it's your sugar?" Shirley asked.

Bobby's combined hell of diabetes and alcoholism always had his body at odds with itself, and the last few days had wrecked him.

"My cravings have cravings," He groaned.

"Does anybody have any cookies?" Shirley inquired.

Jess pulled out a pack of crushed crackers from his pocket and handed it over.

"No thanks, man, I'd choke to death on 'em."

Joe wasn't up to conversation. He just wanted his panhead to be okay. He'd collect it and Smoky and go the hell back to Atlanta. They would have been better off battling it out with the Bayou Runners. Sunlight reflected off the orange and white truck behind them, flashing across the two dozen people around him. Flossie found three cigarettes in a side pocket of her purse. She lit them and passed them around.

Placing a small hand on Jess's thigh, Kitty leaned forward to look at Joe. "How bad is your bike? I didn't see it in the lot."

"It wasn't there," He said.

She hesitated.

"Do you think it's still where you hid it?"

"I hope so."

Beside him, Jess stirred out of his lethargy and nodded.

"If it's there, we'll find it."

"It has to be there," Kitty echoed, but Joe knew it wasn't his bike she was worried about.

CHAPTER SEVENTEEN

The shrill sound of high-pitched racing engines sliced the afternoon sky, piercing their aching skulls. While race fans cheered within the towering walls of the race track, the Regents glumly searched through the scorched remnants of prized saddlebags, booze and half-melted tents. Ugly slung his arms like a windmill, tossing broken bottles and trash to the side. He found a small blue pouch and grinned.

"Bobby!" He yelled.

"Huh?" Bobby Boozer gaped.

"Catch!"

Bobby made a weak grab for the pouch.

"Man, I don't need insulin right now, I need a bag of oranges."

"How about a beer?" Ugly grinned, and tossed him a can of Pabst Blue Ribbon. "That ought to screw up your sugar."

Bobby shrieked, holding the can in his shaking hands, then plucked frantically at the pop top.

"Damn! Oh man, brother, I'd kiss your big blue ass if you'd let me. Oh jeez, this is better than head," He choked down a big swallow and closed his eyes, breathing hard. "Sorta."

Three unmarked sedans pulled up and parked along the road. The races were in full swing, the campground deserted except for silent tents and campers.

"They just won't lay off, will they? Hell, the bastards will fine us for littering."

The Regents bosses had a quick meeting. Whatever was salvageable would go in the back of the last U-Haul. They'd sort it out later at the Atlanta clubhouse. They wanted to get the hell out of here.

Dudley stood with his hands on his hips, squinting in disbelief at the woods. “Where’s our van?”

With all the weapons beneath the false floor. And Smoky. Joe looked around uneasily. The girls rummaged through the overturned tables and grills, searching for food or drinks the ants hadn’t claimed. Except Kitty, who stood wavering on her high-heeled boots, her eyes tracking across the devastation.

“Smoky?” She called, her voice high.

Flossie stopped tossing hotdog buns into a makeshift sack and stood up.

“Where is she? Who saw her last?”

“I saw her run for the van when the cops came up,” Kitty said. “She would have stayed with the van.”

“Not if the cops took it.”

“Smoky!” The girls began calling, clapping their hands, and fanned out. “Here, girl!”

Joe’s heart sank. He looked at Jess, who nodded.

“Go ahead. Good luck.”

Joe took off at a slow lope, entering the woods five yards from the path he had cleared the day before. Maybe the cops in the sedans would think he was going to take a piss. It didn’t look like anyone had been back here. Sunlight shifted, and he spotted an unnatural shade of green. He stopped, then moved quietly forward and pulled back the tarp. The panhead was still there, his partner in crime, escape on a steel horse.

Silent Sam’s duffle bag lay on the ground beside it. But Smoky was nowhere to be seen. No plump little dog hiding beside the bike, nothing black and white in the tangle of sharp vines and broken limbs.

“Smokes?” Joe pivoted.

He could hear the girls calling, their voices urgent.

If she was hiding out here, there was one thing sure to bring her running. Joe swung his leg over the bike, settled down in the seat with a relief that almost made him dizzy, and kicked the bike to life. He revved it several times, then whistled. "Smoky?"

Joe waited, slinging Silent Sam's duffle bag over his back. But nothing moved, or peeked at him from the underbrush. The forest had an empty feeling to it. In his heart, he knew she wasn't there.

Maybe somebody had her tied up to keep her safe until the race was over. She'd been socializing all over the campground Friday. Joe swallowed. No matter where she went, she was still a timid little girl, and always came back to him. Squaring his shoulders, he worked the panhead around until he was back on the path, crunching over poison ivy and twigs.

When he broke through the woods, Jess and Denny were waiting.

"Here." Joe struggled to get the green bag off his shoulder. "Give this to your friend. I damn sure don't want to get caught with it."

"Sam, here's your water pistol," Denny said and tossed the duffle to him. Lowering his voice, he shook his head. "I don't want him going with me to Texas, but I don't know how I'm gonna lose him."

"He understands," Smitty said. "Just tell him it's personal."

"Oh I know he understands. He just won't listen. Can he stay at your clubhouse and hang out with the probate 'til I come back through?"

"Shit, I was going to ask if I could go with you to Texas," Joe spoke up. "I sure as hell don't want to go back to the club house."

Denny laughed. "Port Arthur or the whole pissed-off Regents nation on Fifth Street, huh? Not much of a choice."

"We'll take Sam with us," Jess said. "You leaving now?"

Denny nodded. "I've got to go. I heard a tourist talking about some hurricane in the Gulf."

"There's always a hurricane in the Gulf. It's September." Jess held out his hand. "Wish I could say it's been fun."

"There's always another national," Denny grinned.

Smitty came hurrying up, clutching a bottle of grape Nehi.

"Ten minutes. We're leaving," He said. "Jess, we're gonna stop at that little gas station in Oxford again on the way out. Chat up your old buddy in the overalls when we get there and find some damned beer. I know it's Sunday, but this is Dixie, dammit. Ten minutes," Smitty warned and hurried off to round up the Atlanta crew.

Jess watched him go, then turned his attention back to Kitty and the girls searching the empty campsites for Smoky.

"Shit."

"Why shit? They'll find her. I'll go help. We've got ten minutes."

"It doesn't matter," Jess said quietly. He hesitated, then reached in his pocket and pulled out a pink bandanna.

"I found this where the van was parked. Whoever got the van, got Smoky. She's gone."

Joe stared at him, frowning. He was confused, and more than a little pissed off.

"Then why are you letting them look? Show 'em what you found. Damn, Jess, I was looking for her back there in the woods myself," He swallowed. Shit, he couldn't get sentimental now.

Jess gazed at the bandanna in his hand like he didn't know what to do with it.

"You don't understand. If I tell her—"

But it was too late. Shirley and Kitty came running up, sunburned and panting.

"Jess, please talk to them. Ask 'em for a little more time," Shirley started, then saw the bandanna, and her eyes got big. "Oh. Where…where was it?"

Beside her, something appeared to roll over Kitty, a force lifting her from behind. Nothing Joe could see, but it pushed her forward, making her gasp, and she rocked in her tight boots.

"Everyone else has loaded up what they salvaged," Jess said in measured tones. "Joe, you ride behind the trucks. We'll stop in Oxford for gas, and beer, with any luck. The cops will follow us to the state line so be careful what you do."

"Not without Smoky," Kitty declared.

Jess acted as if he hadn't heard her. He caught Dorrie's attention, whistled at her and the other girls circling the camp, and pointed to the trucks. They stopped searching and glanced at each other uneasily before heading for the road.

"Shirley, take Kitty with you. Joe and I will finish up here."

"Come on, Kit, I found a cushion we can sit on," Shirley smiled weakly.

"Don't tell me what to do." It sounded like her throat was broken, a low growl chopped into words.

Shirley froze, shocked, but the hard words were for Jess, not her. Joe shut his eyes, grateful they had taken the fire extinguisher from him.

"We're all tired and there's nothing else we can do here. It's time to go home," Jess said slowly.

"Then go home. I'm not leaving." Her eyes glowed like a cornered lynx.

"There's nothing you can do here," Jess repeated between clenched teeth. "It's over. We're going home,"

"I'm not leaving without my dog."

"Then you'll fucking walk home."

"No I won't," She retorted, and stared up at Joe. "He'll give me a ride. Won't you, Joe?"

Aw shit. Before Joe could reply, Jess lowered a cold gaze on her.

"No he won't. He's tired of being your hero. Aren't you, probate?"

Kitty didn't take her eyes off Joe. She wasn't playing. Joe didn't move. He didn't know what to say to fix this.

"The dog isn't here, Kit. We have to go. If you get everybody arrested again, I'm not gonna be happy." Jess reached for her arm, but she slapped him away and steadily backed out of range.

"Fuck you, Jesse Whitley. Fuck you."

Shirley made a weird squeak and ran off.

"Kitty, he's right," Joe spoke up quickly. "Smoky isn't here. Whoever took the van, took her, too."

"Can't we look?" She snapped. "Are you saying we shouldn't even try to find her? We should just go the hell home and to hell with her? What if she's scared and waiting for us to find her?"

Her voice began to shake.

"You two just run along home if you're so afraid of the cops. I'll catch a taxi if I have to." She stalked off, her fist crushing the soft leather of her shoulder bag to grip the tarot deck inside.

Up on the road, the box trucks cranked up. The men helped the women into the back, a few gazing across the field at them in concern. They were out of time. Joe looked helplessly at Jess, certain he was at his limit.

"I don't even have a damn bike," Jess said, strangling on his rage. "I'll ride in the back of the garbage truck with everyone else. Stay here with her and let her look. You can be her damned hero again. Maybe she'll learn something if she has to hold a thirty-pound puppy all the way back to Atlanta on your fucking panhead. Good luck."

Joe reached for his last cigarette as Jess headed for the U-Hauls.

"Thanks. I'll need it."

When the remnants of the pack pulled out, Joe didn't turn around. The box trucks left first, gearing up the road past the customized racing trailers and dozens of cop cars. He was certain Kitty didn't even notice them leave. Despite the four-inch leather boots and soft earth, she moved steadily across the vacant camp sites. Her voice was more certain now, calling, then stopping to listen. She opened tent flaps and camper doors to peer inside, and laid flat on the ground to look under vehicles.

Joe watched her, wondering where he had screwed up. Wanting a motorcycle fast enough to leave the bad times behind? Wanting a cat-eyed woman so bad he'd jeopardized the respect of a man he admired? And of course, wanting to beat up an oversized Scottish war lord throwback.

"Well here you are, you dumb son-of-a-bitch redneck. It's just you and the bike and the bimbo again."

Across the campground, Kitty paused her methodical search and looked over her sunburned shoulder at him.

"Yes ma'am," He said under his breath.

Ten minutes later, they discovered their first live person. The woman sprawled in an aluminum lounge chair sagging beneath her weight. Parts of her oozed through the polyester slats. Both plump feet wore dainty pink flip-flops, and were planted on either side of the chair. Joe was grateful she wore panties under the blue floral dress.

"Excuse us," He said, backing up.

"Don't go running off. Took you long enough to get here. Are you two done checkin' everything out?"

"We weren't stealing," Kitty declared wearily. "We're looking for our dog."

The woman narrowed her eyes. "Huh. What kind of dog are you looking for?"

Her pony-tail straggling loose and knees smeared with grass stains, Kitty managed to cordially say: "She's a black and white bull dog mix. About four months old. She's timid and ran off."

"I'da run off too, with that noisy bunch. But your dog didn't run off."

Finally. Joe dared to hope. "You know where she is?"

"Don't know where they went, but them men that drove off in your white van took her."

"Our van?" Kitty said.

"Oh, don't get cute with me, I know exactly when you showed up and who partied with who."

Joe twisted, squinting across the field at the wrecked campsite.

"How did you see all that?"

She reached down beside her chair and pulled up a pair of binoculars. "You think I come to races with my family just to watch cars or motorcycles go around and 'round? Them beer-guzzlers sit there and hope for a wreck just to break the monotony. Now I like them NASCAR boys. Got to see them just a few weeks ago, and I was on the front row. That Bobby Allison is a cute little booger, and so's Buddy Baker. But these motorcycle races? I got better things to do. I'm a man watcher."

Kitty couldn't contain herself. Her jaw dropped open.

"You go ahead and make fun, sugar. One of these days those perky little tits and tight ass of yours is gonna drop like rotten cantaloupes and you won't be so marketable any more. You're short, too. When you run to fat, it's got no place to go except your butt. Then you'll be like me, too big to move, just you and a pair of binoculars checking out the hunks."

"I'll shoot myself first," Kitty declared.

"Nah, you won't be so quick to pick up a gun. You and that good-looking blond fella of yours have some pretty young-uns, put about fifty pounds on you and there you are. You don't have to worry about maintenance anymore. You may not think so, cupcake, but I was damn popular at the USO dances, let me tell you."

"I'm sure you were," Kitty sniffed.

The woman ignored her, prattling along. "That boyfriend of yours and this one here--what are you, son, Cherokee, little bit of Irish? You're definitely my type, all moody, flashing that big smile one minute and dark the next. But an old pro like me—like you're gonna be, toots—my pick for a night of pile-driving would be that tall drink of water with the cowboy boots. He moves easy for a big man."

"What about the dog?" Kitty growled, because Joe couldn't speak.

The woman reached into a cooler beside her, pulled out two RC-Colas dripping with ice water, and handed them to Joe and Kitty. "I saw 'em put the puppy in the van. She'd been sitting under it waitin' for somebody to come back."

Kitty flinched. "Did the cops take her? Or the tow truck people?"

"None of them. It was them two men sitting right over there, watching y'all ever since you got here."

She pointed to a bare spot between two trucks. Joe pulled the caps off both RC-Colas and handed one to Kitty, his mind clicking again. Someone had been watching them? Other than this horny old woman?

"What did they look like? Did they say anything to you?"

"They both needed a haircut, just like you. The smaller one was nasty, had a mouth on him and didn't care if little kids heard him cuss." Since he wasn't a candidate for romance, she dismissed him. "The tall one, though, hoo, he was handsome. High forehead, very neat, kept his hair combed back in a little pony tail, black hair, black eyes, had one of them tickler mustaches, muscular build, wore a shirt that said 'Larry.' Perfect posture, like he worked out."

"Did you get his shoe size?" Kitty sniffed.

"I wasn't looking at his shoes, little girl. But come to think of it, I remember he wasn't wearing shoes. I wondered why he was wearing those old heavy black boots on a hot day like this. Kind of like yours, darlin'." She eyed Joe, and he was fairly sure she calculated his shoe size correctly. "And he had quite a walk."

The woman grew thoughtful, testing Joe's patience, but she had given them a cold drink and plenty of information, so he let her ramble and ogle the fit of his Levi's.

"I know!" She snapped her fingers, and cocked a conspiratorial eye at Kitty. "You know how a baseball player moves? Like a jungle cat, all those muscles working together. Their shoulders and back are always so straight like it's natural for them. You know what I'm talking about."

Kitty finally smiled.

"He walked like a baseball player?"

"Mmhmm. They kept to themselves. Then the cops showed up and they rolled under that truck lickety-split. Had a lady friend with them, dressed like she just got off the night shift at a Dairy Queen, but she wasn't too happy. I seen her sneak off." The woman guzzled her iced tea and smacked her lips. "Had to be bad company if she'd leave that Cajun behind. He was a fine-looking man. As good-looking as you, sugar."

Kitty and Joe stood frozen in shock.

"How do you know he was Cajun?" Joe asked faintly.

"In my day, I spent a fair amount of time working in the Quarter. I knew Lilly Christine, God rest her, and Evangeline the Oyster Girl. I heard that accent so much I can tell you what parish the men come from. That man was Cajun from Lafourche parish. The nasty little fella with him was plain old white trash. They're the ones who snatched up that puppy."

"When did they do this?"

"Right after the police hauled y'all off. And the handsome one did it right out from under the cops, too." The old woman laughed, setting off a tsunami of rippling fat under her dress. "Walked over there bold as brass and took the van before the tow trucks could haul it off."

Kitty swatted irritably at a gnat. "Why the heck would he take the van?"

"He didn't have a choice. Their lady friend took their car when she hauled ass. They stole your van because it was their only way out of here and they wanted to leave real quick for some reason." She smiled up at them. "This has been the best damned race I ever been to. Can I ask y'all something?"

"Sure." Joe stuck his hands in his pockets and held his breath.

"Y'all going to Louisiana after that puppy?"

Joe smiled.

"You can count on it. Thanks for the soda pop."

He and Kitty turned to go.

"Enjoy that bubble-butt while you got it, toots!" The woman called.

Joe took Kitty by the arm before she could turn around and marched her across the grass. "Do not engage. I want to get a head start out of here before those races end."

"She's lying. Lilly Christine my ass. That old bat never saw the inside of the 500 Club."

"She had everything else right. Except, of course, you running to fat in your old age just because you're short." Joe glanced at his watch. "Come on, let's go home. You're got some sweet-talking to do. You have to convince Jess I should go to Lafourche parish, wherever the hell that is."

Kitty didn't speak for a long moment, panting heavily just to keep up with his long stride.

"He won't let you go over a dog." Her voice broke. "He's really mad."

"Foolish child. We're not gonna tell him that."

"What are we going to tell him?" Kitty said, bewildered.

"The truth. We found out a couple of men were watching us, one had a Cajun accent, and they drove off with our van," Joe said. "That's what will count with Jess and the rest of 'em."

"We won't mention Smoky?"

"No, we'll present the facts from a different angle."

"Okay," She shifted her shoulder bag up higher, staggering in her boots. "But I don't have a problem lying, either, if we have to."

Ahead of them, the '65 panhead glinted chrome and black in the afternoon sun.

"Hey, you know what?" Joe said. "You never told me. Do I walk like a baseball player?"

"Huh-uh," She shook her head slightly. "Florida panther. Stalking."

He grinned, and felt good for the first time in days.

"Damn. Thanks, girl."

"Um, Joe?" She stopped by the bike, gazing up at him wistfully with a dirty face. "Before we go home, could we maybe ride south a little ways, see if we can spot the van?"

Joe came to a slow halt, much like a Florida panther would before walking into quicksand.

"I was thinking, maybe they didn't get too far with that cracked engine block," She said.

"You're always thinking, aren't you?"

"He's already mad. It won't matter if we're a little late."

"You are highly optimistic," Joe said. He couldn't say the same about ever getting a Regents patch.

CHAPTER EIGHTEEN

Fueled by raging thirst and plans for revenge, the Regents descended on the small Atlanta clubhouse in the heat of the afternoon. They parked the U-Hauls on the street, slogged up the hill to the bungalow, and wasted little time getting drunk. Smitty directed the Louisville probates to close all the windows and turn up the air-conditioner. The fragmented pack had been hot and dry too long.

"Tell the bootlegger next door I need beer, now!" Dudley told Bugsy. "And help Greasy drag his grill over here."

"Where the hell is our probate?" Bugsy retorted, staring in amazement at the exhausted men pouring out of the U-Hauls. Jesus, whatever had happened was big, and the Regents had been the losers. Bugsy suddenly cheered. "Is he dead?"

"He's busy!" Dudley snapped. "Go get the beer."

As soon as their feet hit the driveway, the Atlanta women ran to the bunkhouse to grab anything breakable or valuable, pleading with Mina to stash their belongings at her house. Smitty overheard them and pointed to the path between the back yards.

"All of you stay at Mina's and don't come back 'til I send for you. It's gonna be ugly here for awhile."

"I got Janis and Jimi, honey." Clutching her collection of black light posters, Dorrie gave Smitty a kiss and waved at her friends. "Let's go."

♦

The old sash windows took blow after blow, the Rolling Stones threatening to bust the wavy glass out of their puttied frames. Angry voices spat beer-fumed plans for revenge into the air already rank with unwashed bodies. By midnight, grievances had escalated to a dangerous level inside the old bungalow. The Regents soaked in the full injury done to them, tossed speed and beer on top of it, and let it simmer. They had lost their money, dope stashes, personal property, even the damned bedrolls. Their bikes lay crushed and dented in pools of oil in the back of a U-Haul. Some men didn't have enough gas money to get home.

The exhausted Louisville and Milwaukee probates lugged beer nonstop from the bootlegger next-door to the bar, followed by a Dayton probate loaded down with bags of ice.

"Where the hell is your probate?" Smitty said to Jess. "He shoulda been back hours ago."

Jess had been wondering the same thing, with some goading from a bottle of Jack Daniels. If Joe and Kitty had stopped at a motel somewhere, they would regret it. If they had slipped back into town and were bunking at his house, they would regret it more. It didn't help that Led Zeppelin was wailing about a woman leaving home for a brown-eyed man. *Stupid bastard.* He knew better than to get close to anyone.

Friends were a liability, a hazard. He couldn't help himself around Kitty, but she understood he had to keep the walls up in public. The only place he could relax was in the bedroom, in the dark, where he could say things no one else could ever know. Jess narrowed his eyes and took another shot of whiskey. If someone else was in that bedroom with her, someone he wanted to consider a friend in spite of himself…

Jess worked himself into a rigid-jawed, black ass mood thinking about the possibilities. He had watched the two of them together, saw how they drew toward each other and weren't even aware of it. How she looked at Joe like he was ice cream and she wanted to lap him up. And Joe, a decent guy with a sense of humor and an edge, always trying to act like he wasn't in love with Kitty, when he couldn't take his eyes off her. Jess knew all her little tricks in bed, the moves that could make a man stone-blind stupid for her, forget who he was or what he had promised. Fuck it, if he lost her, he didn't have shit. He'd kill both of them. Then maybe he'd go home, one last time, and blow his brains out right in the old man's face.

"Put that back together, you son-of-a-bitch."

He stood unsteadily and headed for the back door, stomping through an obstacle course of boots and bare feet.

"Good times, bad times," Bobby Boozer sang under the kitchen table, his eyes closed. "I've had my fuckin' share…"

Just as Jess reached for the knob, the door creaked open. Joe walked slowly up the steps, neck and shoulders stiff.

"Where the hell have you been?" Jess spat. "Where's Kitty?"

"She's at your place. We got caught in traffic from the race."

"All this time?" He moved in twelve inches from Joe's chin, stalling him off-balance on the last step.

"Yeah," Joe became still. "We got a tip on the van. Thought maybe it wouldn't get far because of the cracked engine block, so we went looking. It put us on the wrong side of all that traffic."

Jess frowned, sifting the information until he heard what he wanted.

"Our van? There's a tip? What kind of tip?"

"I'd appreciate it if you'd get out of my face, Jess, I'd give my last fifty bucks for a beer. Couldn't find one of those either, and it's been a long day on that bike."

Jess had not been expecting good news of any kind. He took a step sideways and let Joe pass. The cold ones were hidden in an old washing machine on the porch, and Joe held the icy can in his hand for a moment before opening it. He was so tired he was reeling. Jess relented. It had been a long bad day, even longer for someone riding around on a mission while the rest of the pack wallowed in air-conditioning and self-pity.

"What was the tip? What happened?"

"A woman at the track said two men were watching us the whole time we were there. She said they took the van after we were hauled off. She was sure one of them was Cajun."

Son of a bitch. "Damn. Could she have been lying? Or wrong?"

"No," Joe smiled slightly. "She didn't miss details."

"Dudley will want to hear this. Come on."

Jess hurried back into the dining room and bumped through the crowd to the end of the table.

"My probate's got some news."

"Can ya spill it before you die?" Smitty cracked. "Damn, son, you're toasted. Are you sure you're white?"

Joe held out his bare brown arms like he didn't quite recognize them.

"Half Irish on my mom's side," He said. "I was telling Jess, we had company from Louisiana at the races after all."

He suddenly had the attention of everyone at the table, and Dudley shouted the room into silence. Joe told them about the van, the two men and the woman.

"No shit. The Bayou Runners were there?"

"Only two."

"She gave you a description? We'll run it by our New Orleans Regent, see if his worthless ass can earn that free patch he got. Where's Fat Jack?" Dudley stood up.

"Where do ya think? As close to Alec's ass as his brown nose can get. They're on the porch."

The men wove through the crowd, gaining numbers in the short distance until an entourage piled up at the front door. Big Alec sat on the wicker couch, the most comfortable piece of furniture in the clubhouse, a fan in the screened window aimed at him. The Miami Regents frowned at the sudden invasion.

"Hey," Smitty bumped Fat Jack with his boot, stirring him out of a dazed sleep on the floor. "Wake up and be useful." He gestured to Joe. "Tell him."

"A witness saw a Cajun watching us at the races. They took our van." Joe described the man for the group.

"Fancy mustache?" Fat Jack struggled to sit up and regain his senses.

"It sounds like Guidry," Jess frowned.

The Bayou Runners he once knew weren't all that particular about their looks. In another life, though, Guidry would have been a riverboat gambler. "I haven't heard about him in a while. Is he still with the club?"

"Yeah," Fat Jack said. "He keeps a low profile. He don't party much. He's all about business. Plays card games at the private clubs."

Big Alec eyed two orange moths batting at a lamp shade.

"Was he by himself?"

Everyone looked at Joe. "There was another man with him, and a woman, but the woman left sometime during the night and took the car."

Smitty raised an eyebrow at Alec. "I thought your sources said the Runners got stopped at the Alabama line. And the reporter told us that, too."

"Guess the cops didn't get 'em all." Alec settled into the couch and yawned. "Jack, in the morning, head home to New Orleans and see what you can find out about that van." Too tired to smirk, he favored Dudley with a raised eyebrow. "I'm assuming the van is important to you?"

"You don't want them having the shit in the van, either," Dudley said. "You're the target."

Sprawled on the wood floor, Fat Jack looked crestfallen at being banished so quickly from his new brothers.

"Might be a problem sending Jack home to New Orleans, Alec," Jess said with a cold smile.

"What now, Einstein?"

"If the Bayou Runners were watching us, they saw Jack. With a patch."

Fat Jack's eyes popped. He'd been caught in a trap of his own making. The Bayou Runners knew where he lived and where he worked. The man's face sagged as the danger and full responsibility of wearing a Regents patch sank in. Jess took another swig from his bottle, enjoying the burn. He had no tolerance for people who didn't earn a patch.

"How about a boss's meeting in the morning?" Dudley said.

"How about noon?" The Detroit boss propped himself against the door.

The crowd at the front door lurched back into the house to spread the word of Bayou Runners at the race track. Jess turned to go, Joe wearily following.

"Hey probate," Big Alec called.

Jess stopped, the muscles in his back grabbing. Behind him, Joe turned.

"Yeah?"

"Bring me a beer. A cold one."

Joe paused for two beats, then muscled his way through the gathering without a word. Dudley glanced at Jess, who tried to find a solution in his Jack Daniels-sodden brain. Would they have a problem? Joe was on the final end of a bad forty-eight hours in the Alabama heat. If he didn't come back, Jess would be in a hell of a spot. A disrespectful probate was an embarrassment to the entire chapter, and they would expect him to do something about it. It didn't matter that Jess had planned to dismember him scarcely thirty minutes ago. That was personal.

But Joe returned with two bottles dripping with ice chips. He handed one to Big Alec and one to Wolf, who sat by the porch door.

"Anything else?"

Big Alec didn't reply. He popped the cap off with one thumb and leaned back, closing his eyes. Wolf stared at Jess, then shifted his black gaze to the door. *Get him out of here.*

Jess gripped Joe by the arm and pulled him inside the house. The somber mood had improved into a rowdy uproar. It was easier to blame the Bayou Runners instead of some unreachable Talladega officials for their shitty National. They could lay physical hands on the Bayou Runners. Grousing about the lousy weekend shifted to planning retaliation.

"We are seriously short on transportation." Smitty cornered Greasy. "Find us another van, one that can carry some weight. We're gonna need another car, too."

"No problem."

"Smitty!" Fat Jack worked his way to the Atlanta crew. "Smitty, can I use your phone? I want to call my old lady, and tell her…tell her…"

"What, that you fucked up?" Smitty retorted.

"Sleaze wouldn't be dumb enough to firebomb a place in the middle of the Quarter, but the house would be easy for them to hit."

"Yeah, go ahead, we don't want nothing to happen to good old Francine." Smitty shooed him away.

"Or Gaspar," Jess said knowingly, and Fat Jack glared at him with guilty eyes. Francine would kill Fat Jack barehanded if anything happened to her ankle-biting mutt, and they both knew it. "Better hurry."

"I don't remember him," Joe said, staring at the Miami patch on the man's back as he scurried away.

"He owns a tattoo shop in the French Quarter. It was neutral territory for the clubs, but he screwed that up getting that patch. He didn't even have to probate. Alec gave it to him. Maybe for time served," Jess sneered. It galled him that Big Alec could still surprise him with his sheer audacity for bending the rules when it suited.

"Alec offered me a patch, too. Before he stomped my brains out," Joe said dully. "Who's Gaspar, his kid?"

"Sort of. His wife's yappy dog." Jess set down his empty whiskey bottle on the floor and snagged two beers from a passing probate, offering one to Joe. "What about our dog?"

Surprised, Joe looked at him with half-closed, bloodshot eyes and shook his head.

"The old woman said they took Smoky with the van."

Even deeply under the influence, it dawned on Jess he'd been played, and played well. He steadied himself on a nearby wall. "So all that bullshit about looking for the van? You were looking for Smoky?"

Joe shrugged. "Find one, find the other."

"You were supposed to come straight back here. The cops could have nailed you again."

"It was a risk," Joe admitted. "But they were looking for a pack, not a couple without patches."

The beer was too cold. It didn't slide down all the way. An air bubble caught in Jess's chest. *A couple*?

"Kitty asked you to keep looking."

Joe didn't answer. It wasn't necessary. And it didn't matter.

"Jess, I've got a bad feeling the puppy is gone for good. I just couldn't tell Kitty. She wasn't going to give up. I…I had to make her think she tried. It seemed important to her."

Another pair of probates came stumbling by, their mouths hanging open with exhaustion, arms straining to carry triple-stacked cases of beer. Jess looked over his shoulder to make sure no one could hear him before ordering: "Go to my place and get some rest. See you tomorrow."

"It *is* tomorrow," Joe said. "I think."

"And take him with you." Denny's hang-around stood in the kitchen doorway, bewildered and lost. "He can sleep in the hammock in the back yard. Just get that damned duffle bag out of here."

♦

Kitty woke up from a deep black sleep. The bones in her neck ached from yesterday's long ride, and the cotton pillowcase scratched her sunburned skin. She had dosed herself with vinegar last night in the shower so she wouldn't peel, and smelled like a fresh-dyed Easter egg. In the window, the grumbling air-conditioner muffled noises from the street. The door to Joe's room and the one to the kitchen were both shut. Good, she could go back to sleep. She didn't care about her stranded out-of-town friends, or jail, or the Bayou Runners.

None of it mattered. What mattered was that one awful moment when she finally realized the van had somehow vanished on those endless Alabama back roads, and Joe told her they had to stop searching and head back to Atlanta. But Joe would find a way, she was sure of it.

A wind-up West Bend ticked on the table. One o'clock. Damn. She had slept almost twelve hours and still felt awful. Kitty listened to the voices in the next room until she determined who it was, and knew them well enough to stagger to the bathroom in an oversized tee-shirt and no make-up.

"Finally decide to get your ass out of bed?" Jess said as she passed by them.

Great. Grouchy and hung-over. She couldn't blame him. It had almost killed her to see what had happened to the knucklehead.

"I've got to pee. Is that okay with you?"

She padded barefoot through the kitchen to the hall. When she came back, they were silent, frowning and not looking at each other. Now what? Joe sat damp-haired and slant-eyed in a clean tee-shirt and Levi's, one copper-brown elbow propped on the table, the other hand toying with a crystal sugar bowl.

Jess, who strove to look grubby to counter all the pretty-boy remarks, had accomplished his goal. His eyelids hung puffy over bloodshot eyes, and his hair spun around his head like a straw whirlwind. Where the heck had he slept, on the floor? He leaned back in his chair, his arms folded across a shirt rank with sweat stains. She recognized the stiff "I have spoken" posture. Trying not to inhale, Kitty walked behind him and peered inside the percolator. The coffee pot was half-empty. They had been discussing something unpleasant for a while. It would be up to her to end the stand-off. All she could manage was stupid humor.

"J.W., you are planning on taking a bath today, I hope?" She sniffed while pouring a cup of coffee. Maybe some caffeine would help fill the hollow space under her lungs. *Hang on, Smokes, we'll find you. Don't be scared.*

"What the fuck is it to you?" He snapped, surprising her with the viciousness.

The percolator trembled in her hand and she set it down, the mug only half full.

"I was just kidding," She appeased weakly. "I thought a bath would make you feel better."

Jess reached for his own coffee, took a long drink, then set the cup back down hard on the vinyl tablecloth. "It's after one o'clock. Pack up and get going. The other probates have got the U-Haul switched out and loaded. Rick's expecting you."

Stunned, Kitty turned. Rick in Jacksonville? Joe didn't budge.

"Anybody can haul those bikes to Florida. The Chopper Shop isn't hard to find," Joe insisted quietly.

"We didn't pick anybody, we picked you," Jess replied, his jaw tight.

"You could talk to Dudley. Tell him I'd do more good if I went with the fat guy back to New Orleans. Nobody knows me there."

"And you don't know the Bayou Runners. So what good would it do?"

"If Fat Jack helped me find the van, I'd have a chance of getting it out of there."

"He's right!" Kitty hurried around to stand at the end of the table, her fingertips spread across the wood. "Randy probably knows where Guidry hangs out. We could call him, see if any of the Runners are back yet. Joe can pass for Cajun."

"Would you shut the fuck up?" Jess banged his fist on the table. "This is Regents business. Get the hell back in the bedroom."

Kitty backed up, her eyes stinging. She was too tired for this.

"I don't think this is Regents shit," Joe declared, his eyes narrowing. "I think this is you."

"Jess, why can't he at least try—" Kitty begged.

And then she hit the floor, the mug cracking beside her, hot coffee splashing her bare legs.

"There will always be another dog! That puppy is gone. Fucking deal with it."

Kitty tried to catch her breath, lifting her head from the slick floor. She saw Joe swing like a hammer, knocking Jess out of his chair, but Jess was on his feet and the two of them locked up, body-punching and grunting. They spun into the window, knocking down the shades and curtains.

"Stop it!" Her voice was too high-pitched, they couldn't hear her. "Stop!"

The table crashed over, ash trays and saucers bouncing and splintering. Kitty crawled across the floor and pulled herself to her feet. She picked up a cast-iron frying pan from the stove and weakly swung, hitting them on the arms, their backs, whatever she could manage. She couldn't bear it, she had to stop them.

"Please…" She panted, aiming for elbows and kneecaps until Jess stopped swinging long enough to shove her hard across the room. She hit the plaster wall, slid to the floor and stayed there.

Horrified, Joe turned to look at her for the second it took Jess to swing and knock him on his ass. Before he could jump back up, Kitty put out her hand.

"Stop. Please," She sobbed, drawing her legs up.

Jess bent over a river of steaming coffee grounds, panting. He pointed to Joe.

"Get your shit and get out of here. Now!" He shouted hoarsely.

Just go, she thought, wanting it over, and didn't realize she'd spoken aloud. A dark silhouette passed over her with a rush of cold air. She heard boots cracking on the hard wood floor down the hall, drawers opening, slamming shut, something heavy dragged from under the bed. Then the boots came back swiftly, crunching across glass shards and spilt sugar to the living room carpet.

The front door opened, spearing her burning eyes with light, and closed with a slam. Silence closed in, the air-conditioner humming in the next room. Jess put his head down and squeezed his eyes shut. "Fuck."

Kitty leaned back against the wall, waiting for the room to focus. Crying made her ribs hurt, but she couldn't stop. Harsh white sun illuminated the overturned table, the broken chairs and a torn shade hanging crooked. At her feet, rainbow prisms glittered from broken bits of crystal. Jess stumbled over and crouched down beside her.

"Baby?" His fingers brushed her hair away from her eyes, wanting her to look at him. "Kit, I…I didn't mean it about the dog."

He touched her legs where tiny ruby beads of blood dotted her skin.

"I'm sorry. I didn't mean it. Jesus. I never should have said that to you. Okay?"

"Okay," She whispered because it was what he wanted to hear.

He stood, crossed through the grit to the refrigerator and wrapped some ice cubes in a cloth. "Here. Put this on your lip." He offered with shaking hands.

A trail of blood ran from his nose down his chin.

"You need some ice, too."

"I'm all right."

"The hell you are," She thought, exhausted. "You just lost a friend."

He carefully pulled her to her feet, put an arm around her and lifted her out of the broken glass. "I'll get Mina to come over and clean up later."

She let him carry her into their bedroom and settle her down awkwardly among the pillows. But he didn't join her. He wiped his hair back out of his eyes, and held his hands in front of him.

"It's been bad lately, Kit, like something's pulling me under," He said, panting. "But I shouldn't take it out on you. I didn't mean it about the dog. That was a cheap shot. Christ, your legs are bleeding."

Here he went. When he started talking fast, he wanted her to tell him what the hell was going on.

"Lay with me, Jess."

“No. Your arm’s bleeding. I’ll get the tweezers. You’ve got glass splinters all over.”

“Jesse?” Her fingers smoothed his pillow. “Please?”

“I shouldn’t, I’m dirty as hell,” Jess said, trying to catch his breath.

“No, baby, you’re just tired. Come here and let me hold you. It’d make me feel better.”

Kitty waited for him to wind down. As soon as he settled beside her, she’d roll a joint and get him so high he would pass out. But right now, she had to stay in one place, holding him here in the room without touching him. She lived in terror he would somehow spin away from her into the distance. She dreamed about it sometimes, him turning his back to her, walking away, gone. Kitty lay still on the pillows, waiting until it was safe to touch him.

“Yeah, maybe if we both get some rest,” His eyes wild, he sat down, then stretched out across the blue comforter on his back, his hands gripping the fabric. “When we wake up, things will straighten out.”

Across the room, the door to the small bedroom was shut tight. She knew the closet door stood ajar, and the drawers in the small oak dresser hung open and empty. Joe had swept out the guns and cash from his hiding place.

Kitty thought: “When we wake up, he’ll be gone.”

CHAPTER NINETEEN

An orange U-Haul with Alabama plates headed south across the Fuller Warren, passing the drawbridge tender's windows at a respectful forty miles per hour. Silent Sam leaned his bushy head out the window, sniffing the breeze. Twilight cast the ancient St. Johns River into a formidable greenish-black entity, falling off the horizon into the starry sky. Closer in, along the south banks, he saw tiny lights in the grand old houses of San Marco.

"You ever seen the St. Johns before?" Joe asked, not expecting a reply. "Some places, it's three miles wide. Like out there. It runs through Florida for over three hundred miles."

He fished a dollar from his pocket for the woman at the toll booth. She eyed the U-Haul and the dark rumpled occupants.

"Heading for Miami?" She said.

Nobody stayed in Jacksonville. They were always just passing through, on the way to St. Augustine, Daytona or Fort Lauderdale. He accepted his change with a warm tanned hand and a big smile.

"No, sweetheart. This is home." He pulled away, certain she thought some ancient Timucuan had survived extinction after all.

A childlike excitement overcame Joe when he veered off I-95 for the Beaches exit, landing them on Atlantic Boulevard. Familiar places -- the Krystal, Pulido's Automotive, the austere Bishop Kenny High School, a glimpse of the Old South Restaurant down Beach Boulevard -- waited like old friends.

"It might look like just another town to you but this place makes my heart feel good," Joe said, grinning. He felt like he had been gone years, not just a few months.

The four lanes split apart at St. Nicholas Center, and Joe pointed across Atlantic Boulevard. Although it was closed for the night, The House of Lamps and Shades was brilliantly lit.

"My girlfriend saved up for three months to buy a fancy little chandelier from Mr. Robertson for our dining room. She called it Blue Delft, like we're Delft people. She never had nice things growing up."

Silent Sam gave him a look.

"Yeah, the girl I left behind me, like the old song. Red-headed Colleen. She deserves better," Joe hesitated. "Most of 'em do."

And that would be enough talk about women. He was done with Georgia, and everything in it.

"The old folks call this the Beach Road because Atlantic Boulevard used to be the only way to the beaches. My Daddy remembered when the road was brick. The ride out there must have been hell. See that creek? That's Big Pottsburg. I used to catch bass and channel catfish there." It was like talking to himself. No wonder Denny called the guy his conscience.

Joe knew no one had explained shit to Silent Sam beyond commanding him to help load the truck with Atlanta's damaged bikes and go along for the ride. Six hours later, the man was in a strange town and didn't have a clue what was going on. Typical Regents.

"The guys at the Chopper Shop are cool. They know Denny. They helped me build my panhead. They do some work for the Regents," He assured Sam. "There's no Regents chapter here, but Jacksonville's kind of a midpoint between Atlanta and Miami for the Regents when they travel."

"You'll be okay hanging around with them. I've got some errands to run while I'm in Jacksonville. Guess I should visit a flower shop. Colleen loves those peach-colored roses. Says they're a waste of money, but they match her freckles. I used to send them to her at work."

He finally realized he sounded a little manic.

"I'll shut up now," He said.

Silent Sam raised both eyebrows.

"Really. Watch. I can do it," Joe said, and was elated when Sam grinned and shook his head.

A U-Haul in a neighborhood during the day attracted attention. People kept up with who was going where. But it was after nine p.m. for working-class America. Most folks were indoors for the night, watching television. Joe turned left on Pecan Street to Berry Avenue.

The blue-shingled house looked the same, wind chimes motionless on the carport. Colleen's red Mustang sat in the driveway. Two doors down, his best friend Buddy had a porch light on, which meant his wife Margie was off playing cut-throat poker with her girlfriends. If Sam hadn't been with him, Joe would have stopped and gone inside. He'd known Buddy since they were shirt-tail kids. There would be time for that later. Maybe a lot of time. Joe headed for Mill Creek Road, and Atlantic.

"See that concrete block building? It used to be Wilson's Automotive. As in Joe Wilson." His enthusiasm dimmed. "I built race cars until I totaled the last one in a big race and all my neighbors lost their grocery money. None of us had any money for a while. That's when I decided riding a motorcycle would be faster and more dangerous and wouldn't cost anybody but me."

Sam gave the vacant building a long look. Joe wondered what kind of lost dreams he'd once had.

"Well, Sam, that's the dime tour. Let's go see if the Chopper Shop crew has some beer."

The Chopper Shop sat back from Atlantic Boulevard on a slight rise. It had been a gas station, a florist and a lawn-mower repair shop at various times. Since the Chopper Shop crew moved in, blue sheets covered the big show-room windows at night while the crew partied or worked late. Trucks and motorcycles were regular fixtures by the side door.

The burdened U-Haul groaned slightly rolling up the incline. Joe was glad to see a welcoming glow behind the building. Several men sat at a picnic table just outside the big garage door, their backs to the light, cigarette tips glowing. Before Joe could get the truck in Park, they surrounded it. A stocky man with curly brown hair reached up and pulled the door open.

"Damn, redneck, look at you, you've gone native!"

"Car Punk!" Joe jumped down from the cab and caught the guy in a bear hug. "How are the curtain climbers?"

"Mean as ever. Damn, your face is all beat up again. You still pissing off the wrong people?"

"Joe!" A tall, frantic young man with shaggy hair and striped bell-bottoms zoomed in front of him. "Hey, man, it's great to see you."

"Pooch," Joe grinned and pounded him on the back. "What are you doing here?"

"Everybody's here. When Smitty called and said you were bringing the bikes down, the word went out."

"Everybody?" Joe let it hang. He wasn't ready to see "everybody" yet.

"The scooter trash," Pooch hastily explained. "I didn't tell anybody from the neighborhood. I didn't even tell Dad or Buddy."

"That's fine, Pooch, I'll go see them tomorrow. Tonight, I just want to have a beer with the Chopper Shop crew." Joe shook the outstretched hands.

"Who's that?" Pooch glanced up at the cab.

"Friend of Denny. His name's Silent Sam. A hang-around."

"Is he cool? We want to catch up on the scuttlebutt. They didn't say much about Talladega." No one here wore a Regents patch, and therefore didn't rate getting clued in.

"Well I hope you have all night, because it was one hell of a weekend. My first National set a standard I don't want to see again." Joe surveyed the group. "Is Rick here?"

They kept smiling, but he could see it was forced.

"Yeah. He's here." Pooch nodded nervously.

"Your panhead didn't get messed up, did it?" High Hal spoke up.

"No, it's fine. But you'll get pissed when you see the others. They can wait until tomorrow. Right now, I want to celebrate being back in Jacksonville."

Silent Sam climbed down from the U-Haul, giving the Chopper Shop crew a chance to gape at him before they ambled toward the big garage doors. Pooch fell in behind the others, loping near Joe's shoulder.

"Joe? Things are little different here," He said, his voice low, then dropped back before he had to explain.

♦

They settled down at the picnic table with cold beer and left-over pizza, while Joe brought them up to date with the Talladega fiasco. Silent Sam stretched out on another redwood table in the shadows of a funeral home canopy and went to sleep, unfazed by the traffic hissing by on Atlantic. Without Regents hovering nearby, they could relax and talk candidly.

"And Big Alec came back to Atlanta with y'all?" Pooch lit up a joint to hide his nervousness.

"Yeah."

"That must have been interesting."

Every man sitting there saw him after he got stomped at the Fourth of July party.

"I was too tired to give a shit about Alec. And the Atlanta Regents warned him off."

"Mighty decent of 'em," Hippie Dave said.

The Chopper Shop crew looked at Joe a little warily, like they weren't quite sure it was the same man who had left for Atlanta a few months ago.

"So how long can you stay?" Pooch queried, unconvinced that the feud was settled. He'd known Joe since he was a kid, and Joe didn't forgive easily. If ever.

"As long as I need to."

Despite the beer and pot, an undercurrent worked its way around the table. The men looked at each other, not him, scratching armpits, toying with their beer bottles and gnawed pizza crusts.

“Something you want to talk about?”

High Hal became the unofficial designated speaker. He was articulate and had a large stake in the problem.

“It’s Rick.”

“Where is he, anyway?” Joe squinted inside the building. “Is he pissed off or something?”

“No, it’s worse than that. Look, Joe, we’ve been covering for him. If the club finds out, they’ll go somewhere else and we’ll all be screwed. These guys will be out a job, and me and the other investor will lose our asses.”

“What’s he done?”

“Nothing. That’s just it. He stays wasted. He’s dropping acid for breakfast, lunch and dinner. Babe got fed up and left, some connections we could have made went elsewhere, and he totally screws up anything he touches. You should see the paint jobs he did. We had to call this chick we know who does metal flake, and then Brush aced them up with his pin-striping. Rick knows those bikes are rolling out of here with the customers thinking he did the art work, and he doesn’t care.”

It didn’t sound like the Rick he remembered. Under his no-nonsense rule, the crew produced superb custom motorcycles, and could repair a rat bike that others would have junked. Organized, meticulous and arrogant, Rick also ran a few side businesses for the Regents.

“What the hell happened?”

Eyes rolled, sighs went up around the table, and Car Punk scratched his beard.

“Jim Morrison.”

Joe’s beer bottle stopped in mid-air. They had to be kidding. Any second now, “Don’t You Love Her Madly” was going to blast him and Rick would have a good laugh at his expense. But practical jokes weren't Rick's style.

"Listen," Brush gestured behind them into the big concrete cavern.

Local radio station WAPE boomed through eight speakers stretched through the shop, an evening mix of Santana and Procol Harum.

"He almost made us crazy. He was playing The Doors over and over. I swear to Christ I heard 'Crystal Ship' in my sleep," Car Punk said through gritted teeth.

"Car Punk told him, take the Lizard King tapes to the office and close the door or we were all walking out," Hippie Dave said.

"So he did," Brush said, bewildered. He had known Rick the longest, taking endless verbal abuse like a sidekick in a black and white movie.

"When you told him to close the door, he really closed the door. Is that it?" Joe said.

"That's it. God," Pooch stared at him in awe. "You nailed it. Remember how he always talked about finding the gateway? His head's in a bad place and he can't get back."

"Your head would be in a bad place, too, if you were eating Orange Sunshine with your Fruit Loops," Car Punk retorted. "Thing is, Joe, he's been doing this since Morrison croaked, and the downhill slide is dragging us all in the toilet."

Not much of a talker, Hippie Dave was more business savvy than he let on. "This place was getting a good rep. Customers hanging out all day, and High Hal brought some of his rich buddies around. They put down some heavy deposits for custom work."

"Until Rick screwed one up and told my friend to get fucked if he didn't like it." Hal shook his head, and looked at Joe. "Me and my partner can't afford to lose our investments."

The third partner was Pooch's father. Unlike High Hal and his wealthy Deerwood friends, Larry Monahan was a welder at the shipyards. He earned his money through brute labor in dangerous conditions. He had sacrificed a chunk of his scrimped-together savings to the Chopper Shop venture so Pooch would have something to keep his nervous mind off the things he had seen floating in Vietnamese rivers.

Joe's family had worked at those same shipyards, and he understood what was at stake. He also understood what the men at the table expected of him. And he didn't mind. Here in Jacksonville, he was a problem-solver. He felt better than he had in a long time.

♦

It seemed like he was always waking up on a couch, and never sure where the couch was. Traffic whished steadily outside, echoing off concrete walls. Paint, lacquer thinner and used motor oil exhaled from the scratchy couch cushions when he turned over. With a faint smile, Joe rolled to his feet. It had been a long time since he awakened without dread for what the day held for him.

The display room, which apparently served as a bunk house these days, looked out over the shop. Lined with heavy benches crowded with parts, the concrete floor stretched empty all the way to the big garage door, awaiting the casualties in the U-Haul. Silent Sam sat at a picnic table outside, watching a raccoon and a ragged orange tom cat square off over a pizza crust near the privacy fence. A steaming cup of coffee sat on the table beside a pack of cigarettes. So the man did have some sense of survival.

Joe followed his nose to a percolator plugged into the wall behind a box of STP and fixed a large cup for himself. It was weird how he felt at home here. Maybe because the place was concrete circa 1947, decorated with carburetors and blue and yellow cans of WD-40. Along with Rick's posters of Ann-Margret and Jim Morrison, and one of Jane Fonda upside down with a knife stuck between her legs. Might as well get it over with.

He tried the bedroom first. The door swung open. The unmade bed was empty. Which left the office. Joe knocked and pushed the door open at the same time. A stench rushed at him from the narrow room, urine and soured clothes and burned metal.

"Damn!" He reeled back, then stomped forward and seized the man lying on the couch by the arm.

"Hey…what the…"

"You sorry piece of shit." Joe yanked him to his feet and dragged him into the hall. The odor floated along with him. "What the hell happened to you? You son-of-a-bitch, you gave me your word you'd pay back Pooch's dad for the loan. You aren't doing shit. I oughta kick your sorry ass."

"Who…" Rick slid down the wall.

"Who do you think it is? Didn't you tell me you'd start making payments? Pooch's mom is sick, they need the money. It was a loan, not a gift."

"Joe? Joe, you look different, man. Oh shit, the floor's coming up again, it keeps inhaling." He braced himself against the wall.

Joe couldn't believe it, not meticulous Rick with his Wild Bill Hickok hair and mustache, a carefully groomed façade that drew women like honey bees. Instead, his long greasy hair stunk like a stagnant pond, and his stained jeans and shirt tangled around him. A toothbrush hadn't been near his teeth in a while, and his facial hair had grown together in a revolting clump. For some in the biker world, such an appearance was a way of life. But not for Rick.

"How'd you let yourself get like this?" Joe snapped. "Some rock singer drowns in a bathtub in France and you go off the deep end?"

"It…he…" Rick closed his eyes. "I thought Morrison knew how."

"Knew how what?"

"To get to the other side. The gateway. The door."

"He was a man just like us and shot his talent down a drain, just like you're doing. You're going to lose this place, Rick, and put everybody out of work. I need your help. I came down here with a truckload of trashed bikes, including Jess's old knucklehead. You're the only one he trusts to work on it. Do you even give a shit?"

"About what?"

Joe clenched his fists and counted to ten, out loud. Beating the shit out of Rick wouldn't do any good.

"Okay, you want to cross over, I'll help you. I can do that."

He seized Rick by a sticky boot and dragged him down the hall on his back to the bathroom.

"Oh Jesus, the walls are falling!" Rick's hands flailed. "The walls are falling on us, Joe, we're gonna be crushed."

"You wish." He stuffed him in the small shower stall, then twisted the faucets until warm water belched loose.

"Don't." Rick stuck his legs straight out and clawed at the tile with broken fingernails for a grip. "Get me out. Joe, get me out. I'll slide down the drain."

"Isn't that what you want?"

"I don't want to *stay* there," Rick squeezed his eyes shut. "I just want to go long enough to find my brother. I want to tell him I'm sorry. But I don't want to stay."

Joe couldn't move. *Oh no…*

"Sorry for what?" He managed to say. "You told me the cops killed your brother. They shot him off his bike."

"He was running from them," Rick panted. "He'd just stabbed his wife. Jesus, I want to talk to him, I just want five minutes."

We don't get those five minutes. Ever. Joe felt like he was hanging in the air. If all he had to do was pop some peyote, have visions like his ancestors, talk to the dead—*don't even think about it.*

"It doesn't happen that way, Rick, or Morrison would be standing here telling you you're an asshole instead of me."

Water pelted Rick, plastering the blue denim shirt to his chest. Bones and pale skin showed through where muscle had been only a few months ago.

"She wasn't cheating. Amy just liked to have fun," He leaned back, exhausted. "But he stabbed her. I didn't know people had that much blood in them. You shoulda seen it."

Joe waited. If Rick managed to find a mystical gateway, it would be hard to say who he really wanted to talk to, his brother, or his brother's wife. He had seen that kind of blood. *A flight crew. The mechanics. Our dog.* And five minutes would never be enough. But it was better than nothing.

"If you figure out how to do it, to get one more chance, let me know."

Joe backed out of the room and shut the door behind him.

CHAPTER TWENTY

With the sunglasses, it was hard to tell what Silent Sam may have heard. But he ignored the look in Joe's eyes and helped him get their motorcycles down out of the truck.

"I'll be back in a little while. Make yourself at home," Joe said. "Don't worry about the rest of the bikes. The other guys will be here soon. Let them unload 'em."

He revved up the panhead and pulled out on Atlantic, heading east toward the beach, just because he wanted to, and because he could. No Regents, no "here boy" whistles. A few hours of salt air and a beer, maybe a ride down A1A with nothing but sand dunes and a few old beach houses between here and Vilano Beach, and Josiah Kelley Wilson would officially be home.

Three fuel stops later, and a near-miss with a pelican after ogling a curvy brunette in a tie-dye bikini, Joe returned to Jacksonville via Beach Boulevard. There wasn't much civilization out that way until he reached the Alhambra Dinner Theater on his left and the entrance to Florida Junior College on the right. A classic old landmark within tossing distance of Duval County's next generation of artists.

"I'm home!" He was so euphoric he tested a few lights down Southside Boulevard, the last one skidding left on Atlantic in front of a bus.

He decided a beer would be appropriate, and the Neighborhood Tavern was a good place to start. Tucked up behind a building off Atlantic, the bar looked like a two-stool saloon from the outside. Inside, though, it meandered around pool tables to a big outdoor area in the back. It was a popular place for construction workers in the afternoon. He recognized most of the vehicles in the small parking lot, including a 1951 Chevy truck, restored from bumper to fender, near the front door.

Joe stepped inside and gave his eyes a minute to adjust to the near-darkness. The bar ran down the length of the room, and the stools were packed. The man on the end was lifting his beer, and stopped in mid-hoist. One by one, the drinkers leaned back or forward to stare at the entrance, conversation faltering.

“Howdy, fellas.”

Maybe they couldn’t tell who it was with the light behind him. Johnny Russell kicking on the jukebox with “Rednecks, White Socks and Blue Ribbon Beer,” and Joe headed for the end of the bar. But he could still hear the comments.

“Is that Joe Wilson?”

“Heard he ran off with some bikers.”

“Thought he was gone for good.”

“You ain’t the only one.”

“Hush. That ain’t none of our business.”

He would have stopped to question them, but spotted a beefy, sun-reddened face at the end of the bar. There was nothing bewildered or confused on that face, just a steady gaze.

“It’s too early for trick or treat,” Buddy drawled, lifting his beer in salute. “They don’t have barber shops in Atlanta?”

“Didn’t have time to get a haircut. Stayed busy.”

The man next to Buddy picked up his beer and slid away. Joe eased onto the rickety stool and offered his hand.

“Busy with what, getting knocked around again?”

“You should see the other guy.”

Buddy relaxed.

“Did you get him?” Then he lowered his voice. “Are they looking for you?”

“Nah. I haven’t got the one who messed me up so bad. Yet.”

“Was this just a tussle?” Buddy eyed the bruises.

“Guess so. Over a woman and a dog.”

“Oh. Same old shit.” Buddy sighed.

“What’s going around here these days?”

"Shit's going on all over Jacksonville. Hans Tanzler is gonna clean up the St. Johns, and some bunch from Baltimore is gonna turn downtown into another New York City. They're fixing to do urban renewal all over Hogan's Creek and Hansontown and tear down all them old houses that didn't get burned up in the Civil War or the 1901 fire. Gonna be plenty of work bulldozing those houses, building HUD welfare apartments and parking lots instead." Buddy lit a cigarette. "You planning on sticking around? They'll be looking for supervisors and work crews."

Joe waited while the bartender handed him a beer and left.

"I might. Things got complicated up there. Shit never stops."

"Serious shit?"

"Yep."

When provoked, he'd done stuff here at home that tended to shake up his friends. But there were rules and familiarity with the players, all basically decent blue-collar men who liked to hunt and tussle and would never think of cussing in front of their Mamas, even if their Mamas cussed first.

"I got to get back to work. Why don't you come by the house later? I'll put on some Merle Haggard and jog your memory about where you belong."

"I've got some stuff to straighten out over there at the Chopper Shop. I'm not sure how long it'll take."

"Suit yourself. Margie would like to see you, even if you do look like a bum. She was worried about you when you left."

"I was worried about me, too."

♦

When he returned to the Chopper Shop, the U-Haul was empty and parked by the fence, out of the way. The men looked up when he walked inside the shop, their faces gloomy.

"I didn't know it was this bad," Hippie Dave said.

"These are just Atlanta's bikes. We had three vanloads," Joe told them.

"How could they do this to the knuckle?" Pooch crouched beside it. "It was a work of art. I don't get it."

"Just do what you can. Jess has another bike to ride, but this one's his baby. Where's Rick?

"In the bedroom. He was laying in the shower when we got here, but I don't like taking a piss with a man's head two feet from my dick, so Hal and me carried him to the bedroom."

"Did he have a pulse?" Joe asked.

"He moved," Brush shrugged. "You think he's gonna die?"

"Only if I kill him." Joe fished in his pocket. "Here." He tossed a key to High Hal. "You're a partner. Act like it. You're in charge. Pooch? Here's one for you, too."

"Give it to Brush, he lives here." Pooch backed up, his tennis shoes squeaking.

"Brush, you want to be in charge?" Joe extended the key to the gape-mouthed pinstripe artist, who shook his head.

"I'll do it," Hippie Dave spoke up. "It's stupid to let this place go to shit."

"You're on. All right, let's get to it."

"What's he gonna do?" Pooch glanced over at Silent Sam, who sat sideways on the couch, one arm draped across the back.

The blue sheets were looped out of the way, and he watched the steady traffic on Atlantic, his sunglasses on.

"Looks like a supervisor to me," Joe said.

They worked until seven p.m., cursing each ding and scrape, then headed home.

"Glad you're back." Pooch didn't look up from the frame he had picked for tomorrow's project. "Sure everything's okay now?"

"For the next five minutes," Joe said. He knew Pooch wanted to talk about Big Alec, and apologize for the beating Joe took. And Joe didn't want to talk about it. The kid carried enough weight from far more serious losses. "How much of that shit does Rick have on him?"

"Acid? Too much."

"Where's it coming from?"

"All he has to do is go to a rock concert or a party."

"In Jacksonville?" Joe asked incredulously.

"That shit is everywhere. Some older guy brought a briefcase to a cook-out in Gainesville last month, and he had rows of it, pick your trip. And there's this dude in California named Owsley who makes a hundred thousand tabs at a time and knows all the rock stars. His stuff is really good."

"So there's no danger of Rick running out," Joe said, disgusted. "They've got drugs I've never heard of in a park up there in Atlanta. And sell it in the open, like they're at some carnival."

"You been doing dope?" Pooch grinned. "Rednecks drink beer."

Joe scowled at him.

"Just some pot. And of course good old speed from the Air Force days. It's the only way I could keep up in Atlanta. I still wake up at six every morning, even if I don't get to bed by four. Have you tried any of that LSD?"

Personally, Joe did not think it would be a good idea for Pooch to venture into an altered state of consciousness. The kid had been a nervous wreck before he ever went to Vietnam, and came back vibrating like a tuning fork.

"It can make you paranoid," Pooch admitted. "Depends on what kind you get. It also makes mind-blowing sex. I mean tremendous. This one chick, it was like her nipples were little raisins. I couldn't leave 'em alone, and it turned her on like crazy. I thought she was gonna buck me off into the ceiling, and it was one of those ceilings with all the little plaster points. Man, it would have hurt. You need a guide to keep you cool. If the stuff is any good, it can take you places."

"Like the ceiling."

"Yeah. Speaking of nipples, I got an invite to a party for two in Riverside with an art student from FJC and a world-class bong. She does abstracts. I'll see you in the morning."

"Sure you will. Noon, maybe."

"Maybe," Pooch grinned, and glanced at Silent Sam. "Guess he's got the couch. Where are you gonna sleep?"

"I'm heading home. It's about time I got that over with."

Pooch's grin froze on his face.

"Home? Atlanta?"

"Hell no, that'll never be home. I mean home, on Berry Avenue. The blue house. Colleen."

"Oh." Pooch's eyes began darting everywhere. Not a good sign.

"Is she that mad?"

"I don't know. I don't go by there. She wasn't happy when you left and you know I avoid hostile situations. Well, I gotta beat feet, man. Can't let a bong wait too long on Cherry Street."

Pooch headed for the side door, and then his tennis shoes screeched on the concrete.

"Oh yeah, I forgot. Jess called earlier to make sure you got here."

"Got here? It's only six hours."

"It was kind of trippy. It's almost like he thought…well, he wasn't asking if you got here okay. It was kinda like he was asking if you got here at all, like you were gonna take a detour."

That son-of-a-bitch. Calling to check up on him, like he was an unreliable punk. Joe fumed. The Regents didn't know when to quit.

"Fuck him."

"Wow. Later," Pooch fled.

♦

The florists shops were closed, so he decided to take Colleen out for dinner. She had never rode on the bike. She'd get a kick out of it. Joe took a shower, then realized, like the Kris Kristofferson song, his choices were his cleanest dirty shirt. It ruled out any place fancy, but the Alhambra wasn't on his list anyway. They could sit in a back booth at the Famous Amos if his rustic appearance bothered her.

"Going out on a date with my girl. Don't wait up for me," He told Silent Sam, who responded by yawning.

Berry Avenue was a short zigzag away, down into the neighborhood of small 1940s era homes with compact yards barely able to contain two cars in the driveway. Colleen's shiny red Mustang was parked inside the carport. A light beamed from the kitchen window across its hood. Thanks to the Harley, there could be no doubt that someone had just arrived.

Should he knock? She didn't like surprises. But this was his home, and had been for the last eight years. He'd rented it when he came home from the service, and clever Colleen saved up a down payment and negotiated to buy it from the landlord. The man hadn't wanted to sell, but Colleen could look at someone with those steady serious blue eyes and her upturned nose and parted lips, as if she expected only the best from you, and you'd go ahead and do it.

That wasn't how she looked at Joe when she opened the door. Her strawberry blonde hair was tousled and the freckles across her nose were undusted by powder, as if she had already had a shower, but she definitely did not gaze at him with anticipation.

"Hey," Joe gave her a friendly grin.

Colleen, however, didn't open the door all the way, and held on to the knob inside. "Hello."

"I'm back in town."

"Okay."

Joe paused. "You want to go get something to eat? I'll take you for a ride on the bike."

"Your hair is almost as long as mine."

"I just want to talk to you, Coll, see how you are. We can go to Famous Amos if you want to. Or Beach Road Chicken Dinner." Hell, the neighbors has to be flocking to their windows by now and phoning each other.

The same thought must have struck her. She looked down the street at the quiet little houses, and reluctantly opened the door. "Come on in."

"Thanks," Joe said under his breath.

She let him pass, then closed the door firmly and leaned against it. Joe took a few steps away, giving her some room.

"Okay, what's wrong, other than I vanished off the face of the earth for awhile?"

"Nothing's wrong. I just thought you were gone for good. You took your death wish and went where people would help you out with it." She crossed her arms. "I cried about it, then I figured you and I were past needing each other and it was time to go on anyway. It's not like we were ever in love."

Damn. Joe had not given it that much thought. He apparently had some catching up to do to join the discussion, much less win it.

"Are you saying you don't want me here?"

"Are you saying you've come back for good?" She retorted.

When he opened his mouth to speak and couldn't utter a word, she nodded.

"Exactly what I thought." Colleen uncrossed her arms, and walked into the kitchen. "Do you want a sandwich?"

"Where's Cole?" He frowned, trying another tack. "What have you done with him?"

"He's curled up in the middle of the bed. He gave up on you, too. And no, you can't have him."

"He's my dog, Colleen, you aren't keeping him." He sat down at the kitchen table while she pulled a foil-covered ham from the refrigerator.

"Oh really? How are you going to carry him around on a motorcycle? You left him and you left me. End of discussion. I'll make you a sandwich and then you can leave."

"He didn't even come out to see me," Joe groused. "I shot somebody over him last year on that hunting lease."

"You think he remembers? Or cares? Dogs are lucky, they can move on beyond the stuff people do to them."

"I hope so," He didn't want to think about Smoky. This was going to hell fast, and he suddenly didn't want to fight about it.

"Sorry for bothering you. I'll call before I come over next time. Or do you want me to take my stuff now?"

She kept her back to him, sawing savagely through the ham with a large knife, her spiral curls shaking.

"I packed your stuff in cardboard boxes and put it all in the storage shed out back," She said, her voice not so spunky. "Your tools are at Buddy's. I was going to call your parents to see if they wanted to send someone to get them, but I didn't want them worrying about you. Your mom's called a few times. I made excuses."

"Thanks." His ribs felt like they were squeezing shut. She wasn't kidding around. Was this what fainting felt like?

She put the knife down and wiped her hands on a dish towel. "You'll need the money you sent me. I've still got it."

"No, it was for you."

"For safekeeping. If you rent somewhere, you'll need it for deposits and maybe a down payment on a car. Summer's almost over. I wouldn't want to ride a motorcycle when it's eighteen degrees."

He sat in the gloom, wondering why she didn't turn on the blue ceramic chandelier for some cheer. When she returned from the spare bedroom with an envelope in her hand, he waved it away.

"I don't have a place to keep it. And I can't afford to lose it." He took five twenties from the envelope and handed it back to her. "This'll do for gas money. Look, Coll, I don't have a place to stay. If you don't want to sleep together, that's fine, but I could use the couch."

"Not here." She looked down, her lashes hiding her eyes, and wet her lips. "I told you. I moved on."

Three beats passed before the truth hit him. Hard.

"You're seeing somebody?"

She nodded.

"Somebody I know?"

She nodded again. *Oh no.*

"Pooch?"

"What!" She stared.

"Pooch. Are you seeing Pooch?" It wasn't so farfetched. They were only a few years apart age-wise, even if Colleen was a respectable secretary for an insurance company and Pooch would always be a stoner.

"Our Pooch?" She gaped. "Are you serious? No! I'm seeing Pete Hines if it's any of your business."

Joe frowned, then shook his head.

"Pete Hines?" Damn. Responsible. Serious. A regular gentleman, Pete opened car doors for women and never cussed. Then Joe remembered how Pete never approved of him flirting with other women. What was it Pete said once? "If I had a girl like Colleen…"

Joe felt pole-axed. And he knew he had to leave. He stood up.

"We thought you were gone. He asked me out," Colleen said softly. "And I'm not going to see anybody else while Pete and I are dating. All this free love stuff just isn't me. You know that."

A blush tinted her face a rosy pink. She'd never been with anyone but Joe. Until now.

"So go find yourself another couch. And another dog. I'm tired of being scared all the time worrying where you are and if you're in trouble. Pete makes me feel safe. I'm sorry, Joe."

"Me too," He managed to say.

He took a few steps toward the door, lightheaded, then turned.

"Colleen, I've always wanted what was best for you. So if it's Pete, I'm glad. I'm definitely not good for anybody. I'll call you before I come over to move my stuff out," He hesitated. "And if you need anything, if anyone bothers you, ever, let the guys know at the Chopper Shop. They can find me. Good night."

"Good night," Her blue eyes glistened, but she let him walk out the door.

CHAPTER TWENTY-ONE

Joe headed for the side door to the Chopper Shop, the evening traffic noise scraping the insides of his head. His boot heels scuffed the asphalt, like he was wading in hot molasses.

"You knew it was coming. It was always a friendship with sex. You protected her from that piece of shit daddy of hers when she was little, and she returned the favor when you came home half-crazy from Korea."

"Who are you?" Someone asked faintly, maybe from the parking lot next door or a car stopped at the red light.

"Excellent question," He thought.

Coming home wasn't so easy after all. He'd wanted a good two weeks here to consider his options. Assuming he ever got a damned Regents patch, which wasn't likely after giving his sponsor a black eye, he might eventually enjoy the freedom of the road, and find a way to bust Big Alec's chops. On the way down from Atlanta, a comfortable existence where he knew everyone and who he was and how things worked seemed like the smarter option.

"What do you want?" The voice sounded fearful, and a little peevish. "Answer me. Who are you?"

Joe snapped to attention. The questions came from inside the building. The big back doors were closed for the night. Only the side door stood open. The parking lot was empty except for the U-Haul.

"I will fuckin' shoot, I mean it."

Shit. Joe pulled his .380 from his boot and carefully sidestepped away from the glare beaming from the open door. He edged over until he could see inside the building, and his heart sank. *Break it up, fast.*

"Anybody home? Rick?" He called out. "You there?"

"Joe? Come here, quick. I caught somebody trying to break in."

And the Somebody was sitting on the couch, expressionless behind the sunglasses. Shit, where was the duffle bag with the AK? Or did Silent Sam have the damn thing under his jacket? If he sprayed the room, he'd wipe out Rick and all the Regents' motorcycles.

"Rick, this is Sam. He's a friend of Denny's. A good friend," Joe emphasized. "Denny went home to Texas to see his dad, and Sam's hanging around until he gets back."

He edged closer. "Rick? You hear me?"

Rick wobbled on bare feet, curling his toes, as if the concrete tilted. The pistol in his hand traced squiggles in the air.

"Do you hear me?" Joe repeated slowly, then froze when Rick turned toward him with the pistol.

"Are you sure you know him?" His eyes were black discs, the blue irises gone.

"Yes, I met him in Atlanta. Put the pistol down. I'm not in a good mood and you're making me nervous."

"I can't see his eyes. I don't like that."

"It's what he likes that counts. Put the pistol down. It must be getting heavy by now."

Rick looked down at his hand.

"How did you know? I almost can't hold it."

"It's a good thing I got here in time. Put it down before it breaks your wrist." *Or I will.* Joe calculated fast. It would take four steps to reach Rick, but he had no idea how acid affected someone's reaction time. Suggestion seemed to work best. "Man, I can hear your arm bones snapping all the way over here. Put the damn thing down now, quick."

His mouth wide in horror, Rick let the pistol fall, then held his arm out to see if greenstick fractures had popped out of his skin.

"Go sit down. I'll get you a beer," Joe consoled.

As soon as Rick headed for a recliner in the corner, Joe stepped forward and swept up the pistol.

“So you’re a friend of Denny’s,” Rick said loudly, gripping his arm and panting with imaginary pain.

“He doesn’t talk,” Joe said over his shoulder.

“Damn. That’s rough, man. Bad Helen Keller trip. That’s why he couldn’t hear me.”

“I didn’t say he was deaf. He’s a good listener.”

Joe opened the small refrigerator in the office. Aha. Two Budweisers and a Dos Equii. And some unknown growth in plastic containers that might be early-stage penicillin. Joe returned to the display room, and handed them each a beer.

“I’ve got to go find some ass to kick. I just found out I’m a bum. Everybody cool?” It didn’t take long to pick up the hippie lingo. He’d better drop it before he walked into the Neighborhood Tavern. But then again, maybe a Northside or Westside redneck had meandered into the bar looking for a fight tonight, and waited for him at this very moment.

“We’re very cool,” Rick said. “But I may need you to drive me to the emergency room later for my arm.”

“Heal thyself,” Joe said and walked out.

♦

When he returned, tired and knuckles bruised, they were both on the couch, their bodies boneless from pot. A collection of burned-down roaches circled the ash tray. Someone had wrapped Rick’s arm in white tee shirts, perhaps so he wouldn’t bleed out from the imaginary fracture. Joe glanced down the hall. Since they had claimed the couch, he could have the bedroom. Maybe he could get four hours of sleep.

The phone burred in the office as he walked by, startling him. Rick didn’t budge. Two a.m.. Seven rings later, it stopped. Joe hesitated. It might be one of the crew calling for help, Car Punk or High Hal broke down somewhere. He waited long enough for someone to feed a dime into a payphone, and it began ringing again. The office still stunk so he pulled the cord as far as it would reach, almost to the hall.

"Hello?"

He heard music, bottles clinking, girlish laughter. No one spoke. Joe started to take it from his ear, then heard a sound.

"Who is this?" A soft quiet voice questioned, the last word ending on a high note.

He'd taken a few hard punches to the abdomen earlier at the Tavern, but this one knocked the breath out of him.

"The Knight of Swords," He replied and was gratified to hear her exhale.

He leaned against the door, listening to Steppenwolf in the background. *This is so damn screwed up.*

"Hey," Kitty said. "I was calling to make sure you got down there okay."

"Everything's fine. It's good to be home."

"What did the Chopper Shop guys say about the bikes?"

"They're salvageable. It could take a while to get them running again. Rick hasn't been feeling too hot."

"You're staying until they get them fixed?"

"Yeah. They need my help. At least two weeks." *Or the rest of my life.*

"Oh. Well, I just wanted to make sure you got there okay."

Joe couldn't help himself. "Why didn't you just ask Jess? He already called here to check up on me. He didn't tell you?"

Of course not. He shouldn't have thrown it in her face. She struggled, then gave up.

"As long as you're okay," She said. "I've got to go, I'm at Mina's. I don't want to run up her phone bill."

Joe stared at the poster of Jim Morrison. He didn't want her remembering him as an asshole.

"Be careful, okay?"

"I'm not worried about me," She said softly, and hung up.

♦

He worked relentlessly for a week, waiting for a phone call to summon him back to Atlanta, but none came. Rick stayed in the funky office. He didn't care that two other people now had keys to the shop, or that frames and fenders and tanks littered the benches and floor. Joe worked beside them all day, then headed up to the Tavern each night to hang out with the neighborhood men.

When the weekend arrived, the weather was the sort that made people move to Florida. Joe suggested a ride to the beach for a pizza and to check out the bikinis. Car Punk made a few phone calls and pulled together two dozen riders.

Joe found himself at the head of the pack, the others following his lead as they jammed down Atlantic, the wind in their face. It was a strange feeling, riding down the highway into the sun, leading the way. He sensed he had done it before, in a different place and time.

They drifted from bar to bar, depending on the women and the band, and watched the sun set over the Intracoastal. A good day, a fine evening.

When they returned late Saturday night, the regulars were stunned to see Rick standing in the paint booth, with the knucklehead tank on his bench.

"What's going on, California?" High Hal advanced slowly, cringing.

The shop didn't smell like paint thinner so maybe it wasn't too late.

"Forgot to ask him if he wanted the same colors," Rick said.

"Stick with the original."

"Pooch is almost finished with the frame. I've got to get started on the tank."

"Want me to sand it?" Brush asked hoarsely.

"Only if I get in a jam. I want to try."

"That ain't my idea of a practice piece," Hippie Dave muttered.

Rick glared at them weakly, and they were relieved to see that his irises were once again dark blue.

"You don't think I can do it?"

"No!" Five men replied in unison.

“Well, go screw yourselves. This will be the best tank I’ve done since leaving the west coast.”

“What did you drop to make you think that?” Car Punk said snidely.

“I’m straight,” Rick retorted.

“You’re don’t smell as bad, either. Do I need to go throw some degreaser in the shower, see if I can break up the sludge?”

“You can go scrub it with your Brillo head for all I care,” Rick retorted.

“Women love my naturally curly hair. Everywhere I go, they follow me to ask if they can touch it,” Car Punk declared.

“Is this going to last for a while?” High Hal surprised them with his vicious challenge. “We’ve got too much work to do for you to go tripping. Either you’re with us or you aren’t. And if you aren’t, get the hell out of here.”

“I’m done with it for now,” Rick said evenly. “Kitty called me this afternoon, and talked to me for a long time. She feels this isn’t the right time to cross over. It would have happened already. So I have to wait.”

None of them cared if it was pure bullshit. They wanted Rick back at the helm: handling the volatile Regents, juggling egos, yelling about maintaining order in the parts room so they could find a kickstand without looking all day, and managing the dope trade. Most of the Chopper Shop crew wouldn’t dispute Kitty’s abilities anyway. Sometimes a little psychic intervention came in handy.

“Well, if she says wait, I’d damn sure wait,” Car Punk said sincerely. “I’d—“

He stopped in mid-sentence, staring at the open side door.

A policeman stood there, arms at his side, holster unsnapped. The laughter in the paint booth stopped, but the cop was used to getting that kind of reaction.

“Heard you were back in town,” He said to Joe. “Got a minute?”

Without waiting for an answer, he stepped outside.

Spence Gilbertson eyed his hair and beard without hiding his contempt, but accepted Joe's hand when he offered it.

"How's Brenda?"

"She's a cop's wife. How do you think she is?"

"Tried to talk her out of it, remember?" Joe said with a faint smile.

"What's going on with you these days? You decided you want to be a motorcycle bum?"

"I like riding."

"It doesn't seem to like you."

"Spence, we've been friends a long time. I might be home for good. Don't shit in my hat."

"Looks like you're feeding into their shit instead of vice versa."

"Well, I did find out that their paranoia is justified," Joe said. "You see all those bikes in there? That happened when two hundred of us were arrested at the Talladega Speedway. They tore up the bikes, they burned our clothes and sleeping bags, and I personally saw them stealing guitars, radios and cash. The charges were bullshit, but they had four branches of law enforcement ready to shoot anybody. Not all cops are like you, Spence, that's what I found out."

"You also found out that good old boy stuff you run isn't quite as believable with that extra hair covering your redneck. I never had you figured for someone who'd let himself go."

"My hair doesn't change who I am," Joe said.

"Something did," Spence told him, and stared coldly into the shop. "I shouldn't have listened when you said you'd handle the trouble with that asshole Regents boss from down south. I should have gotten the squad together and shut this place down when he busted Pooch's head open."

"I'm not done with it yet. I told you I'd handle it and I will," Joe insisted quietly. "I want you to leave the Chopper Shop guys alone. They aren't Regents. They're just trying to earn a living."

"So am I, Joe," Spence smiled tightly and stepped away from the door. "See you around."

"Now you're acting like a cop," Joe said, infuriated. "If this place goes under, good people lose their investment."

"And if you don't handle your payback correctly, bad people will kill you," Spence hissed. "You damn near bought it the first time. You won't get a second chance with that guy."

"Yes, I will," Joe thought. "Because Alec won't be expecting it this time. He thinks he got away with it."

♦

Early Monday morning, Rick came out of his office with his hair brushed and pulled back, and a shaky Fu Manchu mustache freshly shaven on his gaunt face. He dragged away the plastic from the paint booth, sat down on a stool and began sanding the knucklehead's tank with cautious strokes. Silent Sam fiddled with the radio dials until he found a country station, John Denver going home to his mountain mama.

"Did you ever go back to California?"

Joe watched him ease the sandpaper over a slight scrape in the paint, testing it with his fingertip to judge the depth.

"No. They were gone. And things change. Even if you're gone a week."

He had that right.

"Maybe what Thomas Wolfe said is true. You can't go home again." Rick turned the tank to a different angle. "Everybody's got their own truth."

"All I know is, I feel better here than Atlanta."

Rick picked up a square of smaller grit.

"You feel like you belong here. Even with the changes."

"Yeah, even with the changes," Joe said.

"Imagine, though, assuming changes are actually evolution. Science. If time goes forward, it should go back. Imagine if you could go back."

"How would you know where to stop?" Joe shook his head.

"Exactly. Would you stop and fix some of the little things, or would you choose some defining moment, something that tore you in half?"

Joe hesitated, and stole a glance at Rick's eyes. Was he stoned again? No, the irises were blue, the pupils normal-sized, focused on his work. Did Rick think like this all the time, or did the acid leave him with more questions than answers?

"I have to keep moving forward, Rick. If I went back, I'm afraid I couldn't find my way home again," Joe admitted.

"Yeah, you'd get caught up trying to make everything right and screw up history for the next couple of centuries," Rick smiled faintly. "Instead of saying what you have to say and coming back home. Whatever home is."

Rick squinted down at the scarred knucklehead tank.

"I can have this ready in a week. If I were you, I'd try to figure out where or what home is to you fairly quick."

PART TWO

CHAPTER TWENTY-TWO

Denny had regrets long before he hit the Louisiana state line. First, that he had given his mother three hundred bucks that he needed for gas back to Atlanta, and second, leaving Port Arthur so late in the evening. Truck stops were few and far between on this stretch of I-10, and the sportster tank on his '69 shovelhead chopper required a fuel stop every seventy miles.

He wanted to run wide open, get the hell out of Texas, but it would provoke the cops from their hidden lairs. He'd wind up in a jail cell too close to home. So he focused on the road signs and tried to keep his speed down. The refinery smell of Port Arthur faded into swamp funk and road-kill. Another ten miles to Lake Charles. Forever to Lafayette, then Baton Rouge.

He had the nerve-ass bad. Going home did that to him. *Home, shit.* A ragged dump with busted screens and soft floors. Mildew growing in the dark corners because the old man had been too cheap to let them turn on the lights. Even when he was gone for weeks at a time on a Gulf rig, he made sure no one ran up the electric bill. Last time Denny was there, the old man came home early from a poker game gone wrong and caught Debbie watching *Shindig*! He took it out on Debbie. And Denny took it out on him.

It took five Jefferson County cops to pull him loose. The judge said he could go to jail or to the Army Recruiter's office. He hadn't been back to Texas until a letter reached him at the Chicago clubhouse a month ago saying the Marlboros had finally caught up with the old man. Denny didn't care, but his mother had scrawled "Please, son" on the blue-lined paper, and he remembered how scarred her hands were from working in the rose fields. Long ago, before she got worn out, she used to pull the old man off him and take a beating for him even when she was pregnant with one of the girls.

When he showed up at the front door, she had been thrilled to see him. She didn't say anything about his long dark hair, the beard cut into a Vee like Satan, or his open denim shirt and dirty dungarees. She stepped back to let him in, babbling. And he realized she really didn't believe he was there, that he had come home.

"I worried about you so much, son. We went months without a letter when you were in Vietnam. I guess…I guess the mail wasn't too reliable over there? It was like that when your daddy was in Italy, and you were just a baby. Our mailman got so tired of me waiting by the mailbox. Some days he wouldn't even slow down or look at me. He'd just wave and go on to Mrs. Blanding's house." The smile on her face tightened. "I don't know what I would have done if I hadn't had you. The waiting was so awful."

To him, the nicotine-stained ceilings seemed lower and the walls closer. But he looped his big arms around her, and cradled her. She had no idea what to do, and stood still. He had never been allowed to hug her when his dad was around.

"And here you are waiting again." He kissed the top of her head. "Mm, you got a perm?"

Since the old man wasn't there to demand all her time, she'd been to the beauty shop. Her straight black hair made her a target. People assumed she was Mexican, living in the wrong neighborhood. His father hurled "Mestizo bitch" at her when he was drunk, like it was an insult.

"Honey, do you know what a Mestizo is?" She asked once when he was ten and they were driving all over town trying to find a pair of shoes that would fit.

"It's what he calls you," Denny replied. "So it ain't nice."

"No, it's fine. It's why we can't find shoes for you. A Mestizo is part Spanish, part Indian. And those Indians were Karankawas. They're supposed to be gone now but guess what?" She patted his knee as they left Kinney's Shoes and headed for Thom McCan's. "We're not gone. You're proof."

"I am?" What the heck was a Karankawa?

"They were over six feet tall. Even back in the olden days, when the Spaniards weren't much bigger than me. Can you imagine what the Spaniards thought when they saw Indians six feet tall? It must have been terrifying!"

That, Denny could follow.

"I'd like to be terrifying," He decided.

Almost twenty years later, his reflection in her china cabinet confirmed he'd achieved his goal. He wondered how she could be so accepting of his appearance, how she talked to him like he'd been gone a month, not years. Maybe it was because she could finally talk without worrying about the repercussions. Denny hung around the house for a week, repairing what he could, bleaching away the mildew before moving the furniture to the middle of the room and painting over the orange nicotine tint on the walls and ceilings.

"My Lord! I'll have to get some new curtains. Look how bright the room is now." His mother stood in the kitchen doorway, her amber eyes sparkling and small hands clasped.

"New curtains would be great," He agreed. "And some pictures. Don't I have nieces and nephews? You don't have any pictures of the grandbabies?"

"Why of course I do." Her smile faltered. "They're in my room."

"Let's see."

Her room was tiny, once shared by the two youngest girls. The top of an old maple dresser was strewn with framed photographs.

"Whew, what's wrong with Sandra's boy? That young'un is stone ugly."

"Denny! He is not. He's the sweetest thing, just like his daddy. Elmer's good to Sandra, he's just homely."

"You aren't hiding the pictures in here 'cause of that boy, are you?" He teased.

"No. It was just easier…well…"

Of course. Any kind of love she openly displayed, even for a grandchild, was a threat to his father's hold on her.

"Pick a few—not little Frankenstein—and we'll set them on the china cabinet. I can hang 'em on the walls, too."

She didn't move. "I should wait."

"Why?"

"He's not dead yet, Denny."

"Neither are these kids." He didn't mean to say it so viciously.

She flinched, then looked up at him curiously, her brown eyes seeing more than he intended. Her capacity for compassion amazed him.

"You're right, son," She said softly. "These children are our family."

"More Karankawas."

Stunned, she almost dropped the photos she had collected.

"You remember that?"

"Sure.*" I remember all sorts of things, and if I told anyone, it would be you, because you could handle it better than most grown men I know. But it would be shitty and selfish to burden you with the things I saw*."

There had been weeping adults, in shock, but it was the kids, dear Jesus, orphans trotting down the road, skinny little sisters staggering under the weight of baby brothers clinging to their necks, dazed toddlers trailing and finally left behind on that bombed-out highway because he couldn't carry them all and his sergeant was yelling at him, and then the NVA hit them again.

"I can't believe you remember that." She shook her head and swept into the living room with a stack of pictures.

"Was it true?" He asked, not moving from the little room.

"Of course. My grandmother told me about the Karankawas, and she was definitely from way back. She looked like an old Aztec like you see on National Geographic, with a big honking nose. Like yours." She wanted him to smile, so when he finally turned around, he took a deep breath and grinned.

He let her cook for him, frying okra and chicken and pork chops, browning bread crumbs and onions on a squash casserole, and his absolute favorite, stirring up bubbling white gravy in a cast iron pan for a pan of cat-head biscuits. Each evening, after supper, she went to the hospital by herself. When she insisted he hand over his filthy clothes for the washer one morning, and hinted he might want to take a bath himself, he knew what was coming

"We've always been clean people, Denny. No matter how hard we worked, we were clean when we went to bed."

Or to the grocery store, or a hospital. That evening, his mother said: "I'm going up to see him. Do you want to go?"

No, but he owed her. After dinner, he fired up the bike and followed her shabby Corvair through the dusty streets. Tension knotted between his shoulders with each passing block. "This is for her and all that thumping she caught so you wouldn't go to first grade with a black eye," he reminded himself.

At St. Mary Hospital, a pre-World War II warren, his boots struck hard on the tile halls. People turned to stare, some discreetly, most point-blank gaping. They navigated a maze of corridors, then went up a lurching elevator to a floor where no amount of bleach could dispel the scent of human decay.

"He's in here," His mother whispered, pushing open the door to a tiny room. "Ed? Ed, look who's here. It's Denny! Honey?"

The old man wasn't even sixty, but appeared mummified beneath folded white sheets, a small fluorescent light over the bed.

"How do you like those 20-watts, you son-of-a-bitch?" Denny thought, but kept his mouth shut.

"He knows you're here," His mother said. "Say something."

But Denny couldn't. There was nothing to say. He backed into a corner out of the way, and waited around a few hours. Despite the best efforts of the nuns and nurse's aides, the room stank like piss and crap and diseased flesh. His mom sat beside the bed, refolding the sheets, combing the old man's hair away from his face. How the hell could she still care?

Two of his sisters showed up after they'd put their kids to bed. They said hello and kept their distance. But when Debbie came bouncing in, she ignored his long hair and rough clothes and gave him a big hug.

"You're still skinny." She craned her neck.

"Not as skinny as he is." Denny gazed at the man in the bed.

"Yeah. Well." She glanced at her older sisters and tried again. "Hey, I'm getting married next month. Johnny Mousteau. Remember him?"

Denny looked down at her. "I thought you were fifteen."

"I'll be sixteen next month. Will you be here? It won't be fancy. And you'd have to promise not to eat all the cake. Mama's gonna make a three-layered white cake with roses." An idea suddenly occurred to her. "Denny, you could give me away!"

"Debbie," The oldest sister hissed, glancing at their father.

"So? I wouldn't ask him anyway."

"He can hear you."

"I don't care," She declared.

"Deborah Sue!"

"Would you give me away, Denny?" She took him by the arm. "Please?"

"I won't be here, sugar." Denny reached to pull his chain wallet out of his back pocket. "Here. Get a nice dress and flowers or somethin'." He handed the twenties to his mother, and gripped Debbie hard by the shoulder. "And tell that little Mousteau bastard if he lays a hand on you, I'll come back and kill him."

"I won't…I mean, I will…" The women stared open-mouthed at the money.

Denny shoved his wallet back in his pocket and edged toward the door.

"Son?" His mother gazed up at him. "Where you going?"

"Got stuff to take care of up north. I can't stay gone too long."

"But..." She glanced at the withered man in the bed. "It won't be much longer, Denny. He'll be gone soon."

"Twenty years ago wouldn't have been soon enough," He told them and stalked out the door.

♦

Now he rode until the lights of Port Arthur faded, swallowed in the thick Gulf humidity. Two hundred miles on the shovelhead made his eyes burn, flushed the questions out of his head. "Why were you like that? Why did you want the air she breathed? What made you beat your own kids instead of loving them and protecting them? A man's supposed to take care of his kids." But it didn't matter now. Once the piece of shit was dead and buried, she and the girls and grandbabies could enjoy themselves.

A sign up ahead flashed *New Orleans*. Seventy-six miles. Finally. The tension across his shoulders eased. One a.m. and traffic became heavy, drunks and gamblers and partying tourists, all descending on the ancient city and French Quarter. He worked his way down the side streets to Dauphine, the rattle of his forty-inch pipes echoing off the brick streets and balconies.

Fat Jack's Custom Tattoos occupied a narrow two-story house near the corner of Dauphine and Toulouse. Nearby, a few girls precariously perched in the open windows of a century-old bordello.

"Hey, Slim, come on up and let's party!" A cute gap-toothed brunette called to him. "Got some new gold!"

He took a deep breath, smelled pot and beer and fried shrimp. Four different blues tunes floated up around the antique grillwork, and a woman had to be dancing somewhere to that raunchy sax. Denny almost smiled. Goodbye, Texas, hello, New Orleans. He waved at the cute brunette, then stowed his helmet and goggles and walked inside the tattoo shop. Fat Jack sat humped over a pretty blonde girl, his eyes never leaving her shoulder where he painted a curving red dragon.

"Need a place to crash for the night."

"You got it, brother," Fat Jack said without looking up. "I'd offer ya something to eat but you know the ol' lady never cooks nothin' but horse cock and beans."

"Thanks, man, I'll pass."

"Grab a beer and check out the baggie. It's some strange shit."

Denny strode to the refrigerator and helped himself to a beer, then rolled a fat joint to go with it. Looking over the blonde in her little pink halter top and hip-hugger bell-bottoms, he wondered why she picked a dragon. She turned her head slightly, checking him out. Or maybe she was just trying to get her mind off her stinging shoulder.

"Is that the new ink they were talking about?" Denny pulled up a chair and straddled it. "The colors kick ass."

"Yeah. Mixed it myself. It don't fade as fast as the old shit. Korean vets been coming in to get their tats freshened up. And some guys going to 'Nam. Say they want I.D. tatted on their bodies in case the dog tags get blown off."

Denny watched the dragon come alive under Fat Jack's needle. The man was an asshole, but he knew his shit.

"I want you to do my club tat with your new stuff."

Fat Jack looked up for the first time. "It'd be an honor, man. You wanta do it now? The cunt can wait."

"No, I got some partying to do tonight. Been on the road for awhile."

"You're a Regent too?" The little blonde smiled, cutting a sideways glance at his denim vest, then flinched when Fat Jack growled in her ear: "Don't ask stupid questions."

"I'm sorry," Her smile vanished and she looked a little queasy.

"Here," Denny offered her the beer. "It's easier if you've got a buzz on."

He meant both the tat and Fat Jack breathing in her ear.

"Thanks."

Denny figured Fat Jack would be busy with the tat for a while. He was suddenly hungry, and wanted another beer. Definitely some pussy. He was getting his second wind, and felt strung from head to toe with hot barbed wire.

"What the hell is in that pot?"

Fat Jack focused on the dragon's fangs. "I ain't sure. It screwed up my balance, like I was on a roller-coaster. I had to sleep here. It's a weird high."

"No shit," Denny frowned as an icy blue tongue flared from the neon sign in the window. "I think your light's shorting out. I'm gonna go find something to eat. See you in a while."

"You goin' to the whorehouse, watch it. They got clap running through the place. Of course, anything's better than what my old lady puts on a platter."

The little blonde's face went from pink to green. Denny decided it was time to leave. He stepped outside and sniffed the air again. Teriyaki, shrimp-fried rice, garlic and ginger wafted from restaurants and tiny cafes in all directions. Two giggling hippie girls toted quart cups brimming with pink fizz. They jumped when he lurched in front of them, splashing their tie-dye tops with rum.

"Now you've got to lick it off!" The tall one laughed, thrusting two soaked tits his way, but her friend grabbed her by the wrist.

"Are you crazy? He's a Regent!" Rum and pink ice splattered in their wake.

The cute brunette wasn't hanging out the window down the street. She either fell, or a trick showed up. Schallinger's Deli over on Bourbon Street was his safest bet, making sandwiches at 3 a.m. The barricades had been moved and the streets were open to traffic again, but his aching ass deserved a break from the shovelhead. It was faster to walk, if he could figure out which boot went first.

Denny widened his eyes several times, and a cluster of drunk tourists quickly split to go around him. It felt like he was going to fall over, hyper-aware of smells and voices and the trash in the street, so close he could pick up the empty bottles with his teeth. Yet he remained upright, floating and striding down Bourbon Street, the buildings rearing back a polite distance from him.

The black women who worked for Schallinger saw stoned and intoxicated people every night, but their faces changed when he swam up to the counter.

"Club sandwich, everything but the hooves," He said clearly.

"Ain't seen you around in a while," One of young women spoke when he put a dollar in the tip bucket. "Ever'thing okay wit' you?"

"Shut up, Chelle," An old woman hissed.

"I just aksin'. Long, tall drink of water like him, he ain't afraid of nothin'."

"What am I supposed to be afraid of, cher?" He asked.

She faltered as the chatter around her stopped, and got busy making another sandwich. The old woman beside her glanced across the street, then back up at Denny, her eyes deep.

"Sorry, baby, she didn't mean nothin'." The woman handed him a sandwich wrapped in white paper.

Denny moved carefully down the sidewalk, and crossed the street, aiming for a bar. Did he look as high as he felt? Someone was staring at him. He opened his eyes wide again. Overhead, the ironwork balconies creaked with people who just couldn't shut it off and go to bed. Beneath them, stoned college kids openly shared a joint, and a middle-aged couple stepped over a woman passed out at the curb. Nobody was paying any attention to his buzz.

"Hey, lovie." A drag queen in a poppy-red robe floated by, blowing him a kiss.

Denny realized he was squeezing the sandwich. Maybe a beer would take the edge off whatever the hell raced through his system. He stumbled slightly going in the door. The bar had two rooms, both facing Bourbon Street. One held a long row of pool tables, the other sported a square bar. On the juke box, Don McLean drove his Chevy to a dry levee. Denny headed for a clean spot at the bar, hooked one boot in the stool rung to steady himself, sat down and unwrapped the sandwich.

"Mister?" The bartender stood frozen. Only his hand moved, wiping a glass over and over with a thick white rag.

It made Denny dizzy so he looked down at the scratched wooden bar and the mustard oozing from the fresh fat bread. "I want a Bud," Denny sank his fangs into the sandwich. "Draft."

"Mister, you might want to go someplace else."

Denny put the sandwich down, mustard and crumbs littering his beard.

"What'd you say?" Was that asshole telling him he couldn't eat in there?

But the bartender had nothing left to say. He backed up, the motion sucking Denny's eyeballs with it. Two tourists on the far side of the bar stared beyond Denny into the pool room, then got up and hurried out the door.

Denny swallowed the thick bread, forcing it down his tight throat, and reached down the bar for an abandoned bottle of Jax. He drained it, and turned to look over his shoulder. A half dozen Bayou Runners headed his way, pool sticks and beer bottles in hand, stealthily slipping on brass knuckles. A short dark man pulled out a blade, flicking it open smoothly.

Christ! He didn't have a damn thing with him except a fuckin' ham sandwich. The serious shit was stowed on the bike. They came in fast and jerky like a movie coming off the reels, spreading out too quick to follow.

"Hey mother-fucker, are you stupid or what? You wanta die, is that it? Coming in our territory with that pussy patch on?"

Denny reached for an empty mug on the bar, but something struck him behind his ear and all reflexes failed. His snakeskin boot jammed itself behind a rung, and the momentum took him to the floor, tangled up in the stools. The men closed in, cracking pool sticks across his ribs, breaking them across his knee caps.

Get up! The stool legs snared his left arm, bending it backward. "Where is my damned foot?" He lifted his right arm over his head, fending off the wooden sticks bouncing across his skull. Bones snapped and lightning pain shot up to his shoulder. Boots sank deep in his guts, plunging between his intestines. He took a deep breath and gagged on the puke.

Oh fuck, I'm gonna die before the old man. See you in hell, you old bastard. Someone kicked him in the forehead, then the nose.

Bone exploded and the tight skin ruptured open. Mother-fucker that hurt! Enraged, he kicked out with the steel-toed cowboy boots, tugging furiously on his trapped arm. If he could get on his feet, he'd have a chance. Broke face or not, he could swing, but they crowded in so close they had to be hitting each other.

"Get his patch!"

Oh shit no. Denny pushed his back against the bar, protecting the regal lion. Knives came out, silver flashes near his face.

"Bastard. You came in the wrong place."

Cold steel sliced between his ribs. It was a new kind of hurt, icy and burning at the same time. Denny took a breath, whistled instead. They were slashing now, blades sawing through fabric and flesh. Someone lost their footing and slid down with a loud curse. Warm liquid bubbled in the back of his throat, weighing his head down on the dusty concrete. A shudder ran through him, disconnecting nerves as it went. He was leaving, but they were taking his patch, he had to stay, fight.

Hands yanked off the remnants of his patch, and he was suddenly cold. They pawed at his wallet. He hovered inside his skull, watching.

"He's got a bike around here somewhere."

"Go find it. Lado, get the truck and drive it around back."

"I'm dead," Thought Denny. "And I just wanted a fuckin' beer."

CHAPTER TWENTY-THREE

They left town at twilight and rode straight through the night. Shown no mercy, the engines pinged and hissed at the fuel stops. A brutal acceleration and they were back up on the interstate, running hard, the lines becoming one long white streak, the wind threatening to tear them from their seats.

Wind-burned and wired, they made a six-hour trip in four and a half hours, chugging down off I-75 at eleven p.m. Joe and Silent Sam throttled up the driveway on Fifth Street and parked by the garage. A beat-up blue Ford van, the Impala, and a big Mercury sat there. Lights beamed weakly at the bunkhouse and a curtain moved, but no one came out. Joe left his gear strapped to the panhead and motioned to Silent Sam.

Without announcing themselves, they strode through the back door of the clubhouse, through the empty kitchen, and found the Atlanta Regents slumped around the plywood table, somber and quiet. Cigarettes burned relentlessly, hazing the dismal crimson glow of the lava lamp. Joe walked through it, scattering the smoke into frenzied trails, and stood by the old couch.

"We're having a meeting, Probate," Dudley said wearily. "What do you want?"

"I've been to a National," Joe said. "Am I going to New Orleans with you as a patched Regent?"

No one answered. They had not slept since they got the news early that morning.

"You didn't get a hundred percent vote," Smitty finally spoke up.

Joe waited a few beats, then swung his blackest look to Bugsy, who chose to study the lava lamp. They let that punk's opinion keep him from joining them? Or had it been Jess, sitting there without saying hello or go fuck yourself, his gaze lost in the smoke. Joe smiled faintly, his lip curled. His insides had turned to stone after the phone call this afternoon, and this sealed it. He belonged to no one but himself. Forget friendships. From here on, he would deal with plans and action. He owed no one but Denny.

"Your club, your call," He said and walked out.

Silent Sam followed him down the back steps and stopped beside his bike.

"I've got a spare work bench in there," Joe pulled his bedroll from the panhead and headed for the garage. "Bring your stuff."

Sam took off his sunglasses and folded them. His anxious eyes held a question.

"We should have gone straight there from Jacksonville," Joe agreed, exasperated. "Like that damned patch matters anymore. If you want to go, Sam, just be careful. I'll be along when these assholes decide to do something. I don't know my way around New Orleans and I'll need them, for a while."

Sam nodded, then stepped forward, offering his hand. "Let's hope for the best," Joe said, and repeated. "Be careful."

♦

He was chilled after the long ride, and the sun-warmed interior of the big garage felt good on his skin. A small pole light behind the garage defined the shadows inside. He knew his way around and didn't bother to turn on the overheads. Joe tossed his bedroll up on the bench and worked the fasteners loose, careful not to let his stash of weapons fall out.

Behind him, the side door squeaked open. Tennis shoes padded softly on the concrete and stopped several yards away.

"Hey," She said.

He glanced over his shoulder. She wore a pair of jeans and a peasant blouse, and had pulled her hair into a messy ponytail. Even in the dull light, he could see her eyes were swollen from crying.

"I'm glad you came back." Each word came out with great effort. She was exhausted. But he couldn't afford to care.

"I owe Denny. He saved our lives in Daytona," Joe reminded her unnecessarily, rolling out his new tee-shirts and socks.

She bit her lip. "I should have seen this coming. I can't believe there was nothing. I didn't pick up anything."

"Maybe it's the Talladega curse," Joe mocked. "Everything went to shit there and just keeps rolling downhill."

"At least we were right about something watching us." She missed his sarcasm. "But I never felt anything about Denny."

"You'd be pretty busy if you picked up shit from everyone around you."

Outside, a car drove by with the windows down, voices chattering excitedly. A rush of cheerfulness, gone quickly, leaving them in an awful stillness.

"Why aren't you at work?"

"Dorrie and Flossie are the only ones who went. They wanted to get out of here," She said hoarsely. "I couldn't go dance and act like everything's fine. Are…are you going to sleep in here tonight?"

"Yeah."

"Joe…would you please talk to Jess before you go to New Orleans? You can't trust anybody there. They've called the goon squad from Louisville and Chicago. It's going to be rough. They don't normally take probates on trips like this. You've got to work things out with Jess now."

"I don't have to do shit for Jess. I owe Denny. That's the only reason I'm here now."

She waited, but he wouldn't look at her.

"Jess isn't doing too hot. He has spells. Like yours, but it takes him a while to get over them."

"No shit," Joe thought. "You should have seen him with the fire extinguisher at the stockade."

He folded and refolded the tee shirts, stuffed another box of bullets in a sock and rolled a pair of Levi's around them.

"We've all got problems," He said. "Right now, the problem is in New Orleans."

“After that’s taken care of, are you coming back to Atlanta?”

When he didn’t answer, she reached in her back pocket and stepped forward. “I brought you something.”

She moved up beside him and laid the tarot card down on a black tee shirt. The card was old, the sides chipping from years of shuffling: his card, the Knight of Swords, charging forward fearless and relentless.

“I didn’t notice ‘till the other day. In this deck, he has a little white dog at the bottom of the card. It’s usually on The Fool.”

“That’s kinda appropriate, wouldn’t you say?” But he refused to look. He didn’t want to be reminded.

“Keep it with you wherever you go. Maybe it will bring you luck. I don’t have to throw cards to know you’ll need it.”

“Kitty, I know I’m expendable. But I’m not doing this for the Regents, or a patch, or your boyfriend. This is for Denny. He saved my life, and he didn’t have to. He chose to help us and went up against the other Regents to do it. That’s a man that deserves respect, to be honored. The rest of ‘em can kiss my cracker ass.”

CHAPTER TWENTY-FOUR

They headed due west, the sun radiating across the cracks in the bug-spattered windshield. It was almost five p.m. when they neared the Alabama state line. The two-lane blacktop had taken them through long stretches of pines and small towns. Just when Joe thought things were going to be all right, that his careful speed-limit driving and fresh-shaven face had paid off, a faded green sign officially announced: "Alabama Agricultural Inspection Station Ahead. All Trucks Prepare to Stop."

"Shit," Smitty said from the passenger seat.

Thirty yards ahead, a small white booth with tinted windows sat at a desolate crossroads, with a Stop sign and pull-out lane in front of it. A tall middle-aged man in uniform sat in a state car, the door open and one leg out, folding up a jacket.

"Keep going," Smitty told Joe. "He's worried about tomatoes, not what we got."

"If he knew what we had in this damned van, he'd be worried enough to radio for a tank division," Joe thought.

He kept driving into the sun, watching the speedometer, counting down until the little white building became a speck in the side mirror.

"Oh shit," Smitty hissed between clenched teeth. "You dumb son-of-a-bitch."

Joe saw the blue lights, and felt them spiral around his intestines a time or two, tying a knot. He sat up straight.

"What's wrong?" Dudley looked up from the van's rear floor. The seven men with him jerked out of their stupor and reached under the sleeping bags.

"Inspection station cop," Smitty told them.

"This isn't a truck," Joe said, half to himself.

"No, it's a van that bottoms out every time we hit a bump," Smitty retorted. The van was a last-minute choice when the other two deals didn't work out for Greasy. "We can't outrun him. He's got a state car and he'll call for reinforcements. We've gotta stop."

"How many of 'em are there?" Dudley questioned.

"Just one," Smitty said.

They fell silent, barely breathing. Just one. Who would do it? Whoever drew the short straw?

Joe tightened his grip on the wheel. "What if he wants to look inside?"

Dudley stared at Joe, leaving no doubt as to what he meant, and said quietly: "Make sure he doesn't."

"Here, show him this," Smitty passed Joe a worn driver's license from his wallet. "You're Jimmy Cobb, if he asks."

Was he supposed to give the cop time to ask? Joe hit the blinker and eased off the highway when he came to wide patch of dirt beside the mucky ditch.

"Leave it running," Dudley told him.

In the side mirror, Joe watched the state cop pull over several yards behind them. He used the door to leverage himself out of the car. In his sixties, he slumped in the uniform, a wide black leather belt cutting into his paunch. He ambled crookedly on the pavement like his feet hurt in those shiny uniform shoes. A few years from retirement.

Mister, I may be expendable, but you damn sure just got promised a trip to a gator hole if you decide to be a hero.

"Keep this on a country station. No hard rock." Joe turned up the volume until the Statler Brothers warbled across the stagnant ditch into the pines.

Heart beating hard, Joe slid from the driver's seat. He met the man about a yard from the back of the van, near the chugging rusty exhaust. Summoning his best lop-sided grin, Joe stuck out his hand.

"Jimmy Cobb. How's everything in Alabama?"

The inspector came to a slow halt.

"Reckon it's all right," He said and reluctantly put out his hand, not getting too close.

His name tag said Raymond Godwin. The skin around his eyes and cheeks sagged down into jowls like a good-natured bloodhound. There was nothing stupid in his frank appraisal.

"Where you heading to, Mr. Cobb?"

The van had Houston County plates. Joe didn't know what address the fake driver's license had on it, and he didn't dare give their true destination.

"My brother-in-law's place down near Daphne," Joe said. The town's name had always intrigued him and came floating back to him now.

"Your van's riding kinda low, Mr. Cobb. You carrying produce?"

Oh mister, please don't do this to either one of us. Joe worked hard to keep a smile on his face. He knew Smitty was watching the mirrors and would signal the others if things went bad. Joe hoped they could not hear him over the chugging exhaust. If they'd just give him time, if they wouldn't panic, if he could keep the man away from the doors…

"I've got a load of junked transmissions I'm gonna try and fix for my brother-in-law. He's the wheeler-dealer, I'm the mechanic."

The inspector assessed the squatting tires.

"How many transmissions you reckon you got in there?"

Joe raised a rueful eyebrow. "Too many, I guess. Some are just pieces but I think I can work with 'em."

The man looked at him with those hound dog eyes and shifted on his feet as if he couldn't get comfortable. Gout, bunions, arthritis, or all three. This man was not the enemy. He was just in the wrong place at the wrong time, like so many other people who went to a job one day and never got to go home. Joe knew he couldn't shoot the man, and if he didn't, he'd get left behind, too, floating face down in the ditch with beer cans and crushed to-go cups.

The highway was empty, the electric lines stretching into the dusk. A high-pitched insect song shrilled in his ears.

"You by yourself?" The inspector questioned.

He had noticed Smitty in the passenger seat as they drove by his station, but wanted to hear what Joe would say. Joe struggled. Greasy could have flimflammed his way through this without breaking a sweat, but Joe felt like he was digging through solid concrete with a spoon to come up with answers.

"No sir, I got some friends with me. They're sleeping."

"I guess you'll have to wake them up. I'd like for them to step out while I look inside the van."

The cicadas reached a frantic pitch. Joe swallowed, and gazed up at the pumpkin-colored sky. Almost sunset. Ten more minutes, the man would have ended his shift and gone home. Instead, he stood there awkwardly, waiting for Joe to escort him to the side door of the van.

Joe reached into his pocket, pulled out the pack of cigarettes, tapped it on his palm and tore the cellophane loose. He shook one out, stuck it between his lips and took his time lighting it. Joe squinted over the man's shoulder at the silhouettes of the big trees draped with moss. When he looked back at Raymond Godwin, the good-old-boy humor had vanished from his face. All Raymond Godwin saw were two deep black pools.

"You got any children, Raymond?" Joe said softly. "Maybe some grandchildren?"

"I got grandsons," Raymond said, bewildered, then he sucked in his breath. His right hand twitched as if he were getting a stupid idea.

"Have a cigarette, Raymond. Keep your hands where they can see them." Joe was counting on Merle Haggard and the spitting exhaust to drown out what he was saying. "Bet you enjoy those little grandsons. Do you take them fishing? My granddaddy always took me fishing."

"Yeah. We fish."

"How long you been with the State of Alabama?"

"Since I come home in '45," He said tonelessly. "They hired me straight out of the service."

"That's a lot of years standing on your feet for the State of Alabama," Joe said. "Bet you're looking forward to retirement."

Raymond's gnarled knuckles trembled when he lifted the cigarette to his mouth. He finally nodded.

"Yes. Yes sir. I want to retire, spend some time with my grandsons. My…my daughter is sick. She's got the cancer. That's why I take care of my grandsons."

"I believe you're a good man, Mr. Godwin, and a smart one. Now if you would do us both a big favor and get back in your car and go back to your office and finish your shift." Joe gave him a moment to hear it through the terror galloping in his head. "And here's the really important part. Don't even think about making a phone call, because they will send somebody back here for you one day, and you won't know it's them until it's too late. It might be the day your grandsons come by for lunch. So, can you do all that for us, Raymond? I'd be much obliged."

Raymond's mouth opened. His gaze went to the side mirror and the dark shapes reflected there. He wavered, a lifetime of training and responsibility warring against common sense.

"Who needs you the most, Raymond, the State of Alabama or those kids?"

A weird breathy sound escaped the man, a cry of surrender, but not defeat, which was a different thing entirely to an ex-military man. Then he abruptly shut his mouth, the cigarette clenched hard. He turned around, a brave act in itself, and wobbled back to the car as if he expected a bullet in his spine at any moment. When he reached the door, the inspector turned, the look on his drawn gray face one Joe would never forget. A man whose day began with breakfast in a sunlit kitchen and had unexpectedly gone dark. He now knew how the close the end of it all waited.

Joe waited until the man got the state car turned around, nearly running it in the ditch, and drove off with no lights on. Then he walked casually to the driver's door of the van and swung himself up into the seat.

"What was that all about?" Smitty scowled, and rapidly squelched Tammy Wynette.

Dudley and the others listened, their eyes locked on Joe. Their lives and freedom could have changed in an instant if he had not handled it right. He managed a tight smile. *How do you like that, you sons of bitches*?

"Told him I was hauling auto parts." Joe shifted the van into Drive.

"We're cool? It's cool?" Dudley gripped a .45.

"Yeah, we're cool," Joe assured him.

With one last glance over his shoulder, he eased the creaking van back on the highway, and drove off into an orange Alabama sunset before they changed their mind and told him to go back.

When Raymond Godwin tucked those kids into bed tonight, he would be a praying man.

♦

They reached Biloxi after dark, but could still see the injury done to the fragile coast by Hurricane Camille two years ago. Prows of shrimp boats reared like sharks from shattered trees, and grand old houses teetered on brick foundations, porches propped by sagging timbers. In the towns, bulldozers had swept the land clean of tree stumps, shopping centers and motels, leaving an eerie dead zone beside the warm waters of the Gulf.

"Pull over up here and I'll drive," Smitty said. "You don't know your way around. Pass Christian was still a wreck last time I went through."

Joe gladly gave up the driver's seat. U.S. 90 had washed away in places, along with bridges and road signs. Snores rattled from the back, but no one invited him to crawl back there and get some shut-eye. He swallowed some speed and washed them down with warm beer. With Smitty driving, Joe focused on the landmarks: bridges, roads, the detours, the scraps of unfinished interstate, and endless water. He wanted to know where he was going, and more importantly, the way back home.

When they reached the New Orleans city limits, Joe leaned forward in anticipation. Instead, he found himself gripping the window sill. The traffic was the worst he had ever seen outside a race track.

“People here drive crazy,” Smitty smirked. “Some of ‘em learned to drive a boat first and can’t tell the difference.

He maneuvered the van down through a dismal neighborhood, away from the lights. Smitty stopped briefly at a pay phone, then worked up and down a few one-way streets, watching the side mirrors. Joe was hopelessly lost by the time they crept into the rear parking lot of a seedy two-story motel. Smitty parked so that the front end of the van was in shadow.

“We’re here, Duds,” He said over his shoulder.

Wincing, Dudley rolled to his knees and pulled himself up on the back of the passenger seat. “See him?”

“He won’t be driving his car.” Smitty put the van in Park and lit a cigarette.

“I see a Coke machine.” Bobby Boozer jammed his hand down in his pocket for some change. “Probate, go get me a Coke.”

Great. Joe edged out the door and stepped down into a crunchy mess where someone had dumped their ash tray. He watched the darkness between the parked cars for any movement, then the untrimmed shrubs against the building, littered with drink cups and napkins. Even the poorest tourists had a choice of motels when visiting New Orleans.

The glare from the big red and white Coke machine was blinding, but he saw a man deliberately move halfway from the shadows. Dressed in a dark shirt and jeans, the man was as coppery brown as Joe, roughly the same age, and wore a rough black cowboy hat with a hand rolled brim. He kept his long hair pulled back out of the way, and there was power in his solid stance. Joe hoped he didn't have to swing on him.

"Any probates wit' you?" The man said in a peculiar accent.

Exasperated, Joe turned his back to him and let the coins slide in the machine. He bought a Coke for Bobby and one for himself, popped the caps off, then faced the stranger again.

"I'm the probate," Joe announced.

The stranger studied him, then walked across the parking lot to the van, letting Joe trail behind.

"You got us a good place?" Smitty said.

"Very good. Favor to Denny. What about this probate?"

"He's ours. What's the problem?"

"I got my orders, too. No rookies where we're going."

Smitty rolled his eyes. "Hey Jess, come talk to this boy."

The man raised an eyebrow, but didn't say anything. Smitty slouched over to the passenger side to let Jess slide through to the driver's seat.

"What's going on?"

"I was told not to take any rookies. Nobody without a patch."

"He's my probate, Randy. He's not a security problem."

Except with women.

"Don't give me no hassle, old friend, you wanted a place to park this, I got it. They doin' it as a favor, for Denny. Got transportation waitin' on you, too, some other things you need. I'll drop off your probate at Fat Jack's 'til you're ready."

"The probate's going with us," Dudley settled it. "He knows what'll happen if he causes any problems. Let's go. I don't like sitting here."

The dark man stood still, but his eyes briefly met Jess's.

"If we get separated, wait for me at St. Charles and Josephine. I want to make sure we ain't followed."

"Tell you what. The probate can ride with you," Jess announced, startling everyone. "He needs to familiarize himself with the area. There's a lot more to New Orleans than the French Quarter."

"There's a lot more to Louisiana than New Orleans," Randy countered.

"You two can swap gumbo recipes, I don't care." Jess reached for the ignition. "Just stay away from the family tree."

A slow grin crossed Randy's face.

"Oh yeah? But ol' friend, family trees are what Cajuns are all about," He said, then turned to Joe. "You from here?"

"No."

"You could pass for one of us."

"Hasn't that been a trick bag around here for a couple hundred years?" Smitty interrupted. "Trying to pass as something you ain't?"

"Sometimes it works." Randy tossed his car keys in the air, and swung a hand at Joe. "Let's roll. You got a name?"

"Yeah. Probate."

CHAPTER TWENTY-FIVE

"You never been here?" Randy Breaux sat low in the seat, one arm propped on the window. His dark eyes watched the traffic lights and the van behind him, skillfully guiding them around the city.

"No," Joe tried to pay attention to where they were going.

They were on Broad Avenue, skirting north of the congested tourist areas. He wanted to know more about this man with the strange accent. Jess had thrown them together on purpose, and Joe wasn't too sure Jess had his best interests in mind anymore. New Orleans might be a good place to get rid of probates.

"That old Johnny Horton song about the battle? I had an uncle who danced to it when he was drunk. He'd pretend to high-step through briars and bushes. And it was a big deal for them to mention powdering the alligator's behind on the radio."

Randy grinned.

"That ain't why most people visit here. Not a gator's behind anyway."

"You've got a lot of history here. I never finished school but I read a lot. Where people come from. How they survived. Where they wind up."

"You're dark as hell. Sure you ain't some long-lost Cajun cousin?"

"Irish, Scots and Cherokee, maybe some Creek," Joe took a deep breath. He might as well get his ass off his shoulders. This guy hadn't done anything to him. "My name isn't 'probate,' either. It's Joe Wilson. My mother's people were Kelleys from Ireland. Of course, not everybody thinks where they came from is important."

"That's 'cause they ain't nobody. In Louisiana, pedigree is everything," Randy informed him. "We're all something, whether we like it or not."

They drove down a narrow street flanked by white mansions which had seen better days. Set back from the street, in the dark, the houses could pretend they were still grand, their beautiful wrought iron gates keeping out the riffraff.

"It's smart to know who somebody is. It could matter one day."

"Yeah, it's like that at home. You had to be careful what you said at the shipyards because you might be talking about somebody's cousin's wife."

"My point exactly." Randy grinned.

"Are you from New Orleans? You sound French."

"Damn. You have a good ear. How'd you pick that up? We came here way back. Louisiana, I mean, not New Orleans. My people are country people."

"But were still speaking French not too long ago," Joe said.

"Does Jess know you're smart? I can't see him wanting a smart probate. He wants the kind he can lord it over."

"He's not so bad," Joe said grudgingly. "I wouldn't want to be him, though."

"Nope," Randy glanced behind at them at the van, and abruptly changed subjects. "You probably won't get a chance to party while you're here, but I'll take you to some of the strip joints if things get slow."

Slow? Randy obviously knew more about the Regents' plans than he did. The only thing he overheard them discuss was going to New Orleans to wait for Denny's Chicago Chapter. If an opportunity presented itself beforehand, they would take it. And he didn't dare discuss any of it with Randy Breaux.

"If things get slow," He echoed. "A friend of mine mentioned a place called The 500 Club and a stripper named Lily Christine?"

"Lily died awhile back. She was a class act. That place ain't so hot anymore. The new girl, she's got what they called Bourbon Street boulders. I like real tits," Randy said. "You want to see a show, I know places to go. If we have time."

There it was again. Joe wasn't sure who was the slickest. But one thing he had figured out. Randy was freelance, not a Regent.

The night air blowing in the windows was hot and sticky. A musky odor wafted in the car, rust and fish and the oily metallic scent of industry.

"I smell a river," Joe said as they drove down a long quiet street of tall, dark warehouses.

Somehow they were heading toward the French Quarter again, on a street named Tchoupitoulas. When he knew Randy better, he'd ask how it was pronounced.

"You're smelling the Mississippi. This street parallels the river."

Randy circled the lengthy block twice before turning up a narrow street beside a three-story brick warehouse and pulling to the curb. He got out and looked around, then motioned the van to pull over and wait.

"Stay with my car. I'll be back soon as I get them situated," He told Joe. "You see anything weird, drive around back but don't stop. Keep going across the parking lot to the next street. I'll have the doors shut but I can hear you."

Damn, how bad was this going to be? Randy seemed to read his mind.

"What they got in that van could get a lot of people in big trouble, including the man loaning us the place to stash their stuff. I ain't aiming to get killed or do time over somebody's carelessness. If they don't like it, they can park their van somewhere else."

Joe nodded, his respect for Randy kicking up a notch.

"You get in a jam and have to leave, Fat Jack's tattoo shop is on Dauphine near Toulouse in the French Quarter. It ain't all that far from here," Randy said, smiling faintly. "I just took the scenic route to make sure nobody followed us."

Joe slid over into the driver's seat. Randy walked briskly up the sidewalk and veered left around the corner of the warehouse. A few minutes later, the van's brake lights flashed briefly, then it crossed in front of Joe and disappeared. Joe checked his mirrors and settled in, his senses tuning in to his surroundings.

Even with his extraordinary eyesight, he couldn't see very far down the street in front of him. Massive oaks dripping with moss obscured the neighborhood. Probably the homes of people who had worked at these warehouses years ago. Was it the Irish Channel? He stretched to reach his bedroll in the back seat. He had stashed an old map from a National Geographic in there before he left home. Maybe he could see the warehouse district on the map and figure out where he was.

Ten minutes passed into thirty. He ate a couple of melted Moon Pies and washed them down with a lukewarm Pepsi. Then he went still, watching the side mirror. Behind him on Tchoupitoulas, a car slowed, the headlights winking out as it came to a stop somewhere in front of the warehouse. He heard a soft click of metal when a door eased shut. Damn, they were right around the corner.

Joe slumped down and reached for the pistol in his boot, then froze. Shit, they were already coming up the sidewalk. The silhouette walked rapidly, then realized the car window was down and stopped. From what Joe could see, the man was skinny and small and wore a jacket, his hands jammed in the pockets. He had long hair that swayed when he jerked to a halt, and he stood there almost seven beats. Joe knew the man had spotted him in the side mirror.

Getting shot in the back of the head on a New Orleans side street was not the way he wanted to die. *Quick*, he had to move quick. Joe reached for the door, shoving it open, his .380 in hand. The stranger drew in a sharp breath, then whirled around and ran. Joe jumped out, already dodging in case the man turned to fire at him-- then he stopped, shocked. It was a girl, with long red hair, her hands out of the pockets, running frantically to disappear around the corner.

"Hey wait!" He called.

He started after her, then heard a car engine kick in. He didn't want to run around the edge of the warehouse into a bullet, but Joe ran anyway. She was alone, her frantic face white as she did a U-Turn and sped down the street the wrong way with no lights on.

"Damn," He said out loud.

All that trouble for a secret location, and apparently it wasn't so secret after all.

"Everything okay?"

Thirty minutes later, Randy walked up to the car, slowly, when he saw that it was parked forty feet closer to the back corner of the warehouses.

"Think so. Haven't seen anyone but a girl with long red hair. She parked out front, came around the corner and took off running when she saw me. I scared her pretty bad."

"How long ago was that?"

"Half an hour."

Randy gazed down the sidewalk toward the river.

"She was probably lost. People get turned around on these one-way streets. There's another warehouse not too far from here where all the rock and rollers go. Best live music you ever heard." He dismissed the girl's appearance. "Bring the car around, I want to get it off the street. It's a spare. Can't afford to lose it."

Relieved to rejoin the others, Joe drove to the back side of the warehouses. The parking lot was empty, a single streetlight washing across the huge expanse of potholes and gravel. Someone opened a set of double doors, tiny in the long expanse of brick, and a dim blue light gave him a place to aim for. He drove inside, and the doors quickly closed behind him.

"Back here," Randy motioned.

Astounded by the size of the interior, Joe followed him, his foot riding the brake. Massive timber supports stood like telephone poles down the length. Four cars and two motorcycles were parked nose out along the brick wall. The van was nowhere in sight. At the front, someone had enclosed the upper story into a loft. He bet it overlooked the Mississippi.

"Back it in next to the Dodge."

Joe tried to look nonchalant as he parked the car and tossed his bedroll to the concrete floor, but he was calculating what he could do with a place that size. And what purpose it currently served.

"Where is everybody?"

"Next door."

Instead of going outside, Randy walked to a dark corner under the loft, and slid back a barn-style door. Light flooded the corner, and voices suddenly stopped.

"Here's your probate."

The Regents stood near a circle of old couches and recliners, the cavernous interior beyond them pitch black. After the long drive, they wanted to stretch their legs. A lamp with a hoop-skirt-sized shade squeezed most of its wattage toward the ceiling, which was too high to be seen. The van was parked a few feet away, the doors open. Ugly stood by one of the timbers staring into the darkness, also intrigued by the vast space.

Dudley toked on a joint, his aching limbs pressed against the brick wall. Since they left Atlanta, he'd been the one to give Joe orders. Jess barely spoke to him, and that was fine. Joe didn't have a lot to say to him anymore.

"You got guard duty tonight, Probate. Tomorrow, Randy will show you around town."

"Where you want him to go?" Randy inquired.

"Wherever he can find some damn Bayou Runners and pick up some intel. They don't know him and he can pass for local. Take him to some of their hang-outs. Somebody has to be running their mouth. I want to know exactly who put Denny in a trick bag and where the hell Sleaze hangs out when he isn't in New Orleans."

"We ain't waiting for Chicago to get here?" Ugly said.

"I don't want to hang out here any longer than necessary. I want to take care of business and get the hell out of town."

"If that had happened to one of our guys, I'd want to take care of it personally."

"Then Chicago needs to get their asses down here. We waited a damn week in Atlanta getting shit ready." Dudley frowned at Randy. "All this time you've lived here and you still don't know where their clubhouse is?"

"I know places they party. I know places some of 'em stay. But no damned body knows where Sleaze puts his greasy head at night after a big haul. Don't think he's stupid. That's where everybody makes their mistake wit' him."

"It can't be that hard to find," Dudley insisted.

Randy smiled slightly. "I used to know people who tried. We never saw 'em again."

"We gonna let him know we're here?" Lindsey from Louisville inquired.

Dudley shook his head.

"I'll give the probate a chance. We can lay low for a few days. Then I'm heading to Fat Jack's and find out how that piece of shit let them steal Denny's bike from his fucking front door."

"He doesn't know you're in town?" Randy said.

"No. Because once he knows, everybody in town will know."

CHAPTER TWENTY-SIX

New Orleans was like no place Joe had ever visited. If he had been there under any other circumstances, he would have had a damned good time. During the first day, Randy pointed out German cafes, Irish pubs, and Jewish art galleries among the strip joints. The signs posted on the club doors left nothing to the imagination, and he could not believe that some of the exotic dancers on the Bourbon Street posters were men.

"What about that one?" He nodded toward a doorway.

"The Gunga Den, it's gonna be a man."

"Do they still have dicks?"

"Shit, you got the tourist act down good. Ain't you ever been anywhere? Weren't you in the service?"

"Yeah, but I did basic in the Bible Belt."

"They the worst ones, son. The police raid that place right now, you watch and see how many deacons from Omaha they get."

Randy showed him landmarks to watch for, the main streets, and where the vehicle barricades were placed each night to protect the shit-faced tourists staggering through the French Quarter. The Dodge crawled down the bumpy streets beneath creaking balconies, past hotels advertising air-conditioning and private courtyards.

"Is that a woman? Please tell me that's a woman."

"Definitely. That's Chris Owens' place. Pay attention here, this next block up is where they got Denny. See Papa Joe's there on the right? You going in there tonight, shoot some pool."

Joe tried not to stare. The bar looked small, with two open doors facing the street. His breath caught in his chest.

"You going with me?"

"No, not yet. Some of 'em know me. You'll do better by yourself. If you get in a jam, cut down the street behind us on foot to Dauphine and you'll see Fat Jack's shop. He won't do nothin' to save your ass but it'll get you off the street. Does he know you?"

"He saw me at Talladega and the Atlanta clubhouse. But he was with Big Alec's chapter shitfaced and acting like a big shot."

"Well, if you have to, remind him you're Jess's probate. He'll make sure nothing happens to you, even if he don't like it."

Joe quirked an eyebrow. "He have something to do with the other probate getting killed?"

"He offered up his house for Big Alec and the Miami crew when they came to meet Sleaze and damn near got killed. So yeah, I'd say the piece of shit had a hand in it, hoping he'd make points with Alec. Instead, it backfired all over him."

"I'm surprised he'd want a Regents patch living here."

"He wouldn't have turned it down when Alec offered it, no way. But he don't wear it around here."

"Alec offered me one, too. Turned it down."

"No shit?" Randy hung a left on St. Peter Street, then another left on Dauphine. "Why?"

"I'd already promised Jess I'd probate for them."

"You're better off, even when it don't seem like it."

Randy pulled over to the curb, and pointed down the block to a narrow stucco two-story building on the left, with a single door and a window.

"That's Fat Jack's. That's where they stole Denny's bike. We ain't going in there today because Dudley wants to handle it. Remember now, Bourbon Street is only one block over, and runs parallel with Dauphine. This cross street is Toulouse. I'm gonna go get us some sandwiches from that place on the corner, and then you're gonna show me how to get back to Canal."

Randy didn't have to tell him his life could depend on knowing his way around.

♦

The first night at Papa Joe's, Joe sat at the bar, unable to enjoy his beer. There was a big gap in the stools, and he couldn't help wondering if this was where Denny had sat. He lit up a cigarette, didn't speak except to order another beer, and watched the men at the pool tables until he knew who was good at the game and who wasn't. A plump woman kept feeding the jukebox, playing "Bye Bye Miss American Pie," and sang along only with the lines about the day she planned to die.

Joe got up and fed a dollar's worth of dimes into the Rock-Ola, heavy on Creedence, Santana and the Eagles, and earned two free beers from the grateful bartender. Shortly before midnight, Joe nodded good night and entered the noisy world of Bourbon Street.

The sidewalks and street rippled, dazzled couples drifting in the neon lights from bars to music halls to strip joints. Hucksters at the door lured them in, assuring them that curiosity and bad behavior were fine. Joe seemed to be the only one without a cup in his hand. A sudden whiff of Teriyaki beckoned him down a side street. He had to step over a drunk guy in a gold suit quarreling with himself, then nearly collided with a cop, but everyone missed each other and kept going. Joe bought four of everything the Chinese place had cooked, then zigzagged his way to Rampart Street, where Randy waited in a motel parking lot.

"Damn, that smells good. How'd it go?"

"Just getting it set up. Tonight, I'll go in there and shoot some pool, let somebody win a time or two, make him my buddy." Joe reached for a teriyaki steak on a stick and tore into it.

"Can you spare an eggroll there, my friend?"

"If you'll drive slow. I'm not sharing with the rest of them."

"I'll make a few passes on Tchoupitoulas before we stop," Randy said. "They're worried about guard duty on the wrong place anyhow. Sleaze's people are watching Fat Jack's house."

♦

On Wednesday evening, Randy managed to find a parking space on Bienville, and presented him with fake I.D..

"James Breaux of Shreveport?"

"That's you. You're family now." The corner of his mouth quirked.

"What the deal with you and Jess and family?" Joe inquired.

"An old joke. He came through here on his way home from the service, but never made it home. He liked it here. Found him a family of misfits."

"He said he used to be friends with Sleaze."

Randy's hand tightened on the wheel.

"So did a lot of people. Ain't life funny?"

Joe closed the car door. "I've got to meet you at midnight again? I might need more time if it goes well."

"Start earlier," Randy advised.

Joe didn't mind the walk. He deliberately ambled like James Breaux of Shreveport would, intrigued by the outdoor carnival where adults were encouraged to let it all hang out, literally. If he got a chance, if things didn't go wrong, he wanted to catch Chris Owens and her burlesque show at the 809 Club, and swing inside a jazz hall to see who was playing sax like Boots Randolph. A cheap beer would go great with the live banjo music at Your Father's Mustache. Curious, he paused at a shadowed doorway where Junior Walker and the All Stars boomed out "Shotgun." A hustler stepped forward to invite him inside.

"Evening,sir. Welcome to the House of Joy, the best Swedish massages you'll find. One girl or two, whatever your pleasure. Light or heavy hand."

"Don't listen to him, baby, you got to experience my body crawl massage to believe it," A woman called in a deep voice from a nearby balcony.

"Your massage ain't the only thing crawling, Claude."

"That's Claudette to you, shrimp-dick."

"Don't make me send Skip up there. He done told you about hanging out on this end of the balcony."

"Oh, I am so scared of Skip," Claudette mocked, hoisting a drink in a shot glass. "My rent is paid in full with the man who counts, so you just send Skippy up here and I'll toss his ass off this balcony when I'm done with it!" She pulled her gown apart and lunged at the empty air a few times, then turned her attention back to Joe. "I'm serious, honey, ignore this panderer of inexperienced flesh and come on up here. I'll put on some Clarence Smith and give you a big discount. You're a handsome one. How about 'Slip Away?' I get chills listening to it. You want to warm me up?

"Maybe later," Joe said and started off down the street.

A shot glass crashed to the bricks, and he heard a man yell. Maybe this was Bourbon Street's version of Wednesday night prayer meeting.

Papa Joe's was jammed, standing room only. The tourists wore polyester and talked loud over the music. The bartender remembered him, and handed him a beer through the bodies crowded around the bar. At least it gave Joe an excuse to retreat to the pool room side and lean against the wall, out of the way. It didn't take long before a few men spoke to each other in an undertone, and one looked at him with dark flickering eyes. Pigeon or pro? He waited, sipping a beer, watching the tables with the idle interest of someone with no place else to go.

"How about a round?"

They were cautious, waiting to see if he was a shark or just bored.

Joe played well, not overdoing it enough to piss them off, and not sloppy, which would have alerted them to a pro warming up. He won a few, lost a few, and mulled over how to maneuver the conversation to Denny and the fight. A stranger asking questions would end the game instantly, so he had to make them think it was their idea. The smart thing would be to come back tomorrow night, but Dudley wasn't giving him much time.

"Where's a guy go to get some pussy around here?"

That topic was guaranteed to start some debate.

"Well you're surrounded by it around here so you must be picky."

"Where you from?" A tall lanky man with hair like clipped straw saw an opening.

"Shreveport. Visiting my cousin, but she works at night so I'm on my own."

"Whyn't you ask your cousin?"

"We ain't like that," Joe replied with a grin.

"I can tell you where not to go," Strawman said.

"Yeah, Stan's got clap from every place around here," A man laughed.

"I'm just looking for a girl wants to have some fun and a few drinks."

"Oh, hell, that's easy," An olive-skinned man chuckled. "Go through them doors, take a left about two feet, then stand there in the middle of the street and pick out something you like. It's what they come here for, man, all those little college girls and the secretaries from Detroit and housewives with their drunk-ass husbands asleep at the motels. Help yourself."

His friends laughed, and Joe knew if he came back tomorrow night, he could get them talking. If Dudley and the crew would hang out at the warehouse another day. He wanted to do this right.

And truth be told, he was having a good time. A man with a blue Hawaiian shirt plundered the juke box for hidden gold among the rock and roll, and loaded up Floyd Cramer and Ace Cannon. The old Dixie Belle's version of "Down at Papa Joe's" had the rum-happy tourists dancing and singing.

Sitting out a set at the pool tables, Joe grinned, leaning in the doorway, then saw the pool players do a double-take. He followed their gazes, and suddenly couldn't breathe. It was the red-haired girl from the warehouse. Tall and slender, she was even more beautiful in a good light. She walked in behind a man, as close to his broad back as she could get without climbing it. Her smooth face was serene, but her eyes never rested. Bright blue and heavy-lidded, they took in everything around her.

"Bedroom eyes," He thought. And what did they call that kind of skin in commercials, peaches and cream? Damn, she was pretty.

He glanced at the man she was shadowing, and almost ruined two days of planning and work. The man was powerfully built, moved with a cat-like grace, his dark eyes on the bartender. His black hair receded slightly, the large forehead giving him an intelligent look. And he spent some time trimming that perfect mustache.

Joe was ninety-nine percent positive he was staring at the man who had watched them at Talladega. And stole the van. And Smoky. He looked a moment too long. The red-haired girl noticed him. Her eyes widened, but instead of calling attention to him, she turned away quickly.

"Holy shit." Joe's heartbeat revved.

Should he leave? Why wasn't the man wearing his Bayou Runners patch? If he'd watched them at Talladega, would he recognize Joe? As casually as possible, Joe stepped back into the shadows and made a sweep around the room. He focused on four schoolteachers from Wisconsin acting up, but watched the new couple out of the corner of his eye as they walked to the bar. The man leaned forward and said something to the bartender, who shook his head. The man thought for a moment, then turned to the girl, who suddenly went from anxious to intimate.

She slid her hand around his waist, leaned into the crook of his arm, and gave him a smile that made the bartender stare with undisguised lust, then glance away in embarrassment. He handed them both a couple of shot glasses and hurried to the customers clamoring for refills.

Joe lit a cigarette. The girl was not trying to conceal her face from him. Her whole focus on the Bayou Runner, who lost some of his fierceness when he looked down at her.

"Damn, he got him a pretty girl again," A man behind Joe commented, not too loud.

"Never seen nobody like Guidry for them pretty women," Strawman said, leaning over the table to make a shot.

"Maybe I'll grow me a mustache, see if it's them rides they like."

"I'd wanta see that gal's face when I was screwing her. My sister used to have a cat wit' eyes like that, all sleepy."

"Did you screw the cat?"

Taking a chance, hoping his grin didn't look as fake as it felt, Joe asked: "Is he one of them Jefferson Parish Guidrys? I remember my cousin mentioning him. She might have dated him, too."

It went wrong. The laughter stopped.

"Your cousin dance for them?"

"I don't know who she dances for," Joe said with the right amount of bewilderment.

The game went on in silence.

"Look, fellas, I'm new in town. If I'm stepping in some shit, I'd appreciate knowing before I offend somebody. I don't want no trouble, for me or my cousin."

They kept playing, and finally the olive-skinned man seated to his left spoke up, elbow level, without looking at him.

"The man's a big shot with the Bayou Runners. It's a biker club. They got women dancing for them at some places. Anybody messes with their women, there's a problem."

"Seems like it would be an ongoing problem if their women all look like that redhead."

"She's the prettiest one I ever seen. Usually their girls do blow jobs at truck stops. You ain't gonna find them dancing at the finer establishments. I ain't too sure that girl's a dancer or just Guidry's latest. She'd be a moneymaker if she worked in a good club."

"I guess I should quit staring at her." Joe tried to make a joke out of it.

"That'd be real smart of you if you wanta hang out. Guidry ain't got a sense of humor about his women. And we got a lot of respect around here for Mr. Guidry."

Joe forced himself to slowly pull on the cigarette and watch the game, instead of looking at the bar. This is what he came here for. He just hadn't expected to hit the jackpot.

"Look-a-that. There's that son-of-a-bitch again." Strawman faced the door between the two rooms, for all appearances concentrating on sinking the eight ball. His friends discreetly glanced at the stranger making his way to the bar.

"I seen him around lately. Who dat asshole?"

"Somebody who wants to lose him teefs, for sure."

"Gonna lose him nuts he keep sniffing after that redhead."

The man was average in height, had long tangled reddish-blond hair, both arms heavily tattooed, and a gloating smirk on his face. Guidry saw the stranger coming, and turned so that the girl was between him and the wall.

"That's right, asshole, you gotta go through him to get to her," Strawman advised.

The local people looked without pretending to hide their interest, so Joe moved from the crowded doorway to a wall beyond the pool table lights where he could watch. The sandy-haired man came to an abrupt halt, his smirk deepening.

Who was he? Former boyfriend or pimp? No one seemed to know. One thing Joe knew: it was not a southern face. He guessed Pennsylvania coal town. Hard and knobby, without a trace of mercy or kindness, this man had lived the kind of life Joe had been spared. A heavy hitter, with the amoral confidence a man gets when he's done certain vile things and discovers it doesn't bother him.

The girl kept her head down, focused on her drink, her shoulder against the broad back protecting her so he would know exactly where she was. Joe thought fast. Nobody here knew the rough stranger except Guidry and the girl, and Guidry knew what to expect from him. Eleven p.m.. Should he head for Bienville Avenue, hope Randy was there early, and bring him back, see who he knew? Maybe they could figure it out. But if he left, and something happened...shit.

The stranger nudged the tourist on the end stool, who glanced up at him with a whiskey-glazed smile. The smile wilted in an instant, and the tourist fled. Guidry set his shot glass on the bar and spoke to the girl. She had already moved to his left side, and they both began to walk away. But the stranger reached out and got Guidry by the sleeve, in the way that an adult would grab an unruly child.

“Dear God!” Strawman said.

“Who that man think he is?”

A very good question. Joe watched as Guidry fixed his black eyes on the man, who smiled unfazed, until Guidry reached across and placed his thumb and forefinger on the man’s hand and applied pressure. With a wince, the man let go and jerked his hand back, glaring in disbelief. Guidry straightened his sleeve, as if something nasty had settled on it, then walked out.

CHAPTER TWENTY-SEVEN

Leaning inward along a termite fault line down the middle, the cottage was about two months from being condemned, if another storm didn't come along first and finish it off. The Bayou Runners weren't worried about the water-stained ceilings or missing jalousie panes. They had a much bigger problem. With Hermy on guard duty at the front door and Lado at the back, they still flinched at every shadow that passed by the dirty windows. The men silently appealed to Guidry, their appointed spokesman. He in turn gazed at Sleaze, who chewed his thumbnail to shreds while his foot beat time on the floor.

"Gimme a minute."

"We ain't got a minute," Hermy said, checking the deadbolt lock one more time. "He could come back any time."

"How we gonna get rid of that son-of-a-bitch, Sleaze?" A younger Bayou Runner begged. "It's about time for a boat to come through. We cain't let him see that."

"We? If you dumb-asses hadn't jumped that Regent, the bastard woulda gone back to New York. Now he thinks we're pussies because you didn't finish it."

"What we were supposed to do?" Lado retorted. "Fuckin' Regent's sitting there with his colors three yards from us and the Trog says 'there ya go, there's your chance.' We didn't have time to find you or Guidry to check with."

"You're lucky the Regents didn't come riding in here and blow up the bar," Sleaze scowled.

"We thought you wanted the Regents here."

"Oh they'll be here," Guidry said. "You can count on it."

"Not like this!" Sleaze yelled. "I can't believe Leon sent his fuckin' spy down here. It wasn't like we screwed up Talladega on purpose. I never seen so many cops, it was like the Regents had an escort everywhere they went."

"They did," Guidry assured him.

"I don't need a Trog babysitter," Sleaze sulked. "I can't shake that mother-fucker unless he's sniffing that redhead's ass."

"That's something else gonna bring an unhappy ending down on us if it don't stop," Guidry warned softly.

"For Christ sake, she's just a cunt. He's a damn Trog. If he wants to fuck her, I can't do anything about it. You know that. Send her back to Vegas or wherever she came from. Christ, I got a boatload of pot heading this way and you're worried about a fucking cunt."

"It ain't about the woman. He's disrespecting us in front of our own people, acting like he's running the show, telling the boys what to do, fucking up everything. Going after a Regent on Bourbon Street, for shit sake?" Guidry glared. "Ain't nothing supposed to happen to upset the tourists. City Hall don't like it, the cops don't like it, and the Italian Chamber of Commerce sure don't like it."

"I already got word to them it's our problem and we'll take care of it."

"How you gonna fix it? Trog Boy's already calling the shots. That dumb ass has no idea how things work in this city. He's gonna screw up everything we're doing and get us killed."

"He's a Trog! He's Leon's man. We can't touch him." Sleaze slammed his fist down on the table. "Mother-fucker…"

"You started this shit, wanting to be something we ain't. You better come up with a solution to keep the people 'round here happy, not troublemakers from New York," Guidry said. "And quick. None of my people seen anybody looks like a biker in town, but Chicago Regents are gonna hit us, mark my words. They might wait six months but it's gonna be bad when they do. And you still won't have what you want from Big Alec."

He looked at the other Bayou Runners.

"Me and the boys, this is our home. We got no place else to go. You didn't ask nobody about this big patch-over. We don't want to be Trogs. We got money to live off, we ride our motorcycles, we're all right. This other shit, you're getting us in a war we can't win."

"And if you can't ditch this guy long enough for us to unload those boats, we gonna lose some big money and piss off the Chamber of Commerce," Hermy spoke up from the front door.

"Damn, don't you think I know that?" Sleaze raged. "I 'bout had a fucking heart attack when I got the call."

"You'd be better off with a heart attack than pissing off the people who own the Quarter. I got some phone calls to make, get things ready for the boats. I ain't telling them we can't handle it right now," Guidry declared and walked out.

"We ain't cowards." Three men stood up. "But Guidry's right. We got a sweet deal already, we know the players. Why screw it up?"

They tromped out the front door into the sunlight, followed by four more. Sleaze watched them go, regretting ever clueing them in on the deal with Leon, a patch for a patch. He counted on their loyalty, their desire to hold on to their territory, but they wanted to do things the easy way.

"What you need is a diversion."

"What?" Sleaze glared at the young probate, who should not have been listening and damn sure shouldn't tell him what to do.

"When the boats get here. You need a diversion to get that Trog some place."

"For instance?"

"Give him the girl."

Tempting, but he knew Guidry wouldn't appreciate it. And he needed Guidry. Guidry knew a lot of people.

"That Trog's done raped her a couple of times so it don't matter."

"You know for sure?" Sleaze glanced at the remaining men, who nodded.

"The night you sent me to pick her up from work," His enforcer spoke up. "He got in the back seat with her and told me to drive. She sure didn't want it. And Hermy seen her on the stairs at Sherry's club with her clothes all messed up, and the Trog came out of the room behind her. She asked us not to tell Guidry. You know how old-fashioned he is about women. What's his is his. If he finds out, he'll lose his temper and do something about it and then we're all dead."

"So why not give her to the Trog?" The probate persisted. "She's used goods and the Trog wants it. Arrange for her to be in a hotel some place, like it's a present for him."

"He'll see right through that," Sleaze shook his head.

"Maybe not. He's really got it bad for that girl," Lado moved from his post at the back door. "And her hanging tight with Guidry just makes it that much more interesting for him."

The probate smiled. "If she disappears, who cares? Guidry will find himself some more sweet meat and we'll have our dope shipment."

Sleaze gazed at the probate, with his lazy eye that never caught up with the other one and his nose smashed from the beating Guidry gave him on the way home from Talladega. The kid didn't know when to shut up. But he sure knew how to get revenge on someone, and Sleaze liked that, even if it was the only friend he'd ever had.

"Yeah. Shit. Whatever works. Leon ain't getting in on our action. We get our dope and money, I'll figure out another way to get Alec's patch, even if I have to go to Miami."

"Could I go with you, Sleaze? I brung you the Chicago patch. Well, me and the other guys. If you get a team together—"

"Shit! Boss, the Trog's coming up the sidewalk," Hermy called urgently from the front door.

"Fuck. I ain't got time for this," Sleaze headed for the back door, and was nearly run over by his men.

Sighing, Hermy unlocked the front door, and stalled as long as he reasonably could. The Trog knew no one wanted to talk to him.

"Got to be somewhere," Hermy finally said and hurried down the sidewalk to his sportster. The Trog watched him go, smiling, then walked inside the dingy little shotgun house. He was surprised to see only the probate and Lado, a small black-eyed Cajun with a permanently twisted jaw. Someone told him the man had an accident with a boat propeller.

"Where's Guidry?"

Lado shrugged. "He don't tell me nothing. But he ain't here."

"What about Sleaze?"

"Think he was heading out to Jefferson Parish, taking care of business."

"That's funny. From what I've seen, none of you coon-asses can take care of business."

They exchanged glances.

"We did what you told us."

"I heard you didn't finish it."

"We was in the Quarter, man. We got a deal with the cops. Ain't no killing in the Quarter. And hell, we thought he died." Lado shook his head in wonder. "Anybody else would have died."

The probate had enough brains to stay quiet for a change. And Lado already knew what the Trog was going to say.

"I'm tired of waiting on the Regents to show up. I want 'em down here so Leon can see if you can handle it. So go ahead. Tonight, finish what you started. And bring back something so I'll know you did."

He sat down on the couch.

"I'll wait here."

CHAPTER TWENTY-EIGHT

Yvonne loved the night shift. The halls were empty of the naïve student nurses she wanted to strangle, and the weeping, praying families. Sometimes the elevators would clank open to reveal a young man sneaking his Uncle Alphonse some gin, or a husband smuggling in a little toddler too young to visit her ailing mama during the day. Yvonne dealt with them kindly, but firmly. Thirty minutes, then go home.

Unlike the day shift, when the managers and staff and doctors competed to look the busiest, the skeleton crew on the night shift covered for each other. If somebody needed a nap, or had to make a quick trip home to see if their husband was out catting around, the women on her floor kept their mouths shut. They might gossip among themselves – "Poor Rosaleen, dat man no good" – but the daytime managers never knew what went on at night on the seventh floor.

The man at the end of the hall looked up. He knew what time she punched on the clock. He had finally decided to sit in the chair she brought him, instead of on the floor. The other nurses were content to let her work the east hall each night. After doing her first rounds, she picked up her clipboard and coffee.

"Michelle, I'll be in 714 if you need me."

"I'll just wave at your friend down there, tell him to get you. Bet he won't leave that chair, even for you."

Yvonne pivoted down the hall, her white shoes soundless on the tile, holding her breath. No faint calls for help to the bathroom, or more common, pleading for more medication.

"Just be quiet for thirty minutes." Yvonne glided by the ten rooms between her and the man in the chair, and came to a halt in front of him, her hand on her hip.

"I feel like a natural-born fool, cher. I know you been going in his room for water and the bat'room, but I finally realized ain't nobody been feeding you."

With the heavy jacket on, it was hard to tell exactly how big or skinny he was, but his skin was pale and drawn under the beard.

"Brought you an oyster po'boy." She held out the brown bag. "They'd fire my ass if I brought you a beer but I got you a Pepsi with some ice. How about that? And there's some of my mama's pound cake, too, and I don't share that with nobody, here? I got to keep my figure, 'case your friend in there wants to take me dancing."

He slowly took the bag, and she thought "oh lord, honey, don't look at me with those big blue eyes, you got more pain in there than anybody on this hall." But she saw the question, and was pleased he would trust her.

"Aw cher, didn't I tell you before? He's gonna be all right. That man's tough like an old crocodile. Don't you worry 'bout him, I been taking good care of him. I was first in my class. I can talk proper when I want to, that's how I got to be supervisor so young," She sniffed and struck a pose. He almost smiled. "But up here, these people don't care about all that silliness. They want somebody knows her stuff. You eat that sandwich now, make you feel better."

Even though it was her nature to pat and touch people, Yvonne knew not to stand too close to him. Hospitals were always full of sad people. She straightened her uniform, used her tongue to wet the fresh lipstick she had just put on, and pushed open the door.

"Knock knock." She always said that, softly.

One of the few things she did not like about working night shift was waking up sleeping patients who desperately needed rest. But she didn't have to worry about this one. They kept him knocked out because he had nightmares that sent his blood pressure soaring.

Someone on day shift had pulled back the curtain. The view of New Orleans at night from a dark seventh floor room never failed to mesmerize her. If she got rich one day, she'd rent an apartment like this, sleep during the day, turn out the lights at night, and just watch.

"It's pretty out there tonight, cher. All them cars going places, people working or loving or leaving. And all those little lights across town."

Yvonne set down her coffee, popped the lid off and let the chicory scent fill the room. She checked his skin and veins around the IVs, the liquid in the tubes, the bags dripping fluid down one bubble at a time, made sure everything was working, then leaned in to sniff. The day shift was responsible for bathing, but she knew they were scared of him and his unholy entourage standing guard.

So she had taken over the sponge baths. He always had a funny odor, rich and woodsy like a shady southern forest. Fanciful, but she knew her smells. Her nose drifted along his arm, feeling the heat from the relaxed brown bicep, studying the inked lion tattoo above the rough white cast. When she lifted her head, she heard him take in a deep whistling breath, as if he had sensed her.

"It's okay, darlin'. It's just Yvonne. I'm gonna sit here and have my coffee, then I'll get you all cleaned up. Everything's fine. Your friend is out there having him a oyster po' boy. Sure wish I knew his name."

She paused by the mirror, settling her white cap better on her thick dark braid, and tugged on her uniform again. Yes, it was a little tight but she couldn't help the way she was made. Or walked. Her most recent boyfriend used to call her Sidewinder, and he wasn't complaining.

"Sam."

Yvonne looked over her shoulder. Had that come out of his mouth? More importantly, was it a word?

"Baby, did you say something?"

The scabbed mouth moved slightly.

"Sam."

Oh lord, please let him talk sense. Even slurred, his agonized ravings about burning children and bombs falling was too much. She always had to shush him. Yvonne rushed to the far side of the bed, and on impulse, picked up his hand and curled the big fingers around her breast.

"Baby, if you'll say something that makes sense, you can play with these all day. And I don't let just anybody do that."

She waited anxiously, her chest rising and falling against the limp fingers. Then she felt something stir, a connection of muscle and will. The big palm pressed against her nipple in a caress that shot heat to several important parts of her body.

"Oh Lord," She gasped aloud without meaning to.

"His name…is Sam." The lips barely moved but it was enough.

His eyelids creaked backward, and wonderful amber brown eyes trailed around the room until they came to her.

"Am I dead?"

The deep Texas drawl rushed over her. *Damn, Yvonne, ain't you silly? The man's in Critical Care and making you blush.* She hastily set his hand and arm down, careful of the IV needle in the crook.

"No. You aren't dead." She smiled. So far, so good. He was definitely coherent.

"Where am I?"

"Charity Hospital. New Orleans."

"I'm in New Orleans?" His heart rate shot up on the green monitor and his fists curled. "Shit…I've gotta get out of here…"

"You all right, Denny," She leaned in close to his ear. "Your friends from out of town are here. They're gonna take care of things. Sam's just outside the door. During the day, they got people watching you, too. You're safe. You need to rest."

"Where's my stuff?"

"It's gone, honey. It's all gone. But you're going to be okay, and that's what matters most."

"I want…a pistol," He told her.

"I'll bring one up here when I come in tonight. I got a sweet little .22," She assured him, without having any intention of doing so. With any luck, he'd forget this whole conversation before breakfast.

He closed his eyes, and she thought he'd gone back to sleep.

"You said…if I made sense…"

She grinned.

"You ain't in no shape to play with nothing right now."

He blinked with some effort, his gaze drifting to her uniform, then up to her face.

"Like to try. Damn, you're beautiful. But you know, don't you?" He mumbled before the morphine took him down.

"Ain't done me much good so far."

Yvonne stood there a few minutes, grateful to her mother for the prayers and charms, and a few other things the hospital would not appreciate, like the herbal poultices she put on the cuts and stitched-together places between his ribs, letting the skin take the homemade medicine inside to heal where regular medicine was failing. If the doctors noticed the unusual smells, they didn't mention it. It wasn't all that uncommon at Charity Hospital where the poor came.

She was irritated with herself for the elation she felt. Sure he was special because of the various connections, but he was still a patient and she couldn't even tell if he'd once been handsome.

"Fool, letting a broke-ass biker take up room in your head." A man who couldn't take her out to dinner at Brennan's or the Rib Room, spend money on her, put gas in her beautiful car, or pay her rent. He only had that one asset, as far as she could tell, although his eyes were nice, too.

Something hard hit the door, pulling out of her reverie. Was Sam knocking to let her know the junior nurses needed her? She walked around the bed and nearly caught the door in her face when it jumped open a foot.

"Easy, darlin', I'm right here," Yvonne scolded.

She recoiled when a hand suddenly lunged around the wood, clutching a shiny knife twelve inches from her eyes.

"Holy Jesus!"

She threw herself at the door, digging her shoes into the tile floor, but a hundred pounds and fifteen pounds wasn't going to do shit against a huge door made to open inward. She only had a minute, or even less. *Think, Yvonne, think*!

"Oh mon Dieu mon Dieu," Gasping, she shoved a hand down into her uniform pocket, pulled out three syringes and jerked the caps off with her teeth.

The door trapped the straining arm, but he still sliced and lunged at the air. God she hated knives. Yvonne braced her shoulder against the door and pushed hard with her shoes. It was enough to hold the arm still for a second, long enough for her to shove the three big needles two inches deep into the wrist. They struck bone and nerves, and a man shrieked. She pulled the needles out and struck again and again like a viper. The fine metal finally twisted and bent, but she didn't dare stop. She hit a vein, spurting blood down the arm. It pulled back, along with the weight against the door.

Panting, Yvonne frantically looked around the room for a weapon, but the day shift nurses kept it clean and free of clutter.

"Damn it." She kicked the trash can over with her foot, looked at the soiled napkins and plastic bags. Nothing she could use.

A woman's scream sounded down the hall. Her gaze latched on the IV pole. The base was very heavy, enough to stabilize bags of medicine when it was pushed or pulled. Yvonne unsnagged Denny's big glucose bag and hung it on the headboard, then swept the pole around.

She paused at the intercom, hit the button and screamed: "Call my brother!"

"Yvonne, stay in the room, they right by your door! Big George on the way with Security. I called the police, too. You okay? Oh my God! Oh…oh dear Jesus, Vonnie, stay in the room!"

Thumps buffeted the door. She slid down, her back braced against it, and reached for the phone on the night table.

"Put me t'rough," She shouted at the switchboard operator. "Get me an outside line."

Her fingers trembled so bad she had to start over twice, then finally got the number to go through.

"This Yvonne. He there? Hurry!" She slipped fast into Cajun patois as the thuds against her back grew stronger. Blood crept under the door and she closed her eyes in relief for just a minute when she heard her brother's voice. "Randy? They tryin' to get in the room and I got nothin' but a damned IV pole…Randy? You there, baby?"

CHAPTER TWENTY-NINE

The New Orleans police arrived on the seventh floor at roughly the same time as the Regents, a group of men they had been advised to watch for and remove from town. Both sides declared a temporary truce, equally impressed by the mess at the bottom of the stairwell.

"Do you recognize 'em?" Ugly nudged Jess with a smirk.

"I might have seen that foot before," Jess gazed over the rail. "But I couldn't be sure, not from up here."

A few sleepy patients ventured to their doors and were promptly ushered back to bed by the shaken nurses. A middle-aged homicide detective in a gold polyester suit sat in a chair beside Yvonne. Her cheeks burned red above her white uniform, and she had taken off the jostled nurse's cap, pulling loose a few twirls of dark hair in the process. She sipped from a paper cup provided by Randy, who hovered over her. Every man there watched her put the cup to her lips, swallow, then pant slightly.

"I couldn't see what happened," She said. "All I saw was an arm come in the door waving a knife, so I pushed back against the door."

"There's blood all over your uniform, miss," He did a close, careful inventory.

"That's 'cause I was sitting down braced against the door. The blood came under it. I don't remember much else."

"Where did that chair come from?"

He pointed to an overturned chair in a sticky brown puddle. She stared, swallowed, then wet her trembling lips and gazed at the man with large dark eyes.

"Lord, I don't know. I had just gone into the room to give the man a sponge bath. I'm the only one who can do it without hurting him. They say I'm very gentle." She put a hand on his thigh to steady herself. “Next thing, there comes that knife and I threw myself at the door. I put my back against it and slid down and braced myself with my feet. Do you want me to show you?”

“How bad would I have to hurt myself to get a room up here?” A young detective pondered.

“That’s Yvonne Breaux, you idiot. Remember she dated Donegan for a while. That man can’t even tie his shoes anymore. He ain’t nothing but a husk. Filed for bankruptcy, too.”

Smitty and Dudley watched from a safe distance.

“She ain’t gonna tell ‘em shit,” Smitty said.

“So the mystery man down in the emergency room is safe?”

“He’ll make a big recovery once the cops leave. We’ll get him out of here, if he’ll go.”

Smitty shook his head. “How the hell did he manage to throw both of them off the rail?”

“Who knows?” Dudley shrugged. “Too bad Chicago got him first. I’d sponsor him.”

“You’re fucked up,” Smitty said.

They heard Ugly laugh suddenly in the stairwell, and an echoing laugh from far below.

“Hey, it’s an ear, all by itself, stuck to the wall. Hey man, if you don’t need it for evidence, I want it,” He called.

“Pipe down,” Jess said. “Just in case anybody’s still asleep up here.”

“They should move Denny to another floor.” Dudley looked down the hall toward the elevators.

“Can’t. This is Yvonne’s floor. I wouldn’t trust another nurse with him, he’s hurt too bad,” Smitty said. “Randy’s got some swamp rats who’ll do guard duty twenty-four seven. I’ll ask her if they can move Denny closer to the nurse’s station.”

“Sleaze has lost his fuckin’ mind, ordering a hit like this,” Dudley declared under his breath. “Wonder if he knows it went bad yet.”

They both eyed the cops.

"Bad or not, one thing you can count on. As soon as one of them can slip off to a phone, Sleaze will know *we're* in New Orleans."

"Well then, what are we waiting for?" Dudley finally grinned. "Tomorrow we hit Bourbon Street and make it official. The Regents are in town."

♦

The regulars at the pool table welcomed Joe like an old buddy. He bought a club sandwich next door and wolfed it down, hoping it would stop the gnawing hunger in his guts. Feeding the probate during the day wasn't on anybody's radar, and the hundred dollars he got at Colleen's had dwindled to forty. At least this nighttime assignment gave him a chance to buy his own food, and he had plenty of choices in the French Quarter.

"Don't she never feed you?" It wasn't long before the locals swung the conversation around to his cousin-the-dancer.

He eased out of it the smart way, complaining she warned him about discussing her business around a pool hall.

"She's gonna throw me out if I don't shut up about her, and I can't live on the street. My job in Shreveport don't start up again for another two weeks."

"You need a place to stay, my wife and me got a couch that opens up. Our apartment's kinda small but you're welcome," Strawman spoke up, and Joe felt bad.

It had been his experience that the people with the least were quick to offer it, whereas people who could afford to be generous often looked the other way. He enjoyed the company here, and the lying felt wrong, even when he was trying to help make something right. This would probably be his last night here anyway. The Regents agreed that the man dogging Guidry last night had to be a Trog, simply because Jess said Guidry wouldn't have taken shit off anyone else. Dudley declared that Joe had gleaned more information than they had hoped for, and wanted to pull him back to fulltime warehouse duty. Randy intervened, buying him this one last night on Bourbon Street. It looked like a dull one.

Joe spent the evening shooting pool, sitting out a few games because of his thin wallet. They rattled on about their families and shrimping, and he couldn't steer it back to the Bayou Runners without being obvious. It appeared the evening was going to be a waste after all. He didn't even notice the phone behind the bar ring until the bartender gave the place a sweeping look.

"Ovide! Guidry back there?"

"No, ain't seen him tonight."

"Okay. He ain't here, man…Jeez, settle down, I'll tell him…sure." The bartender put the phone down. "Jeez."

"Dere him is, across the street."

"One of you holler at him. It's important."

Strawman loped over to the door.

"Guidry!" He waved, easy to spot. "Telephone."

Joe watched the man work his way through the tourists. He envied him that calm. Joe wondered if he had been among the ones who attacked Denny. He would be a hard one to bring down. The bartender handed him the phone and he moved into the corner to make the call, his back to the customers. The call didn't last long, and when he turned around, his composure had taken a devastating hit. White-faced, his eyes burning with fury, Guidry set the phone down and walked out.

"Somebody fixing to get their shit stomped," Strawman said under his breath.

"He don't risk his hands 'less he's got to. Wonder if it's that wise-ass. I'd like to see him hurtin'."

"His hands?" Joe raised an eyebrow.

"Mr. Guidry plays cards. Private parties when rich tourists come looking for a game. The clubs call him. You play?"

"I don't have money to lose. If he's that good, why does he hang around a biker gang?"

"He likes ridin'. Cards is just something he's good at. One finances the other. He splits the difference," The olive-skinned man explained with a snort, the closest he'd come yet to a laugh. Maybe because he was extremely drunk.

Randy's advice to know the enemy was getting complicated. The more Joe knew, the more questions he had. Treating himself to a final beer, Joe volunteered for another round of pool.

"Hoo shit, looka there, Hermy ain't wearing his patch."

"That ain't good. He's proud of that patch. Something's wrong."

"Something's up tonight," Strawman agreed. "Hope them assholes from New York ain't back." They were between rounds, and he put the pool stick down. "About time I went home anyways." He looked at Joe. "I'd find somewhere else to hang out if I was you. The Bayou Runners keep bad company, and if they're upset, somethin's happened."

"I don't care what he's upset about, I'm leaving, too," Another man nodded and walked out.

Joe saw the reddish-haired little Bayou Runner speak briefly with the bartender, who pointed down the street after Guidry. The man took off, his freckled Irish face grim.

"Take a chance," Joe told himself, and emptied his beer bottle. "I reckon I'll follow your advice. I ain't looking for a fight. Not tonight, anyways. Good night, fellas. Thanks."

He stepped outside with a few others, and paused to light a cigarette until they were gone. At the end of the block, the nervous Bayou Runner had caught up with Guidry. They had an agitated conversation, Hermy chattering away, distraught, and Guidry looking as if he'd explode. Then both men turned off Bourbon Street and headed at a fast pace down Orleans Alley. Joe set off after them.

When he rounded the corner, he hesitated. Even in the shifting swarm of revelers, he risked getting noticed because he would have to double-time it to keep up with them. They were watching, too: Hermy peering over his shoulder, Guidry scanning the crowd in front of them. They crossed Royal and veered down Pirate's Alley, its sixteen-foot width jammed, weaving through the herd, alert to everything around them.

Joe stopped short at a small café. It was just too risky to match their pace. He glanced at his watch. Five minutes 'til midnight. Randy was waiting seven blocks away. Hell, he didn't even know what the big deal was, he could be walking into a very bad place for a Regent, even a probate. Reluctantly, Joe lingered outside the café until they disappeared, the headed back north.

The steady din buzzed in his ears, and he suddenly felt tired. Between guard duty at the warehouse and hanging out at the bar in the evenings, he'd had four hours sleep since his arrival. He'd done enough. The fun time on Bourbon Street was over. Time to go find Randy and let the Regents decide his fate.

The street beyond him was dark, with only a few businesses open, hunkering beneath those oppressive sagging balconies. Joe glanced up at a jungle of ferns and planters tugging at the old building itself. He stepped off the curb to detour away from it, and collided with a brick wall. Startled, he put out a hand to steady himself and found it twisted and locked behind him in an iron manacle. His face ground against old clay bricks. What the hell? Reflex kicked in, and he shifted to pivot out of it, but the man knew the move. Joe heard the faint click of a switchblade an inch from his left ear.

"Why you following us, boy?"

Shit, you dumb ass, they doubled back on you.

"What are you talking about?" Joe bluffed, his heart pounding.

"Who are you? Talk fast or bleed fast, it don't make no difference to me. Who you work for?"

"Albert Breaux Construction. In Shreveport." The blade nipped his skin. "What do you want? I don't have any money."

"You been dogging us since Papa Joe's," Another voice growled, but he heard the anxiety behind it. Hermy was scared, and that made him almost as dangerous as Guidry. Why was he scared? Two of them versus him, corralled in some piss-stinking doorway, coarse clay scraping the enamel off his front teeth and his arm grating out of the socket.

"I'm just looking for my girlfriend," He gasped as his shoulder creaked another half inch. "She was going to Pirate's Alley."

"You were setting quite a pace, mister."

"She's drunk. I didn't want her wandering around alone."

"I didn't see no girl with you last night."

Joe's chest collapsed. Damn, the man remembered seeing him the night before? Or one of the pool players tipped him off. Either way, he was in serious trouble.

"Look at my driver's license. I ain't lying."

His wallet was jerked roughly from his back pocket. Their attention would be absorbed with it for at least a minute. Joe calculated feigning a collapse to grab the .380 from his boot before Guidry sliced his artery. Fat chance. Be still, he told himself, just be still. And it wasn't like he had a choice. What the hell did the man do for a living besides play poker, wrestle cattle? The pressure on his arm was excruciating. Another quarter-inch and the shoulder would pop. He waited, listening. Money rustled. There went his last forty dollars.

But it seemed to take forever for them to examine the license. Damn, was there a flaw on it somewhere? If that wall would just give three inches, let the pressure off his arm socket…

"Where'd you get this?" Hermy almost chattered.

A chain-smoker's hand held the open wallet at the side of his head. He couldn't see what they were talking about.

"What?" Joe shut his eyes tightly. If he vomited all over himself, he'd be embarrassed, if he lived. All those years he'd done that move and had no idea how damned bad it hurt.

"Where'd you get this card?" Guidry demanded between clenched teeth.

Card? Oh yeah, the good old Knight of Swords. He felt more like The Fool at the moment.

"A friend gave it to me."

Silence fell behind him.

"Your driver's license says you're James Breaux. You related to any Breauxs around here?" Guidry rasped.

"I ain't getting my family in this. You got a problem with me, do something about it or let go of my damn arm. I told you who I was."

The alley became quiet again, then Guidry said a few words in a soft patois. They waited to see if he understood, then Hermy responded, very briefly.

The pain suddenly reached an all new level, but it was because his arm slid back where it belonged. He gasped, bent over to clutch his wrist, and was surprised to see his wallet flung at his feet.

"You damn lucky who you know," Guidry spat. "And I'm in a hurry. Don't waste my time again, boy."

The darkness swallowed them up. Joe collapsed against the wall, groaning, and let loose all the cursing he'd held back. He managed to pick up the wallet and pry it open. The money was gone, but his driver's license and the tarot card were still there.

"Oh Kit." Man, if she could see him now, she would not be very impressed. But he was. Even long distance, she was pulling his ass out of the fire one more time.

Joe squeezed his eyes shut. A woman's braying laughter rocketed into the sky from the next block. He moved that son-of-a-bitch Guidry up ahead of Big Alec on his payback list. How'd they do that down here, challenge each other to a duel? "Lead pipes at dawn." That son-of-a-bitch. Pain ratcheted from his shoulder, and he gritted his teeth. Maybe he had some change left in his pocket. He wanted some booze to steady himself before hauling ass to Rampart Street.

In the Vieux Carre, his yellow, scraped face and wild eyes were dismissed by everyone but the strip joint hustlers, who shut up when they saw him. A ragged dive with ice cream smeared all over the sidewalk promised a shot for the dollar he gripped with his left hand.

"How much is a whiskey sour?"

"Fifty cents at the bar. No offense, buddy, but you look like need straight Irish whiskey. Same price."

"Thanks," Joe nodded.

The man poured, went to help someone else, then came back.

"You got enough for another one. This ain't Pat O'Brien's."

The drinks carried him from cold and sick to hot and dizzy. A search of his left pocket came up with a few dimes and quarters. One more shot, to fuel his anger and drown the embarrassment, and he had to go. Randy would be worried or pissed by now. Joe left the scant change on the bar.

The sidewalks took on a slant, the paving uneven. People moved like fat bumper cars, bouncing off each other, backing up, showing their teeth. Was he drunk or was this the downside of the adrenaline rush? Ahead, down the tunnel of hotels and houses and restaurants, four lanes of traffic rushed by on Rampart. He focused on the lights as he lurched along like Frankenstein's monster.

One a.m., and a loaded Southern Tour bus cruised by in the traffic. Didn't anybody sleep around here? He came to a breathless halt at Rampart, disoriented, then headed south. The buildings here were commercial, seedy, and poorly lit. Last night, Randy had parked a few blocks down by a coral-colored building, one of the few that still had a grillwork balcony. Joe squinted. He saw the grillwork, but the Dodge wasn't at the curb.

He stopped beneath a dark awning to work his pistol out of his boot and stick it down the front of his shirt. A humid breeze gusted from a rattling old truck, stirring up a beer carton in the middle of the street. Had Randy given up? The Regents didn't give a shit, but Randy had been straight with him so far.

Joe leaned against a stucco building. The front windows had five-inch sills, covered in dirt and cigarette butts. He sat down on one, breathing heavily, and counted his Kool's.

Three cigarettes later, Randy had not shown up. The change Joe left behind in the orange juice and beer suddenly seemed important. It might have added up to cab fare to a street near the warehouse. At least he had a Plan B. "You're the one who wanted to be a probate." Joe pushed off the sill with his left hand. "Nah, I wanted to skip this part." He took a deep breath, trudged around the corner back to the lights and noise along Conti Street, and headed for Dauphine.

♦

"Fat Jack's Custom Tattoos" flickered in eye-scalding neon from the small front window. Beside it, the door stood open and the lights were on inside. Two young men in long surfer style shorts and striped tee-shirts sat on a lacerated black vinyl couch. A third lay rigid on what looked like an old gynecology table. The beer fumes gave depth to the air. The young men grinned and moved over, pulling more polyester stuffing loose from the cushions. Joe sank down beside them. Fat Jack glanced up for a brief second.

"You want to look at the book or you know what you want."

A beer, the bathroom and a bed, Joe thought, but said "I'm not sure."

"Suit yourself."

"He's getting a Hydra." The youngster closest to Joe nodded at his prone friend.

"The constellation?"

"Huh? No, it's a five-headed beast, man, and it lives in the swamps and it's predatory."

"And it hurts," The kid on the slab groaned.

"You mind if he smokes another one? Maybe it'll help," The surfer asked Fat Jack, and that was the last thing Joe heard for forty-five minutes.

When he woke up, he had a broomstick in the middle of his chest, pushing hard. Fat Jack sat on a stool, glaring at him.

"You ain't with them?" He said, irritated.

Joe jolted awake, slapped away the broom without thinking, then dug his boot heels into the floor. Oh shit that hurt. He grabbed his arm.

"With who?" He glared.

The three surfers wobbled at the door, their red lids half-closed.

"He thought you were gonna get a Hydra, too. High-Dra-a-a-ah," The kid breathed. "See you later, man. We gotta find something for his pain."

"I don't know how you bums can feel shit," Fat Jack retorted.

Wheezing with laughter, the boys stumbled out the door. Fat Jack gave the clock a scathing look, leaving no doubt he wanted to go home. He started packing up his inks.

"How about an eagle? You look like an eagle kind of guy." He could do eagles in his sleep.

Annoyed past caution, Joe stared him down. What the hell, he'd been batting a thousand in the Stupid League tonight.

"Nah. I want with a lion. With a shield, and a couple of crossed scimitars. You know, those old-fashioned swords. Dripping blood. You done any of those?"

Fat Jack set down the ink with a jolt, his left hand snaking toward the pistol he kept under the table.

"Who are you?"

"People keep asking me that tonight. You don't remember? We met at Talladega."

"What?"

"Short term memory loss? You were with Big Alec, I was with Jess and Dudley."

Fat Jack blinked rapidly.

"Oh. Sorry, man, it was crazy there. You're with the Atlanta Chapter?"

"I was with the bunch that got hauled off in the school buses to jail while you hung out in air-conditioned splendor with your boss."

"What can I say, man, Big Alec invited me to hang out with him. That's the breaks. You got a bug up your ass about it…wait a minute. I remember you from the Atlanta club-house. You had a beard…you're a fucking probate!"

"Yep."

"Shit, you come in my place of business talking to me like this? You mother-fucker, you got some balls." Jack stood up menacingly.

"Yep. But I was told if I needed a safe-house, you're it. I've had a real bad night and my ride didn't show up."

Fat Jack slowly sat back down. "How come you're in New Orleans by yourself?"

Joe let him think about it.

"Are they on the way?" Fat Jack asked.

"I'm not supposed to discuss it. They said if you needed a reference to remind you I'm Jess's probate."

Jack struggled with it all, his arms leaving sweat smears on the table. He nodded, bluffing confidence.

"Me and Jess go way back. Glad to know they're gonna get all that shit straight about what happened to Denny."

"I'm sure they will," Joe pinched his nose between his fingers, wincing again as his shoulder shifted in the socket. "You got a beer you can spare? I got robbed tonight."

Playing the host, Fat Jack feigned sympathy as he stepped to a small refrigerator in the corner.

"You gotta be careful late at night, man. The cops look out for tourists, but you don't exactly look like you're going to the opticians' convention." He handed Joe a cold bottle and paused, barely able to conceal his gloating delight. "Hey, they didn't get your probate patch, did they?"

Joe twisted off the cap and took a careful swallow.

"No, I wasn't wearing one," He said. "Just like you."

CHAPTER THIRTY

He awoke to find himself alone in the tattoo shop, traffic sounds coming in the window. Not surprising, with the street barely a yard away. Eight a.m., he reckoned, early for the French Quarter. People passed by on the sidewalk, close enough for him to hear their high heels clicking or the familiar clank of a Zippo lighter opening. Like the tourists, he was surprised to discover that people actually lived and worked here.

Joe stood up and found his way to the bathroom among the cubbies and halls hidden by old curtains. There wasn't too much he could do about the damage, just tame his dusty hair with a wet comb and wash out his soured mouth, hoping the water was good.

A phone sat on a heavy government surplus desk, but he had no numbers to call.

Across the street, an old Falcon pulled up to the curb. From the passenger side, a heavy-set woman with sharp dark features struggled to heave herself out. She held a suitcase, a large paper grocery bag, and a small dog. The driver, another woman, spoke to her and reached out the window to pat the woman's arm. She hurried across the street, and to Joe's amazement, set the suitcase down and pounded on the door of the tattoo shop.

"Open up, asshole."

Joe waited, but Fat Jack didn't appear. Reluctantly, he went to the door. The dead bolts were tricky with one hand but he managed, and held the door half-shut with his boot. She glared up at him, and the snag-toothed terrier flared its lip as a warning.

"Where's that fat turd?" She bumped the door open with her suitcase.

"You mean Jack?"

"Who else?"

"I don't know." Joe stepped out of her way, and his mouth started watering. He smelled garlic, oregano, tomatoes, and onion. "Damn, miss, what is that?"

No one had called her miss in thirty years. She stopped, eyed him and clutched the brown paper bag closer.

"It's my husband's breakfast. Where is that son-of-a-bitch?"

"I really don't know. I missed my ride home last night and had to camp out here."

"Well, he musta missed his ride home, too, or just decided to stay here because he was too chicken-shit to come to his own house." She set down the dog and the suitcase, picked up the broom and beat it against the ceiling. "You up there? You don't come down, I'll give it to this man who needs a bath something fierce."

Joe flinched.

"You know where I can find a tub?" He asked. And how about some of the chicory coffee panting through the bag at him?

"You ain't looked too hard. There's a shower right around the corner from the toilet, behind that wall. You might get some ink on your feet but from what I can see, it'd be an improvement."

Okay, deferring to her wasn't going to work. She had been a hateful beast a long time. Heavy steps creaked overhead and a sliver of plaster fell, narrowly missing the dog. It leapt sideways and shrilled at Joe, who decided walking three miles to the warehouse wasn't a bad idea after all.

"Shut the fuck up before I wring your damned rat neck," Fat Jack said from somewhere at the back end of the building.

"You touch that dog, I'll kill you dead," The woman warned.

"You can shut up, too, Francine. What the hell are you doing here?"

"They all…" She slashed Joe with a cautious glare. "Who's he?"

"A friend of Jess's," Her husband confirmed.

"Oh. Well, he's fixing to go take a shower, ain't you, Mr. Whiskey-stank?"

"Christ, in my shower?"

"What the hell you used it for lately, yanking your dick?" She retorted, and pointed to Joe. "Go on, this ain't your business."

He couldn't agree more. He navigated behind a closet, a sink and toilet, and finally spotted a shower head and two faucets in the darkness. It was too dark to inspect, and he was tempted to leave his boots on, but desperately wanted some hot water on his shoulder. Ten minutes later, the heat had burned a hole through his aching trapezoids, and the loud voices still sniped in the front room. Joe snatched up a towel from a stack behind an unopened pack of Dixie cups, and wondered if Mr. and Mrs. Fat Jack would loan him enough change for a street car.

"You dragged me in this mess with your big shot ideas and we got crazy people circling the house. Then last night they all of a sudden vanish, like somethin' about to happen. I ran next door to my sister, but her husband sure don't like it. He says you gonna get everybody on the block killed. So I'm staying here tonight and I tell you what, Jackson Bulliard, they burn that house down with all my mama's things, I'll cut your fat throat while you asleep."

"Fuck you, Francine. Waddle your ass right back down Canal Street to your sister's house and stay put. I don't need your shit down here while I'm doing business."

Joe sighed. There just didn't seem to be a good time to ask for a dollar. He stepped around the corner, and the dog went berserk, advancing with savage barks.

"Shut up, you!" Fat Jack kicked at it.

"Don't yell at him," Joe frowned. "He's just doing what she's trained him to do—protect her. It's his job to keep her safe."

Francine's fork stopped in mid-air, a huge sauce-coated shrimp dangling in front of Joe. Her sharp beady eyes looked at Joe like a squirrel who had unexpectedly found a hoard of acorns.

"That's right. He's protecting me," She jabbed the fork toward her husband. "Fool, you. Ain't never give that dog credit. Look how Gaspar gets between me and this fella—what was your name?"

"Joe. From Atlanta."

"You know a lot about dogs."

"Usually they like me," Joe said. "That's how I knew you had trained him. I never had a dog bark at me before."

"That's right. He gets savage, somebody get too close. Come here, my boy." She pulled the shrimp from the fork and ripped it in two. "Here's some shrimps for my Gaspar."

Fat Jack grunted and slid back from the table in disgust.

"You're all full of shit. He's working you, Francine."

"What's he working me for?" She retorted. "We gonna run off together? Hah!"

"He's a probate. Got robbed last night, didn't you say so?" Fat Jack looked up at him smugly. "Right now, if you flipped a penny at him, he'd kiss your fat hairy ass. He's got no money, no ride, and can't even buy himself a cup of coffee."

Joe counted down from ten.

"You such a bastard," Francine spat. "I told you before, I ain't cooking for your trashy friends no more, but damned if I won't give a stranger a cup of coffee if he needs one." She fished in the brown paper bag. "Get you one of them cups outta the bathroom, Joe from Atlanta, I pour you some."

Knowing her husband's temper, she made sure the cup was beyond his reach when she poured the coffee.

"Thanks," Joe said, and caught her doing a subtle survey, finally curious.

A swath of blue flickered across the far wall, catching their attention. For the first time, Joe noticed a small round mirror clamped to a shelf, angled to reflect the front door. Which he had not locked after Francine's entrance. An Olds Cutlass parked at the curb across the street, the rear bumper barely visible from the window.

"Who's that?" Fat Jack stood as the car doors slammed shut.

Francine grew pale and scooped up the dog. Joe sipped his coffee and watched the men cross to the sidewalk.

"It's just my ride. Finally."

Randy came in first, easing the door open. He scanned the room quickly, and smiled in relief.

"Thought I'd find you here. Your sponsor thought you was in a canal somewhere. I told him you followed directions."

"And I told him it'd be a first." Jess stomped in the door behind him.

Randy sniffed the air. "Whew, got any more of that coffee, Miss Francine?"

"I'll go down to the corner and get some," She said, taking the hint. She turned to leave, then hesitated.

"Here, these go good with that coffee you got," She handed a small white bag to Joe.

It contained two layered pastries, covered in powdered sugar. Joe's burning stomach was very grateful.

"Thanks, Miss Francine," He winked at Gaspar. "See you later, killer."

Randy rubbed his jaw until the woman and her dog waddled through the back hall, then raised an eyebrow. He choked back his comment when he saw Fat Jack's expression.

"Glad you're okay," He said, then took a closer look at Joe's scraped face. "Any problems last night?"

Joe didn't want to talk about it in front of Fat Jack, but they didn't leave him much choice. He stalled, savoring the pastry. Before he could get his story together, Fat Jack sneered.

"He got robbed. Lost his money. You shoulda seen him come staggering in here, looked half-dead. Some probate you got, Jess."

"What happened?" Jess said coolly.

Joe bit into the pastry, determined not to inhale it.

"I followed Guidry and a guy they called Hermy from the bar. They were both upset about a phone call. They spotted me tailing them, doubled back, and wanted to know who I was." He took a sip of coffee. He wasn't about to go into details over getting caught in a trick bag. "When they saw my ID, that seemed to settle it."

"Fuck, you were lucky," Fat Jack breathed, then scowled. "Damn, they coulda followed you back here. You stupid son-of-a-bitch—"

"They were in a big hurry to go somewhere else," Joe retorted. "Guidry said I was damned lucky about who I knew. Asked me if I was related to any Breauxs around here."

"What'd you say?" Randy said.

"Told him to leave my family out of it. They took the money and gave back the wallet and took off."

"You're full of shit," Fat Jack declared.

"It's right here." Joe finished the first pastry, wiped his hands on his Levi's, and opened the wallet. "I think this is why they returned it. They wouldn't even touch it to take it out."

He pulled out the tarot card and held it up.

Jess flinched at the sight of it, stunned, then he clamped his mouth shut and gazed hard out the window. Randy, however, stepped forward and took the card gently from Joe's fingers. He turned it over, touched the old paper reverently, and handed it back.

"This is quite a gift," He said, avoiding looking at Jess. "Don't lose it."

Joe eased the card back into his wallet. "So what are we doing now? Am I done on Bourbon Street?"

"You and I have new orders," Randy said. "Plans have changed. While you were getting robbed last night, they tried to get Denny."

"Shit, in the hospital?" Fat Jack exclaimed.

"Yeah."

"Is he all right?" Joe said anxiously.

"They were not successful. They met with resistance at the door," Randy pursed his lips. "Some homeless guy happened to be roaming the halls, and there was some kind of misunderstanding."

"Is the homeless guy okay?" Joe said.

"He got cut up a little, left the ER this morning. The two Bayou Runners, however, are on ice."

"Fuck," Fat Jack's eyes widened.

"They know we're in town. You're on red alert," Jess told him, his blue eyes cold. "Dudley and I are staying here. He'll be here shortly. And we called Chicago and told them to get their asses down here or they're going to miss all the fun."

"Maybe I should close shop for a few days," Fat Jack pondered nervously.

"Where would you go, Jack, Miami?" Jess sneered.

"Hitting your place would draw too much attention," Randy said. "They're already in trouble with their Italian connections for stomping the shit out of Denny on Bourbon Street."

No one asked Randy how he knew.

"And you'll have Jess and Dudley here to protect you," Randy continued, smiling faintly, pleased to see the man's face bulge with fury. "And Gaspar with his sharp little teeth. Ain't nothing gonna happen to you, big man."

"He'll be all right," Jess said, tossing a bedroll to the floor harder than necessary. "Fat Jack knows how to duck."

CHAPTER THIRTY-ONE

"What do you know about it?" Guidry had three Bayou Runners lined up on a couch in the upstairs of the old house.

He sat on a hassock where he could watch the door and the stairs. Hermy stood at the front door, listening for anyone else approaching. This meeting was unofficial.

"I don't know why the hell they went after that Regent, Guidry. Neither one of them said shit. We were playing cards at Sammy's place uptown and they just got up and left."

"What time did they leave?"

The three men exchanged glances.

"Wasn't quite midnight. Maybe eleven?"

"It was the Trog who told 'em to do it," Hermy said. "They were alone with the Trog yesterday after everybody hauled ass. I saw 'em come out a good ten minutes after he went inside."

A young Bayou Runner with no front teeth leaned forward. "Guidry, you got to talk some sense to Sleaze. He's gonna get us killed. He's got everybody after us but the coloreds. I ain't no pussy but I didn't sign on for all this shit."

A tall man with orange hair stood against the wall, nervously pulling on a cigarette.

"I need that money from the load coming in. That deal can't get screwed up. I owe some folks who helped out my uncle after Camille trashed his shrimp boats. I got to have my share of that money, Guidry. Sleaze ain't thinking straight and I ain't too sure he won't cut the Trog in on it."

Guidry stroked his mustache.

"Nah, he isn't that crazy. Not when it comes to his money. But he's letting everything else go to hell. Did you find him?"

"He's on the way. Gonna take him some time to get here. Maybe tomorrow."

"He knows what happened last night?"

"I tol' him. He's mad. Wasn't his orders."

"Anybody seen the Trog?"

"The Trog is with him," Hermy said wearily.

"On business?" Guidry stared.

"Oh shit! I knew it, I knew he'd cut him in." The Bayou Runners on the couch went wild. "That stupid idiot, he's gonna ruin it for us."

"I don't think it's boat business," Hermy said. "He went up north of here."

The Runner with no teeth leaned forward, his anxious breath sour. "There's only one way to get Sleaze's attention. What about a vote?"

They all became still. The day's heat had built up in the old house with nowhere to go. It was pushing ninety in the small room, and it was suddenly hard to breathe. No one spoke. A vote to remove Sleaze was serious shit, especially if it didn't go their way. And even if it did, there would still be a lot of loose ends to deal with. Sleaze had brought down Hell on their heads.

"Let me think about it," Guidry said softly. "Meanwhile, nobody goes to the Quarter. Stay here or close by until he gets back. No patches on the street."

"Here comes the rest of 'em," Hermy said, and shouted down the stairs. "Up here."

They waited for the other Bayou Runners to join them, panting and sweating.

"Okay, this everybody? All right. Anybody that don't already know--last night, we lost Lado and the probate. They did something stupid and didn't clear it with nobody, and they are in the morgue at Charity Hospital," Guidry said. He took a deep breath, and looked at each one of them. "Anybody else here decides they want to freelance to impress that Trog? I got some news for you. The Regents showed up at the hospital last night."

The men tried not to react, but a few paled and hastily stepped away from the windows.

"How many? Who's here?"

"The ones who count," Guidry said. "Nobody was wearing patches, but from the descriptions, sounded like Atlanta. Jess, Smitty, Ugly and Dudley."

"Christ."

"That ain't very many," A rangy man declared.

"It don't need to be many, Virgil," Guidry said. "And I'm sure there's more. Somebody followed me and Hermy last night that's connected to 'em."

He and Hermy exchanged glances, but didn't mention the tarot card. Not everyone respected the power of such things.

"Who did Lado and the probate? Did they lose their patches?"

Hermy's sweaty red face took on a green tint.

"The cops couldn't tell."

"Huh?"

"They got tossed down seven floors. Cops said it was like trying to shovel jello salad. Busted them out of their clothes. Couldn't tell what belonged to who."

"Jesus, who did that to 'em?" The toothless man shuddered.

"Whoever the Regents had on guard duty. The cops said he looked like a hobo, took a few cuts, went down to the ER and disappeared. None of the nurses saw the fight." Hermy hesitated. "Yvonne Breaux almost got hurt. She was working night shift."

"Yvonne Breaux? Didn't you date her years ago, Guidry?"

"You talking about Randy Breaux's sister?" Virgil smirked. "Hell, everybody's dated her."

"Watch your mouth," Guidry said quietly.

"That's another reason that whole damned amateur night assassination attempt was bullshit," Hermy said. "If that woman had got hurt, you'd all get picked off one by one. Randy Breaux's got kin from Vicksburg to Lake Charles. You fuck with his family, they might wait ten years but they'll get you."

"I ain't afraid of his fancy coon-ass or his family. He ain't even in a club."

"You'd be afraid of his mama if you knew shit," A long-time Bayou Runner from Vermillion Parish muttered under his breath.

"That's enough about them," Guidry said. "My advice is stay out of the Quarter and stay together, either here or the farmhouse. Anybody got a car, use it instead of your bike. And no patches on the street."

"What the hell good is any of that gonna do? We still got to do something about the Trog."

"It'll keep your ass alive until we figure out what to do," Guidry said, losing patience

"What about a vote?" The toothless man persisted.

"I told you, I've got to think about it."

"But you're VP. You or Hermy have to bring it up."

"What are you wanting for him? Out of office, or out of the club?" Guidry said.

"I…I just want it to scare him. Maybe he'd straighten up."

"Wait a minute." Virgil, who had arrived late, stood up and frowned. "You're talking about a vote on Sleaze's patch? Straighten up how? He can't help it if the Trog showed up. All he wanted was a patch from that Miami Regents bastard and we were working on that."

"Oh, working on it like Talladega? Crawling with fifty kinds of cops? Besides, he doesn't want the patch for us, he wants it for Leon!" Toothless retorted.

"I didn't see your ass hanging back when he offered a cool grand for the patch. Every damned one of you went on that ride."

"What the hell was I supposed to do, stay here and keep the Trog company? He's psycho. He'd cool you in a second. But he's your hero, just like Sleaze."

"Yeah, Virgil, if you hadn't charged ahead and cut up that Chicago Regent, we wouldn't be up to our ears in Regents in our own back yard," A tall Irishman taunted. "Whose idea was that? You sucking the Trog's dick?"

"Eat shit, Fahey," Virgil glared.

"Sleaze didn't even ask us if we wanted to patch over to the Trogs. He didn't call a vote or nothin'."

"That don't mean he deserves to get voted out. He's handled shit for us around here for a long time."

Guidry let them rage and ramble, listening to who sided with who. His blue cotton shirt stuck to his skin, and he finally stood up.

"Enough. First things first. What are ya'll worried about the most?"

They exchanged glances, hating to admit to their basest nature.

"The dope," Guidry answered for them. "We can't afford to lose our end of the business. It'd be the end of us. So we are all gonna go across the river and lay low. We wait. Let the Regents tear up New Orleans looking for us, we won't be here."

They relaxed.

"The boats come in, we take care of business, and then we make some plans. Maybe we'll do some fishing." That got a laugh. "We'll have money, we keep the boat bosses happy. Our contacts will know where the Regents are staying by then. They might even decide to leave, now that they got two of us. We can take care of it smart. And if Sleaze wants to keep acting the fool, I'll let him know I'm gonna bring it to the table. Or get him a bus ticket to Miami to go get Big Alec's patch himself. You want a ticket, too, Virgil?"

Virgil didn't smile back, which was fine with Guidry. He'd made his point.

"That all makes sense, Guidry," Fahey said. "But we still got a problem."

"No," He said. "If we have to, we'll drug Trog Boy when the dope comes in. I figure we've got a week, two at the latest, before they call back. They'll wait 'til after the full moon."

Nobody was about to tell him that Sleaze had already decided that the diversion for the Trog had long legs and long red hair.

♦

The woman who ran the whorehouse met him a block down the street from her place on Burgundy after sunset. The rusty old truck looked like some produce hauler from the sticks. He stretched across the seat to open the door for her, and she slid in, making a big effort to calm herself.

"Ain't seen you in a while," She said, her new green dress rustling.

"It's been busy," He said.

"Yes, I been hearing stuff."

"I appreciate you sending me a message. You found out something for me?"

"There's some men at Fat Jack's that ain't customers and they ain't tourists. The girls have seen 'em before. One's a good-looking blond fella with blue eyes, used to see him in the quarter a lot. And another fella, walks with a limp and got big old horse teeth."

"You sent one of the girls around to see?"

"Shit, Guidry, I still got them military binoculars you gave me years ago," She laughed. "I wouldn't trust them little peckerwoods girls to go see, they wouldn't come back. Celeste saw Randy Breaux come out of there with a dark-haired man she said looked like Waylon Jennings the morning after the accident at Charity."

She hesitated, trying not to scratch the dried hair spray on her scalp.

"Was it true what we heard? Did them boys get thrown seven floors?"

"Yep."

"Damn. Is…is Yvonne okay? I heard they tried to cut her."

"You better go on back, cher. I don't want you getting in trouble if someone sees you wit' me. I appreciate you letting me know. You been doing all right?"

There was the opening she had hoped for. And he was easy to talk to.

"I'd be grateful if you'd pass it on that I was helpful. Last time the man came to collect, he wanted free pussy. I pay enough, Guidry, without them grease-ball collectors banging my girls. I can't keep 'em if they have to turn tricks for free. There's too many other places for them to go work. If you see any of the bosses, if you'd just mention I was helpful? We don't want no trouble in the Quarter."

"I'll make sure the right people are aware you doing your part, cher. And I 'd appreciate it if you let me know if anything else funny goes on over there," He squinted down the block. "Looks like you got two customers at the door, sweetheart, better run. Thanks again."

She grabbed the door handle and was halfway down the sidewalk in five seconds. Guidry reached over to shut the door. He wanted to circle the block and check out Fat Jack's shop for himself. But it would be risky and he knew her information was good.

"Damn, Jess, what you doing? Go home, take Denny with you. You got two of ours now and them three in your cigar box last year. Fuckin' leave," He urged silently. "It ain't ever gonna be even. Somebody's got to stop. The wrong people are gonna get hurt." Like Yvonne Breaux. In the privacy of the dark truck, he allowed himself a harsh breath with ragged emotion. It threatened to flare into a rage, so he gripped the steering wheel before it took over. Lado and the probate were lucky they died.

♦

When he got to the farmhouse, the big steel gate at the road was closed. The toothless kid had been stationed as a guard, a shotgun crosswise in his arms.

"What's going on?" He pulled up, eying the distant lights down the lane. It sounded like they were having a party.

"Just want to make sure you're by yourself and ain't nobody hitched a ride in the back."

"You think I'm a fool?"

"Course not, Guidry. I'm just following orders. Sleaze is back, and he's wired, man. He's brought some people with him, too."

"What kind of people?"

The kid sighed, and shifted the shotgun.

"Nobody I wanted to know."

The truck rumbled down the rutted road, blue moonlight flooding through the pine trees. This night would have been better spent romancing Madeline, her wearing a simple but expensive blue dress like some politician's wife, take her out U.S. 90 to Mosca's for supper, then back to the apartment. She liked to wear panties and bras that matched the dresses. He liked the way she moved, the way she looked at him with those heavy-lidded eyes as if she wanted to know exactly what he was thinking. It had been a challenge to surprise her. They did things different in Vegas.

"Shit man, get your brains on business, not that red hair."

He counted seven cars around the farm house, and the front porch teetered under the weight of a dozen armed men. Sleaze stood against a post barely supporting the tin roof. Guidry was surprised it didn't splinter when he wrapped one arm around it so he could toast him with a bottle of Jax in the other hand.

"Mr. Guidry has returned," Sleaze rasped. "Come on up here and look who I brought back to help us in our time of need."

Great. Wired to the gills. As were the two men he pointed to, settled on the edge of the porch, shoulders hunched in their thin tee-shirts, biceps and chests rock-hard from daily prison work-outs. Racine, he remembered well, Mississippi white trash who lived to brawl and stayed in and out of prison for robberies and assaults. He could not recall the other man's name, but knew he was a cousin to Muller, the enforcer who vanished last year along with two others, and wound up in a cigar box, thanks to Jess.

On the far end of the porch, the Trog sat on a battered milk can, his back against the unpainted wood siding. The Bayou Runners watched and waited.

"You on paper?" Guidry asked the two new arrivals.

"Of course," Racine shrugged his tattooed shoulders. "But I ain't worried about it. I come down here to make me some money."

Hell, what had Sleaze told them? Not the dope boats. And had he said it in front of the Trog?

"They want to join the fight for old time's sake," Sleaze grinned, his black eyes brilliant. "Racine's got a grudge with…which one was it?"

"Smitty. That punk stole a car from me and left me stranded."

"If you get his patch, it's mine," Sleaze reminded him.

"No problem. I don't want it. I just want to bust his head. For old time's sake."

"And Muller," Sleaze vibrated. "Well, that's self-explanatory."

"My cousin went missing last year when I was in Angola," The man told Guidry. Wasn't nothing I could do about it. But I'll by God do something now."

The man shared his cousin's shaggy dark hair and German features. And probably his rap sheet full of rapes.

"Either of you wanting to probate for us?" Guidry hated to mention it, but he had to find out what Sleaze had promised them.

"Hell fuckin' no. I just wanta find out what happened to my cousin. I owe him. He saved my life twice in Angola. Twice." Stoned, he thumped the porch with his beer bottle.

"Well ya know what? I can solve that little mystery for ya," Sleaze cackled. "It's about damn time anyway."

The Bayou Runners exchanged puzzled glances. Guidry blazed a warning at Sleaze but he ignored it and went tripping into the house, arms swinging for balance.

"What the hell is he on, he looks like Charles fuckin' Manson," Fahey growled.

"What's he talking about? How does he know what happened to Muller? They all just vanished. Didn't they?"

Even the Trog watched from his milk can when Sleaze came whirring out of the house, clutching a cigar box against his chest.

"This ain't the place for that," Guidry tried again. "That's the man's family you're talking about."

"Sure as fuck is."

With a grin, he opened the lid and clumsily tossed out the contents on the porch as if he were freeing captured insects. The men jumped back. Only Hermy moved forward to touch one with his boot.

"Don't do that. I think that's Muller. Or maybe it's Jitters," Sleaze laughed.

Hermy stepped back. The drunken cousin rolled onto his knees and crawled across the wood planks.

"What is this?" He picked one up. "What do you mean it's Muller?"

Sleaze staggered over and pulled out the edges for him.

"See? '1%er.' Your dumb fuck cousin got himself a tattoo he didn't earn, and pissed off a psycho medic I used to know. Here's Lem. And Jitters. And Muller. No way of knowing who died first."

"But what is it?"

"The tat was on his chest. Someone surgically removed it." The muscles on Sleaze's face tired, unaccustomed to constant grinning. His mood took a sharp left into a bad place, and the smile turned into a grimace. "He shouldn'ta died like that. It had to be hard."

The man dropped the curled dried skin.

"That's from his chest? His fuckin' chest?"

"Jesus Christ!" The men on the porch cringed.

"How long you had them, Sleaze?" Hermy said, stunned. "Why didn't you tell us you knew they was dead?"

Guidry stared at him, poker-faced, his mouth shut. It had gone too far now. The Trog stood up and walked over to the dried objects, crouching to look more closely.

"How are you so sure who did this?"

"Cause he mailed 'em to me. He wanted me to know."

Hermy and several other charter members put it together. They knew one man with the skills, and mindset, to exact revenge in such a manner.

"This is because of that bullshit ambush last year. When the kid probate got killed," He declared, spooked beyond caution.

"No, it's because these three went and got themselves one-percenter tats they had not earned."

"You know who did this," The Trog repeated, touching one with the tip of his finger.

"Yeah. He used to be a Bayou Runner. Patched over to the Regents a while back." Sleaze wet his lips, swaying on his feet. "He was a medic in the war."

The Trog was silent.

"We heard he was in town, too," Virgil spoke up, determined to sway things toward Sleaze. "Ain't that right, Guidry?" He taunted. "Weren't you telling us that the cops at the hospital described Jess to a tee?"

Guidry glanced at Hermy, who understood where this was going. They were smart enough not to rise to the bait. But the Trog didn't care about their club politics.

"If I was y'all," He said, exaggerating a southern accent, "I'd want the psycho medic gone, and quick. Before he finds you first."

CHAPTER THIRTY-TWO

"What day is it?" Sleaze hung off the bed, one foot on the floor to steady himself. Maybe he had finally roasted his brain. It was hot and wiggly along the edges where it touched his skull, like it was well-done.

"I don't know."

"How long did I sleep?" He tried again. It was dark outside and dark in the room. Everything was downright murky except the pink fringe glowing behind his nose.

"About thirty minutes," Virgil burrowed into the sleeping bag on the floor. "But you been up three days that I know of."

"I've pissed myself."

"Nobody'll notice."

"I'm gonna be sick." Jesus, this was the worst, the absolute worst.

What the fuck had Racine concocted? Even the damned Trog had finally shut up. Sleaze staggered to the shower, crashed into the wall, turned on the cold water and slid down, waiting for the water to put out the fire in his head.

"Sleaze, you up there?" Someone called from downstairs.

"Fuck off. I'm dyin'."

"There's somebody at the gate. They won't talk to me. They want you or Guidry."

"Go find Guidry." He opened his mouth to catch the cold well water. The clogged pipes barely produced a mild spray but the drops still hurt his bad teeth when they hit. He grabbed the knobs and pulled himself up so he could get closer to the shower head.

"Guidry ain't here." Hermy trudged up the stairs. "I told 'em to come back later, but they're from town, says they got a message."

"My brain's on fire." Sleaze groaned.

Hermy waited patiently.

"I'll drive you down to the road. It might be important. Somebody else might be dead."

"I see music on your face," Sleaze gasped. "What day is it?"

"It's two days since you threw them tattoos on the front porch." Hermy accused. "What kind of music? Can you hear it, too?"

Sleaze was not in the mood for criticism or questions. He turned off the water and stepped out of the shower dripping in his clothes, balancing his wild head in his hands.

"Help me downstairs and bring a car up to the porch."

Hermy rode the brakes all the way down the lane just to keep the big engine under five miles per hour. Sleaze hung out the window puking.

"Who is this guy?"

"I don't know him. He says Peggy sent him and he ain't talking to nobody but you or Guidry."

"Peggy. She…she's the old whore who runs the brothel, right? Across the wall from Fat Jack's?"

"Think so."

"How the fuck did this guy find us?"

"He lives out here somewhere. He's married into her family."

"Good damned thing this ain't the other place. If it was that easy to find…Jesus, pull up, I ain't getting out. Hey you. You wanta see me?"

The man walked up to the car and peered inside cautiously.

"You Mr. Sleaze?"

"I was two days ago. Right now I'm a poisoned mother-fucker. What have you got for me?"

"Miss Peggy wanted you or Mr. Guidry to know she's seen some more strangers over at Fat Jack's. One of 'em was a big man, she said resembled a cave man. They came by about four a.m. and went off some place with the blond man she already told you about. They're driving an old Dodge Dart, light-colored."

Sleaze blinked, opened his mouth wide to pop his jaw. She had told him what? Aw Jesus, he couldn't remember. How could he forget the old whore tipping him off about where the Regents were? Christ, was he finally losing it?

"When did she tell me this shit? What day did I talk to her?"

"Wasn't you, Mr. Sleaze. She told Mr. Guidry a couple of nights ago about them strangers at Fat Jack's." The man drew back from the car a little. "She just wanted y'all to know there was more strangers showing up. Mr. Guidry asked her to keep an eye out."

Sleaze opened his parched mouth to speak, but he didn't know what question to ask. He pulled up the front of his wet shirt and sucked the moisture out of it. The inside of his head lifted upward, a peculiar pressure separating it from his hair. He tried to think.

"Let's go," he managed to say.

Hermy worked the car back around and headed down the lane.

"Did you know about this?"

"No," Hermy said tonelessly.

"Why…what's he doing? Why didn't Guidry tell me?"

"Cause you been crazy lately, Sleaze. He's trying to keep everybody from getting killed and you won't listen to him."

"He should have told me. He was here all day and didn't say nothing about knowing where the Regents are."

"And you were shooting up all day, too," Hermy said, then softened it by saying: "And he hates that Trog. He ain't gonna talk in front of him."

"The Trog's got nothing to do with it." Sleaze chewed his lower lip until he tasted blood.

"He's got everything to do with it," Hermy said. "Guidry wants us to lay low 'til that boat comes in. We get our cut, the boys ain't getting killed, and the Chamber of Commerce stays happy with us. Then if the Regents ain't gone home, we make our move, make your fuckin' Trog happy."

"Nothing's gonna make him happy."

"You the one brought in Racine and Muller's kin. You're wanting a fight."

"None of the rest of you have any fucking balls!" Sleaze snarled and puked out the window again.

"Last ones had balls wound up like scrambled eggs sharing a drawer at the coroner's office."

"I didn't send those two idiots after Denny. They didn't even tell me."

"They didn't have to. The Trog knew. That was good enough for 'em," Hermy explained patiently. "He's the one seems to count around here."

"I know Guidry ain't working with him." Sleaze came back full circle. His chest hurt now, a dull ache he had never felt before. "So who's he working for?"

"The Bayou Runners," Hermy said softly. "Your club."

"That's right. It's my damned club. Not his. I put it together. Maybe he needs reminding." Sleaze leaned forward to squint at the porch. "What happened to those tats?"

Hermy closed his eyes for a brief minute. Two nights ago, and he was just now asking.

"Muller's cousin picked up one. Virgil got one. And the Trog took the last one."

♦

Across the river from New Orleans, on a desolate strip of U.S. 90, late-night gamblers could order dinner at 1 a.m. at Mosca's Italian Restaurant. If he'd been able to take the motorcycle, with her on the back, the ride would have calmed him down. But the Harley was parked in the garage, and he'd borrowed a car for the twenty-five minute drive. She sat close to Guidry on the seat, one hand lightly on his shoulder, like an old-fashioned date.

After they returned from dinner to the upstairs apartment, she closed the curtains and asked him to turn on the air conditioner in exchange for a massage.

"How do you stand the heat?" She said in her husky Lauren Bacall voice. "It's eighty degrees at night in September here."

"How hot is it where you're from?"

"Get naked and find out."

She said she came from Las Vegas, but never talked about where she lived, or grew up. He never asked. He only kept on with it because she'd been quiet during dinner. He hadn't felt like talking much, either. This was what they both wanted, behind the safety of thick cypress doors, relaxed from the drive and a bottle of burgundy wine. Her firm thighs straddled his hips while she worked her fingers through the leaden tissue and muscle in his upper back.

"Etienne, your shoulders are in knots. What's got you so tense?"

"You sitting on my ass, girl, with that hot fanny of yours."

She laughed, and dug into the muscles under his shoulder blades.

"It's the least I can do after you bought me a nice dinner."

"I got to buy you dinner to get you to laugh?"

She grew quiet, and he regretted ruining her good mood. They had both been preoccupied all night, struggling for conversation.

"I've been worried about you. You set me up in this nice apartment and then vanish. I appreciate you keeping me safe but when you didn't come back…" She moved forward to put her hand over his and kissed the side of his face, her long red hair sweeping across the pillow. "With everything going on, I worry. I'm not complaining. I just wasn't expecting all this other stuff when I came to New Orleans."

"Thought you were going to make big money dancing in a nice club, go out to dinner with gangsters, ride around town in a limousine?"

"Well, you got the money part right, anyway," She laughed.

"And that hasn't worked out for you, either."

"No. You've been good to me, but I want to get out there and make my own money again," She laughed low. "What the hell. I was looking for adventure and romance, and sure as hell found it."

"If you want to go out, see some sights the next couple of days, you won't be bothered. I'll leave the car here."

Her intriguing movements stopped.

"You didn't…uh, do something to him."

"No. He's busy, a place across the river," He said. "I can keep an eye on him there."

And take care of his ass first chance I get.

Her fingers pushed and dug against the resistance remaining in his shoulder, and he heard her sigh. In his experience, that meant bad news.

"Etienne, I want to talk to you about something and I don't know how," She said softly. "I'm thinking about going back out to Vegas for a while, until this is over. Unless you think it's going to end soon." She hesitated. "I'd rather stay here but I can't hide forever. I'm not asking you to discuss business, I know you can't do that. But can you at least tell me if your people are going to do something about that other club soon? If they…what's that?"

The cajoling tone hardened and her hands eased away.

"Look. On the floor," She said. "It wasn't here when we left this afternoon."

She slithered to the far side of him as he lifted up, both staring at a white envelope on the cypress floor, partially hidden under a dresser.

"I locked the door when we left," She said, suddenly frightened. "I know I did."

He reached under the mattress for his pistol.

The apartment was basically one good-sized room in the upstairs of an old Garden District mansion: a kitchenette on one side, the bed against the far wall, and a wardrobe for a closet. A tiny bathroom had been squeezed in around the corner, the single bulb casting a rectangle of light across the kitchen counter. There was no place for an intruder to hide.

"Somebody must have slid it under the door while we were gone."

"You have a boyfriend, cher?"

"I'm not seeing anyone but you."

Annoyed, she crawled over him, retrieved the envelope, examined it, and handed it to him. "My name ain't Guidry."

He set the pistol down on the sheet beside him, and ran his tongue along the back of his teeth. Who the hell would know where to find him tonight?

"Have you told anybody you livin' here? Grocery store? Cab driver?"

"No. You said not to."

Only three people knew he lived in the apartment next door to this one, and Madeline was not one of the three. The landlady must have seen them go out, and knew which door to slide it under. The handwriting was scratchy and the envelope contained a half sheet of notebook paper. He read it twice before recognizing Hermy's scrawl.

"Whore sent messenger. More people seen at jacks. S. upset you didn't tell him you knew. Called a big meeting. Made bad plans. H."

Damn. Madeline watched him, her intense focus on his eyes, like she was trying to see inside his head. He got up and walked over to the gas stove and lit the paper. When the flames burned his fingertips, he let it fall in the sink.

"Is it bad?" She whispered.

"Vegas might be a good idea after all."

CHAPTER THIRTY-THREE

The Dodge Dart sat parked down a deserted side street in the shadows of an old oak, facing the backside of the warehouses. From that angle, Joe could see the three warehouses on the end, although not for long. Silvery fog crept in from the river, consuming the solitary streetlight. He would have to move shortly, but had run out of places to park where he couldn't be seen. He also had no way to let Randy know his whereabouts. This was the worst part, he and Randy agreed.

"If we just had a shoe phone like Maxwell Smart, we could at least make some phone calls."

"To who, Agent 99?"

"I don't know. Each other? I could call you, make sure nobody come up behind you and slit your throat like they do in the horror movies." Randy made a face and gurgled.

"While you're in there watching skin flicks."

"Hey man, you picked the short straw. Tomorrow night, it's your turn."

"As long as they stay gone, I'm catching up on my sleep."

Taking turns on guard duty had worked out for both of them. In the absence of the Regents, they decided it was pointless to station two vehicles on watch. So the winner watched TV or slept inside the building, while the loser spent the night trying to stay awake in a muggy car. Joe didn't care. He was dead broke and his only source of food and cigarettes came from the unattended stash in the warehouse.

Joe kept the windows halfway down, and could sometimes hear party boats leaving the Canal Street docks for a moonlit cruise on the Mississippi.

Down the street, the noisy rock and roll warehouse sent drum vibrations and bits of guitar riffs he tried to recognize. Statesboro Blues? The Allman Brothers were regulars there. Marijuana rode in on the wet crystals, and he took a deep breath.

A car moved slowly down Tchoupitoulas. Two a.m.. Most likely a stoned college kid heading back to Tulane from the concert, unable to see the street signs or landmarks. Joe smiled. He remembered being so drunk that his own street didn't look right and he pulled into the wrong driveway. He also remembered the next morning when his dad dragged him from the car across the wet grass to their house. Good old days, as long as nobody got hurt.

Two ghostly orbs floated toward him as the car turned up the side street. Joe hastily slumped down and became completely still when the vehicle pulled over under the street light, the roof shadowing the occupant. He reached for his pistol. Let it be a lost tourist or college student wanting to puke.

The driver's door opened, and the streetlight shimmered across red hair. The girl wore a windbreaker despite the humidity, and had a hand jammed in the pocket, which meant she had a pistol or knife. Easing the door shut, she hurried across the street to the parking lot. A shoe phone would be pretty handy right about now.

She started at the warehouse on the end, went to the single door, and to Joe's surprised, she knocked. Her knuckles made no impact on the thick door, so she slapped her palm against it, then kicked it. He couldn't see her face clearly, but her agitation was plain. The girl looked over her shoulder at the chain link fence and dumpsters and old buildings surrounding her, then slapped the door with her palm again.

"Hey!" She called. "Open up."

Again, she waited, and he heard her mutter "damn it!" She stepped back, studied the door for a sliver of light, then hurried to the second warehouse. Bingo. The big double doors were solid, the hardware old but secure. She took off her shoe and pounded on it. Joe cringed. The noise echoed through the wet air. What the hell did she want? He debated confronting her. If she didn't have that hand in her pocket, he would be less reluctant. And she was Guidry's girlfriend. This could be a trap, the oldest trick in the book, sending a female to lure someone out.

Joe exhaled, his fingers tightening on the .380. Down on Tchoupitoulas, another vehicle crept through the mist. It passed by, then stopped and backed up. The headlights switched off, and the car eased up the side street and stopped just below the streetlight. Damn, he was right, it was a trap! He sat up straighter. The driver waited, the window down. Joe was sure they could hear the sounds of her shoe thudding against the door. Someone slid out of the car. Definitely a man, moving quickly and quietly across the street to the side of the warehouse.

Shit, he needed to signal Randy. *Don't answer that damned door.* But if he gave away his position, it would definitely compromise the warehouse and all that firepower inside. Would they give up and leave if no one came to the door? Joe thought about starting the car and driving by very slowly to see if they would spook. But before he could do anything, the driver stepped around the corner and deliberately stood where the girl could see him, backlit into a large black shape. The girl glanced sideways, screamed, then covered her mouth.

"What are you doing here?" The man said.

No Cajun accent. Not Guidry.

"What the hell do you want?" The girl retorted, her voice high.

"I asked you a question, cunt. What are you doing here?"

"I came to see a girlfriend, if it's any of your business."

He looked up at the windowless brick façade.

"She must not have been expecting you."

"You were following me?" She spat with righteous indignation but she had slid her shoe back on and was steadily backing up. "What the hell is your problem? Guidry'll cut your nuts off."

"He hasn't done it yet," The man taunted.

"That's 'cause I didn't tell him what you did. Or tried to do, with your limp little needle-dick. No wonder you've got to take it from a woman. Who'd want to fuck that three inches you can't get hard? You piece of shit."

"Guidry's a good fifty miles from here, Red, at their little country place. They're real busy right now, and damn sure don't give a shit if I'm gone for a while. I ain't worried about him or if you like what I do to you. I want to know what you're doing here."

She took two more steps, then turned and bolted. Her long legs gave her a brief advantage, but the man knew she would run, and caught her by the hair. He yanked her around, slapped her hard across the face twice to end any resistance, waited a second, then hit her in the jaw with his fist.

"Do ya like that, cunt? You want to suck some dick with a broken jaw? Bet that'll feel real good."

She hit the gravel, wheezing, but her hand came up with the knife and she slashed clumsily at his ribs.

"Goddamn!" He caught her wrist, twisted it until she dropped the knife, then punched her in the stomach. "You're gonna tell me why you're here. It might take all night, but you'll be thrilled to tell me what I wanta know. Get up."

He grabbed a handful of her hair and started toward the car. She pedaled to her knees, then vomited. He pulled her head up and backhanded her until blood smeared a red mask across her face.

"Let her go."

The Trog glanced up, startled. Out of the mist came a furious face, an extended arm and a silver barrel with a small black hole.

"Mind your own business, cowboy," He told the stranger.

The girl choked, spitting blood. The Trog bent to yank at her hair, concealing his left hand while he reached under his shirt to pull out a snub-nosed revolver. He drew in a deep breath, feeling the power of the cold steel in his hand. Pulling the trigger was orgasmic, rendering the smart-mouthed cunt into a white silent heap, and then the do-gooder stranger who had been too chicken-shit to fire when he should have.

Two quick pops exploded, the sound ricocheting up the red brick wall into the wet night air. The Trog exhaled and tumbled over, his shoulder dredging a short path in the gravel. The girl sank to a crouch, her arms over her head, shuddering.

Joe couldn't move, stunned by how quickly it had ended. He stood with his legs braced, the .380 still extended. Damn. He had shot the guy. Without even thinking about it. Without intending to. But his brain registered the snub-nose coming around toward the girl's head, and sent a message down his arm to his hand.

"Did I do that?" He almost said out loud.

The girl gagged again, a wet red trail running down the front of her jacket.

"Jesus, did I hit you?" Joe shoved the .380 in his boot and hurried toward her.

"No, please, I didn't see anything. Please let me go." Terrified, she scrambled away from him. "I won't tell, I swear."

"I'm not going to hurt you." But he had no idea what to do with her. She'd just witnessed him shoot this man in a damned parking lot. If he were back home, he'd know what to do…maybe. Shit shit shit!

Wood creaked somewhere in front of him. Out of the gauzy veil came a fast-moving form. Randy, with a pistol in each hand, a 9mm zeroing in on the Trog, the .38 searching the mist behind Joe.

"Shit, what happened?" He hissed, and kicked the pistol away from the Trog's hand. "What fuckin' happened?"

"He followed her here. About killed her. He pulled down on me."

"Was he by himself?"

"I didn't see anyone else. His car's over there beyond the streetlight. So's hers, this side of it."

"This is the same girl came here your first night?"

"Yeah. She's Guidry's girlfriend, the one I saw at the bar."

Randy stared, panting. "What are you doing here, girl?"

"I won't tell. Please don't kill me. Please."

"Are you by yourself? Don't lie to me." He stepped forward and put the pistol to her head.

"Damn it, what are you doing?" Joe gaped.

"I'm by myself." She wept. "I came to…to find an old friend. I had a message for him."

Sirens rose up in the distance, the sound raising the hair on Joe's neck.

"Shit. Watch her," Randy ordered.

He hurried off into the mist, boots crunching like firecrackers in the gravel, and returned with the Trog's car. He pulled up beside them, looked around, then opened the trunk.

"Give me a hand."

The Trog weighed at least two hundred pounds, but adrenaline had them both buzzing, and they weren't worried if he was comfortable wedged around the spare tire. Randy tossed the snub-nose in.

"Go get your shit out of your car and lock it up. Quick," He told Joe.

"Want to move it off the street?"

Randy glared at the girl. "No. We still don't know why she came here."

Joe hurried to the Dodge, listening to the sirens. They weren't moving fast. If someone had called in the shots, it'd be anybody's guess where it happened. The girl sat in a crumpled heap, her arms cradling herself. But her battered face lifted, triumphant, as Randy closed the lid to the trunk.

"Give him the keys to your car," He told her when Joe returned. "Help her up, we've got to get out of here."

What the hell were they going to do with her? Joe eased the girl to her feet. She had to be wondering the same thing.

"You know somebody named Dudley?" She sniffed, and winced.

Randy paused. "What you know about Dudley?"

“What do you know?” She countered.

“I know we don’t have time for bullshit,” Randy snapped.

“He’s boss of the Atlanta Regents, right? Smitty’s the VP, Bobby Boozer’s enforcer. So now, you tell me their old ladies’ names.”

“Flossie,” Joe spoke up. “Dorrie and Suzette.”

The girl’s eyes closed in relief. “So you are Regents?”

“Close enough.”

“And the rest of them are over at Fat Jack’s,” She said tiredly.

“How the hell do you know that?”

“The Bayou Runners all know that, they’ve got spies all over the damned place. Everybody’s related to everybody else. I couldn’t go to the shop, so I came here to warn you. The Bayou Runners are going to hit the tattoo shop some time tomorrow.”

Randy glanced at Joe.

“Now why would Guidry’s girlfriend want to warn the Regents? They’d peel your skin off and feed you alive to the gators. And why the hell do you keep coming here looking for Regents?” Randy was extremely irritated that his safe house had somehow been compromised.

“I’ve only been Guidry’s girlfriend for two months,” She said, wiping her mouth with her sleeve. “He thinks I’m a dancer from Vegas. I was sent to hang out with the Bayou Runners, and it was a lot easier to get close to Guidry than Sleaze.”

Shit. Joe remembered how the smug Trog followed them everywhere. Had he just offed her boyfriend?

“Who sent you?” Randy asked, waiting to see just how bad the situation could get.

Despite her broken nose and cut face, she looked at him with a proud smile and announced: “My old man sent me. Big Alec. I’m from Miami.”

CHAPTER THIRTY-FOUR

Randy Breaux helped carry the red-haired girl up the back steps, introduced Joe to his sister, and grabbed a fresh set of clothes. Joe followed him down. They stood in the street between the two cars, the heavy Spanish moss muffling their conversation.

"I'll take care of it," Joe said.

"You don't know where to go. I do."

"It's my problem." Technically.

Two feet away, in the trunk of the stolen Crown Vic, lay the problem. A Trog, no less. A favorite soldier of Leon, the legendary boss of the Troglodytes MC.

Joe felt like he had just let go of a rope he had been hanging onto for a long time. He was falling…

Randy stared at him for a long minute.

"You can't lose it now. Anybody finds out about this, you are dead, you hear me? That is a mother-fucking Trog." He stopped, his gaze going up to the window of his sister's apartment. "I ain't too sure we might have to take care of that, too."

"The girl?"

"She could put you in Angola for life, or send you to the chair. This is Louisiana, Joe. You gonna gamble your life on her not telling her big man all about it?"

Randy didn't move, but Joe felt him pull back. If he couldn't trust Joe, Randy had just set himself up for a big fall. How far would he go to protect himself and his family? As far as Joe would go.

"She won't tell, Randy. She's a Regents old lady. They know better. Don't think about hurting that girl because of me. You do it, it's on you."

"I don't like loose ends but we ain't got time for this." Randy shook his head. "Soon as you get done upstairs, ditch her car and head for Fat Jack's to warn 'em about the Bayou Runners. Damn, I can't believe Sleaze keeps pushing this. He's lost his damn mind."

"You're the one who gave the Regents a place to stash everything. Whose side are you on, anyway?"

Randy bit his upper lip, and admitted: "I never thought the Regents would get a chance to use them. I thought the Bayou Runners would hide out. Just goes to show you, you can't out-think a dope head."

"Your way of keeping an eye on everything," Joe remarked. "For the locals."

"Local businessmen. I got friends in the Regents and Bayou Runners. I'm not in a good place here."

Joe glanced at the trunk.

"Did this solve a problem or create a problem?"

Randy laughed. "Hell if I know."

Joe finally smiled.

"Hey, you still got that tarot card on you?"

"Sure."

"I told you before, it's quite a gift. Knight of Swords. It keeps you safe."

"How did you know?" Joe said, surprised. "Shit, I don't even remember deciding to pull the trigger. It just happened..."

Randy rubbed away a mosquito with his sleeve, and glanced at the Crown Vic. "I've got to go. Believe what you want. You were in the military. Maybe it was all that training. What matters is, you beat him to it. Now we clean up and shut up. He ain't much of a loss in my book."

♦

The two women in the expensive, spacious apartment acted like it was normal for people to show up covered with blood at four a.m..

"What's your name, Peaches?" Yvonne was all business, a terry-cloth robe over her red silk pajamas as she rigged up an IV in her spare bedroom.

"Her name's Madeline," Joe said from the door.

"Wha' ya doin'?" Madeline mumbled when Yvonne tied off her arm.

"You ain't gonna wanta feel what I've gotta do to your nose." She said, sinking the needle in on the first stick. "All right, cher, you're going on a little trip to sleepy land. If you feel like you're gonna puke, say so."

"Who you?" Madeline tried again, hanging on.

"She's a night supervisor over at Charity Hospital," A heavy-set blonde woman assured her. "You got lucky. We've both off tonight and she ain't busy, which is a miracle. Somebody musta had to get back to his wife before breakfast."

"You're real funny," Yvonne said, "It was too damn crowded down there tonight anyway."

"Guess it would be kinda awkward to give your favorite patient a sponge bath in front of all his friends. Boing boing!" The blonde lifted her finger several times.

"Don't be talking nasty in front of my brother's friend and this dead girl. Hmm, Miss Madeline's got good veins, she just don't have no blood in 'em. She in a car accident?"

"No. Somebody beat her," Joe said.

Yvonne winced, then glanced at him.

"How about you, baby, that shower do you some good? You want somethin' for your nerves before you leave, help yourself to the cabinet." She shook her head. "I sure thought Randy's clothes would fit better than that. I'm usually a pretty good judge of size."

"They don't feed their probates," He said.

"Put them dungarees in the washer. I'll get 'em back to you somehow. But we gonna burn that shirt, it's half rags anyways." And looked like he'd been to a hog-killing.

"You said Denny's room was crowded?"

"More of his friends. From Chicago."

Finally. Joe poured himself a stiff shot of whiskey, and watched her set ice packs around the girl's face.

"Madeline was…is…very pretty." He said in case they could do something about it.

"Somebody didn't think so."

"Need my shtuff," Madeline mumbled, her eyelids fluttering toward Joe. "Can you take me?"

"You can't go anywhere right now, cher." Yvonne bathed the dried blood from her shoulders. "You got a bad habit?"

All she needed on top of this was addiction withdrawals.

"Money. At my 'partment," Madeline swallowed, imploring Joe: "Take me there … 'fore Guidry comes back."

Yvonne paused, the wet cloth in her hand.

"Oh Lord," The blonde woman said under her breath.

"What Guidry you talking about?"

"Etienne," Madeline sounded like she was caressing his name.

Yvonne glanced over her shoulder at Joe and narrowed her eyes.

"Who is she? No bullshit from you with that grin, it won't work on me. I want to know who's in my house. I thought she was one of yours. How does she know Guidry?"

"She was sent here to find out what she could about the other team," Joe hesitated, wondering how much they knew about the clubs and the war. "Guidry's one of their people. He was her way in. He was easier to con than Sleaze."

The blonde woman kept her eyes down, and swallowed hard. Yvonne yanked a strip of tape from a roll and ripped it in half with blood-red fingernails.

"Guidry don't know yet about none of this."

"No," Joe said.

"My stuff," Madeline whispered through the morphine.

"Don't be worrying about your stuff," Yvonne snapped. "We'll get your stuff and your ass on a bus back to wherever you come from as soon as you can move."

"Etienne…" Madeline gurgled.

"Etienne Guidry is a proud man." Yvonne leaned in close to her smashed face. "Don't you dare try to apologize to him just to make yourself feel better about what you did to him. It would embarrass him to death if he knew what a double-dealing con bitch you are. He's better off thinking you crawled away and died."

"Vonnie," The blonde woman pleaded. "She's stoned. She doesn't know what she's saying. If you don't want her here, I'll take her over to my place. Randy wants to keep an eye on her, remember?"

"I'm gonna kill my brother for bringing her here. Hold her still, I got to fix her cute little nose."

Joe decided it would be a good time to leave.

♦

He assumed the car was stolen. Joe parked in a dismal lot at a by-the-hour motel near Congo Square, and wiped his prints off the wheel and door. She had bled all over the passenger seat. He checked the glove compartment and found a small bottle of mouthwash and a soap sample from a motel. The back seat was empty, but the floor behind the passenger seat had a surprise. A lump of denim unrolled into a shoulder bag.

He'd been raised to skirt wide around a woman's purse, including his mother's even if it sat half-open with the grocery money poking out. None of the kids dared help themselves to a stick of gum, or even ask about for one, because it would look like they had been snooping.

"Sorry, Mama, but I'm starving and I'd be scared to death if I had any sense right now." Joe stuck his hand deep in the denim bag, finding lipstick, mints, a hair brush, tampons, a switchblade, change and nail polish. She had supplies for any female emergency, and then some. But it was her money he needed. The bottom of the purse swam with change, and he found fifty dollars in bills stashed in a small beaded bag.

Crunching a mouthful of mints, Joe got out of the car and headed for the side street at the back of the motel. He pushed through a gap in the fence, and glanced around. A dark toothy grill grinned from the concrete curb. He plucked her driver's license from his pocket and tossed it into the grate. Madeline DuPree had officially vanished forever.

♦

With Ugly at the wheel, a half dozen Chicago Regents gaped like tourists at the intoxicated partiers lying on the sidewalks in the deserted French Quarter. Charged up after visiting Denny, they passed around a joint and a baggie of speed. They left three men behind on guard duty, and a very unhappy hospital staff.

"How come he looks like a pumpkin?"

"They said the medicine does that," Ugly explained. "Messes with his color."

"As long as he's all right, man. I swear, I thought we were gonna have a funeral."

"Nah, Denny's a tough mother-fucker. He don't need intestines."

"That's twice those bastards tried to kill him," The Chicago enforcer said. "I wanta make sure they know who they fucked with."

"Those two guys down in the morgue could tell 'em, if they could find their lips," Ugly laughed.

"Yeah, wasn't that some shit? When we get back, I want to call a vote about the hang-around. I want that son-of-a-bitch watching my back. Who knew, right?"

"Wonder how long it took for them to hit bottom?"

"They got what they deserved. That was low, going after a guy in a hospital," Ugly said.

"Hey, brother, stop here so I can get some beer, I'm thirsty as shit. Where's some place to eat this time of morning?"

"You'd have to ask Jess, he knows where everything is. He used to—holy fucking shit! That's our probate. What's he doing here?" Ugly leaned out the window. "Hey! Get over here."

Joe hurried across the street to the van.

"Everything cool? Why aren't you at the safe house?"

"Randy's there," He lied. "He got word about a hit today.I was heading for Fat Jack's to warn everybody."

"On foot?"

"Long story."

"Get in," Ugly said.

♦

They stopped at a pay phone and got directions from Jess to meet at an all-night burger joint. The place was empty except for two bombed insurance secretaries from Savannah hovering over a cold pizza. The women promptly left, and Bobby Boozer grabbed the pizza. An exhausted, pimple-faced waitress who may have been fourteen helped them shove tables together, then pulled out a tablet and pencil.

"Is this all one check?" She trembled.

"Yeah. Tell the cook we want thirty hamburgers all the way and seven baskets of fries," Jess said, sliding into a chair between Ugly and Smitty. "While he's cooking, bring us some beer."

They waited until the girl delivered the first round of beer and hurried to the kitchen to help the frantic cook before addressing Joe.

"Let's have it," Dudley said.

He sat between Bobby Boozer and the Louisville boss, finally on the downside of calm.

"Randy got a tip that the Bayou Runners are going to hit Fat Jack's sometime today or tonight. They know you've been staying there."

"Was this information good?" The Chicago enforcer stared him down. Joe didn't sound very excited about it.

"If it wasn't, he wouldn't have been sent," Dudley spoke up.

"Told you it would work. All we had to do was let 'em know we're in town and they can't help themselves," Smitty gloated.

"They're gonna hit the tattoo shop? Isn't that kinda public?"

"And it don't leave 'em an easy way out of there. Those streets are a bitch."

"They're getting bad advice from their Trog buddy and I'll bet he's rushing him," Dudley said.

"And they have friends everywhere, so they're really not taking much of a chance. We're the ones the cops will haul off," Jess said.

"So who's got any brilliant ideas? Or stupid ones?"

"The brilliant idea would be to close up the shop and not be there," Jess said.

"What's wrong with you?" A Chicago enforcer scowled. "This is perfect. We can nail 'em all."

"In a major tourist city? You better have a private jet on stand-by to get your ass out of here quick," Jess retorted.

"Sleaze ain't that stupid," Smitty said. "He just wants to make a show. Bet he doesn't know we just got reinforcements. I'd say let's teach him a lesson."

"Without a massacre?" Jess said drily.

"You with us or not, grandma?" Waco, a fellow Texan of Denny's, sneered. "I thought you and Denny were tight."

Smitty saw the acetylene torch ignite in Jess's eyes and quickly intervened.

"Jess is right about taking it easy. It's not a good place for either side. But apparently they don't know when to quit. How about a little spanking?"

He let them savor the idea along with their beer. Grins broke out as they nodded, rocking back in their chairs.

"I like it," Dudley said. "But we'll have to move fast, get our shit from the safe house."

Joe stared steadily at his beer, trying to make it last.

"They would have to hit late at night. After midnight," Smitty said. "Once the barricades are down and the tourists have left. I'd guess three or four a.m.. Daylight would be too risky for them, too many local people around."

"Anybody got a map? I want to see which way these streets run."

They pulled out pens and grabbed napkins to write on. The men familiar with the area huddled together, speculating. They wanted action, and the Bayou Runners were bringing it to them. But Joe did not get caught up in the excitement. He kept cycling back to Madeline and Big Alec. He'd come here to avenge Denny, and instead that damned bastard had outwitted all of them by sending in a girl two months ago to find out what she could. And created a disaster for him. He was too tired and sick to get mad about it.

A deep fryer crackled with pounds of French fries and the flustered waitress and cook darted around the kitchen like wind-up toys. The little waitress loaded two trays with more cold beer, and headed their way. Joe got up and headed down a long dim hall for the men's room.

He splashed his face with water, then leaned on the sink, his elbows locked and his eyes closed. This was for Denny. He had to hang in there for Denny. He had those incredible high buzzes of energy, so he had to expect the lows. The door behind him swung open, then hissed shut. Joe stood up straight, his gaze on the sink while he washed his hands.

"You all right?"

Oh. Here we go.

"Yeah." He scrubbed his fingers.

"I don't think so. Something happen?" Jess leaned against the wall by the towel dispenser.

"Are you psychic now, too?" The bad thing was, he desperately wanted to tell Jess. He wanted someone else to confirm what he should do, or not do.

He couldn't hurt Madeline even to save his own ass, but he was afraid that Randy could. He wasn't too damn sure if Randy wouldn't off him, too, if he felt threatened. Kitty's words floated back to him. "Don't trust anybody."

"You showed up with fresh clothes and after-shave and a mouthful of mints, and I don't think you and Randy are fooling around," Jess observed.

"Nothing happened. I'm just tired."

"Your boots must be lying."

"What?"

"Your boots. Attention to detail, probate. You washed off everything, including you, except the boots."

Joe didn't respond.

"Is Randy okay?"

"Yeah," Joe nodded. "He's all right. It's settled."

Jess opened a fresh pack of Marlboro's and offered him first choice. Truce? Not yet.

Joe said slowly: "I would like to know how Randy knows where the tarot card came from. It's kind of important at the moment. You've never said who the hell he is to you, but you threw us together for a reason."

Jess took a deep drag and watched the blue smoke head for the ceiling.

"Randy knows where you got the card because he's the one who gave her the deck. When he runs across them at pawn shops or antique stores, he buys them for her."

Joe frowned. "Randy knows Kitty? And you don't care if he buys her presents?"

"Nope. She's his little sister."

Joe stared at him, so stunned he didn't flinch when someone hammered on the bathroom door.

"Can you two wrap it up? I'm about to piss myself."

Jess smiled, a genuine grin that showed off his perfect teeth, and said: "Is that enough of a reference for you? You can trust the guy with your life."

Joe tried to return the smile, but wondered: "How about someone else's?"

CHAPTER THIRTY-FIVE

"Boss, it's two-thirty. We shoulda left by now."

Crickets jangled like metal combs grating in a tin can and the moths hit the porch light overhead with bee-bee pops. Sleaze raised his head, full of white energy, and peered down the lane for the hundredth time in two hours. Where were the headlights? He had this set up, ready to go, and the Trog still hadn't shown up.

"Where the hell is he? I want the mother-fucker to see this. We're gonna show him what we can do."

When they got word the Regents were staying at the tattoo shop, the Trog had grinned at him and said: "What are you waiting for? How about some patches? I'd love to make that call to Leon."

And Sleaze wanted him to. And now the son-of-a-bitch was off somewhere, right when he finally had everything in place.

"I ain't worried about impressing a Trog, I want to pay back those bastards for killing my cousin. You know which one tortured him. That's who I want and I want him alive." Muller's bloodshot eyes swung around, his rifle carelessly following in a sweep of wind.

"Yeah, Sleaze, let's do this. Who gives a damn about that Trog?"

"Maybe he's already there, waiting for the show," Virgil suggested, knowing what mattered to Sleaze.

Sleaze stopped pacing. "That's it. He's holed up some place to watch! Shit. And we're dicking around like idiots. All right. All right, let's go."

Hermy stuck his head in the front door. All the Bayou Runners were already waiting impatiently on the porch, except one.

"We're leaving," He called.

"Good luck."

Sleaze bopped down the steps, assigning men to the trucks, two cars for diversions, and a truck with a camper top. Hermy came down the steps behind him and headed for the camper.

"Where's Guidry?" Sleaze pivoted.

"Right here." He came to the screen door.

"Come on already."

"I'll handle guard duty. In case Mr. Trog comes back and wonders where all of you went."

"Kenny's got guard duty. Get your ass in the truck. Quit fuckin' around."

"I ain't going."

"What!" Sleaze screamed, and the Bayou Runners froze. "You mother-fucking pussy. What do you mean you ain't going? You saw what he did to Muller and Lem and Jitters. You want him coming after you in the middle of the night?"

"He sent the trophies to you, not me. You fixin' to get these boys killed over something that never was about them."

Sleaze flushed purple, clutching his rifle tightly. The Bayou Runners backed up, slinking close to the shadows for cover.

"You son-of-a-bitch!" Sleaze spat. "When I get back, I'm pulling your goddamn patch."

"Come and get it," Guidry said, and walked back in the house, letting the screen door slam. "I'll wait."

♦

With Muller's cousin riding shotgun, Virgil drove down Dauphine, creeping along in the primer-paint truck. A dank acidic smell from the silent street stirred their hair. Rifles rested across their laps and in the floorboard. They didn't give a shit that they rode past centuries of history, where bordello madams and blind pool players and illiterate jazz geniuses had made and lost fortunes. They believed their violence would become a new legend in the French Quarter.

"Is that it?"

"Next block, left side."

"I don't see no sign. Does he turn it off at night?"

"Heard he was a cheap bastard. Damn, that moon is lighting up the whole truck."

"You see any lights upstairs? There's a balcony down the side. Look quick."

They passed by the shop, and Virgil craned his neck to peer out the back window.

"I think I seen a cigarette up there." He relaxed and grinned. "Let's go tell the rest of 'em."

The Bayou Runners parked near Congo Square, their heart rates soaring near stroke level. A gray haze surrounded their vehicles from the cigarettes they chain-smoked.

"Okay, we gotta slow down long enough to fire 'em up, then haul ass, you understand me?" Sleaze could barely draw breath. His lungs bellowed for air, and he clawed at an itch rippling down his arm. "We gotta run these mother-fuckers out of town so we can take care of business. Did you see the Trog? He might be watching from the whorehouse."

Exasperated, Muller clenched his fists.

"I wasn't looking at nothing but that tattoo shop. We gonna bust down the door or what?"

"Jesus, no. I've done told you, we're gonna shoot the shit out of the place and haul ass. There's no way inside except the door and the window, and that door's two inches thick. We try to go busting in there, they'll kill us all. There's no place for cover. We're making a statement so the Trog can see we've got balls. You wanta do anything personal one on one, do it on your time."

His rotten teeth ached as air whistled through the roots. Christ, he'd already told the stupid shit this was a drive-by. They could shoot until they reduced the old bricks to powder, and with any luck, they'd nail some of the occupants, but this was not some eye-to-eye cowboy shoot-out in the street. This was noise and destruction of property and a "Fuck you!"

Sleaze grinned at the thought of the Trog watching the whole thing, and it relaxed his crew.

"We're gonna scare 'em so bad they shit their pants," Virgil declared. "Lock and load, boys, let's send 'em back to Atlanta, show Sleaze's Trog what we're made of."

Four men crowded into the truck with the camper topper and braced themselves against the sides, working rubber plugs into their ears, rifle barrels poking through the torn window screens. Sleaze elected to ride in the cab of the old truck with young reckless Kenny as the wheel man. Virgil was in charge of the overloaded car at the rear.

They crept down the silent streets, and Sleaze waved them to a stop at the corner of Dauphine. Headlights flickered out. He slid the back window open, propped up his pump shotgun barrel on the ledge, and told Kenny, "Go slow enough for me to blast 'em. If somebody's awake and fires back, step on it."

Kenny liked the idea of stepping on it.

"Don't even give 'em time to act, boss," Kenny gloated knowingly, the hardcore image he wished to project ruined by his smooth bare face and wisp of a mustache. "Catch 'em unawares."

Sleaze signaled the men behind them on Toulouse, and they pulled around the corner onto Dauphine.

"Damn that moon is bright," Kenny whispered, creeping past the old hotel. "Okay, boss, get ready to light 'em up."

He let the truck ease forward a few yards past the shop, giving the two other vehicles room, and stuck a finger in his left ear. Sleaze had the safety off on his Ithaca 12 magnum shotgun and was ready to rock and roll. He pointed the nose up at the balcony and the two shuttered doors, and braced his shoulder for the recoil. Sleaze took a deep breath, then hacked it out in disbelief when one of the other men fired first. Those stupid bastards! They were supposed to wait until he fired. Glass shattered, stinging his face, and Kenny flew forward.

"What the fuck—oh shit *shit*!"

Pops like firecrackers echoed between the brick houses and walls. Sleaze let loose with the shotgun, shoving Kenny. "Go go go!"

Kenny fell over on the door, his mouth exploded open like a wet rose.

Christ! Sleaze ducked to the floor as bullets sprayed the truck, and wrenched Kenny's shoe off the brake. Hanging on to the wheel, desperate to keep it straight, he mashed the accelerator with his right hand. The front end of the truck hit something hard but kept going and he didn't let up, gritting his teeth at the smell of warm shit oozing out of Kenny.

Behind him, Hermy took the old Chrysler up on the sidewalk to go around, the passengers screaming and ducking instead of returning fire. The two vehicles collided, running fender to fender, scraping concrete and cast iron gates all the way down Dauphine.

Peppered by precise fire from somewhere overhead, Virgil reversed the camper truck, tires screeching as it backed up to Toulouse, then rocketed away, the topper swaying.

A sudden quiet descended. Groggy residents and tourists awakened to wonder if they had dreamed the brief, intense exchange. Gunpowder floated in through open windows. Must have been teenagers with cherry bombs. Or thunder. They rolled over and went back to sleep. Over on St. Ann Street, a cream-tinted van started up and drove quietly to Toulouse. It parked in the shadows near an old hotel long enough for nine men to hurry from the gated courtyard and get in. Then it proceeded at a reasonable pace toward the warehouse district.

Fat Jack waited ten minutes, sweat pouring from under his flopping breasts down the front of his white wife-beater, then dialed the operator.

"Get me the po-lice. Somebody shooting up my shop. This is Fat Jack, I'm on Dauphine. They know me."

They wouldn't bother to show up, but he'd done what he was supposed to. He put the phone down with trembling hands and walked around back to make some coffee. There was no point in going to bed; he wouldn't be able to sleep for a week.

♦

At four a.m., it was easy to hear sounds in the distance. Some folks were already heading to work to beat the heat. But these vehicles came south, slowing at the open gate. Guidry stood in the yard beneath a magnolia to watch the headlights coming down the dusty lane. Two vehicles, one missing a headlight. His heart sank.

The old truck sputtered into the yard and pulled up beside the house. Behind it limped the camper truck. He looked down the lane, and didn't see the Chrysler. As soon as they stopped, the doors opened and the men piled out, some staggering to the porch, a few not making it. He tried to do a head count and was amazed to see Sleaze riding in the back of the truck. Alone in the cab, Hermy jumped out gagging and shoved off his jeans.

"Who's hurt? Where's the car?" Guidry asked.

"Had to park it. The radiator got hit." Hermy turned his head to puke in the grass again. "Holy Jesus, I been sitting in someone else's shit since New Orleans. It's done come through my jeans. Oh God."

He stumbled over to the water hose in his jockey shorts and sprayed himself down, shuddering when the water ran ice cold. White-faced and gritting his teeth, the tall Irish Bayou Runner staggered over and snatched the hose away from little Hermy, aiming it at his bloody shoulder.

"You shot, Fahey?" Guidry frowned.

"Ask who ain't shot, it'll be quicker."

Sleaze stalked across the yard, hitting himself on the head with his fists, and kicked a five-gallon bucket into the side of the house. The noises he made sounded like a man trapped in boiling water.

"Where's Kenny?" Guidry looked at Fahey, who shook his head.

His ambitions silenced, Virgil stomped up the steps and went inside the house, his palm pressed against his ear, followed by four others bleeding and desperate for a drink.

"Where's Kenny?" Sleaze mocked and suddenly stopped, his fists clenched at his side. Then he stooped over and picked up a handful of oyster shells. "You wanna know where Kenny is? He's fucking dead!"

Sleaze flung the shells at Guidry, who dodged, letting them clatter across the front porch.

"If you had gone, he'd be here on guard duty. He wouldn't be dead."

"What happened?" Guidry said between clenched teeth.

"They knew," Hermy gasped. "They was waiting on us."

"They let us get right in front of 'em and then opened up," Fahey said, his teeth chattering from the icy well water. "Would you look at this, see if it came out? I can't feel a hole."

"What I wanta know is how they knew?" Sleaze would not relent. "And how come you didn't go? How come you stayed here?"

"What are you saying?" Guidry looked at him.

Guidry saw fury, yet a pathetic despair. Sleaze didn't want to believe Guidry had betrayed him.

"You didn't tell me Peggy tipped you off about the Regents staying at Fat Jack's. Then you don't want to go, you don't want anybody else to go, and goddamn if we didn't get blown to shit." His sallow face peppered with shot, Sleaze's small eyes blazed back at him. "What the hell's your game? Who are you working for?"

"I tried to tell you this ain't the way to handle it. You let Leon push you into a damned war we didn't need. Everything was fine, Sleaze, 'til they showed up last year. It's gone to shit ever since."

Sleaze swallowed, and shook his head.

"You've never backed down from a fight. You always went."

"If your Trog saw all that, we can hang it up." Fahey pressed a sock against his bleeding shoulder. "He's probably laughing himself stupid."

"Shit." Sleaze plopped down on the porch steps and dug his fingernails into his scalp.

"Where is Kenny?" Guidry asked for the last time.

Hermy wrenched the faucet off and stalked up the steps in his soggy shorts.

"He's where Sleaze put him because the boy shit his pants. Don't worry, he's dead."

"Fuck you. Did you want to ride all the way out here with him in the cab?" Sleaze countered wearily, then changed tack. "Get your truck, Guidry, you and Muller can tow the car back here. They shot the shit out of it. It barely got to Lawson's Corners. We can't leave it by the side of the road."

"Let me guess," Guidry said tightly. "Kenny's in the trunk."

Unexpectedly, Sleaze laughed and reached in his pocket for a cigarette.

"Coulda been you. But you decided not to go." He fired up the lighter, took a long hit, then proved that despite the meth, the generations of petty criminals in his lineage, the roll of genetic dice that gave him a conscience he couldn't deal with, he still out-thought smarter men. "And still no sign of your friend the Trog. Ya know what, old buddy, if Leon comes down here looking for him, I won't be the only one asking questions about whose side you're on."

CHAPTER THIRTY-SIX

It was quiet in the foyer. Guidry shut the door, and paused to listen to the old clock ticking on the side table. He smelled lemon furniture wax. It was clean here. He wanted to be clean again. The landlady's door opened, her expression pleasant, but guarded.

"Hello, Mr. Guidry, I was hoping I'd catch you. I was wondering if your lady friend had moved out. I haven't seen her in a few days."

His eyes flickered up the stairs. "She was thinking about going home for a little while. Her mama was sick."

"Oh. Well, I'll wait then. Let me know if you want it for another month."

"Thanks, Mrs. LeBlanc."

He made himself walk slowly, and fished out the key from his pocket. He waited by the door, listening. When he didn't hear voices or the radio, he unlocked it and stepped inside. The bedside lamp was on, the bulb blazing hot to his touch. A faint sour smell came from the sink, an unwashed cereal bowl, a rim of curdled milk scumming the sides. Her clothes hung neatly in the wardrobe on perfumed hangers, her sparkly heels lined up on the floor. Her prized Magnavox stereo and turntable sat on the tiny dresser, along with the Jefferson Airplane and Emerson, Lake and Palmer albums.

Guidry couldn't find her purse. He checked the bathroom. Her toothbrush was dry. So was the wash cloth stretched over the tub faucet. He sat down on the bed and surveyed the small room again. Her and the Trog both gone. How long? He thought hard, his hand on the bedspread. He'd last been here three nights ago. When had anyone last seen the damned Trog?

He got up, locked the door, and hurried down the stairs, shaken by the thought he had once again been too busy to check on her, to spend time with her, take her dancing. To see if she needed him.

His blue truck was parked two blocks over, a brisk walk past dusky old mansions that looked a lot better now that the sun was almost gone. Virgil sat smoking a cigarette, waiting. He had not complained about the detour, even when he'd been told to wait in the truck. Sleaze had pitted them together to search for the Trog, and they were both irritated and tired. Hermy had spent the day calling the hospitals, while Muller and Racine headed for Pontchartrain Beach.

Leon had finally called that morning, and didn't bother to conceal his surprise or suspicions when he could not contact his lieutenant.

"He's got a thing for a whore down here. We think he's having some fun with her," Sleaze concocted at the spur of the moment, shifting the blame to the Trog.

Guidry overheard him, got a queasy hunch, and didn't protest when Sleaze sent him out with Virgil.

Now he stared out the windshield, and hardly noticed Virgil wheezing slightly.

"Now what? We gonna search the whole French Quarter?" Virgil grimaced. "These boots are new. They're killing me. Why don't we go on back? Maybe the asshole showed up or someone else found him."

He lit a joint and picked at the scab on his ear where a .22 had grazed it. Starting at noon, they had hit all the dive bars an out-of-town biker could possibly have ventured into, including neighborhoods that braver men would have avoided, and left each one with no clues. The bartenders and waitresses didn't act fearful or secretive, so they were most likely telling the truth.

"I think we can rule out The Rib Room and Brennan's," Guidry said sarcastically. "He mighta gone to some strip clubs, though. We'll go check."

"You're driving," Virgil shrugged.

They had only gone two blocks when a police car lurched out of a church parking lot and hit the blue lights.

"Shit." Virgil squeezed the joint out and got ready to toss it. "What the hell, man, you got a bad tag?"

"This is my damn truck, it ain't stole," Guidry said, frowning. "Wait here. He'll smell it if he gets too close."

He slid from the truck slowly, keeping his hands where the cop could see them as he walked back to the cruiser.

"Well hey there," He relaxed. "You 'bout scared the shit out of me. How you doin'?"

"I'm fine," His cousin said, his big worried face saying otherwise. "Hoping I'd run across you. You got a minute?"

"Sure." Guidry moved closer to the car so Virgil couldn't hear.

"You still got that little Chevy you bought from Aunt Pauline?'

Guidry felt his chest sink an inch, and fought to keep his shoulders straight.

"Yep."

"You loaned it to a friend lately?"

"Why?"

"Found it abandoned over there near Crozat. There's blood on the passenger seat. I ran the tag and saw it was still registered to you. I had it towed. You want to report it stolen?"

Guidry felt a tingle in his arm, and the ground shifted under his feet.

"It was stole about three nights ago," He finally said. "I'll come down and fill out a report tomorrow."

"I can do it now," His cousin glanced down at a clipboard. "You parked it in front of the dry cleaners on Tulane and went down the corner for a beer. When you come back, it was gone."

"Yes." He bit his lip under the mustache.

"I know somebody who can change out the seat. Be a week or so, though."

"It's that bad?" Guidry winced.

"Yeah, Etienne, it's that bad. We need to go have a beer later?"

"No, it's okay." He put his hand on the door. "Thanks, Emile. Thanks for everything."

At the next red light, Virgil lit up what was left of the joint and burned it off, tucking the baggie down in his boot. He tried not to grin. Guidry looked like a gang of vampires had lit on him and sucked the blood right out. His skin was clammy white against his black hair and his eyes stared ahead. Twice Virgil had to warn him about rolling through a Stop sign. It was good to see Mr. Cool looking shook for a change. Virgil smiled to himself. Things were shifting his way without even trying. Now if they could just find the Trog. He kind of hoped the guy was in a jam, where he could step up and help him out. That Trog was a scary son-of-a-bitch, and Virgil relished fantasizing about being the one he owed.

They parked and descended on the north edge of the French Quarter. An eerie cluster of black clouds drifted in from the west, hurling gusts down the narrow streets in short bursts. Trash fluttered around the tourists, and the jazz music sounded flat inside the halls, the sax and horns pumped full with heavy humid air. They tried several strip joints, quizzing the barkers and a few of the women, but no one remembered a man matching the Trog's description.

Tourists nervously crowded inside the bars, their good spirits replaced by edgy irritation as people jostled for drinks and the waitresses fell behind on orders. Guidry and Virgil worked their way down to a section thick with bars, wind blasting at canopies and clothes. Virgil was gratified to see Guidry distracted, like he was trying to solve a puzzle and walk at the same time. Gloating took the sting out of Virgil's blistered ankles.

"I'm gonna stop for a beer," Virgil announced. "You want to meet back here around ten? I'll hit this side of Orleans, you can take the other side."

Without waiting for an answer, he left Guidry standing on the sidewalk and strode inside the bar. Two tourists careened off toward the door, and he settled on an empty stool. He could feel Guidry's shocked gaze on his back, and he grinned.

"Get used to it, asshole. I'll be the one wearing a VP patch soon. Good old Sleaze done promised me. And when he patches over, he's taking me with him." He lit a cigarette, imagining the weight of that patch on his back.

A full-fledged Troglodyte, running dope with crazy-ass Sleaze, getting a bigger cut of the action. And the respect. Man, people pissed their pants and hid their daughters if a Trog walked down the sidewalk.

If they could just find the bastard before Leon called again, or showed up. He'd be Sleaze's right-hand man, in on the meetings and the action. Virgil reached for his beer, and had to grab it fast when two men roughly brushed against him to lean across the bar.

"Hey, come here," They beckoned to the bartender.

Startled, the bartender glanced at Virgil, expecting him to retaliate, but Virgil had sighted in on the sunburned arm that had almost claimed his beer, and stopped breathing. A tattoo decorated the heavy bicep. He glanced sideways again. A roaring lion, a shield crossed with scimitars. Virgil didn't move. Two Regents stood next to him, their black tee-shirts ringed with salt stains, the flesh of those white-scarred arms pungent. His injured ear burned. It could have been one of them who shot him the other night.

The bartender paled but headed down to their end of the bar. "Help you? We got cold drafts, two for one tonight."

"No. We're from out of town. We're looking for some friends of ours, thought they might hang out here. They're with a club called the Bayou Runners. Ya know any of 'em?"

"Holy Christ. Don't do it, mother-fucker," Virgil stared down at his watch, steadying himself while the bartender gasped for words.

"Don't know any clubs, sir. Sorry."

"You sure?"

Could he reach the door? *Don't run, just get up and walk.*

"Very sure, sir. I don't ask nobody nothing."

A customer at the far end of the bar hooted and tapped his empty glass. It was the excuse the bartender wanted, and he sped away. The two Regents stared and one sighed heavily.

"Maybe this wasn't such a good idea after all. Nobody knows shit in this city."

"All we need is one," The larger man said under his breath, and put his hand down flat beside Virgil, unwilling to leave. The knotty knuckles looked like the guy practiced boxing on concrete blocks. Another tattoo on the inside of his forearm sported the old classic "Death before Dishonor," and something about Chicago. Their cold brutal faces would have made the Trog run out the door.

Virgil closed his eyes, thinking: "I'm going to die right here where I stabbed that Regent in the guts."

"What about you? You ride?"

Virgil wanted to reach for his beer, but knew he'd choke. Maybe that would be better. It'd sure as hell be faster.

"Me? Yeah, I've got a...a Honda. A Gold Wing."

"A Honda?" The man and his friend laughed, easing the tension. "Mr. Gold Wing, you know any motorcycle clubs around here?"

"Just my Honda club." He felt a buzz suddenly hit, like he was rising from the stool, a euphoric chorus in his ears.

"We're supposed to meet a friend of ours tonight. He's with the Bayou Runners, mostly a bunch of Cajuns. You know any Bayou Runners?'

Virgil swallowed. Sweat broke out across his upper lip. His gaze flickered down the bar for a half-second to make sure the bartender's back was turned. Then he glanced over his shoulder and nodded slightly.

"See that guy just inside the bar across the street? The black ponytail and mustache? Denim shirt? He's some big shot with the Bayou Runners." Virgil took a hit off his cigarette and watched the tip glow. "Maybe he's the friend you're looking for."

CHAPTER THIRTY-SEVEN

The rain blew in that night, sheets of icy needles, dampening hair and clothes, and turning the white nurse's uniforms into peep shows. Joe didn't care about any of it because Ugly had showed up at the warehouse at 5 a.m. with a summons.

"Get your shit, man. You got guard duty in Denny's room."

Joe couldn't move fast enough.

"Man, you're grinning like a chimpanzee," Randy said in the elevator. "Straighten up, act serious, he's got a room full of people."

"I haven't seen him since he left for Texas. He probably thinks I don't give a shit because I never came to see him."

"He knows you're a probate and ain't got a choice. Besides, he's been busy worrying about my sister practicing her gris-gris on him."

"That would be your older sister, the nurse?" Joe inquired sarcastically.

"Do yourself a favor and don't call her old."

"Why didn't you tell me about your younger sister, the psycho fortune-teller?"

"Jess asked me not to."

"It's as simple as that?"

"Yes. I have a lot of respect for the man. You'd be well-advised to show some respect, too."

"He doesn't make it easy," Joe said.

" 'Cause he don't know how. He's crazy in love with that girl, emphasis on the crazy. She likes to play around and broaden her horizons, as she says, but you aren't in the play category if she gave you that card. You can't expect him to like it."

"It's a little more complicated than that."

"Always is when pussy is involved. Get laid somewhere else, Joe. Tell you what, if you're still here after they settle this, I'll take you out to the house, introduce you to my mother."

"Your mother?" Joe exclaimed as the doors opened.

"Let's go," Randy strode past the nurse's station. "Good morning, my beauties."

"When we have a minute, I want you to draw me a family tree so I know who belongs to who around here."

"That would be telling," Randy said, making a left down the hall. "They got Denny in the Presidential Suite. And I believe you know this fella?"

Joe surveyed the stranger sitting in a chair outside the room, but couldn't quite place him. Freshly shaven, he wore a new denim jacket and faded jeans. His thick dark hair was combed back in a neat pony-tail. He turned to watch them as they approached down the hall, and stood up.

When he saw the man's eyes, Joe knew.

"Sam? What'd they do to you? Who cut your hair?"

"Delilah," Randy replied for him. "With her little nurse scissors."

Sam extended his hand, emotion working across his face. Joe accepted it, clenched it, overwhelmed at what the man had done to protect Denny. And now allowed this transformation, so he could remain the guardian of the gate.

Randy tapped on the door and waited until someone inside opened it and glared at them.

"Oh, it's you," Smitty said. "Hey, Duds, the pizza boys are here."

"Pepperoni at five a.m.?"

The walls appeared to be braced by the backs of two dozen men, but it was the man in the bed who grinned and beckoned weakly to Joe.

"Probate. Get your ass over here."

Joe fought to keep his emotions under control in front of all these Regents. The beating had been horrific. And Joe had not been able to help him or do a damn thing about it.

"Good to see you," Denny said, and lifted the cast. "I'd shake, but it upsets the nurse."

"And you want to keep her happy," Joe replied, thinking, "Damn, do not look at his nose."

"I would love to make that woman happy."

His Chicago brothers laughed, eying Yvonne, who leaned against the sink adjusting her hair up under her cap.

"I'll let you know when I think you can manage it," She retorted, then sighed. "Well, gentlemen, day shift will be here in about an hour. I got to go do my final rounds. You men behave."

Joe had to give her credit. Except for her brother, every eye in the room was on her rear end all the way out the door, and she still sashayed with a total lack of self-consciousness.

"How does she do that?" A Louisville Regent marveled.

"And why ain't she down there on Bourbon Street making some money instead of up here emptying bedpans? She could make a thousand bucks a night just walking across the stage."

"She's picky about who sees her naked," Randy told them with a straight face, and watched them all gape hungrily at the door.

"All the years I've known you, and you never told me about her," Denny said to Randy.

"He's real good at that," Joe said, then glanced across the room.

Jess sat on the window sill, the glass behind him streaked with rain. He pulled his gaze from the sky and studied Joe.

"He's promised to introduce me to his mother," Joe said. "Says she's the prettiest one of all."

Jess grinned sideways, only slightly reassured, then returned to his seventh floor view of a rainy New Orleans dawn.

♦

Regents came and went at the hospital, openly wearing their patches. Joe watched them, hoping it was over. They had made their point with the ambush. When the Regents came back to the warehouse that night, stinking of gunpowder, congratulating or mocking each other about the good and bad shots, it sounded like the Bayou Runners had been wiped off the face of the earth.

"We nailed all the drivers," Ugly roared. "They were climbing all over each other trying to haul ass."

"I told you Sleaze was mine and you went for him anyway," Jess said tightly.

"As long as that little bastard is gone, who cares?"

"We don't know for sure that he's gone," Smitty spoke up, looking at Jess oddly.

"Sleaze was in the first truck, brains went all over the windshield. To me, that's gone," Ugly protested. "Lighten up. Damn, Doc, somebody could give you a million bucks and you'd bitch about it."

Randy bought a Times-Picayune to take to Denny for a souvenir, but there was only a brief article about a Mr. Jackson Bulliard reporting someone had fired shots at his tattoo shop on Dauphine Street. Randy also brought a couple of sandwiches, even though he knew Yvonne was taking good care of Joe. They sat on the window ledge, tomato sauce dripping from the hoagies.

"They're about done here. They're packing up shit at the warehouse," Randy told Joe. "It's getting into the hurricane season. I'm sure the Yankees want to get the hell out of here in case we get a big one. They won't leave Denny, though, and he ain't up for that trip."

His long form lay motionless, propped up so his snoring didn't suck the oxygen out of the room.

"Did they put a big hurt on the Bayou Runners?"

"Not like they think. But it's about even. They need to leave, Joe. Don't you want to go home?"

"Not to Atlanta," Joe said, with regret. He liked it here.

"Ask your sponsor. Now that you know your way around, they might let you stay here 'til Denny can travel. Unless you've got more pressing business."

"Just wondering what happened to that redhead," Joe thought.

♦

Jess showed up with a bag of hamburgers, waving them under Denny's nose until he woke up.

"Their morgue is right across from the dining hall. See if these taste like real hamburger to you."

"I don't care," Denny assured him. "My belly button's touching my back bone. Where's everybody?"

"Louisville and most of Atlanta are leaving, if they can get Bobby and Ugly out of the strip joints. They're coming by later to say goodbye," Jess said. "I've got to go, too. Couple of things came up in Atlanta."

"What about my crew?" Denny frowned.

"You'll have to ask them," Jess said. "Dudley's staying. And Sam and the probate." He glanced at Joe. "You'll be reporting to Dudley until I get back."

"You're coming back?" Denny tried to aim a french fry at his mouth.

"Yeah, I'll hang around until you're fit to travel. Might go up to Chicago with you to make sure there's no complications on the way. You got some pretty serious injuries, Denny."

"I appreciate that, man." Denny pulled the hamburger apart. He studied it, and picked a tomato loose, then put it back down, suddenly tired.

"You all right?" Jess went into medic mode, picking up Denny's wrist to check his pulse.

"Just tired…putting on for everybody."

"That's bullshit. We're your brothers. You don't have to pretend you don't feel like shit."

"Naw man. It's my patch, Jess. They got my fuckin' patch." Denny closed his eyes. "I ain't worried about being handsome again. And I know my bike's in parts somewhere between here and Arkansas. But my patch, Brother, losing it hurts worst of all."

♦

That night, Joe waited for Yvonne, and met her outside the door.

"He's really depressed. Can you sweet-talk him a little?"

"This may surprise you, Joe, but I don't like group parties."

"Nobody's here. I haven't seen Dudley since yesterday, and the rest of 'em left, too, except his guys, and they're keeping a low profile somewhere."

"The rest gone for good?"

"I don't know. I hope this is over," He admitted, then reluctantly asked, "Do you still have company at your place?"

Yvonne shook her head.

"She's been gone. I kept her doped up, but she called a cab when I was asleep. Just as well. She did what she was told, now she can go home like a good girl where she belongs."

"She had a rough time of it."

Yvonne wet her lips with the tip of her tongue.

"I'm sure Mr. Guidry took very good care of her. As long as she's gone for good, I don't care."

"And as long as she keeps her mouth shut," Joe thought, "And as long as your brother wasn't driving the cab she called." He honestly didn't know what would be worse.

♦

Fat Jack was dismayed to find the Regents leaving. He knew the Bayou Runners had not taken a hit like the Regents presumed. It looked like he would have to sell out and move to Miami after all, and quick. He didn't mind starting over--a good tat artist could always find work-- but he didn't like doing it so fast. And he sure as hell wouldn't tell Francine. Maybe he'd send a postcard...

Dudley ruined the rest of Fat Jack's day when he showed up and ordered him to report for guard duty at Charity to replace Joe.

"I can't leave my shop. I could miss a phone call. Big Alec's been calling about some girl."

"I'm not in a good mood, Jack," Dudley said, sporting a fresh black eye. "Get your ass over to the hospital."

"I gotta check with Big Alec," He protested. "He's my chapter president."

"Then call him. You've got two minutes."

Jack agonized over interrupting Big Alec long distance with no news, or pissing off Dudley, who stood three feet away. With a groan, he picked up his cigarettes and pistol and followed Dudley to the car.

♦

"Christ, I'm dead," Denny groaned when Fat Jack walked in.

"Nah, Sam's got the door and Yvonne's got night shift," Dudley said. "Don't worry, you're covered."

"You're taking the probate? He's only been here two days. I finally relaxed."

"I'll bring him back," Dudley said. "Just need him for a little errand."

Dudley didn't say anything on the elevator, but his face drooped with fatigue. He leaned against the wall, bracing his aching hips against the constant stops. Joe let Randy ask the questions.

"We got trouble?" Randy asked once they were in the parking lot.

"Not yet. We're taking a ride," Dudley said.

"Should we run by the safe house, pick up some supplies?"

Dudley thought a minute, then shook his head.

"No, let's get this over with."

They rode in silence across the Mississippi River, down into a dreary neighborhood. The concrete block houses huddled close together as if they expected a beating from the sky. Overturned trash cans spewed ancient garbage into the mucky soil. Small water oaks struggled for life in the sunken yards. It didn't help that the sky was clouding up again, throwing a dismal cast to the untended places. Joe didn't see any people. Was this neighborhood abandoned after some disaster made it unlivable? Hurricane Camille, maybe. Wasn't there anything worth coming back for?

They pulled up in front of a dull yellow house with curtains that puckered as if they were stapled to the walls inside. A weird shiver rippled through Joe. He worked his shoulders in circles to hide it. Under the carport, he recognized the van the Chicago Regents drove down from Illinois, the side doors open.

"The Knight of Swords wouldn't get nervous just because the place looks like the setting for a Halloween movie. Straighten up. Whatever it is, it's bad, but it ain't you."

The enforcer stepped out of the house, his troubled eyes surveying the empty street. Waco came out next, wiping his hands on a bloody rag.

"Ain't too much I can do about that bathtub. Let's just leave it. We ain't coming back here anyway."

The enforcer nodded and stepped up into the van.

"Your local expertise is required," Dudley said quietly to Randy. "Need a good place to dump some trash."

"Lots of places around here," Randy shrugged.

"Somewhere you can hang out for a while without getting seen."

"What's today, Monday? I know a place."

Dudley handed him the keys and climbed into the passenger seat.

"Take us there. Don't attract attention. Probate, get in the back."

Joe set his beer down and pulled himself inside. His eyes adjusted to the gloom, and his heart skipped a beat. In the back corner near the rear doors sat a bundle, the head covered with a blood-soaked sack, the denim shirt soaked halfway down, arms bound tightly. In slow motion, Joe moved across the hard steel floor and sat down behind Randy's seat. Pressing himself against the metal seam, he focused on an old beer can under Dudley's seat and did not look up again. Randy turned, glanced around the back, then casually adjusted the stick shift into Reverse.

"Let's go," Waco stepped in the side door, and that was the last thing anyone said for an hour.

It rained just enough to turn on the wipers, smearing bugs and dust across the big windshield. Randy kept his window down, and a steady damp breeze gusted in above Joe, tossing his hair. He sipped at the warm beer, propping the bottle on his knee. The road grew rougher, the old shocks sparing his tailbone nothing. Then the van slowed and veered left, crunching down a shell lane. Mossy branches hung low enough to brush the van's roof.

They came to an easy stop. Joe listened. He heard a blue jay, a mockingbird and light rain pattering on the roof. They were deep in the country.

"You've got quite a sense of humor," Dudley said to Randy.

"Ain't no better place."

Dudley motioned for them get out of the van. The Chicago enforcer opened the side door and stiffly hopped out, tossing two shovels to the ground. His chest tight, Joe eased down into a flat scraggly expanse of grass. He stood just outside of a leaning pair of wrought-iron gates to a cemetery.

Dudley walked several yards from the van, his boots striking noisily on the shell lane. "I don't know how long we'll be gone. We're making a trade."

"For what?" Randy asked.

"Him for Denny's patch."

"Chicago got one of them?" He lifted an eyebrow toward the van.

"Yeah, but he wouldn't talk," Dudley exhaled. "Maybe he really didn't know where it is. Anyway, I'm trusting you to handle this 'til we get back."

"Fine." Randy surveyed the cemetery. "So if you're offering them a trade, you're saying Sleaze didn't get nailed in the ambush."

"No. He's been seen. If he'll just hand over that damn patch, everybody can go home," Dudley said. "We'll come back another time for his slimy ass. Jess hasn't given up on nailing him."

A faint mist tapped the leaves overhead.

"Over here, Probate." The Chicago enforcer beckoned to Joe. He looked exhausted and frustrated, and had a busted lip. "Saw you hanging out with Denny at Talladega. We're trying to make things right for him. Here's your chance to even it out."

He opened the back doors, reached in and got a handful of rope, and tugged. Joe saw a brief flash of handcuffs, and a hand that was almost black, before the body crashed down hard on the shells.

"I'll take care of it," Joe promised.

"I hate these places," The enforcer shuddered, surveying the neglected graveyard, and got back in the van, calling to Dudley. "Can you find this place again?"

"If I can find our way out, I'll find our way back here."

They left Randy and Joe standing in the lane, watching the van disappear behind a grove of trees

"Now what?" Joe glanced skyward.

"It's going to rain. We find a place to wait where we don't get soaked. Wish I'd brought a beer. You got some candy?"

"I've got gum and two cigarettes. Is there a store near here?"

Randy snorted.

"Okay. Is there a caretaker's house?"

"They haven't had a funeral out here in over fifty years. There ain't no caretaker." Randy forced the gates open until the bottom rails dug into the earth and refused to budge. "The only reason it isn't overgrown is because the trees keep out the light. There's a tomb over there made up to look like a little house, under a cedar tree. That's our best bet. Anybody comes out here, which I doubt, can't see us, and we'll hear Dudley when they come back. Come on, let's see how much this bastard weighs."

They walked over to where the man lay on his side, fresh blood on the sack.

Randy pushed at a bruised bare foot with his boot.

"Hey. You want to get dragged or can you walk?"

The wet sack billowed out with strained breathing. Someone rasped a few words in Cajun, something about Dieu. God?

Joe moved his pistol to the back of his belt and waited for Randy's signal to lift the man But Randy didn't move. He stared in disbelief, then his mouth twisted like a child about to cry. His arms flung out as if to steady himself against a gust Joe didn't feel. Then it all let go. With a swipe, Randy yanked a knife from his back pocket and squatted down on the sharp shells.

"Damn it. Mother-fucker. Shit!" He raged, sawing through the rope until it fell from the man's arms. Then he grabbed the loop securing the sack around the Bayou Runner's neck and hacked at it. "Hold still!"

Stunned, Joe grabbed his pistol and stepped back. Were they supposed to finish the man off? What the hell had set Randy into a frenzy? Joe held off, waiting to see if Randy was going to slit the man's throat. Instead, he swept the ropes away, then carefully pulled the damp sack off and slung it aside. Squatting on the shells, he held the man up by the arms, staring at his damaged face, black eyes wet.

"Damn it, why didn't you just tell them? All they wanted was that fucking patch. Damn, Etienne."

Guidry swallowed.

"They'da killed all the boys."

"So you were gonna let them kill you?" Randy retorted.

"Odds was against it."

"Put that pistol away," Randy snapped at Joe, and crawled behind Guidry. "What's on your wrists…oh hell. Handcuffs?"

"What are you doing?" Joe watched, incredulous. "That's the bastard who robbed me! He's a Bayou Runner. Jesus, after what they did to Denny? What are you doing?"

"He didn't do nothing to Denny," Randy raged.

"Orlando… dear God… quit pullin' on me," Guidry gasped.

"Get his arm, Joe, we're gonna stand him up."

"Not the right one," Guidry warned. "Don't touch it."

"I owe you a bum arm," Joe glared.

Randy lapsed into a rant in patois, working a shoulder up under Guidry's left side.

"If you ain't gonna help, get out of the way," He told Joe.

"You've lost your damned mind," Joe accused, but roughly grabbed the bad arm and hoisted, not caring that it almost put the man on his knees.

CHAPTER THIRTY-EIGHT

It was fairly easy to find the girl. Virgil took Guidry's truck, parked at the curb, and waited. On the second night, she showed up, getting out of a cab down the block.

He was very surprised when she didn't go to the big mansion under the live oaks. Instead, she walked right up to the truck. Her face and arms were all bruised up, but she moved pretty good, and tried to smile.

"Hey. If you'll talk to me, I'd like to—"

Then she saw his face.

"Shit!" She exclaimed and ran back toward the taxi. Virgil caught her at the door.

"Hey, what you doing to that girl?" The cabbie said.

"Lover's quarrel," Virgil grinned, despite the fists pounding his face. "It's okay."

He dragged her to the truck, his hand over her mouth. She got in a couple of good shots to his ribs. He went around to the passenger side, where the cabbie couldn't see him, and hit her hard enough to knock her out.

♦

The lights were blazing at the farmhouse, but the two Angola cons sat alone on the empty front porch, sharing a pipe. Virgil left the girl bound up with duct tape in the car until he could find out what was going on, and walked inside. Hermy sat on the stairs, his fingers sunk in his hair, his head down. Virgil was amazed to see the Bayou Runners pacing, not partying, while Sleaze sat on the edge of the couch, smoking a cigarette and plucking at the pellets in his face. Beside him, the green phone sat important and ready, the plastic line stretched across the room.

The men stalked around, panicked, like nutria flushed out a den without a clue about which direction to go. Except for Sleaze. He stared at the mildew rippling down the wallpaper, his beady eyes lightened to clear amber.

"Leon call again?" Virgil speculated.

"Yeah, but we're not worried about him right now," Irish Fahey said.

"His Trog finally show up?"

"Not hardly."

"Then what's going on?"

"The Regents called," Hermy swallowed, despairing. "They've got Guidry."

"What?" Virgil's eyes sped from face to face. "Shit, that's bad."

"He's alive, at least. They want to swap him for the Regents patch."

Virgil didn't have to feign surprise. *Alive*? How?

"Are you sure he's alive? It could be a trap."

"That's what I'm thinking," Sleaze said vaguely. "Where you been?"

"Out looking for the Trog. Somethin's happened to him."

"No shit," Sleaze retorted but didn't move.

Damn, had he gone so crazy they sedated him?

"We need to ask everybody where they last saw Guidry," Fahey interrupted.

"You can be sure he's hid someplace we can't get him," Virgil said. "He's probably already dead. They're bluffing to get the patch."

"Damn, Virgil, if it was you, you'd want every coon-ass we know out there looking." Fahey glared.

"How do we even know he ain't working with them? He knew where they were and didn't tell us, he kept going behind Sleaze's back, and he didn't want to go on the drive-by run," Virgil ticked off on his fingers. "If he'd gone, that woulda been him getting blown out of the front seat, not Kenny. Was that just dumb luck?"

"You're full of it," Fahey spat.

"Maybe not," Sleaze said tonelessly.

The men gaped at him, then protests went up.

"He'd never do that to us! His daddy fed me and my sister when my parents died. You too, Sleaze, you wore rags to school 'til his father got you something decent. Guidry's from good people. He'd never go against this club."

"But what about the Trog? What if he killed him over that girl, or gave him to the Regents? The girl's disappeared, too."

"No, she ain't," Virgil smirked. "I know right where she is."

Smug, he strode out to the car, opened the trunk and set her on her feet.

"Damn, what you got there?" Muller and Racine jumped off the porch and hurried over, grinning.

"Guidry's cunt. She might know something about where that Trog went."

Eyes glinting, they hurried behind him into the house.

"Well shit, Virgil, you finally surprised me. Sit her down," Sleaze said, and leaned back in his chair. "Looks like someone already worked her over. Go ahead."

Racine moved in close to her face and pulled the duct tape off. "Where's the Trog?"

She gasped for air, looking frantically around the room for Guidry, for any of the men who had been nice to her or, shown some respect.

"Look here, I don't like this," An Orleans parish man spoke up. "She's Guidry's old lady."

"You don't like it, leave," Virgil ordered.

He saw them shift, look at him differently. *That's right, things have changed.* When Sleaze didn't intervene, three men got up and walked out.

"Where's the Trog, Red? He's been sniffing your pussy since he got here. Now he disappears and you're all busted up. Did you get in a jam and have to cut him?"

"No! I haven't seen that asshole in a while," She insisted, breathless.

"Well then, when's the last time you saw Guidry? He do something to the Trog?"

Her lips parted, and she looked around the room again, confusion sliding into desperation.

"What's happened?" Her voice broke.

"The Regents say they got him," Racine said, watching her eyes, liking the fear. "When's the last time you saw him?"

"What—oh no. No. Are you sure?"

"Nobody's seen him in a couple of days. Regents called and said they have him, they want to swap for something."

"Then swap!" She shouted. "What's the matter with you? Give them what they want. They'll kill him if you don't."

"She's right," Fahey tried again. "We do it smart, take the patch some place neutral, leave it. Then let 'em know where to find it. We don't have to shoot it out with them. All they want is the damn patch, let 'em have it."

"Who's running this club?" Virgil turned on him.

"I'm beginning to wonder myself," Fahey retorted. "How about it, Sleaze? That's our VP they've got. Even if they've killed him, I want his body for a decent funeral, not to rot in a ditch somewhere. Why are we even standing here discussing it?"

"Because Virgil is right. If he's dead, we'd be giving up a Regents patch for nothing. If he's gone over to their side and abandoned us, we may be walkin' in a trap no matter how we play it." Sleaze lit a cigarette, as calm as any of them had ever seen him. "There's only one way to find out."

They all looked at him expectantly.

"We ain't giving 'em the patch," Sleaze announced.

They stared at him, exchanged shocked glances, but it was Madeline who jumped up, took two steps forward and spit in his face.

"You little bastard! You sawed-off chicken-shit fucker."

Sleaze came out of his stupor and back-handed her across the face. He pointed to Racine and Muller.

"Take care of her."

They each seized an arm and pushed her toward the stairs. Screaming and kicking, she dug her shoes uselessly against the wood floor. Averting his eyes, Hermy moved to the side as they went up the stairs. She kicked again, throwing them off-balance in the narrow space and slid down two steps. She landed even with him and panted in his ear: "He had Guidry's truck."

"Huh?" Hermy said.

"Virgil. When he grabbed me, he had Guidry's truck." A fist came down and grabbed her hair, and she squeezed her eyes shut. "Fuck all of you chicken-shit bastards!"

CHAPTER THIRTY-NINE

Joe wondered what Rick and his acid hallucinations would make of this place. Time stopped for everyone at the gates. Here, beneath the mossy old trees, the dead slept and the living waited. Worn and cracked, the old headstones and tombs bore green-tinged dates from the eighteen-hundreds, half-hidden by decades of leaves and fallen limbs. *Yes, we were once here.* Alex and Rena Allemand. Octave and Sophie Molaison. And the small ones he couldn't stand to look at, like: *Aurelia, Beloved Daughter Age 5 Mo. May 10, 1883*

Ignoring the rain, Joe roamed the cemetery to take his mind off his dry mouth. He was used to hunger, but the thirst was a different kind of hell. He finally spotted a trail of rain water dripping down a crack from the top of the tomb, and scooped it up on a leaf, spitting out the bugs and twigs. It took another five minutes to gather a leaf full, and Randy carried it inside for Guidry.

When the van didn't return by dusk, they resigned themselves to spending the night there. Joe found enough oily magnolia leaves and dry twigs to make a tiny fire on the threshold, more for comfort than real purpose. The smoke kept out the mosquitos, and the fire reassured them that they were capable of taking care of themselves.

He stood at the door of the empty tomb just inside the drip-line from the elaborately sculpted eaves, watching the moon track through the cedar trees. Behind him, Randy sat with his legs outstretched on the clammy stone floor. He had retrieved the cotton sack and taken off his own shirt to make a pillow for Guidry. When drifting clouds obscured the moon, it plunged them into a gloom where they could barely see their own hands. Joe fed the fire stingily, just enough to keep the embers glowing.

Now that he could relax, Guidry faded into a miserable sleep, pain bringing him out of it with relentless malice.

"You tell anybody I'm letting a man sleep with his head on my thigh, I'll cut your throat," Randy warned Joe.

"It's your business if you want to make him comfortable." Joe said, determined to stay furious. "I swore I'd bust his knee caps when I saw him again."

Guidry muttered: "Who he is?"

"Jess's probate," Randy said.

Guidry didn't say anything, and they thought he had fallen asleep again. Then he spoke in a quiet patois to Randy, who smiled faintly. Joe heard "tarot" in the middle of it. Soon everyone in south Louisiana would know he carried a tarot card for protection courtesy of Kitty Breaux.

"I'm also a good friend of Denny's," Joe emphasized, eyes cold.

"Oh. What time it is?"

"Two a.m." Randy said.

"Reckon…it went bad?"

"The Chicago Chapter won't leave 'til they get the patch. I don't know if they wanted blood, too."

"They got enough of mine," Guidry closed his one good eye. "They had that arm chained up for two days over my head. Hope I don't lose my hand."

Randy grimaced and lied. "It doesn't look nearly as bad as your face. And you're moving your fingers. You'll be playing at the clubs again in no time."

"Dumb shits kept working on it, didn't know I'm left-handed."

"How the hell did they get you?"

"Come up behind me in the Quarter, hit me in the head. We were looking for that damn Trog."

"You and who else?"

"Virgil. From Gretna. Look here, I need a favor."

"The nearest house is twenty miles from here or I'd have done lit out," Randy said. "And they could come back any time. We have to wait for them to line up the trade."

"Not for me." The fractured bones in his hand shifted, and he sucked in his breath and held it until the bones settled down. "A girlfriend. Redhead. Long legs."

Randy shot a warning look up at Joe.

"Left all her stuff behind. Trog was after her. They both gone."

"What can I do?" Randy said.

"Find her."

"Pretty girl?" Randy asked.

"You know it."

"Prettier than Yvonne?"

"Nobody's prettier than Yvonne, even if she picked my pockets to buy that fancy car."

"You let her, 'Tienne."

"Kept hoping she'd like me again."

"Why, you enjoy having your heart cut out and fed to you with a silver fork? It's safer to go hang out at Tulane or Loyola, find one of them free-love hippie girls," Randy shook his head. "What about you, Joe, ever been married?"

"No. I lived with a girl a long time, up until a month ago."

"Damn," Randy said snidely. "And still found time to go mess up somebody else's romance. I can't believe Jess hasn't killed you."

They both heard what sounded like a chuckle from Guidry.

"Bet Kitty won't let Jess kill him."

"Why don't you give that mouth a rest?" Randy countered, hiding a grin. "I wouldn't want to be talking with it."

"If I talk, it takes my mind off the rest of it." He shifted, moving his shattered hand from his chest to the cold stone.

"Y'all have fireflies here?" Joe suddenly asked, peering out the door.

"Not this time of year. And not this time of night."

"I'm seeing something green and glowing floating in the air."

"Ah shit," Guidry shut his eyes. "Your little sister done sent her spirits."

Randy watched it dip and dance along the cedars. “No, he’s right. It’s a lightning bug. Must be lost.”

“Maybe nobody answered his signal but he won’t give up,” Joe said.

“Must be looking for Yvonne,” Guidry mumbled.

“Nah, there can’t be two of y’all that dumb,” Randy cracked, but Guidry had passed out again.

Joe watched the firefly until it danced upward toward the moon and vanished. He wanted to believe that Kitty had sent a spirit, even a flashing flying bug, to let them know it would all be okay.

The next morning, he plundered until he found an old glass vase at the base of a sprawling magnolia. He rinsed it with water dripping from the tomb’s roof, and scoured it out with his shirt before patiently waiting for it to fill again.

“Here,” He handed it to Randy. “He’s probably thirsty.”

“He’s pissing blood. They need to come on.”

A warm sunrise glimmered through the trees, an intense tropical red. Not a good sign. Randy gave Guidry two chugging swallows, then laid the cotton sack back over his face. Mosquitos had scented warm blood, and their high-pitched whining in his ears was almost unbearable.

“There’s no more water,” Joe said, standing by the gates.

“There will be later. Look at those clouds.”

Morning cicadas sang at full-pitch, sawing on his nerves.

“What if they don’t come back? He should be in a hospital.”

“They aren’t dumb enough to walk into a trap. Might have took a while to get a message to Sleaze through the gumbo grapevine.”

“Or they could have set up the Bayou Runners and had some problems. I could see ‘em doing that. They can’t do anything easy,” Joe said. “They never listen to Jess.”

Randy chewed his thumbnail.

“Jess don’t necessarily do it easy, but he makes it so they don’t forget. And I never known him to involve innocent people just for the hell of it." He swiped at another mosquito. "Tell you what, if they don't come back by this afternoon, I'll walk out of here. Don't know what the hell I can do that won't get us both killed, though."

He looked expectantly at Joe.

"He ain't the enemy, Joe. You got my word. And I want your word if I leave, you won't hurt him. He can't fight back."

"I wouldn't do that," Joe said. "Whatever he is to Yvonne, I'm not pissing her off."

Humidity built up before the storm like a sauna, and they were soon hot and thirsty again. Joe listened hard, heard thunder rumbling in the distance, and searched for more vases or containers, but could only find broken pieces.

"Are you sure there's no civilization around here?" Joe said. "There had to be people living near here to have a burying ground. If you want to go scout out the area, see if there's a house, I'll try not to shoot Mr. Guidry 'til you get back."

"I know the area and I know the cemetery. There ain't shit."

"Wait. You hear that?" Joe interrupted, tilting his head.

"Thunder?"

"No. A dog barking. Listen. Over there." Joe stepped into the overgrown lane and headed for the road, following the sound. The barks grew faint. He picked up his pace, mad at the wind sighing in the pines and his own noisy boots grating on the shells.

"I don't hear it." Randy stuck his nose in an empty pack of cigarettes and inhaled.

Joe stopped, concentrating. "I know I heard a dog barking."

"Maybe it was chasing game. I want to hear a van."

Instead, thunder rippled in the west, ending in a series of booms.

"Damn," Randy said. "The skeeters are gonna eat us alive in that tomb."

"How come it's empty?"

"I knew you'd get around to asking. Let's just not—what the hell are you doing?" Randy exclaimed and stomped over to the tomb where Guidry had managed to prop himself in the doorway. "You need to go piss again?"

"No." He swallowed, his face clammy with sweat from the effort of standing. He pointed with his left hand. "I want to talk to your friend there."

Joe stared at him.

"What have you got to say to me?"

"I just remembered where I seen you before. You were at Talladega. With the little bull dog."

Joe stood very still, unable to speak. Man, that hurt. Guidry smiled faintly through split lips.

"I know where the van and dog went."

"She's alive?" Joe struggled.

"Last I heard."

"It won't make a difference for you, Etienne," Randy said harshly. "He's a damned probate. We're just the help. We don't make the decisions. Look at him. They don't even give a shit if he's got food to eat."

The air hissed out of Guidry, leaving him looking like a bruised balloon, but he set his jaw.

"The only thing that's gonna help you is give 'em what they want," Randy insisted.

"I'm thinking we're all in a world of shit. Somethin' went wrong or they'd been here by now. For all you know, Sleaze might be on the way here instead of your Regents friends. Hope you got more than a couple of rounds."

Randy stood up straighter.

"I don't know nothing but my stomach is hurting and I would cut my own toes off for a cup of cold water from Aunt Pauline's well and a Goody powder to chase it. That's what I know."

"What about the dog?" Joe said stubbornly.

Guidry was sinking fast, nausea hanging in his throat and a buzz in his ears. But he managed to say: "I get out of here alive, I'll tell you where she is."

"Damn it, don't mess with us about the puppy! She's been dead," Randy declared, surprising the other two men.

"No, she ain't," Guidry said wearily. "Why you getting upset? It's his dog."

"It's Kitty's, too," Randy said with bare emotion, his dark eyes riveted on Guidry. "She's been grieving over the puppy since it went missing. She finally got a dog again, and you stole it."

"It sure wasn't on purpose."

Randy shook his head. "She's been calling me about it. I told her it was dead so she'd quit worrying, but she said her damned cards told her the puppy was alive."

Guidry had held on a minute too long. Gripping the doorway with his left hand, he turned and slid down the interior wall.

"Well then Orlando, her hero's got an incentive to find it and take it to her." He closed his eyes. "Since we're all dumb sons a' bitches when it comes to your sisters."

The three men waited, sweating and swearing as the day's heat built and the insects maintained their high-pitched shrilling.

"We've got to find a bigger clearing with a breeze. I can't take these skeeters much longer," Randy said. "Why don't they bother you?"

"He ain't half olive oil," Guidry mumbled.

"Shut up."

"Both of y'all shut up," Joe said, and leaned outside the door, cocking his ear. "I hear a car."

"Wait a second," Randy strained to see through the trees. "Make sure it's them."

He relaxed when he saw the van turn off the road and come down the lane.

"They're back! Now we can get out of here." Randy clambered to his feet. "Can you walk to the van, Guidry, or have I got to tote you?"

"I'll walk. Give me a second. Up and down ain't so clear right now."

Joe hurried across the sandy yard and trotted over to the van, breaking into a relieved smile. Until he came up to the passenger window. Dudley and Waco sat quietly, their faces sunken and grim.

"Where is he?" Dudley stared out the windshield at the lane.

"Over by the cedar trees," Joe said.

"You have any trouble from him?"

"No. He's been sick. His hand looks like blood poisoning. Can we drop him off at a hospital?"

Although the sun wasn't in his eyes, Waco squinted, and drew a short deep breath.

"Let's go," He said to Dudley, and reached behind the seat to pick up a big white pillow.

Joe hung back as they walked through the gate with slow heavy deliberation. Standing at the carved stone doorway, Randy's sarcastic greeting died on his lips. He shot a questioning look past them to Joe, but Joe didn't have an answer.

"What the hell is this thing?" Dudley stopped at the door of the tomb. "He's in here? You cut 'em loose?"

"Damn, Dudley, he ain't going anywhere, he's all busted up."

The men ducked to step inside the small room, glancing warily upward for spider webs, then at the leaves and moss and broken glass kicked to the back of the interior, and finally settled on Guidry. He sat against the wall, his left hand braced against the floor, the fractured hand in his lap. The expectant hope in his one good eye shifted when he saw the pillow.

"Okay, Mister Bayou Runner boss," Dudley said. "You have one more chance to tell us where the patch is."

"What you mean?" He stared.

"Last chance. Where's Denny's patch?" Dudley said.

"The trade," Guidry said, bewildered. "You couldn't find Sleaze?"

Waco worked a cramped knot from his jaw and rubbed it with his hand.

"Oh we found him all right. Sleaze said no deal. He doesn't want to trade for you," He said simply.

Joe shot a glance at Randy. Good God, were they bluffing? He looked for some connivance, some malicious humor on their faces, but Dudley's bloodshot eyes told him he meant what he said, grim and final. He had spoken an awful truth. Waco stood between Joe and the door, crouching hunchbacked to avoid the green mold on the ceiling, one hand loosely holding the pillow.

Randy stooped beside Guidry, his dark eyes stunned, a pulse beating hard in his neck.

"So it's back to you again," Dudley said. "You've got to get your own self out of this shit. No dickin' around. Where's the patch? Tell Randy where it's hid, he'll drive us there, and you can go."

"Sleaze wouldn't trade?" Guidry couldn't believe it. There had once been a skinny kid named Vincent Minarde at his father's table, thin legs swinging, too short to touch the floor, chattering away the whole time he ate. "He eat fast like that 'cause he's afraid he won't get no more, but he's got to talk, too, 'cause he finally got somebody paying attention to him," His father had explained. "Be kind to that little fella, son, he's got nothin' but himself."

"I was his friend. I was the only damned friend he had for years."

"He took a vote. You lost. You took that beating for nothing," Waco sneered. "Your own club didn't think you were worth saving."

"Where's the patch, Guidry?" Randy spoke up, a faint note of hysteria in his voice.

Guidry closed his eyes.

"I told y'all before. I don't know," He said quietly.

"No, what you told me was 'fuck you' every time I asked," Waco retorted, tugging on a pair of brass knuckles. "You still gonna lie for those sons of bitches who turned on you? Maybe I hit you too hard in the head."

"Damn it, just tell them," Randy shouted. "I'll find the fuckin' place. Tell me where it is!"

Dudley winced, shifting in the cramped space. "He's not going to tell, and he's out of time. I can't stand here much longer." He reached behind him and brought out his 9mm.

Randy took a deep breath.

"Dudley, our families go back a long way. I'm asking you as a favor to my family to let him go. If he knew anything, he would have told you at the house."

"He don't have no family," Waco retorted. "I told Sleaze if he didn't trade we were gonna leave him to rot some place where nobody'd find his bones, and Sleaze said fine, Guidry don't have any family. Nobody would miss him."

Eyes blazing, Randy put a hand to his chest in an oddly European gesture. "He is a friend of my family."

Dudley glared at him as if he'd been slapped, then drew himself up, his rusty eyes furious. "Don't you ever threaten me with your goddamn connections. I don't give a fuck whose bastard son you are."

He nodded to Waco, who stepped forward and pressed the pillow against Guidry's head, pinning it to the wall. Guidry's left hand came up, got Waco's wrist in a vise and shoved.

"Damn it, don't do this," Randy shouted. "I'm asking you."

"We're done. He's got nothing left to give us."

Dudley put the pistol up to the pillow and pulled the trigger.

CHAPTER FORTY

When the storm finally let loose, it sent a line of squalls from Bogalusa down to the Gulf. Small torrents of rainwater swirled in the parking lot at Charity Hospital and headed downstream to Tulane. A van pulled up in the middle of a deep puddle and let two men out.

Before the Chicago Regents pulled the side doors shut, Dudley leaned forward and said in a hard tone: "I'll see you two later."

They drove off, heading for a bar west of town to regroup. Randy and Joe had not been invited.

"He might think so," Randy said, his dark eyes cold.

They walked to the Emergency Room entrance. Randy went to a bank of pay phones and started calling. He spoke rapidly, and the last time was not English or Cajun-French. Joe would have sworn it was fluent Italian.

"Why you looking at me like that?" Randy moved away from the phones.

"You're an ongoing surprise," Joe said.

"I like to hear that," Randy said.

"Now what?"

"I got Denny covered. This is the part that ain't gonna be fun. Let's go."

♦

Water puddled on the back steps, cupped where the wood had worn despite the fresh coats of paint. They moved slowly up the side of the house, listening to a soft patter coursing through thick magnolia leaves. The upstairs apartment had the closed up, curtains-drawn appearance of an absent owner, or one who didn't want to be bothered. Randy plucked a key from a hiding place and took a deep breath. He knocked a few times, then unlocked the door and stuck his head inside.

"Yvonne?"

They walked inside, boots muddy, clomping harder than necessary across the kitchen. The blinds cast a gray haze of light across the expensive furniture and oak fireplace mantel on the far side of the room. Joe smelled left-over coffee and cinnamon.

"See if she's got some milk in the fridge, I'm needing some sugar," Randy said.

"Vonnie?" He took off his hat and set it carefully on the kitchen counter.

"That you, Orlando?"

"Yeah. You got company?"

"No. Do you?"

A few minutes later, she walked in the room yawning, her pink pajamas rumpled, her long black hair tumbling around her shoulders. "Oh hey, Waylon. Why don't you warm up some of that coffee on the stove? You look cold. I got to work tonight. Trying to get a few hours sleep before I go in. This rain got me chilled."

Joe got a sauce pan from the cabinet, and fired up a burner on the propane stove. Randy opened the refrigerator door, pulled out a gallon of milk, and poured himself and Joe two cups.

"What you boys been up to?" She yawned again, and took a few lazy steps to curl up on a deep red sofa.

"You working overtime?"

"Might as well make me some extra while I can. And things go a lot smoother up there with Joe on guard duty. You be there tonight?" She smiled at him.

Oh shit. "Jump in here any time, Randy," he thought, watching the coffee steam.

Randy finished his milk first, then strode around the sofa to sit next to her, avoiding her curious glance until the very last minute. He took her hands loosely in his.

"Can you call in sick tonight?"

Her sleepy smile faded.

"If I need to," She said, searching his face. "Is…is Mama okay?"

"Mama's fine."

"Kitty? Jess?"

"They're all fine," He said.

She let out a little breath, then inhaled sharply

"Well, you're here, and them's the only other people I love so I ain't worried about nobody else," She declared, and as the truth of her inventory occurred to her, she insisted defiantly, "There ain't nobody else I care about."

"I want you to pack up some stuff and come with us, Vonnie." Randy rubbed her hands.

"Etienne?" She whispered, her dark eyes wide, her fingers wrapping around his, keeping her grounded. "What…what do I need?"

"He's been beat up pretty bad. He's pissing blood. I'd say his hand is fractured and his fingers are broke up," Randy said, watching her eyes fill. "You aren't gonna come apart on me, Vonnie, are you?"

She shook her head, pressed her lips together and swallowed.

"You can get upset later and throw shit, but right now we need your help. Okay? And we have to hurry, it's a ways from here."

Joe poured a shot glass full of blackberry brandy and handed it to her. Yvonne took it and knocked it back, breathing hard, dark eyes flashing behind the tears.

"Who did it?" She asked. "Was it because of that girl?"

"I'll tell you about it on the way out there. Go get some stuff together. He was getting shocky when we left. Grab some blankets, Joe. And Yvonne?" Randy closed down on her hands, squeezing hard enough to get her attention. "It's better for him if everybody thinks he's dead. Do you understand? Everybody. Including his so-called friends."

She couldn't focus on anything but the physical, what she knew. "I can't set broken bones in a hand. He'll be crippled if somebody don't do it right. I know a girl at a clinic owes me a favor. They have an X-ray machine. It's over in Metairie."

"If you're sure they won't talk, we can try that."

She sat up straight as an idea occurred to her. "Was it his left or right hand?"

"His right."

"Then it was somebody who didn't know him good," A feral darkness flared in her eyes.

"Vonnie, don't. Not now. Go get dressed and damn sure bring something for pain."

She drew in a sharp breath. It was the last word that reached through her anger and brought it back where she couldn't bear it. Not pain. Not her Etienne.

Twice, Joe closed his eyes and almost dozed off, green fireflies dancing behind his eyelids, but each time the car braked, he'd snap awake, expecting trouble. Yvonne rode in the back seat, plundering through a kit she had brought. She looked younger in jeans and an old sweatshirt, with her hair pulled back in a loose ponytail.

Randy turned on the shell lane, then stopped the car.

"Vonnie, the Regents worked him over because they thought he had something to do with Denny getting hurt. And Sleaze has pulled some shit and kicked him out of the club. He's about half dead from it all. He don't need to know about that redhead so shut up about her."

She glared back at him, then sat up and watched in disbelief as the cemetery gates came into sight.

"What the hell you bring him here for? What's wrong wit' you? This a damned graveyard. I thought he was at a house."

"I didn't know it was him, Yvonne, they had a damned sack over his head."

"You jackass, how you not know it's him? Jesus and Mary, we known him since we was kids! Let me out. I mean it, let me out!" She thumped him on the shoulder.

Randy slammed on the brakes.

"Get the hell out then. Go walk in the rain in your fancy sneakers, see how long they last."

She jumped out and stalked off in front of the car, nearly breaking her ankle on the rough shells.

"For someone who doesn't like him, she's sure upset," Joe observed. "Why the hell did she dump him?"

"She didn't dump him. Guidry broke up with her before she could break up with him."

"I bet your family reunions are interesting," Joe reached for the door handle.

"Hold on. Let her find him first, get all that cussing and boohooing over with."

"He sees his little Cajun baby, he'll think he's died," Joe smiled.

"And gone to hell."

♦

While they waited outside the back door of the clinic, Randy sent Joe down the street for dinner. Guiltily, they sat in the parking lot wolfing down two huge sandwiches. Joe couldn't remember the last time a beer had tasted so good. After the meal, he felt better, but a full stomach and hours of rain beating down on the car put him to sleep. When Randy opened the driver's door and slid inside, Joe woke up reaching for his pistol.

"Easy there," Randy said.

"Go on back to sleep, darlin', you were snoring hard." Yvonne sat in the back seat, a fat pillow in her lap, stroking Guidry's hair.

"Damn, why didn't you wake me up, I would have helped," Joe said.

"Oh, Etienne's loaded with the good stuff and ready to dance, ain't you, baby?" Yvonne smirked fondly.

"Sure," He opened his eye for a second, then passed out again.

"He's okay?"

"He will be," Yvonne said. "That hand's gonna hurt a long time. They had to rearrange it. That was some shit those fellas did."

"Now what do we do?" Joe said.

"I'm taking you back to Charity and you'll go upstairs to Denny's room and act like nothing happened. I'll take care of this."

"I don't know what's happening here. This has gone crazy."

"Do like Dudley said. Go watch Denny. This is my territory, I got it covered." Randy smiled faintly. "Maybe we're just a dumb ass redneck probate and a gumbo-eating bastard, but we ain't done yet."

They watched Joe head for the Emergency Room entrance, exhausted and more than a little confused about whose side he was on. Yvonne moved up into the front seat so Guidry could stretch out in the back.

"We got to get these people the hell out of here," She said.

"Yeah, my hospitality is about done," Randy said.

"All this time, they been sitting in that room, laughing and cutting up with me. And then they go do this." Yvonne reached over the seat to adjust the newly cast hand so it wouldn't slip off Guidry's chest.

"They didn't know he was a friend of ours, and they can't know you were his girl, Vonnie. You've got to act normal for his sake. You can't be giving somebody the evil eye," He said. "Or gutting them."

"They run up on my blade, it ain't my fault."

"You want them to leave or not?"

"This was because of Denny's patch?" She frowned, speculating.

"Etienne wouldn't tell them while they did all that to him, he damn sure isn't going to tell you," Randy hissed.

Yvonne pursed her lips.

"Then we can't just give them what they want so they'll leave. It has to be handled different. Sneaky."

"That's what I been trying to tell you."

"And what you gonna do about Sleaze? A lot of people gonna get killed or go to prison if he messes up."

"I can't believe he let that happen to Guidry." Randy shook his head. "But I'll take care of it."

"You can't do all this by yourself. What about Joe? He's their probate but he sure don't seem happy."

"No. He's a good man."

"Kitty thinks so." Yvonne looked at him sideways.

"Yeah, she done called me, too."

"So what we gonna do?"

"*You* are going to use that nursing degree to make sure Guidry lives to make little mustached babies with some hoochie dancer from the Quarter. That's what you're going to do. I need some time to check up on a few things. And I'll see what I can do with the probate."

"Can you trust him?"

"He's been through some shit here, and hasn't cut and run yet. He has an old-fashioned sense of justice. I haven't known anybody like him in a long time. I think if he was on his own turf, this would have been over. But they aren't giving him a lot of options or any respect."

"If it gets serious, can you trust him? You already did once and we've got a loose end running around."

"I'm counting on him to do the right thing, not necessarily what they tell him to do. There's only one way to find out what he's thinking," Randy said and grinned at her. "He probably needs a break anyway. I'll pick him up, run him out there tomorrow."

Yvonne smiled faintly.

"Make sure she knows you want him back."

CHAPTER FORTY-ONE

Waco and the enforcer walked into Denny's room with two fresh cups of coffee. They eyed Joe, braced against the window sill, but didn't speak. Joe didn't care. He saw why Jess liked sitting here, with a view across a city that never slept. The Regents sat down on the floor, finished off their coffee, then stretched out on their bed rolls. Joe had to give them credit for loyalty; he personally knew the floor was hard as a rock.

When the sky lightened, he estimated he had about four more hours before Fat Jack or one of the Chicago Regents relieved him.

"Where's the Beauty of the Bayou?" Denny mumbled with his eyes closed.

"How do you know she isn't standing right beside you?" Joe said.

"Because I don't have a hard-on," Denny said. "Or coffee."

"Well, I can't help you with the hard-on, but I can go downstairs and get some coffee."

"Nah. Just wondering if I lost a day. I'd swear she told me she'd be here last night."

"A sugar daddy might have showed up in town unexpectedly," Joe suggested.

"Oh. And I thought she was impressed with me."

"You know how women are."

"Guess I don't. I'm ready to get out of here anyway. What's the hold up?"

"They're waiting 'til they're sure your guts can make the trip," Joe said drily.

"Is that all? Hell, dope me up and slide me in the back of a station wagon. Get me out of here. I'm serious, son."

"You're getting pretty good care here."

"I know. And nothing personal, probate, even with all the friendly heat, I feel like a sitting duck. Sooner or later, they're gonna hit Sam or they'll hurt Yvonne, or both. Their rookies tried it and blew it. But I might not get so lucky again."

"Denny, you've got half of Chicago in here. Nothing's gonna happen."

"Would you be comfortable laying here?"

"No. I'd want to go home," Joe admitted. "Maybe they'll come up with another plan to get your patch and then you can all leave."

"Is that what they're waiting on?" Denny frowned.

Joe glanced at the two men on the floor and listened to make sure the snores were genuine.

"They already tried once and it didn't work out."

"Shit," Denny eased back on the pillows. "I figured the patch was long gone."

"No. And they want to make sure you and that patch go home together. No matter what."

Joe didn't realize he'd dozed off standing up until the big door squeaked open. In the hall, breakfast carts clattered by and the day shift went from room to room, waking anyone who had managed to pass out for five minutes during the night. Surprised he hadn't fallen off his window perch, he pried his eyes open quickly.

"Go with him, probate,." Dudley pointed to the door.

Randy stood there, along with three cold-eyed young men who drifted into the room and took up position. Joe picked up his jacket and headed for the hall.

"Now what?" He muttered under his breath.

Randy waited until they stood outside the elevators and said: "I told him we had to go take care of Guidry."

"As in…"

"Trash removal. They don't know if he died or not, and they don't care. They just wanted to show you and me a lesson for interfering, like stay out of their business. So fuck them. It's a good excuse for a day off. Unless you want to sit in that hospital room until your tailbone grows to the floor."

"No thanks. So what are we really going to do?"

"Fishing."

♦

Joe was relieved to see Randy head in a different direction, far out of the city where the deep canals beside the roads weren't littered with trash and the houses and farms were cared for. Outbuildings sported fresh coats of paint and azalea bushes waited for spring in the shelter of live oaks that had been there since the Louisiana Purchase. When they veered off a highway to a hard-packed dirt road, the farms thinned out, separated by acres of thin timber.

Another turn at a set of rural mailboxes, and the road narrowed to a goat trail. The ruts were deep, the grass a little overgrown and woods rustled on either side, tangled with wild grapevine. But fresh tire tracks bent the grass in places, and a Beware of the Dog sign looked new.

The lane finally opened up onto an expanse of grass and huge old live oaks and a one-story cypress farm house with a new tin roof.

"Where the heck are we?"

"BreauxVille," Randy said, and parked the car under a shed.

"This is your place?" Joe squinted through the trees at a large expanse of water.

"Yep. I got some cane poles around here somewhere. Or how about something to eat? I hadn't have breakfast yet."

"Man, this is nice," Joe stepped out of the car and stretched.

Overhead, morning clouds raced across the sky.

"I didn't want you to think all of Louisiana was shit." Randy headed for the house.

The front porch felt solid, the cypress boards not giving a quarter-inch. Randy opened the unlocked door and led him into a gloomy parlor. The long windows were open, the screens catching a breeze shaded by the porch. Randy steered him past a tiger-oak dining room table and glass-fronted curio cabinet to the kitchen.

"Reminds me of my grandma's house," Joe said.

"It goes back a grandma or two."

Randy set a percolator brewing, and crouched to look in the refrigerator.

"Let's see what the old lady left in the fridge. She hates it when I stand in the door with it open, ha ha."

"Any chance of me getting a shower? I can't remember the last time. I think it was at Yvonne's that day with Madeline. I've been washing off in Denny's room but it ain't the same."

"Help yourself. Down the hall toward the back. Take your time. I'll make us some sandwiches."

Hot water rippled over his aching grimy skin and he forgot about the sandwich or coffee or anything else. Finally. If the water held out, he might feel human again for a few hours. A burring of an old-fashioned phone made him pull his head away from the water to listen. He had not imagined it, but it wasn't his house or his problem.

"Hey," Randy knocked on the door. "I've got to go take care of something. I'll be back in a little while."

"Everything okay?"

"Yes. A friend's car broke down, they need a ride. Make yourself at home."

"How long can I stay in here?"

"The water'll get cold in a little while. Here's some clean Wranglers out here on the hamper."

The house became quiet. Damn. Privacy, time to think.

"I could stay here a week," He thought, drying off. "And then I'd be fit to go home."

Barefoot, he padded down the hall to the kitchen, and made himself a cup of coffee to go with a large ham and cheese sandwich. Joe sat down at the tiger oak table where he could look out the window at the lake and watch the driveway. The more he looked, the more he saw. The yard didn't end in abrupt square, but sauntered off into the trees. There was a good three or four hundred feet cleared along the lake, and a dock. And a boat.

The leather recliner in the living room looked new.

Joe chewed slowly, thinking about Dudley taking offense when Randy used his family connections to plead, or threaten, for Guidry's life. There was more to Randy than he had figured, but Randy did things smart, kept himself comfortable and didn't flaunt what he had. Joe felt his allegiance sliding.

Out past the front door, a car appeared in the lane, a burgundy Ford Fairlane, the chrome grille catching the sun. It drove across the grass past the windows to the side of the house. A woman stepped from the car, by herself. Randy's old lady. He should go make his presence known so he wouldn't scare her to death, walking in on a shirtless, barefoot man raiding her refrigerator.

Behind the kitchen, in a utility room where a brand new Maytag washer and dryer sat, a screen door led to the side porch.

He stepped out with a friendly grin that he hoped was non-threatening. The woman was reaching in the back seat for a brown grocery bag. A good-looking woman-- no, a downright pretty woman, her soft face reminding him of a dark version of Colleen, full sweet lips, her dark hair pulled back with a hair band, white sunglasses.

"Hello. Didn't mean to startle you. I'm Joe. I'm a friend of your husband's."

"My husband?" She set the bag down on the porch slowly.

"Yes. Randy dropped me off here. He had to run an errand."

"Honey, Randy isn't my husband, he's my son," She said and headed back to the Fairlane. "Would you help me bring the groceries in?"

"You're not quite what I imagined a voodoo priestess would look like," Joe admitted.

"Thanks. I think."

"Kitty referred to you as Mama Therese. I thought you'd be shorter."

"More along the lines of a gremlin?" She stacked frozen meat in the freezer, rising up on her tiptoes.

Joe checked to make sure she couldn't see his reflection in anything, then watched her rear end tighten up in her white slacks with each toe lift.

"Not a gremlin, but I wasn't expecting Gene Tierney, either."

"Why thank you, that's a tremendous compliment."

"The women in your family, that I've seen so far, have an unusual look," He said.

She smiled deeply and said: "I hear you've upset the domestic harmony up there in Atlanta."

Joe slid back from the table, exasperated. "Did somebody put it in the newspaper yet?"

"No. You never heard of the gumbo grapevine?"

"It wasn't intentional," Joe shook his head. "If you're a mystic, maybe you can explain it to me. First time I saw Kitty, I knew her. Which is impossible because she's a lot younger than me, and we hadn't been in the same area at the same time. But I still know the girl and she acted like it was perfectly normal, like she'd been waiting on me. Worse yet, she decided that I was in charge of protecting Jess, like anyone in their right mind would want that assignment."

Why was it so easy to talk over an old kitchen table? Or was it the women in this family who made a man confess his soul's desires?

"And your attraction to her followed an unnatural course?"

Joe refrained from admitting that the unnatural parts were sometimes interesting.

"Listen, I'm not judging," Therese said. "I would like to know your side of it, since I have you here in my kitchen."

Joe raised an eyebrow. "Have I been set up?"

"Do you mind? Don't you need a break?"

He took a deep breath.

"I don't even know what I'm doing anymore. I came here because a friend of mine got hurt, and it's like there's no end to it. I wanted to get it over with and go back home."

"Atlanta?"

"No, Atlanta isn't home. I'm from Jacksonville, in north Florida. Before that, rural Georgia."

"But you're probating for the Regents, right?"

"I don't know," He said. "It just keeps getting more complicated. Thought I'd be riding my motorcycle, hanging out, and damned if I don't stay in the middle of trouble."

She smiled back, her eyes soft and kind.

"I don't have to do cards. You want me to tell you what I see? You draw lightning. It's all around you. All that energy, like you want out of your skin? And all you've done since you've got here is let it build up." She kicked off her pumps and slid on a pair of tennis shoes. "Come take a walk with me. You might want to put on a shirt because of the mosquitoes."

♦

The breeze off the lake remained steady, rippling the moss in the trees. A copper rooster with patches of iridescent greens scratched beside a small plain hen a few yards away. The chickens looked at Therese, who told them "it's not time."

"How long have you been here?"

"Before the kids were born," She said, heading down the lane.

"It's a nice place."

They walked slowly, enjoying the sun and the breeze. She went past the mailboxes at the curve, then headed for an overgrown lane he hadn't noticed when he and Randy drove out there. She picked up a long hickory stick propped beside a post.

"It's warm enough for snakes."

He'd left his pistol at the house, and wished he hadn't.

She gestured behind them at the mailboxes.

"That's where the bus used to pick up and drop off the kids."

"Where are all the people for those boxes?"

"They're all gone. Grown up and left, or died off. Except me. My sister used to live up here."

She followed a path crowded with scrub oak and wild azaleas and stunted pine trees. In ten minutes, they reached a clearing. A small cypress house sat there, silent and dark. The porch was swept clean and the screens were intact, but nothing could disguise the vacant, empty feeling of the place.

"I try to make it look lived in, or at least taken care of, in case some vagrants decide to move in."

"It wouldn't exactly be easy to find," Joe stood in the yard.

"No." Therese dusted off a spot on the porch and sat down, her back to the front door. "Nobody's lived here since she died."

Joe waited.

"I'm going to trust you with something a lot of people don't know. My kids say you're a good man, and you can hold a secret. I'm telling you this because I want you to understand why you have to leave Kitty alone," Therese said.

She pointed to the two faded ruts leading through the woods back to the mailboxes.

"Kitty used to walk to the school bus stop from this house. Her dogs went with her every morning. They'd go wait for her when it was time for the bus to let her off. If I was up here visiting my sister we'd get tickled, watching those pups get up and grin at each other and go trotting off down the lane. A person could hear the school bus once it got close, but I swear those dogs heard it turn off the highway two miles away."

She gazed up at him, her eyes dark.

"Kitty's my sister's girl, not mine. They lived here. One day Randy came home from his part-time job and told me the dogs weren't at the bus stop when he went by that afternoon. The next morning, Kitty wasn't waiting for the bus. I figured she had caught measles or something, and Elvie was too lazy to come tell me. The third day, Randy came up here to check on them," She paused, her lids lowering. “There was blood all over the place. Elvie was missing, and the two dogs were out back, shot to death. Randy finally found Kitty curled up under her bed.”

Therese gazed down the lane.

“Elvie was always into stuff. We didn’t know who did it, or why. I also didn’t know if they came by when they knew Kitty was at school, or if they didn’t even know about her. Randy brought her home-- God bless him, I’ve never seen that boy so scared and upset before or since-- and from then on we said she was ours, to keep her safe.”

“You’re sure your sister is dead?”

“I know. In here,” She touched her breastbone. “But for a long time, what I didn’t know, Kitty thought her mama had killed her dogs and gone off and left her to find those dogs murdered like that.”

Joe flinched, his heart bruising his lungs.

“It wasn’t such a stretch. There were times when Elvie could have done it. She had a crazy temper like Yvonne if someone hurt her, and was always sorry later. But Elvie wouldn’t have hurt the dogs. She always went after whoever hurt her.” Therese smiled faintly, and smoothed down the front of her slacks.

“That’s a rough thing to run in the family.”

“You get used to it. Mostly, it’s hard on the person who has to live with all that fire and ice inside them. Like you and your lightning,” She gazed up at him and lifted her hair up off her neck with a casual gesture. So that was where Kitty learned it. “I had a hard time with Kitty. She wouldn’t talk for almost two weeks and was scared of everything for years. She wouldn’t go anywhere without Randy or Yvonne, but she went a lot of places she shouldn’t, looking for her mama.”

“I’d threaten and embarrass her, drag her fourteen year old ass out of a bar, and she’d cry all the way home and go back out the next night, looking for Elvie or someone who knew her.”

"And then Jess walked into one of those damn bars, and it was like she could finally save something. He was a wreck. If a helicopter flew over, he'd shake or hold onto the chair arms for thirty minutes after it passed. The man never slept. When he stayed with us, he'd sit out there on my porch in the rocker at two in the morning and watch the lake. And she'd sit on the floor beside him, like a puppy."

Therese looked directly at him, and he found it didn't bother him when she said: "So you've got to let it go. You can still love her, Joe, and I hope you will, but no matter what she says or invites, don't cross that line again. You might want her, but Jess needs her. And they both value your friendship and respect, even if they have strange ways of showing it."

Therese stood up slowly, dusting off her slacks.

"I can't stay here too long, I get depressed." She reached over to him and took his hand, her fingertips drifting over his rough knuckles. "I wonder if I could talk you into going back home with me and letting go of some of that lightning before it burns you up. I think it'd be good for both of us."

CHAPTER FORTY-TWO

Hermy's tailbone hurt and his chest ached worse, but he would not give up. He had watched the old house for three days now, coming by in the evenings when it was time for lights to go on in the windows. So far, the upstairs apartments remained dark. He thought about giving a note to the landlady, but if someone else found it, it could get him killed.

He sat on the passenger side of the car, like he was waiting for someone inside one of the old houses. People came and went, young couples and hippies trying to save the fine old mansions, and the slumlords determined to wring out the last dollar of rent before the houses were condemned. He passed the time watching them come home with groceries and schoolbooks, chatting in the tiny front yards or on the porches as the streetlights came on. He got to where he felt like he knew them, but none of them paid the slightest attention to him.

By eight o'clock, it was dark. By ten, he knew he needed to get back to the farmhouse, but he hated giving up. Hermy was trying to summon the courage to go pick the lock on the rear garage and see if Guidry's motorcycle was inside when the back door of the car opened and someone got in right behind him.

"Hello, Hermy. Been a while."

A crackling rush of terror sent his heartbeat into overdrive, and he lost the ten seconds necessary to bolt and run.

"Who—who—"

"You don't remember me?"

"Oh. Randy? Randy Breaux?"

"Yep. What you doing over this part of town?"

"Waiting on a friend." And trying to breathe again.

"Do I know the friend?"

"Why are you in the back seat? What's going on?"

"Who are you waiting on?"

"Stop playing games with me," Hermy snapped. "I know your sister used to date him. Guidry's had an apartment in that house for years. You know it, too."

"Well, that's a lot of knowing, but you still haven't told me why you're here."

"Waiting on him," Hermy said, and slumped. "I think somethin's happened to him."

"Why would you think that?"

"Our business ain't none of your business. You hang out with the Regents when it suits you," Hermy said boldly but couldn't contain his misery.

"I'm a middle man, Hermy, it's no secret. But I only answer to a few people who want everything nice and smooth. You boys upset the Chamber of Commerce with that idiotic drive-by at Fat Jack's the other night. Y'all messed up again, lost your VP? I'd hate to see something happen to Guidry because of Sleaze's ignorance. Yvonne might go after that little bastard."

"It ain't funny, Randy. The Regents called and said they had him, and nobody's seen him since. The boys are worried sick."

"What did the Regents want?"

Hermy calmed down enough to think straight, and turned around, his arm across the seat, his Irish-green eyes resigned.

"You already know, don't you? Look, man, I just want to make sure he's okay. And I want him to know that the boys didn't have no say in the matter, and they're sick about it."

"There wasn't a vote?"

"No. Sleaze and Virgil decided it was a set-up and they weren't walking into no trap. Virgil keeps telling everybody Guidry has turned. They didn't call no vote. Half the boys are ready to walk out. Sleaze has lost his mind about that Trog patch, and he's doing meth and horse tranquilizers and some kind of mushrooms. He cools off, then the next minute he's chewing the siding off the house. But to turn his back on Guidry? I never thought I'd see him get that crazy." Hermy shook his head. "If Etienne's okay, let him know we didn't have nothing to do with it. Fahey and Charlie went and looked for him, but we didn't even know where to start."

"Did the Regents happen to say where they found him, how they got him?

Hermy hesitated.

"No, but there was this red-haired girl. Virgil snatched her up some place, and she told me Virgil was driving Guidry's truck when he grabbed her."

"What girl? I'd like to talk to her."

"She ain't around no more." Hermy said, ashamed, and pulled in a deep shaky breath that capsized his belt buckle. "Them Regents gonna go home now? They got them two idiots at the hospital who sliced up that Chicago Regent to start with. Now Kenny and Guidry's gone, and they didn't have nothing to do with it. Virgil's walking around scot-free and I know he stabbed the Regent. He loves a knife. Thinks it makes him a big shit. He's even wearing Guidry's cut-off."

"Sleaze lets him?" He had finally surprised Randy.

He took a drink from a warm beer.

"Fahey tried to take it from him, but them two Angola assholes beat him for it. Told you, Sleaze is nuts. I'm gonna get myself killed too. I shouldn't be talking."

"No, you shouldn't but I appreciate it," Randy said.

"You'll tell him we had nothing to do with it?" Hermy pleaded. "If he was to come back, we'd call a vote to get Sleaze out. We were wanting to do that before this happened."

"That kind of explains why it happened, don't you think?" Randy reached for the door handle. "Go on home and take care of business. You're wasting your time sitting here, Hermy."

"Okay." Hermy wasn't sure if that meant Guidry was dead.

"Oh, one more thing. But maybe you've explained it to me, if Sleaze has burned out. I was wondering why he hadn't called in some favors with his friends down there at NOPD to clean house. Doesn't he have some boat business coming up where he needs the Regents out of the way?"

This time, Hermy turned full around to gape over the seat.

"Damn, what don't you know?"

"I'm just the middle man, Hermy. And I want it to be business as usual for our local people. We all have to keep the Chamber of Commerce happy. They're not having a good year. Remember that. See you later."

♦

Randy drove out to his mother's house and parked in the fading grass by the shed. He waited a while, smoked a cigarette until he was sure they knew he was there, and got out of the car. The days were getting cooler now and he liked the fresh air. The side screen door banged shut, giving them another warning, and he walked into the kitchen.

"I knew I smelled chicken. Is that etouffee?"

"It will be," His mother told him.

Joe sat at the table, slicing onions and green peppers.

"How's that friend of yours with the broken-down car?" He said drily.

"I never did find them."

"Don't code talk around me, Orlando," Therese said.

"It ain't for women to know," He said, reaching for a biscuit. "Pass me the syrup."

"Get your own," Joe told him. "What news do you have of the outside world? Am I still a Regents probate or do they think I'm dead?"

Randy smiled slightly.

"Do you care?"

"Of course he does," Therese spoke up. "Men aren't happy unless they're in the middle of a war. It's your nature."

"Oh ho, so speaks the women's libber."

"And you've come to get him and take him back to the war zone."

Randy poked a hole in the biscuit and poured cane syrup in the middle.

"Yes, I have. But we'll wait on the etouffee first."

"It won't be good for at least another two hours."

"They ought to be here by then."

"They who?"

"Whoever you're making that five gallon pot for."

♦

Approximately an hour later, Yvonne's black Galaxie 500 convertible pulled into the yard, with the top up. Randy and Joe had already adjourned to the porch for a smoke, and stood when she pulled up beside them.

"Hey, old man, the lou-lou ain't got you yet?" Randy stepped down to open the passenger door.

"I'm not helpless. Back off," Guidry growled.

"Okay, smart-ass, try and open it yourself. But if you scrape up Yvonne's car with that cast—"

"Open the door for him, Randy, so I don't have to kill him. He's wearin' my nerves thin already," Yvonne glared. "Can't even see and he wants to tell me where to turn, and shouting at me 'slow down, slow down!' all the way here."

She got out of the car and stomped up the steps into the house.

"Holy God," Guidry edged from the passenger seat and hobbled to the porch. "Let's sit out here, give my ears a rest."

He wore gray sweatpants and a gray tank top, and held his white-plastered right hand gingerly in front of him.

Randy went inside and came back out with three cold beers.

"You look better. How's your eyeball?"

"It's still in there. I just pretend it's gone so she'll leave it alone. She's got to mess with everyt'ing else. Look, she trimmed my mustache while I was asleep, huh? I can't get my britches closed or open fast, liked to have pissed myself, so she goes and buys me this matching outfit like I'm some French Quarter fancy boy. I'm gonna ask Therese if I can stay out here. Maybe Vonnie will go on back to work."

"Man, are you crazy?" Randy whistled under his breath. "You want to get rid of Vonnie, that'll damn sure do it. But it might be a lot more permanent than you planned."

"She's got to quit punishing me for that. Damn already, it wasn't like her and me was dating. She was just a kid."

"Oh I don't know if she's done yet. What year is it? She might have another decade of abuse lined up for you."

Joe frowned at a pine sapling near the edge of the lake.

"Are you saying what I think you're saying?"

Randy took another hit off the rolled paper, and answered in a low voice: "Guidry and Mama had a little fling years ago, and Yvonne caught 'em. She ain't forgave either one of them."

"While you were dating Yvonne?" Joe asked. "I'm surprised you're above ground."

"I didn't know Yvonne had a crush on me. She's always had moods," Guidry said irritably. "And it wasn't like me and Therese were serious. It just sorta happened. What nineteen year old male isn't gonna take up a grown woman on an offer like that? Beg your pardon, Randy, for talking about your mama."

"That's all right, Etienne, it was just lousy timing. For everybody."

"Who's that?" Joe spotted the car first, crawling down the lane, and reached for his pistol.

"Damn, she let somebody follow us?" Guidry leaned forward to look.

"Cool it. I invited him out here," Randy said.

"You told him what happened?" Guidry relaxed when he recognized the car.

"Not all of it. That's up to you. Your Aunt Pauline told him you didn't up or call for your Thursday card game with her and her lady friends. He flagged me down yesterday. Didn't believe me when I said you were okay. He wanted to see for himself you were alive."

They watched the car roll to a stop. Guidry's cousin Emile got out, still in his patrolman's uniform. He had seen a lot in his career with the New Orleans police department, but this time it was family, and it made a big difference. He stood beside the car, gazing at his cousin with relief and horror at the damage, his eyes and nose reddening.

"Let's go help Mama with dinner," Randy said to Joe.

"You might want to stow that joint, too."

"Hell, Emile smelled it before he got past the mailboxes. Damn, I'm starving, I hate when it makes me have an appetite."

Ten minutes later, Therese lifted the lid off the pot, allowing a rush of garlic, onion, celery and chicken to puff through the screens.

"Yvonne, go ask Emile to stay for dinner, please." Therese pulled another tray of biscuits from the oven.

"I t'ought nobody was supposed to know Guidry was alive," Yvonne hissed at Randy. "I about knocked the poor mailman off the sidewalk for looking too long at my windows."

"Emile ain't gonna bring Guidry no harm," Randy said. "Stop yapping and try to be a gracious hostess for once in your life."

"What about me?" Joe said. "Should I go sit this out in one of the bedrooms?"

"You're one of us now, whether you like it or not. Just don't talk too much. Emile don't need to know who you are," Randy advised, and then his eyes glittered. "Give Mama a pat on the ass once or twice, he'll just think you're some sugar boy she dragged home."

"Seems to me I got dragged here for her by her own son."

"I didn't go with her to Mass on Mother's Day," Randy said. "Had to do something to make it up."

Therese put the lid back on the pot and gave Randy a kiss on top of his head with a wicked smile at Joe.

"You're forgiven, baby. Your Mama still loves you."

All grievances and disputes were put aside once everyone sat down at the old tiger oak dining table. Therese set a box fan in the window to draw out the heat and sat at the end of the table opposite Yvonne. She put Emile on one side of her, and Joe to the right, and proceeded to flirt and wait on them.

"You should have been a police investigator, Miss Therese," Emile said between bites of homemade biscuits.

"Why is that?"

"I just told you half my life story, and you didn't even appear to ask."

Joe remained silent, as was his right, and occasionally favored Therese with a warm look as he had been advised. He agreed with Emile. She was very easy to talk to, and she had a way of putting everyone at ease, except her own daughter. At the end of the table, however, Guidry was two hours overdue on his pain medication, determined to tough it out, and sinking fast. His bruised forehead was shiny with sweat, and he was having a hell of a time chewing.

Yvonne cut Guidry's food into bite-sized pieces, arranging it in a row on his plate, until he finally exploded.

"I don't need some woman making baby food for me," He glared. "Why you always got to fuss over people? Tend to your own business!"

Yvonne froze, her cheeks flaring bright red. Carefully, she set the fork and knife down beside him, then swallowed and put her hands in her lap. She stared down at her plate, her eyes turning pink around the rims. An awkward silence fell, with Guidry scowling and chasing his food around his plate in frustration.

"Yvonne?" Joe said.

"Hmm?" She darted an embarrassed glance at him.

He handed her his plate.

"I'd be much obliged if you'd saw mine up for me."

She dipped her head, swallowed again, and smiled through wet eyes.

"Oh I t'ink you can manage all by yourself."

"Yeah, but it isn't the same," He told her, his dark eyes teasing her just long enough for her to get the joke.

She rewarded him with the kind of look the old-style Hollywood actresses gave their leading men, and took his plate.

♦

"I want to talk to you," Guidry announced after dinner.

Joe eyed him across the demolished pound cake. Dessert had sent everyone into a sugar stupor around the table. Guidry had ignored Yvonne's icy reminders that he was past due on the pain meds, and the man was definitely feeling it. His dark face had a yellow sheen, and his fingers twitched with cramps inside the cast. He had given up on eating with one hand, and drank glass after glass of ice tea, his broad shoulders slumping further with each tick of the grandfather clock.

Joe stood and followed him to the front door. The sun tracked over the lake, a tropical punch orange streaking the clouds. Both men paused on the porch to look at it.

"I don't have much time for small talk. I'm fixing to eat some dope and go to bed. Here's what I have to say. I want the Regents out of my town before any more of my people get hurt."

"Guidry, I'm just a probate. Which is barely one step up from a female in their club. You know all that. I carry no weight." He favored him with a lop-sided grin, and admitted: "Before I got the call about Denny, I had decided to give them back their damned probate rocker. I wasn't raised to be somebody's dog."

"You would be making a mistake to give up that patch."

"And here I thought you were going to recruit me for the Bayou Runners."

"No. It ain't for you," Guidry said. "We ain't travelers. Too many of our people died on the way here after they were exiled. We're staying right here in our swamp. It's home now. Bayou Runners do whatever we can to earn a living and keep gas in the motorcycles. But the Regents? They can't settle down, and they thrive on war."

"You sure learned a lot about me just by breaking my arm."

Guidry looked square at him.

"If you hadn't had that Knight of Swords card on you, your head woulda been broke open. I wasn't in a good mood that night. I thought Yvonne had been hurt. And that's another thing. You cut your own meat, mother-fucker. That ain't for Yvonne to do for you."

Joe took a deep breath, and continued: "You keep saying 'we.' Does that mean you haven't given up on your club? I'd be pretty damned pissed if the Regents did that to me. But that's your business."

"I know who turned on me," Guidry said, his black eyes burning. "I'll settle it in good time. But right now I want your people out of here. And I think, probate, you can convince them to go home."

Joe wanted to tell him they wouldn't leave without Denny's patch. It was like leaving a country's flag desecrated on a foreign wall somewhere. More than most people, Guidry was well aware of the fact. And Guidry could not or would not tell him where the damn patch was. So what the hell was this all about?

"I'm keeping my word to you. I told you if I got out of that cemetery alive, I'd tell you where that puppy is."

Joe took a deep breath and stared sharply at him. Was this a set-up? Damn, he wished he could trust somebody.

"I don't believe she's alive," Joe said. "And I don't appreciate you bullshitting me about it. She was a good little dog."

"I might bullshit you, but I would never lie about something that important to Kitty. She gave you that card, she knows something about you. You're special to her."

Joe shook his head. "I took it because it made her happy. It's all bullshit."

"That so?" Guidry smiled. "You all think we just a superstitious backwater bunch, sitting around eating gumbo, talk funny even though they'd beat a kid for talking French in school. Some kids didn't speak enough English to know why they was gettin' beat.

You can make fun all you want, but some folks down around here has a gift. Kitty glows with it. She has since she was a kid. And I think you know exactly what I'm talking about. If Kitty sees you as a Knight of Swords, and she honors you with a protection, that tells me something about you. You can keep on thinking you're a dumb-ass redneck, but you're wasting your talent, or your destiny, or whatever you want to call it."

He pushed off the porch rail, and took an unsteady breath.

"I've got to go inside. You want to know where that puppy is or not?"

It was probably a trap, a pay-back, a big joke at the expense of the probate who wasn't all that important to anyone. But if there was a chance Smoky was still alive, that she had been waiting all this time for his dumb ass to find her, he had to risk it. Joe smiled.

"Draw me a map."

CHAPTER FORTY-THREE

When Joe walked in the front door of Fat Jack's tattoo shop, Dudley did a double-take, observing irritably that he was relaxed, confident and well-fed.

"You missed your calling, probate," Dudley narrowed his eyes. "Grave-digging suits you."

"Easy, man," Randy glanced around. "Who all's here?"

"What's left of Chicago. Upstairs." Dudley sat on the metal desk, blue neon glowing in the window behind him.

"They gonna stay for the hurricane?"

"I'd like to leave myself," Dudley said wearily. "We got four Bayou Runners. I'd say we're even."

But not the patch.

Randy nodded. "Soon as Jess gets back to escort him, a wise Regent would stick Denny in a van and go the hell home. They probably wiped their asses with his patch and tossed it in a swamp somewhere."

"You think so?" Dudley studied him.

"I woulda heard somethin' by now if it was still around. With Sleaze turning on their VP like that, I imagine the club has split up. Or they're so crazy on meth, they're planning something stupid again."

"Then why didn't their VP just say the patch was gone while Waco was pile-driving his guts?"

"Maybe he didn't want his people getting hurt if he sent you somewhere for it, even on a wild goose chase. He was a stand-up guy," Randy said. "You want us to go to the hospital and relieve the guards?"

"No. Those people you brought have done a great job," He admitted, but looked tired. "Chicago's getting something else lined up. We'll need you two with us."

Randy sat down on the couch and got comfortable. "Okay." Joe reluctantly joined him. More action? Who would get hurt this time?

The Chicago Regents came downstairs thirty minutes later, hollow-eyed and grim.

"What's the latest on the hurricane?" Waco asked him.

"This is South Louisiana. There's always gonna be a hurricane. The old timers watch the barometer." Randy lit up a cigarette. "It was still over by Texas, last time I checked. You fellas got something planned, we need to do it soon."

"Man, I'm so hungry I can't think straight. What was that bar we went to last night and got those big roast beef sandwiches?" Waco ran his fingers through his greasy mane. "Dolpho's?"

"Sounds like a good idea," Dudley said, but followed Waco's sudden wide-eyed stare to the window.

"What the fuck? Watch out—"

The door crashed open wide. A rush of uniformed men hurled into the small room, brandishing M16s, riot shotguns and .44s, shouting: "Hands over your heads *now*, mother-fuckers!"

Stunned, Joe couldn't move, then raised his hands slowly. He did not want any of them having an excuse to shoot him. Waco stood stock-still. Dudley tried to shift his weight before raising his hands, and two shotguns swung toward him. The room was too small for all those men and weapons, the barrels were inches from the Regents.

"Hold on," Dudley said. "Easy."

"Get your hands up now, scumbag, I'm not telling you again."

"I'm trying. Got a hip problem."

"Fuck your hip problem. You're all under arrest."

"For what?"

"We found a stolen car with bloodstains in it. A witness said they'd seen a couple of men near it, wearing Regents patches."

They looked at each other in bewilderment. Only Joe caught the impact in the gut. How the hell could they know about him ditching that car? And he wasn't wearing a patch, and there had not been two men, and where the hell was Madeline anyway, back in Miami?

"You mother-fuckers against the wall!"

Christ, was it going to be the St. Valentine's Day Massacre all over again? The Regents lined up, shuffling in the small space, their hands over their heads. Reluctantly, Joe started to get up, but in a smooth move no one saw, Randy blocked his shoulder with his.

"Get up there." A sergeant lowered his shotgun on them.

"You said Regents, sir," Randy said. "We ain't Regents. This my cousin from Shreveport. He wants a tattoo. We're waiting on Fat Jack."

"That so?" The sergeant glared, the end of the barrel dancing in their faces.

"I don't know 'em," Dudley spoke up. "They ain't ours. Looks like a couple of your bright-eyed little coon-asses to me."

The helpless feeling in the pit of Joe's stomach got bigger. He should get up, go with them, and find out what had happened. Damn, who the hell could have seen him with that car? It didn't make sense.

The Sergeant eyed Dudley.

"Oh. You assholes think you can just come into the French Quarter and start shit and nothing happens. Well, you made a big mistake. Boys, let's get this bunch searched and run 'em downtown where we can have a little chat."

"You two get out of here," a patrolman glared at Randy and Joe.

"Yes sir, cap'n," Randy nodded. "Come on, Charlie, you'll have to get your tattoo somewhere else."

They edged past the weapons and uniformed men, Joe expecting a shotgun blast at any second. Outside on the sidewalk, men circled in a frenzy, uniforms along with detectives in suits and shoulder holsters, all armed and mad. Tourists craned their necks from a safe distance, while the locals hung out the windows. Joe followed

Randy down the street, matching his pace, his stunned gaze straight ahead. He couldn't believe it. What the hell had happened?

"We've got to do something," He urged Randy.

"We will. Bright and early tomorrow morning, while the Regents are getting their brains beat out by Guidry's cousin Emile and his friends, we're going after your puppy."

♦

Joe spent a restless night at the warehouse, irritated at Randy and worried about Dudley. The man's hips were a constant source of pain, and yet he'd been stand-up in the face of the cops, and let Joe walk out of there.

"I couldn't tell you." Randy loaded a sack with ammo. "You had to be as surprised as the rest of them, or the Regents would have thought you set them up."

"Instead of you. Damn it, why couldn't we have just told them we were gonna go look for the dog?"

"Because they woulda wanted to know who tipped us, and demanded to go with us, and would have blasted the shit out of the place. Not all the Bayou Runners are bad people, Joe. Some of 'em are just like you, they want to ride their bikes without any complications. They don't deserve to die because they don't know how to get out of a bad situation. Those Chicago Regents would slaughter them. And if your dog got hurt, that's her sore luck."

Joe watched him.

"Are you sure we can trust Guidry?"

"Sure. Just don't ask Yvonne to slice up your meat anymore, or I ain't responsible." Randy said. "He wants his people safe, Joe."

He picked up a rifle and tossed it at him.

"Better get ready. Don't expect they're gonna welcome us with open arms."

"Are we shooting 'em or not?" Joe said, exasperated. "Make up your mind."

"They ain't all bad, but some of 'em ain't so good." Randy looked up. "You afraid you can't handle it without your Regents buddies? I thought you just wanted to get your dog and haul ass home, fuck the Regents and your patch."

"I want the puppy. For Kitty. And me."

"What about the Regents?"

Joe swallowed, and glanced around the dark empty warehouse.

"I feel like I should have gone to jail with them," He admitted. "I feel like I betrayed them somehow."

"Well, then I guess you ain't done with them yet."

♦

Randy pulled a tarp off a white F150 truck and tossed the keys to Joe.

"This thing's got a kick-ass engine. Why don't you check it out? We've got to leave in about thirty minutes. That fog ain't going nowhere."

Joe started the engine, decided he like the sound of it, and drove the truck up and down the big echoing expanse of pavement inside the adjoining warehouses. Randy poured out the last two cups of coffee, dumped the grounds in a plastic bag, and looked around.

"Something wrong?" Joe asked.

"Nah. Just might be awhile before I get back over here. I want to make sure everything's secured and shut off."

"But what about their vans? How are they going to get home?"

"Joe, they're gonna be locked up for awhile," Randy told him, his dark eyes serious. "It's up to you and me to get this settled. If you want to take your puppy and haul ass back to Jacksonville, I'll loan you this truck. If it don't get shot full of holes today."

♦

Fog hovered in the trees, dripping from the Spanish moss to hit dead leaves with soft tapping noises. Drops speckled the cracked windshield of an old Plymouth station wagon. Virgil came around the side of the asbestos-shingled house, dragging two muddy lengths of chains, and dumped them in the horse trailer with a harsh clatter. Muller came up behind him with a hay fork and a huge come-along winch, and tossed them inside.

"That's about got it." Virgil wiped the rust on his dungarees. "Now if they'll just call."

"Maybe they're waiting for the fog to clear. I wouldn't want to bring a boat up the channel in this shit."

"Stop worrying. The guy's been doing it for years. It ain't a problem." Virgil unzipped his pants and pissed beside the trailer.

The door opened, and Racine stepped outside.

"We all set? They just called."

Virgil said "Everything's loaded" and pissed on a mosquito hovering too close to his dick. After zipping up, he strode up the steps and swept past the ex-con, closing the steel door behind him.

"We're ready," He said, walking by a yellow laminate counter loaded with empty beer cans and sardine tins.

He helped himself to a beer, and wiped his running nose. The mildew odor coming from the refrigerator could choke a hog.

"What the matter?" He finally said when Sleaze didn't budge from the table.

"It's the weirdest thing." Sleaze stared at the wavy glass in an old window above the tin sink. "I been thinkin' about a place I hadn't been to in years."

Virgil figured he was talking about Nam, and didn't push it.

"They had a juke box with old music on it. I can't quit humming that song and I don't even know what it is. Some old Roy Orbison. Slow dance stuff."

His hand tapped out a rhythm on the scrap of vinyl tablecloth, and his mouth jerked with a high-pitched keen.

"You need to lay off that shit you're mixing," Virgil said. "The meth worked better for you."

"I ain't laid off the meth. This is some shit Racine fixed me up with. I been up three days."

"If I was you, I'd watch what that asshole gives you."

Sleaze smirked, his beady eyes once again familiar and shiny.

"You worried about your VP status? Maybe I'll give it to Racine instead?"

"Racine ain't in the club."

"You think you earned your VP patch?"

"What's that supposed to mean?"

"It means, Virgil, that I have sudden moments of clarity. When I put shit together. Even without the mushrooms. Even when it's too late." Sleaze stubbed out his cigarette on the table. "Let's go."

They stepped out the door, leaving it open. Sleaze stood on the concrete steps, studying the fog, listening to it patter on the tin roof. It started an echo in his head, tat-a-tat-a-tat, soft and far away.

"You drive," He told Virgil.

Racine and Muller reached for the door handles of the station wagon, but Sleaze stopped them.

"You ain't going. You haven't earned it."

"What the fuck?" Racine said, furious. "It's all you've been talking about. If we helped you unload the dope, we'd get a cut."

"I changed my mind. I got other shit for you to take care of when fuckin' Leon comes down here. You'll get paid. But this trip ain't for new people."

"Mother-fucker, you said—"

"It ain't up for discussion. Let's go, Virgil."

The station wagon pulled off, the horse trailer rattling behind it.

♦

Fog consumed the white truck, a row of saplings hiding the glass windshield. If Sleaze had been driving, he would have noticed the damp grass broken down just off the dirt road. But Virgil was behind the wheel, frowning, worried about the leather cut-off he wore. It had "Vice-President" stitched across a pocket, and the Bayou Runners patch on the back. Guidry had thoughtfully left a hundred bucks in an inside pocket. It was two sizes too big on him, but he did not want to lose it, especially to those assholes Racine or Muller.

The horse trailer banged behind him, like it was smacking the back of his skull. Sleaze sat slumped and quiet, his morning dope cocktail making him thoughtful. Probably trying to remember more old songs. Roy Orbison? Damn. He hoped Sleaze didn't get weak and screw up things with Leon. Virgil had plans.

♦

Randy waited until the clanking faded and bird song resumed. A squirrel fussed at them from a nearby oak. He nodded at Joe, who reached for the ignition. The truck crept from the small lane onto the dirt road. The house wasn't far, the fog hanging at the edges of the miserable yard.

"There's our van." Joe sat up straighter. "Guidry wasn't lying."

The van rested on concrete blocks, the tires long gone. The engine dangled overhead by chains from a tree that looked like it was about to crack in half.

"Can't see shit," Randy muttered. "How the hell we gonna spot her?"

Both of them tensed up when they saw the two Angola cons standing in the yard. Muller was picking up empty beer bottles and slinging them against the side of the house, glass crashing.

"Do you know 'em?"

"No. They aren't Runners," Randy said under his breath. "Careful."

Joe lifted his hand on the window sill in a salute. "Morning."

"What's your business down here?" Racine scowled.

"Well, we were lookin' for some fight action, but I musta turned wrong somewhere. I can't see my own ass in this fog." Joe glanced across the yard, confused. "Ain't nothing happening here, right?"

He turned to Randy. "I told you we come down the wrong road."

"What kind of fight action you talking about?" Muller stopped tossing bottles, although he kept one clutched in a tight fist.

"Dogs," Joe smiled. "We pick up the losers. There was a big fight last night somewheres around here, and they said a few didn't do too well."

"What do you do with them?" Muller asked, curious.

Joe grinned at Randy, then looked back at the two men with a sheepish glance.

"Chinese restaurants."

"Damn," Racine cringed.

"Hey, they cook it up so you can't tell. And there's a big restaurant I won't name, but they make it into stew. Tourists think it's gator."

"Are you shitting me?"

"Nah. Those big dogs carry a lot of meat. It's a shame to waste it on canal fish."

The two men exchanged glances.

"What do you give for a dog? That's a nice truck. You must make good money."

"We don't pay for 'em," Joe said. "But we'll get it out of your way. You got one you don't want to feed no more?"

"Maybe. Whyn't you take him out there and show him the ones we got? I been holding my bowels, can't last much longer."

He climbed the steps slowly, catching Muller's eye before he went inside the house. Joe kept a dumb grin on his face. He slid out of the truck and followed Muller across the yard. Mud squished beneath his boots, along with bottle caps and broken glass and flattened beer cans. Beyond them, the yard fell off into a tangle of brush and weeds, and he smelled stagnant water. A canal of some kind ran behind the property. The ground grew softer, less reliable, and his smile faded.

They came to a big cypress, the sides peppered with holes and a plastic target nailed to the tree about head-high.

Bark suddenly shredded near his ear, then he heard the pop. Shit! He ducked, then a huge *ka-boom* went off from a different direction, shattering the windows in the house. Muller had crouched behind the tree, and was reaching inside his shirt.

"You don't want to do that," Joe told him, the Colt a scant foot from the man's head.

"Hey, it don't have to go like this," Muller said, still fumbling under his shirt.

"It didn't." Joe moved the nose of the pistol over an inch and pulled the trigger.

Muller's shoulder exploded and he went over on his back, screaming.

"Where's the dog?" Joe shouted.

"What dog? There ain't no dog, you asshole."

"A puppy. A black and white bull dog."

"We ain't got no dogs. The last one starved to death," Muller groaned, rolling in the mud, and yanked out an old .22.

"You don't know much about me, do you?" Joe fired. The screaming stopped.

Across the yard, Randy reloaded and fired pointblank into the house through the open door, giving Joe cover.

Joe hurried to the steps. "He said there's no dog. I didn't see one. Where the hell is she?"

"I ain't seen a dog anywhere. Not even a chain," Randy said. "Wanta go ask the one in the house? I don't know if I got him or not. Wanta go look? You got the lucky card."

"Why not?" Joe said.

He slid inside, the Colt at arm's length, ready. The refrigerator and far wall were spattered with crimson droplets like an abstract painting.

"Picasso's been here or you hit something."

The rooms were a foot deep in trash, the furniture rank. He kicked his way into the next room, and saw red drops dotting the linoleum.

"Anything?" Randy swiveled, keeping an eye on the truck and the yard.

Joe shook his head and pointed to the trail across the floor. It went straight through the house and out the rear door. He hesitated. The woods were white with fog. He would be the target. But they had to make sure.

"You hear that?" Randy stood still.

They both heard it, a little outboard engine, the sound familiar to anyone who spent time on the water.

"There's a canal back there," Joe said. "He's getting away."

Randy hesitated, then shook his head. "Let him go. He'll probably bleed out. Damn, they're nasty sons-of-bitches. Look at this place."

"This isn't the main clubhouse, then. I can't see Guidry putting up with this. My damn boots are sticking to the floor."

"I'm gonna go roll that dumb-ass closer to the canal for the gators. We'll check around, see if we can spot your dog."

Joe went with him, steeling himself. He didn't want to find a little skeleton with a collar on it tied to a tree. He couldn't stand it. Why the hell would Guidry lie to them? Him, sure, but Randy? And he had not figured the man for someone who would lie about a dog that meant so much to Kitty.

"Smoky?" He whistled, and clapped his hands. "Smokes?"

Come on, just a little noise, a whimper and he could find her. Joe clamped his jaw down. Kitty would be devastated. He glanced up when Randy suddenly put a hand on his arm and shook his head.

Joe listened, and finally heard a thump.

"Hello?" A faint voice called.

They waited, turning their heads to pick up on the sound's source.

"Is somebody there? Please?"

"That's a girl," Joe whispered.

Carefully, he and Randy eased up the back steps and stood in the house, listening. A plywood door hanging off its tracks opened on a short dark hall. Joe made out three doors, two with a strip of morning light beneath them.

"Door Number Three," Randy hissed.

They waited, uncertain if it was a trap, silence singing in their ears.

"Please? Somebody. God, please help me?"

"Where are you? Come out here," Randy called.

"I can't. I'm chained up…please don't leave me here."

There was no mistaking the genuine despair in the woman's voice.

"I brought a flashlight. Don't move 'til I get back," Randy told Joe.

When he returned, the flaring beam lit up the narrow hall, and a door with a deadbolt on the outside.

"Are you to the left or right of the door?"

"Left….your left."

"Can you get behind a dresser or something?"

"Wait." Metal clanked across the wood floor. "Okay."

Joe stepped back and stuck his fingers in his ears. Randy raised the shotgun and blasted the door jamb to pieces. He kicked the fragments loose and both men cringed at the odor that rushed out. Sewage and old semen and rusty blood. Joe aimed the brilliant beam around the room. Someone had nailed plywood across the windows. In one corner sat a stained bucket and ragged towels on the floor.

A metal bed was pushed against the far corner. A mattress flopped over one end of the bed, a patchwork of dark stains across its crusty surface. It slowly moved like an unwieldy jellyfish until they saw a pale face emerge above it.

"Please get me out of here," She whispered.

"Oh my god," Randy uttered,

Joe pointed the flashlight at her, and recognized only the long red hair.

CHAPTER FORTY-FOUR

Joe gave her the softest blanket in the stack. She sat between them in the front seat of the truck, leaning against him. All they had to drink was a half cup of cold black coffee, which she sipped carefully. Randy rolled down the windows.

"Sorry about the smell," Madeline said. "They wouldn't let me loose even for the bathroom."

"How long have you been out there?"

"I don't know. I couldn't tell when it was daylight." She closed her eyes. "Is it over? Are they all dead?"

"Not hardly."

"What…what about Guidry? They said the Regents had him."

"He's okay."

"Really?" She looked up at Joe with those heavy-lidded blue eyes, and he was sorry the tears weren't for him. "Don't lie to me, okay?"

"He's not lying," Randy said. "Guidry's busted up, and it'll be a long time before he plays cards again, but he's alive."

She let out a shaky breath, relieved, tears spilling down her face.

"It's been so weird today, like I knew something was going to happen. You know the air gets just before a hurricane? Sleaze came in there to talk to me. I don't know what the hell he's shooting up. He's so damn calm he talks like a college professor. I thought he'd come in there to kill me, and instead he just leaned against the door and talked."

"What'd he say?"

"He kept whistling a Roy Orbison tune, asked me if I remembered dancing to it. Then he says 'oh I'm getting you mixed up with someone else. She wasn't tall at all. She was a little girl with a face like a cat and came walking in the door with Doc. I never been so glad to see anyone. I seen him on fire and I thought he was dead.' " Madeline pulled the blanket tighter. "Like that. He didn't even sound like himself. And he told me at least ten times. Then he says 'you know what, you were a good old lady to Guidry. You stuck up for him. You spit in my face. I admire that. I shoulda listened to you.' That's when I figured Guidry was dead."

She took another sip of the coffee, closing her eyes. Then they flew open.

"Wait! Go back!"

"What?"

"Go back to the house."

"That's not a good idea," Randy said carefully.

"You have to. There's a Regents patch there. I saw it."

"Are you sure?" Randy glanced over at Joe. The girl sounded like she was coming unglued. Besides, the gators may have found Muller.

"You think I don't know a Regents patch?" She retorted.

"Where did you see it?"

"On the wall in the middle room, before the kitchen."

"Did you see a patch, Joe?" Randy said, certain Madeline was delusional. "I missed it."

"The place is a pig sty, and we were too busy looking for a man with a .44," Joe said, and an idea formed out of nowhere. He felt stupid, and wondered what else he had not caught on to. "Turn around, Randy. I'm kind of slow, but I finally figured out why I was sent there."

Smoky may have been the bait, but she wasn't the trophy. In a stranger's eyes, at least.

Randy slowed down, and found a wide place in the road where he could turn the truck around.

"How come they let you see it?" He asked her.

"Same reason they talked about where their big drug shipment was coming in today," She said bitterly. "I was already dead to them."

Randy put the truck in Park and gazed over her head at Joe, dumbfounded.

"Madeline. Sweetheart, if you can remember any details of where they were going, we would be much obliged."

While they bumped back down the road to the wretched house, Randy and Joe forced themselves to stay calm. The girl had been through hell, and half of what she had said was babble. But they wanted to believe she was right.

"Do you mind if I wait here?" Madeline huddled. "I can't go back in that place."

"Honk the horn and lock the doors if anyone shows up," Joe told her, and bounded up the steps.

Exhilaration coursed through them as they cleared the rooms. Randy held out the powerful flashlight along with the shotgun, tracing the stained walls. Joe found a broom and started shoving. The floors were hidden under an odorous soup of broken beer bottles, chicken bones and overturned furniture.

"I don't see it. I knew we wouldn't have missed it," Randy said. "They probably hit her too hard and busted something loose. She sounds out of it. Seeing a patch was wishful thinking. She wanted to see Regents riding to her rescue. And Alec ain't even bothered."

"She's a lot more rational than I'd be," Joe retorted, kicking trash across the floor. "It's got to be around here somewhere."

Randy swept down and speared denim on the end of the shotgun.

"Great. A denim couch. In a hundred pieces. Be careful, Joe, there's used needles all over the place."

"She said it was on the wall. If they took it down…wait. Wait. Son-of-a-bitch. Over here!"

Triumphantly, he swept it up from a filthy chair near a window.

"Look. Chicago!" Joe clenched it in his hands. The old cloth, the personal patches, a tiny Texas flag, the stitches, the sweaty smell of hot sun and gasoline. "Shit, man, we got it. We've got Denny's patch!"

"Damn. Guidry almost got killed over it and they didn't even give a shit enough to put it on the wall," Randy said, and reached out reverently to touch it.

"Looks like somebody got mad and threw it. They knew they'd screwed up. The Trogs set off a shit storm for them. Sleaze has to be sorry he ever laid eyes on them."

"If he isn't, he will be soon," Randy said.

♦

When the two men kicked a path back outside, Madeline was standing in the yard, the garden hose on full blast, washing herself off in the chilly well water. Even with the bruises and cuts and starved thinness, Joe found himself staring. The girl was beautiful. What kind of man would want to hurt or ruin something like that? For that matter, what kind of man would stand there and stare at her after all she had been through? Madeline stood up straight, shivering, and narrowed those beautiful blue eyes at him.

"Don't y'all have a dope shipment to catch?"

♦

Randy flew along the back roads, passing startled old couples in puttering Oldsmobiles and an occasional farmer on a creeping tractor with inches to spare.

"I think you hit that squirrel," Joe said.

"Give me a damned break, Yvonne," Randy retorted. "Feel that air? Bad weather's on the way."

"Where are we going?" Madeline burrowed under Joe's arm to avoid getting slung through the windshield.

"Where you'll be safe."

"I just want a real bath and a disgusting greasy hamburger."

"I'll treat. You've got more guts than most men I know," Joe told her.

"Whining doesn't work nearly as well as an Italian stiletto, and I don't mean a shoe."

"When this is all over with, would you go dancing with me?" Joe said.

“Why don’t you just buy me? It’d be a lot cheaper. I’m sure Alec would give you a great price on used goods,” She slid further down in the blanket. “He hasn’t sent anyone to look for me, has he?”

Buy her?

“I don’t know if he has, Madeline,” Joe said slowly. “I’m not his favorite person. He and I got off to a very bad start. And at the moment, I’m the only Regent in town and I’m a probate, not a patched member. Nobody tells me shit.”

“Everybody’s gone? How am I going to get home?” More tears. Joe was relieved. Tears were normal with the women he knew. Like a rain gage, it let him know how bad things really were.

“They’re not all gone. Dudley and the Chicago Chapter got busted. I’m running under the radar so if Alec called, I wouldn’t know. But I’ll make sure you get home safe. After we get a steak somewhere. Medium-rare? Baked potato with the works?”

She wiped her eyes with the back of her hand.

“You’re either desperate or don’t have any standards at all. But I owe you two. That’s twice now.”

“And we’re not going to talk about it. Ever,” Randy said.

“I don’t know what you’re talking about.” She wiped her eyes again. “Damn, I can’t stop crying. But I would like to know how you found me. If you can tell me.”

Randy let Joe handle it. They weren’t heroes. Nobody had sent them to rescue her. They wished they could tell her Big Alec had ordered them to find her. But lying was pointless.

“Finding you was pure chance. I guess your guardian angel finally got their ass in gear,” Joe began. “That van in the front yard? It was ours. We had it in Talladega. I wanted to get it back. It had something very important in it.”

“The stuff under the floor?” She said hesitantly.Weapons weren’t casually mentioned in her world. “I know where it is. I was there when Guidry came back from Talladega. He was so mad because he had to pour oil in it all the way home. He stopped by the apartment for a minute to unload his bike and that other stuff into the garage. It's still there, if you want it."

"He didn't take it out to their clubhouse?" Randy asked.

"He didn't want them to have it, or even know about it," She said. "The Trogs kept coming around and making promises. Guidry didn't like the way things were going. He has a weird way of thinking, like he's always playing chess in his head."

"He let you see the stuff?"

"Oh no," She smiled slightly. "This ain't my first rodeo. I was spying from the upstairs window. He'd told me to take the puppy up there to keep her out of his way. She wouldn't leave him alone."

She reached for the coffee cup and drank the last nasty gulp at the bottom with a shudder.

"What kind of puppy?" Joe asked hoarsely.

"A pretty little thing he picked up somewhere. Some kind of bulldog. Black with white socks. Scared shitless."

"What happened to the dog?" Randy asked, because Joe couldn't.

"He wanted to keep her but he was gone all the time. So he gave her to the landlady."

"His landlady?"

"Yes. But I think Baby has about worn out her welcome. She's always chewing the furniture. The landlady said she must have hung out with a rough crowd," Madeline said. They were both steadily looking out the windshield, and Randy noisily cleared his throat. She suddenly smiled. "Oh! Are you serious? You were looking for Baby, not me? Well shit, I guess you found both of us. Denny's patch was just a bonus?"

She waited for confirmation, but Joe still couldn't talk.

♦

Randy slowed down long enough to turn off the paved road in a controlled slide, then gunned it for the final two miles to his place, going as fast as the rutted dirt road would allow without hurling them out of the cab. Joe leaned forward, his hand on the dash.

"Seems like I'm always asking, but who's car is that?"

"I don't know it," Randy said. "Those are Georgia plates."

He pulled the truck near the front door and stopped. Joe got out first and turned to help Madeline. She was weaker than she had let on, and struggled to keep the blanket around herself.

"I can't go in somebody's house like this," She said. "I still stink. I'll wait here on the porch."

"No, you won't." Joe put an arm around her and picked her up.

When they got to the top step, the screen door opened. Joe felt his stomach tighten. Madeline's mouth gaped open. She and Guidry stared at each other in mutual shock.

"You are okay!" She exclaimed.

"The car." Guidry stared. "The police found the car full of blood. Damn, Madeline, what happened to you?"

He stepped forward, glaring at Randy and Joe, his fist clenched.

"Where'd you find her? Those fucking Chicago Regents do this to her?"

"Shit," Randy scratched his eyebrow.

"The Regents?" Madeline stared, her face pale. It was that damned Virgil! He picked me up in your truck and I've been chained up in some shit-hole ever since. He told me you were dead, 'Tienne. And he was sure of it."

"Virgil," He uttered on a long, slow exhale.

"Yeah, Virgil," She said, lips trembling.

"She's not heavy, but I'd like to set her down somewhere," Joe said. "If it's okay with you."

Stunned, Guidry held the door open for them. They trailed into the house, reviving at the aroma of hot cinnamon and apple pie, like things were normal instead of falling apart.

"Shit," Joe came to an abrupt stop.

Three plates of apple pie sat on the dining room table, along with three cups of coffee. At the end of the table, Therese looked up, her eyebrows raised at the new arrivals, but it was Jess who put down his fork and actually smiled.

"Damn, Madeline, did they make you ride in the back of the truck? You look like you've been in the hurricane."

"Fuck." Randy melted backward.

"You know Madeline?" Guidry gaped, confused. "Jess, how do you know Madeline?"

She glanced frantically at Joe, who eased her down in a chair before she collapsed, edging it a safe distance from Guidry.

"I've known Madeline…how long's it been, Rusty…three years?" Jess calculated. "Is Alec here, too? He didn't tell us he was heading this way."

"You might want to shut up," Joe told him, without hope.

"What are you saying?" Guidry stared.

Perplexed, Jess studied the miserable faces around him.

"She's one of Big Alec's old ladies," He told Guidry. "Where'd Alec have you stashed, Rusty? I never ran into you down here and it's hard to miss that hair."

Joe closed his eyes and groaned. Jess took a bite of pie, chewed several times, then laid his fork down carefully on the edge of his plate.

"The hair…the redhead?" With a sinking feeling, Jess put it together. "The redhead you told us about with…aw shit."

Madeline crumpled, dipping her head to hide her face.

"I'm sorry," She whispered to Guidry, unable to look at him. "You were good to me. I'm so sorry."

"Don't be," Guidry managed to say. "My own people did this to you? I apologize, Madeline. Good Christ."

"No, not the Bayou Runners," She rushed to assure him. "They never came out there. It was those two cons and Virgil. But I lied to you and led you on. I'm sorry."

"Guess you just did what you were told. And you did it pretty damned good," He said, his dark eyes lost. "Excuse me."

He took a few steps backward, then headed for the front door.

"I think I'm going to be sick," Madeline said.

“Come with me.” Therese stood, and put an arm around the girl. “We’ll run a hot bath for you.”

The men watched the two women trail down the hall, then Joe did the only thing he could think of. He picked up Guidry’s discarded apple pie and a fork, and dug in.

“Damn. Why did it have to be him?” Jess said, stung with guilt. “Shit.”

“You’re about brilliant, Sherlock. No wonder my little sister thinks the sun rises and sets in your ass,” Randy sneered.

“What kind of prick would send an upscale girl like Madeline into a club like the Bayou Runners? Guidry’s the only one who knows what deodorant is,” Jess retorted. “Fuckin’ Alec. That son-of-a-bitch.”

“Shut up, she’ll hear you,” Joe glared, at his limit.

“Don’t tell me to shut up!” Jess slammed his fist down on the table.

“Damn, why don’t you just whip ‘em out and compare?” Randy declared and headed for the living room. “Go ahead, throw ‘em on the table and I’ll go get a yardstick.”

Joe realized he had once again stepped across the probate line. But not much longer.

“Look. I don’t want to do this anymore, Jess. Okay? Truce. This isn’t ever gonna stop. I piss you off if breathe in your direction. I’m trying my damnedest, but I’m a grown man and I’ve had it.”

He paused, and made his decision in a split second.

“I’ve got one more thing to take care of and I’m out of your life,” He announced, shocking Jess and Randy into silence.

Outside the kitchen window, a slight mist crept up across the porch, touching the window. It calmed him. He could go on.

“Madeline told us about a drug shipment coming in,” Joe said. “Thought you’d want to know. Sleaze will be there.”

Jess leaned back, putting some distance between him and Joe. He studied an oak rocking chair in the corner, his mouth in a hard line. “And?”

"You want to settle it with him or not?"

Jess shrugged, but his blue eyes burned when he looked up at Joe.

"It's past time. You going?"

"Yeah."

"Why?"

Joe hesitated.

"I'm the Knight of Swords, remember? For a little while longer. I've got your back, Jess. I just can't handle being treated like a punk all the time."

"So it's about probating, not Kitty."

Joe leaned across the table, and put his palms on either side of Jess's plate.

"Kitty is the best thing that ever happened to you. You've got a once-in-a-lifetime romance, Jess. I couldn't screw that up. And I don't want to."

He pulled back, giving Jess some breathing room.

"You're tired of being a probate, is that it?"

Joe shook his head and let out an exasperated breath.

"Damn tired."

Jess slowly rose to his feet, and glanced at Randy, who sat motionless on a hassock by the front door.

"Nobody walks out on me," Jess said in a low voice. "Me or the Regents."

Too fast to follow, he reached under the table and swept up a small duffle bag. Horrified, Joe took two steps back, wanting to reach for his pistol but couldn't make his waving hands do it, not Jess. All he could do was hang in the air, backing up, as Jess tore the bag open and tossed something at him, hard.

"Fuck you, mother-fucker."

Instinct made him catch it instead of ducking. It was soft, unbending in places. He recognized the smell. His own smell, the aftershave they all ragged him about. It was his own denim cut-off that Jess had kept ever since they came to New Orleans. Joe couldn't believe how much this hurt. It was done.

All that shit he did for them, the dark stuff he couldn't change or undo. Hell, even the good times, when the Atlanta bosses warned Alec to leave him alone, when Denny beat down his own crazed Regents brothers to drag Joe to safety, riding down the highway with them at ninety miles an hour.

"You're fucked now," Jess warned. "Put it on! I'm not losing another probate."

"What?" Joe had a headache.

Jess glared at him. "I've got to make this official? You'll wish I hadn't."

He strode around the table. Before Joe could move, Jess slugged him square in the chest.

"Put your damn patch on, probate." He yelled, but a smile started in the corner of his mouth, and spread. "I mean, *Brother*. Put your patch on."

Joe stared back at him, wheezing slightly and wavering on his feet.

"Are you…is it…" He held out the cut-off and turned it so that he could see the back.

The Regents lion, the shield, the curved scimitars dripping blood. And "*Regents MC*" on the banners.

"Put it on, Brother," Jess said. "And we'll have a toast to Rider, the newest member of the Regents MC. You got a hundred percent vote, Joe. And you earned it."

"This is why you went back to Atlanta?" His husky voice embarrassed him. "Damn."

Joe slid his arms into the denim, feeling the weight of the patch settle heavily on his back. Dumbfounded, all he could do was watch as Jess pulled a bottle of his favorite whiskey from the duffle bag, and poured two shots into Therese's best crystal glasses.

"I think I said this to you once before, a while ago, when you went with me to make something right. There's no going back. You understand that, right?"

Glasses clinked, and Joe felt the burning rush all the way to his toes.

"Looking back never worked for me, Jess. Thanks. For everything."

"I hate to interrupt the ceremony, but you might want to step it up a little," Randy said from the front door, He stood, and put on his cowboy hat. "Guidry left with my truck ten minutes ago."

CHAPTER FORTY-FIVE

Guidry drove fast, skirting down roads better suited to john-boats instead of a truck, but he risked it to make up time. He had not counted on Jess showing up at Therese's, but it had been a good thing after all. Therese gave them the neutral ground to speak freely, to tentatively plan, to say as much as men on opposite sides of a war could. But it was hard. They could never be comfortable as long as Armand's ghost was in the room with them.

How could a man stop thanking someone for saving his brother from a horrific death? The sheer bravery of it awed him. He rarely saw Jess any more, but when he did, his heart ached with gratitude all over again. And even when Jess put out a hand to stop him, Guidry desperately tried to find the words to express what it meant to him that when a med evac chopper went down, and everybody managed to crawl or fall out except Armand, who was too badly injured to help himself, and the damn thing was on fire and people were screaming to run because it was going to explode, corpsman Jess Whitley had gone back inside to drag his brother out on his own badly burned back.

Armand died a painful death in a hospital, but not a horrific one, alone and screaming for help and incinerated alive because no one cared. Jess Whitley had cared.

He knew all this because Sleaze had been there, and told him about it. Or maybe it was little Vincent Minarde who came home and related the story in his aunt's living room while they all wept and prayed. By the time Jess came through Louisiana to look him up, as Armand had requested before he died, he had reached God-like status in the parish. Guidry had never quite been able to see him as anything less. Which made the last few months hell, playing with the cards the Trogs had dealt, friends against friends.

"You just a plodder, son," His father once told him. "Nothin' wrong with dat. At leas' you take your time to t'ink."

Unlike Armand, who went after things like he was shot from a cannon. Thinking through a situation at all the different levels gave Guidry an edge when playing cards or chess. Sometimes he was just a little slow. Like with Madeline.

His fingers curled around the steering wheel.

"Ain't the first time a woman made a fool out of you."

At least he expected it from Yvonne. Most of the time, it was worth it.

Misty rain blew in the window, and he saw several cheap polyester blankets in the floor. He stopped by the side of the road long enough to reach across with his left hand to shake them out. A sawed-off shotgun, a box of shells, a rifle and a .44. *Why thank you, Orlando*. It would be enough.

The wide metal farm gate swung in the gusts, awkward to manage with one hand and a key for the bouncing padlock. After securing it, he got back up in the truck and wound his way across a wide pasture where cattle grazed and stomped the earth. Tire tracks etched a trail in the thin grass, circling cypress ponds and marshy spots, heading for a row of trees in the distance.

The truck's engine announced his approach. The rifle lay on the seat behind him, the butt end toward his thigh where he could reach it with his left hand, and the .44 was wedged in a side pocket on the door. The truck passed into the woods, fog creeping through the saplings. A man in camouflage behind a hidden blind let him pass, but the second one didn't. Stuck between them, he kept a boot on the brakes and waited.

"What you wanting down here?" A toothless youngster peered at him over the top of a shotgun, then nearly dropped it.

"Godalmighty. Man, it's good to see you. Charlie, look, it's Guidry!"

"How things lookin' down there?" He nodded ahead at the narrow road.

"Okay." The men awkwardly shook his hand. "You want us to go with you?"

"No, you stay right here. This is where I need you. And don't let nobody else come down here." He held up a warning finger. "Don't kill'em. Just stop 'em."

"Yes sir." They stepped back into the forest, grinning.

The narrow lane wound down through scrub oaks and trees felled in storms decades ago, until the ruts widened out on a clearing. Gray rain clouds jetted across the marshes in the distance. The men stopped their work when the truck came to a halt at the edge of the water. They hung motionless in the wind, a hush descending until the only sounds heard were the whistling gusts.

He slid from the truck, and the confused dark men on the boats watched in amazement as the Bayou Runners ran over to shake Guidry's left hand and pat him on the back.

"Christ, you're looking rough but I'm glad to see you." Fahey got there first and embraced him in a careful hug. "Don't want to crack something. Where are you broke?"

"I'm not broken," Guidry told them, his dark eyes steady.

Some openly sagged in relief. A few others chose to look at the water and the storm coming in.

"You counted it yet? How does it look?" Guidry addressed Fahey.

"Still counting. Quality's good. They got here early. They were nervous at first, because of the new location, but they're okay. My brother's with 'em. He'll make sure they get out okay if the weather goes bad."

"I appreciate you handling it 'til I got here," Guidry told Fahey.

The Irishman stuck his hands in his back pockets, and swallowed. "Least I could do."

"I'll go talk to them. They been paid?"

"Hermy was waiting on you. I think that's what made them nervous. No bosses, and no money. Guidry, when we get back, we're gonna vote first thing--"

"Hermy told me you all voted to go along with this. I know who my friends are," Guidry told him. "I ain't worried about any other voting right now. We get done with this today, we gonna celebrate this paycheck. We ain't had a hurricane party in a long time. I'm thinking a crab boil with some shrimp and mudbugs and Jax beer in the barn. That's somethin' you County Galway boys specialize in, ain't it?"

Hermy sat grinning on a truck gate. "You coon-asses give us a good run for it."

"We'll see who gives up first. Okay, let's get to it. We've got to beat that rain."

Relieved, they picked up their speed. They had a *conciliateur* they could be proud of, someone who could hold his shoulders straight despite a bad beating, and reassure the dealers with calm confidence they would have no problems.

Guidry lifted his head. The Bayou Runners would be all right: they had enough bales to keep them and the Chamber of Commerce happy, with no interference. Not bad for a plodder. He headed for the dock, hoping his final bluff had worked. Etienne Guidry refused to fold, especially when the stakes were high.

♦

Virgil wanted to smoke another cigarette, but his throat was already raw. A stack of butts lay on the dirt outside his window. Sleaze stretched out in the front seat of the station wagon, his head tilted back and his arms crossed over his chest. But he wasn't snoring. If he wasn't asleep, why wouldn't he say something? Had he finally overdosed? Nervously, Virgil shot a sideways glance, waiting to see if the crusty black tee shirt moved.

"It's almost noon," He said, risking the man's wrath.

"They'll get here when they get here. They're dope runners, Virgil, and the weather sucks."

"You let Racine get the phone. He coulda lied. For all we know, he called 'em back after we left and cancelled the drop."

"Racine isn't an idiot. He's got the redhead to play with, he'll hang around 'til I throw him another bone. That's how it works."

Virgil thought it sounded like a dig at him.

"Where's our guys?" He tried again. "This is weird. It's like we're in the twilight zone."

Sleaze suddenly opened his eyes.

"Did you hear that?"

"What?" Virgil sat up straight, peering across the marshes. "What did you hear?"

"I ain't sure, but it sounded like a fuckin' pussy losing his nerve."

"Damn it, this don't bother you? I think we oughta go to the farm house, see what's taking 'em so long."

"And while we're gone, the boats show up, and no damned body's here." Sleaze sighed, and shifted his arms. "I been thinking. I bet Guidry killed that Trog. Wish I coulda seen that. He was something when he lost his temper. I'd push him and push him, and he'd just grit them teeth at me. But other people? He didn't take no shit. That's how his Daddy raised us. Don't take no shit."

Virgil switched on the windshield wipers for a minute, clearing the rain and silt from the glass. The empty docks and water stretched desolate in front of them.

"Well you ain't got to worry about him or his temper no more. Or the Trog. Two birds with one stone." He decided to try one more cigarette. "When Leon comes down, he'll figure we're even, and patch us over."

"No, when Leon comes down, he's gonna kill any of the boys he can find, and hurt the rest of 'em really bad."

Virgil wrestled with it. Why wasn't Sleaze upset and raving and pulling his scraggly fuckin' hair out? He looked like he was in some kind of trance.

"Well, what are we gonna do? Hey, you know what? Listen! Screw the boats. We can get the dope money and lay low while

Leon's in town. He can do what he wants to the rest of 'em, and then we show ourselves about the time he's wondering how he's gonna get the dope trade set up. How's that? Or hell, we could just take the money and split. Fuck this shit. That's a lot of damned money."

"I guess you and I do kinda think alike. That's really depressing," Sleaze said, and got out. "I'm gonna take a piss."

Virgil put his cigarette in the ash tray. The wind bumped the door against his legs, nearly knocking him on his face in the dirt. Hell, he'd piss all over himself if he wasn't careful. He hurried to the back of the station wagon and faced the woods, bracing himself.

Sleaze squinted across the water at three large boats in the distance, heading for port. He zipped up, and slowly reached inside the station wagon for his jacket as the wind picked up.

"Well, Virgil, I believe you're right," He said. "Maybe they called the farmhouse and said it was too rough. It don't look like they're gonna show."

Virgil sighed in relief. He wanted to get out of here, away from the dead fish and bleach bottles and shit floating up on the tide.

"You and Hermy's the only ones know where it's hid, right? Half one place, half another?"

He glanced up, and saw Sleaze standing at the back of the car, his face like some worn wind-etched figurehead on an old ship.

"You been paying attention."

"Hell yeah. That's what a good VP does, man. We can go on back, wait 'till they're passed out, and go out to the barn and get it. Half for me, half for you. You want to take one car, go to Mexico? That money'd last a long time in Mexico."

"Nah" Sleaze said. "I like to travel light."

"Cool. Whatever." Virgil felt better, in control again. The money would last a very long time if he was the only one who had it.

"Say Virgil?"

"Yeah?"

"Take that patch off. It don't fit." Sleaze gripped a .22, the barrel aimed dead center of Virgil's chest, a scant six feet away.

"Huh? What…what's wrong with you?"

"You think I don't know it was you? You fuckin' cocksucker, getting over on me?" The true Sleaze evolved in a second, eyes black, that ugly little mouth of brown teeth spitting curses, his hand shaking only slightly. "You take off that goddamn patch right now. I don't want to get your stinkin' blood on it. Ain't nobody ever wearing that cut-off again. It was Guidry's, you lying bastard."

Virgil smiled, and pulled out a knife, twisting it in the air.

"Come and get it, asshole."

Enraged, Sleaze squeezed the trigger, once, twice, clicking empty chambers.

"Did you think I was going anywhere with you with a loaded gun?" Virgil screeched and flung the knife with a practiced hand. Sleaze flew sideways, catching it in the arm. Virgil pulled another .22 from the back of his shirt. "I got your bullets right here."

He took a step toward him. Open-mouthed, his eyes wide, Sleaze scrambled to reach the passenger door. The pop startled him, busting the rear window right by his face.

Behind the car, Virgil ducked. How had the little bastard moved fast enough to get another weapon? The second pop was louder, and tore the pistol from his hand.

"That's better."

"I told you I'd get it the second time."

The voices came from the woods directly behind him. Virgil gaped as three men stepped out from the trees. Two wore Regents patches and the third man he already knew, wearing that damned expensive cowboy hat in a storm. His wrist throbbed. The shot had hit bone. He swallowed hard, determined to stay on his feet. He could see his pistol in the dirt just under the car.

"How's it going, Sleaze?" Jess said.

"I been better."

"This must be Virgil. The traitor to our mutual old friend."

Sleaze nodded, clutching his arm.

"That's him, the piece of fucking shit. I gotta take this blade out, okay? It's hitting a nerve or somethin'."

"I wouldn't. It's all the way through," Jess observed.

Virgil silently counted to five, steeling himself to dive and grab the pistol from the dirt.

"Check that son-of-a-bitch," Jess gestured to Joe. "Oh. I forgot. Can't do that anymore. Okay. Orlando, I'm short a probate. Your turn."

"My pleasure."

Handing his rifle to Joe, Randy stepped forward and grabbed Virgil by the hair. Instead of frisking him, he seized his injured arm, yanked it up behind his back, and proceeded to ram his face repeatedly into the cold steel roof of the station wagon.

"This is from my sister, and this is from me!" He snarled. "This is from Aunt Pauline. And this one's Emile's. Oh, and let's not forget Madeline."

"Hey, slow down," Jess warned. "We want him for later."

"And you thought I had a bad temper," Joe said.

Randy wrapped his fingers tighter in the man's hair and stretched his neck backward to look at the nostrils blowing blood.

"I was just getting started. Guidry took a lot more than that, mother-fucker, can you?"

"Jess. That bastard's wearin' Guidry's cut-off," Sleaze said. "Would you get it off him? I was gonna, but he got the drop on me."

"What the hell do you care?" Jess retorted, but signaled Randy to strip it loose.

Sleaze hung his head. "I fucked up. I was stoned and I fucked up. 'Tienne was doing shit behind my back, man, and it wasn't adding up. Everything he did…"

"Was for your damn club," Jess concluded.

"I didn't see it. And this piece of shit kept playing me." He lifted his head to glare at Virgil.

"So this is the famous Sleaze?" Joe inquired.

He was amazed that the recognition seemed to please the man. Sleaze slowly got to his feet, peering at Joe with his manic dark eyes.

"I'd shake, but I got a knife in my arm," He said with a creaky laugh, and had to bite his lip when the pain got away from him. "Who are you?"

"I was Jess's probate. Now I'm Jess's brother," Joe said simply.

"Oh." Sleaze leaned against the car, his fingers tight on his elbow, trying to shut off the nerves. "You got ya another probate. This one's a lot bigger."

Blue eyes crystallized in his direction, and Sleaze put up a hand.

"I ain't making fun, I ain't! Just making an observation. I'm glad for ya. Really. I know you don't believe me."

"You getting soft in your old age?"

"No," Sleaze shook his head, gasping slightly at the incredible pain sawing against the bone. "It's just…you're educated, Doc, you tell me. How did it all go so fuckin' wrong?"

"Greed meant more to you than friendship," Jess said simply.

"Um…Jess?" Randy had been going through Virgil's pockets. "Does this look familiar?"

The wind would have snatched it from his fingers if he tossed it so he handed it to Joe.

"What is it?" Joe peered at it before passing it to Jess. "It looks like a dirty fortune cookie."

Jess scowled at Sleaze, who stared back at him slack-jawed.

"How did he get this? This was a personal message for you."

A girlish scream gurgled from Virgil's throat.

"That was you? You crazy fucker, you did that? Uhnn…" He fainted, nearly dragging Randy to the ground.

Sleaze paled and began swaying.

"You fall on that knife and it's going to hurt," Jess told him.

"I never okayed those tats," Sleaze gasped. "I never. I got more respect. Them three did it on their own."

"Ancient history. But how'd this asshole get one?"

"I dropped 'em. Guess Virgil picked one up for a souvenir."

"What do they call that?" Jess frowned.

"Prophetic?" Randy ventured.

Dull-eyed, Sleaze looked at Randy, who stood with his boot on the back of Virgil's neck.

"Will you get Guidry's patch to the clubhouse? I don't want anyone else wearing it."

Jess decided he had let him agonize long enough.

"I think Guidry wants it back. After he gets it dry-cleaned, of course."

Ferret eyes wobbled around the circle of men.

"What do you mean? That ain't funny."

"Trust me, he doesn't think so, either."

Sleaze blinked frantically, nerves behind his eyes short-circuiting.

"He's alive? That big dumb bastard's alive?"

"Yeah. He's alive. No thanks to you."

Sleaze's mouth fell open in shock. "So he was working with you? Damn, and all this time I kept thinking I shoulda done something to save his ass…shit. Man, I even dreamed his Daddy was standing in the kitchen, looking at me…"

Jess watched the water turn dark. The approaching storm brought in a musky alligator odor. What would the gators do until the storm passed, sink deep into the murky water with bits of wild fur and bones, and wait? The sky darkened, and a change worked over him. He couldn't calm down, couldn't find the place within that took over and acted appropriately when something needed to be settled. It could not go on. The wrong people would get hurt.

"You two want to get Benedict Arnold out of here?" He said, staring stonily at Virgil, who had managed to sit up, trembling, huddling in his own shit. "Wrap him up in a blanket. I don't want him going into shock."

"Want me to take him to Guidry?" Randy asked.

"I haven't decided yet. I know 'Tienne would like to talk to him, but," He toyed with the crumpled tattoo in his hand. "It's been awhile."

Randy frowned. "Nothing personal, my friend, but maybe you should take up chess."

Jess shrugged. He had to wait a second, steel himself so he wouldn't give himself away, then said: "I'd like some privacy here with my old friend. Y'all wait for me by the car."

Sleaze watched them force Virgil to his feet, jibbering in terror, and half-carry him into the woods. Disgusted that he had ever bought into the man's bullshit, he was suddenly, overwhelmingly tired. At least Etienne wasn't dead. Jesus, what a relief. His bones became dust, and it felt like the wind was going to blow him over. He leaned against the station wagon, huddling in his jacket.

"Etienne wasn't a rat?" He wanted to hear it again.

"He wasn't a rat. He was your friend. The only one you ever had, from what I've been told."

"Good. That's good. If I hadn't got into that shit so heavy…" He lifted his long lids, and smiled slightly. "What am I saying? I been a doper since I got my first dose of cough syrup."

"You fought it off for a long time. Some people don't bother."

"Nam did it. Blame it on Nam." Sleaze gazed off into the trees. "Then we came home. I was trying to remember the name of that little bar. Where was it?"

"I don't know. I was lost."

"We were all lost. We came back lost. I thought you died over there. None of them medics I knew made it home. You guys were always the ones crawling through the grass to get everybody else. Guaranteed kill for those little Charlie bastards. I saw you on fire when that helicopter went down. And then we both wind up in a little bar in south Louisiana."

He wasn't stalling. He knew there was no point. Jess let him talk, an ache building between his lungs.

"Man, I was glad to see you. You walked in the door with that little cat-faced girl and all her relatives was gonna kill you, 'til they seen how she looked at you. They played the old stuff at that bar, Roy Orbison and Elvis and Nathan Abshire."

"I remember," Jess nodded.

He remembered slow-dancing with Kitty. He had just met her. Randy had been there, giving him the evil eye for holding Kitty so close. Yvonne smiling, snugged up against Guidry in a corner booth. And Vincent Minarde, as small as the native Montagnard people, sat at the bar by himself. Jess had thought one of the little Yards had stolen a ride over to America, the way Sleaze rushed over to greet him and shake his hand. They both remembered.

Sleaze wet his lips and let out a ragged breath.

"I'd appreciate it if you'd make it quick. For old time's sake."

Jess nodded, tightening his grip on the pistol, squinting as the gusts tore at his watering eyes. Damn it. He'd sworn to Guidry he would do this, not a problem, because Etienne said despite it all, he didn't know if he could. And it had to be done.

"I wanta look out there, where my people come from," Sleaze said. Supporting himself on the car, he turned awkwardly toward the water, his jacket fluttering madly. "I don't want to see it coming. Remember how they used to say that? Ya never see the one that gets you."

He steadied himself, and looked over his shoulder at Jess. His dark eyes were calm. He let his lungs empty.

"They were right."

Sleaze smiled and twisted a quarter turn, a .22 Mini Mag in his hand, fingers tightening.

"For old time's sake, you son-of-a-bitch."

Jess stared in shock, fumbling to find the trigger, the ground falling away from him.

Out of nowhere, a hard wind seemed to pick up the old station wagon, shattering the windows. The car jumped, the tires exploding. Still grinning, Sleaze flew apart, spiraling, gone in a red zephyr.

Jess held onto his pistol, transfixed, wanting to make sense of what had just happened. Blood and shattered glass, green paint and broken bone danced in front of him. Behind him, a gray heron took wing from a cypress tree, flying recklessly into the bleak sky.

"Damn," Jess whispered. "Damn, Vince, where'd you go?"

Joe edged out of the woods, cautiously drawing close to him, bracing a sawed-off 10-gauge shotgun across one arm. The clouds opened up, pelting them with a soft rain. Joe stood there without speaking until the color came back to Jess's face. It would be a long time, thought, before he stopped seeing the colors in the wind.

"Can we go home now, brother?" Joe said.

Jess lowered the pistol, desolate, the cold rain stinging his face.

"Where's home?" He asked, once again lost.

"Wherever your friends are," Joe told him.

EPILOGUE

Before heading east to drench Georgia, the hurricane left a trail of water-logged destruction across Louisiana. The survivors knew what to do: how to pick up what was salvageable, how to put things back in order, how to go on, until the next one.

The storm had littered the cemetery grounds with cracked oak branches and sodden Spanish moss. Madeline carefully picked her way around the sunken places, setting vases upright and moving broken limbs off the older fragile stones. She found a tiny flag, and looked around for a stone engraved with a branch of the military. She didn't have to look far.

"Was Alec glad to hear from you?" Joe leaned against the car.

"He didn't even come to the phone," She said, intent on an Infantry marker with an empty metal holder.

Joe wondered if the sidewalk artists in Jackson Square could do her justice, with that red hair and white peasant dress in the sunlight.

"So what are your plans?" He asked.

"I don't know. Nobody but Guidry knows who I really am. And I doubt he'll tell anyone. I thought I could go play tourist in the French Quarter. And there's a place out there on the Tchopodopee Street called The Warehouse, where all the kids go. Fleetwood Mac has played there, and the Allman Brothers are regulars. It's where The Grateful Dead got their song 'Truckin'. " She smiled slightly. "Busted down on Bourbon Street?"

"Sounds like it'd be fun. Acting our age. If I remember how."

"Am I talking too much?" She held up a muddy rosary, the broken beads coming apart in her hand. "I don't get much chance to talk at the clubhouse. And it's not like he listens."

"Unless you're telling him how wonderful he is."

Madeline glanced up at him, shocked, and laughed. Then she clamped a hand over her mouth.

"I shouldn't have done that. I forgot where I was."

"I don't think they mind," Joe said. "It sounds like music when you laugh."

He could say off-the-wall stuff like that, and she didn't act coy or cute. Just interested. He found himself saying strange stuff just so she'd look at him with those weird blue eyes, like she wanted to know what he thought and how he thought.

"Look over there, isn't she beautiful?" An angel with outspread wings and a serene face beckoned Madeline. "Somebody must have loved that person. I'll be right back, I want to look at the name."

Joe glanced over his shoulder at a cedar tree near an iron fence. Beyond the fence, flashes of color from early morning traffic went by, a regular day after a good cleansing from Mother Nature. A world away, in the shade of the cedar, Jess knelt beside a small marker. He'd had a hard time finding it, and had been there a while, sweeping off the mud and twigs. When it was clean and the sun deepened the engraved name, he pulled a scrap of cloth from his pocket and placed it carefully on the wet stone.

"I got him for you, okay?"

They had come here so he could offer a final gift to the young probate Lee, an apology for a life cut short. There hadn't been much left of Sleaze's patch, but Joe hoped Jess would find some peace from settling the debt. It would be one less young ghost following him.

Joe had not told Jess what he found when they hastily cleared out the old dock landing. Trampled in the dirt, he recovered the tiny .22 Mini Mag that Sleaze had concealed until drawing on Jess. Joe thought it would make a good gun for Kitty, just right for her small hands. But when he looked it over, he saw that it was rusted shut, the tiny trigger broken. It wouldn't have fired.

Joe gave it some thought, while they had all sat and waited in the primitive glow of the old lamps at Therese's house for the hurricane to pass. Jess and Sleaze had once been friends, rode Harleys down swamp roads and past cattle ranches and fields of cotton and sugar cane. Fresh from a war, they shared the guilt and relief that they made it home when thousands didn't. Was the man so far gone he'd forgotten the gun was useless, and had every intention of blowing Jess away? Or was the little pistol a last minute idea to square things, to make Jess think he had to shoot him?

After the storm, Joe had tossed the pistol in the lake, swearing the dark water to secrecy. Even when a rabid beast was better off put out of its misery, it was hard going for the person assuming the responsibility. Unless the person happened to be a Knight of Swords, and took on the burden for a friend.

With a last look at the shady corner, Jess rose and walked across the grass toward the car, his eyes lit by the sun, the soft earth sinking beneath his boots. He had his arrogant face back on, his fine nose and chin tilted in a superior way, even though there was no one in the graveyard—living, anyway—who cared. Joe figured he just couldn't help it. Jess stopped beside Joe, gazing at Madeline as she scraped off lichens from a woman's name.

"Alec would never sell her to you," Jess told him quietly.

"I bet he'd sell her to you," Joe speculated. "If he thinks she's damaged goods. He'd think it was funny."

"The joke would be on him. Rusty's a class act. She's too smart for him. She's too smart for you, too, but that's her choice."

"I'm smart enough to go slow. She's been through a lot."

Jess checked his watch. "Denny's come up with some hare-brained idea. He's decided he doesn't want to go to Chicago yet. He wants me to take him back to Texas so he can give away his sister at her wedding. Can you imagine that joker in a tux?"

"On a hospital gurney?"Joe grinned. "So. You going?"

"Wouldn't miss it. He needs another week of bed rest before he tries a trip like that, even with an escort. Yvonne's doped him to the gills so he'll behave. I'm going to call Kitty, see if she wants to drive over here and go with me."

"Did you tell her about Smoky yet?"

"Yeah," Jess smiled. "She shattered my ears with some kind of Cajun yodel, lasted at least five minutes."

Joe forced himself not to comment.

"I appreciate you letting me tell her," Jess said. "You could have stole the thunder. Again."

"You're her hero, Jess. I was glad you were cool with me giving Denny his patch."

"First official duty as a patched Regent, retrieving a stolen patch for a Brother," Jess said. "I told Lee you were a lot more trouble than he ever was, but you redeemed yourself. Denny thought his patch was long gone."

"I owed him," Joe said.

"Well, I'd say you're even. That's the first time I ever saw Denny choke up."

"It'll be the last time, too, I bet."

"No, not if he's giving his little sister away. Damn, do you think they all look like him?" Jess winced. "Like a bunch of little buzzards?"

"In little white dresses. You'll have to take pictures." Joe wished Jess would invite him along, then shook his head. He had to stop thinking like a probate. "Want an extra driver? I want to go."

Jess looked at him, surprised, and shrugged. "Sure. Why not?"

Holding her ruined sandals, Madeline walked toward them, Smoky trotting behind her gingerly through the muck with a small twig in her mouth. They both stopped a few yards away, uncertain if they were interrupting a business meeting, and just generally uncertain about where they were in life these days. No one seemed to know where to go from here.

Madeline was relieved, and a bit startled, when Jess smiled at her and said: "So, Rusty, you ever been to Texas?"

THE END

About The Author:

W. T. "Roadblock" Harrell grew up in Jacksonville, Florida. An admitted adrenaline junkie in his early years, he raced on NASCAR-sanctioned tracks in Florida and Georgia with many of the great drivers from that era. Fast cars led to fast motorcycles, and RoadBlock joined a 1%er motorcycle club in 1971. In the years to follow, he lived the high-speed 1970s biker lifestyle of sex, drugs, and rock and roll. That way of life ended abruptly when RoadBlock was sent to federal prison for thirty years.

The world raced forward during that time, but because of his long confinement, RoadBlock remembers the towns and events as they were: before cell phones, personal computers, the internet and bumper-to-bumper highways. His untarnished--and unvarnished--memories proved to be a great resource for this fiction series about the adventures of Joe Wilson and the notorious Regents Motorcycle Club. RoadBlock provides the reader with an authentic look at a long-gone era.